ALL GOD'S CHILDREN

ALL GOD'S CHILDREN
Thomas Eidson

MICHAEL JOSEPH

LONDON

MICHAEL JOSEPH LTD

Published by the Penguin Group
27 Wrights Lane, London w8 5tz
Viking Penguin Inc., 375 Hudson Street, New York 10014, USA
Penguin Books Australia Ltd, Ringwood, Victoria, Australia
Penguin Books Canada Ltd, 10 Alcorn Avenue, Toronto, Ontario, Canada m4v 3b2
Penguin Books (NZ) Ltd, 182–190 Wairau Road, Auckland 10, New Zealand

Penguin Books Ltd, Registered Offices: Harmondsworth, Middlesex, England

First published in Great Britain 1996
1 3 5 7 9 10 8 6 4 2

Copyright © Thomas Eidson 1996

Photoset by Datix International Limited, Bungay, Suffolk
Printed in England by Clays Ltd, St Ives plc
Set in 10/13pt Monotype Baskerville

isbn 0 7181 4136 9

The moral right of the author has been asserted

For Sally and Dick . . .
sisters and brothers don't
get any better

PROLOGUE

Liberty, Kansas. December 3, 1891

Like a frigid hand of ice gripping the back of her neck, the winter wind blew in across the prairie, over the quiet farmyard and into the garden where they stood staring at the coffin. She shivered.

'Christ, the Way, the Truth and the Life,' she muttered to herself, gripping harder at the hand of her five-year-old son, Zacharias. She could feel the boy heaving in silent sobs. Samuel, her oldest at thirteen, held her arm in support, while the twins, Joshua and Luke, ten, held each other as if they might fall down if they let go.

No one had spoken since the elders had carried it out of the barn and into this frozen place, and she knew they might not unless the Spirit moved them.

'Christ, the Way, the Truth,' she repeated silently. Thinking about Matthew and their years together. Fifteen years. Where had it all gone?

A low gray fog drifted in over the tops of the towering prairie grasses that surrounded the farm, hovering in a thick bank near the road, then sending vinelike fingers probing amongst the carriages and the legs of the horses blanketed against the winter cold, then edging across the yard and into the garden where the two groups waited. Two distinctly different groups.

Pearl Eddy and her children stood in front of the smaller body of people, all of them bundled in somber black and gray and hatted: twenty members of the Society of Friends. They'd driven in their carriages some fifty miles from the tiny Quaker enclave of Blackwell to be here with the Eddys, the only Quakers in Liberty.

'I want to see my father,' Zacharias said, staring at two boys standing close to the long plank box on the ground before the open grave. They were snickering nervously, each trying to get the other to lift the coffin's lid.

'Thou may not,' Pearl whispered, gripping his small hand harder.

'Why?'

'Because thy father is with God,' Pearl said, avoiding the truth.

Someone sneezed in the second group of mourners clustered in a large semi-circle behind the Quakers. These were the towns-people, come to pay their respects. And she could tell from the sounds of them clearing their throats and coughing quietly that they didn't understand the silence, wondering when the service would commence and they could get out of this burning cold.

She was grateful for their presence, knowing how much they had liked Matthew, comforted by the fact that there were friends if not relatives present. She tensed slowly at this last thought, feeling sadness for her boys and loneliness as she had never felt it in her life.

An only child, Pearl's parents were dead, and on Matthew's side there remained only his mother, Lillian, and two elderly aunts. None had been able to make it in time for the funeral. She forced her thoughts away from Lillian, wondering if she would have come even if there had been time. Pearl stood straighter. She would not think such thoughts on this day, she chided herself.

But she could not stop thinking about Lillian's letter. It had arrived earlier this morning in response to Pearl's wire telling her of Matthew's death and it had been brutally to the point. Lillian had addressed it to Miss Pearl Hoeffer, her maiden name, then written a simple proposition that had stunned Pearl as if it had been a physical blow.

She'd offered to raise her grandson, Zacharias, in her fine home in Newport, Rhode Island. Pearl would be allowed one visit each year, but Lillian would adopt the boy. In return, Pearl would be paid $5,000. She fought the urge to sob, listening to the mourners blowing on their hands and stomping their feet to keep warm.

The twins, Lillian had continued, would be placed with Matthew's well-to-do aunt in Boston. Similar terms. Samuel would be found a boarding school until college. Similar terms. Pearl, gasping for breath, hated Lillian for sending this letter.

She was shivering now, recalling the last of it: 'Allow me to remind you of your unfortunate handicap. I assure you that you will not be able to provide for my grandchildren. And I also assure you, I will not have Eddy blood mistreated. Accept this offer or remember: if you fail to provide suitably for my grandchildren I will have the authorities remove them from you. Liberty, Kansas is not so far that my retainers cannot learn of your affairs.' Pearl was shaking so hard that she feared she might collapse.

'Mother, do thou want to sit down?' Samuel whispered, gripping her arm tighter.

She shook her head and braced herself against the cold, her loss, and her fears. Pearl had never understood what had caused Lillian to dislike her. Whether it was a mother's natural protectiveness, a feeling of superiority, or what. There was no question the Eddys were an old respected Rhode Island family – Episcopalian merchants, lawyers and politicians – while her own parents were immigrant Dutch farmers. Her thoughts began to cloud with memories of her parents and Matthew. She struggled for control.

Whatever Lillian's reasons, she had shunned Pearl from the moment she'd learned of their meeting at Yale. Five generations of Eddys had attended the New Haven college and Matthew had dutifully gone. But he wanted nothing of commerce, law or politics. Instead, he dreamed of farming as some men dream of wealth or power.

And when Matthew met this small Dutch girl, who did not attend the college but worked in the library, this girl who understood the land and animals, he fell in love. Fell so hard that although he never became a Quaker, he lived as one. Or tried. This thought caused Pearl's breath to catch in her throat. It was the reason they were standing here today, standing before this open grave. She shoved this thought roughly away, forcing herself, instead, to think of Matthew's quiet sensitivity. Moments later, she laughed softly. He was not a very good Quaker.

'Mother?' Samuel questioned.

'I am fine. Just thinking about thy father.'

The boy nodded and returned to staring at the wooden box.

Their decision to move to Kansas had sealed Pearl's fate with her mother-in-law. No matter how many times Matthew had explained that it was he who wanted to move to what Easterners called the 'grass sea' for free land, Lillian would not believe him. Believing instead that it was Pearl stealing her boy away.

'I want to see my father,' Zacharias moaned. 'I have to tell him something.'

'Zacharias, hush,' she said softly. 'Thy father is gone from this earth.'

The boy was sobbing hard now and Pearl felt like joining him but she controlled herself.

'We commend our brother to God,' Elder Fredrick Gray said in a loud clear voice that pierced the frigid afternoon air in the same way it did Pearl's heart.

'Take me to him,' she whispered to Samuel.

Slowly he guided her forward toward the coffin, the two town boys backing awkwardly away. She knelt and put her hand upon it, while Zacharias stood with his hands on her shoulder staring down in shock, not willing to believe that his father was inside the wooden box, soon to be in the earth.

Pearl leaned forward and whispered, 'Goodbye, Matthew. I will never forget.' Pearl knelt there a while, then stood and blinked her eyes. A moment later, she said, 'Zacharias. Thou wanted to say something to thy father.'

The boy leaned in tighter against her, clutching her hand in both of his. 'Just that I don't want him to go,' he sniffed. 'Please, pa, don't go,' the boy pleaded.

Pearl put a hand on his shoulder. 'Zacharias,' she said reassuringly, 'thy father is with God. That is a glorious thing.'

'I want him here!'

'Thou must accept God's will.'

The boy stood shaking his head back and forth, tears flowing.

That was it. The service was over. When the townspeople saw Pearl and her boys moving away from the grave, they realized there was to be no more said or done and an audible muttering of surprise rose amongst them and then, suddenly, Rose Sherman, an old friend of Pearl's, began singing 'Rock of Ages' and slowly people began to join her until all were singing. All but the Quakers. They stood in respectful silence waiting for the song to be over, so they could say their farewells.

They would go as they came, quietly and gently, in stark sobriety. They would not linger to eat the mounds of food that the women from town had brought to Pearl's house, nor stand around talking weather and crops, laughing and trying to lighten death's load the way she knew the townspeople would. No. They would simply go their steady, somber way, love and peace in their hearts. She knew them well. She was one of them. And that scared her.

Matthew had been her bridge to this town, to this other world. She shuddered, knowing he had died because of it. Now she would have to make it alone. She and her boys. 'Follow Christ to find that life which is life,' she said, quietly, shaking hard.

Then she heard the scream. The two boys had opened the coffin and stood staring into it as if frozen by the cold. Then one of the elders hurriedly shut the lid before anyone else could see inside.

CHAPTER ONE

Liberty, Kansas. March 15, 1893

It was late and Pearl Eddy was trying to breathe again, clutching at the letter that Hank Fegan had read to her and trying to get air. Mr Fegan had left an hour ago, letting himself out the back door and leaving Pearl sitting in the darkened parlor of her old house. She had made the man read it five times. And now she could repeat the words herself:

> My Dear Mrs Eddy:
>
> Our records show that you have not cleared two loans for farm equipment. We have allowed this debt to remain on our books due to our sympathy during your mourning period. However, we are certain you agree, this matter must be attended. Therefore, we respectfully request payment in full, in the amount of $500, within sixty days.
>
> I know that I do not need to remind you that under the terms of this obligation these monies must be repaid or your land, buildings and chattel sold to cover them.
>
> Sincerely,
>
> Alfred Snipes
> Manager
> First American Bank

Pearl was gasping for air again. She had not known about the loans. Her hands were trembling badly and she locked her fingers together and held them in her lap for control, her mind dredging up the deeply buried memory of Lillian's threat to take her boys. Though it had scared her, she had ignored it. Ignored it until this moment.

She bit hard at her lower lip. She didn't have $500. She'd been making ends meet during the past year and a half from seamstressing and the garden. Barely making them meet; things fraying badly at the edges. Her throat tightened. Lillian Eddy was a lot of things, Pearl knew. But she was not a person to make idle threats.

Pearl took a deep breath and held it until she thought she was going to burst and then let it out through clenched teeth. She had no more than half the needed money. She squeezed her hands together until they hurt. No . . . no . . . no. She would not lose the house. She would not lose her boys!

Pearl sat for a long time trying to focus on the silence inside her, listening for the inner voice of the Spirit. It did not come to her. But she did hear a sound: a harsh whisper of sorts. She tensed, thinking for a moment that it was a runaway horse somewhere outside in the darkness. But no. Something else. Something indistinct seemed to be rushing out of the prairie night toward the old house. One of the boys coughed in the bedroom and she was momentarily reassured. But then she heard the vague noise again; it seemed to be moving rapidly over the distant rooftops of town, then out across the three miles of intervening grasslands, until she finally distinguished the sound of human voices.

Ten minutes later, a noisy crowd was hurrying down the road toward the house. That's when it happened. She was certain of it. Her back doorknob turned and the door squeaked open. Pearl stood and faced the rooms behind her, listening.

Moments later, she heard another noise: someone moving in the kitchen. She took a sharp breath and pulled the boys' door closed, then turned toward the hallway, her ears probing the shadows, her heart pounding. Nothing. No movement of the air. No sound. But someone was in her house.

Pearl was taking her breath in little gulps. She backed reflexively against the bedroom door, listening with her mouth open so that her breathing wouldn't interfere with her hearing. There! The cellar door had opened, then closed: the latch clicking sharply in the darkness, the sound of footsteps descending the steps. Cornered. No windows. No way out. Would the intruder realize this and suddenly lunge back up the stairs?

She crept across the parlor toward the hallway, her hands shaking. Then she stopped, suddenly feeling foolish. This was not right, she told herself, sneaking around, afraid of every little sound. She pulled herself up to her full height. Her hands still trembled but she felt better and stepped cautiously into the hall and locked the cellar door.

She was still calming herself when she smelled it. She bent and sniffed, the odor familiar, but oddly out of place. Uncertain, she searched until she touched it. Yes. Blood. Drops ran across the hallway floor. The person was hurt. Something caught inside her chest.

Moments later, someone was pounding hard on the front door and she moved and opened it, expecting Sheriff Haines, but it was Jake Bidwell who spoke.

'Mrs Eddy.'

Bidwell had worked on their farm and she had midwifed his second child. She did not care for the way he lived. He worked little, drank hard and was rough on his wife.

'We're hunting a man,' Bidwell said, looking boldly past her into the shadows of the darkened house.

She recognized the voices of others as workers in the carriage factory south of town, or loafers around the saloon and livery.

'Buck-nigger,' one of them continued.

She stiffened.

'Colored,' Bidwell corrected, slurring the word.

'Robbed old man James – attacked him and his boys.'

'Are they alive?'

'Busted up.'

The men pressed around the door.

'Where's the sheriff?' Pearl asked, her voice shaking slightly. She couldn't get her thoughts off the memory of a young Negro lynched across the Missouri line the year they had come out to Kansas. 'Cause of death unknown, but severe,' the newspaper had reported.

'Bad nigger,' one of the men said to Pearl. 'We'll search your place, then be –'

'Do not use that word,' she snapped. She was trembling.

The man who'd just spoken took a step forward. 'Like I said, we'll search your place.'

Pearl had opened the door fully intending to turn the intruder over to the sheriff, but now, having touched the blood and listened to the men, something shifted hard inside her. The Negro wouldn't survive the night in their hands. She squared her small shoulders in the doorway.

'Where is the sheriff?'

'Doesn't matte –'

'No,' she interrupted.

'We're hunting a gawddamn criminal – chased him down this road –'

'Thou will not search my house. My children are asleep. I thank thee.'

When the door clicked closed, her legs went weak and she leaned against it for support. Moments later, she hurried into the kitchen, scooting quickly through the darkened hallway as if she were being chased. Again, she forced herself to slow down and braced a chair under the cellar door handle, wondering if it and the lock would hold the man. Probably for a while. Then she remembered that he had beaten the three Jameses. He didn't sound normal. Perhaps a madman – with a madman's strength.

She put an ear to the wood. Nothing. She backed away and took a deep breath, then cleared her throat. 'I know thou are down there,' she said tentatively. She waited for the man's response. If he heard her, he said nothing. She pulled the door to the parlor shut so that she wouldn't wake the boys.

'Please do not try to fool me,' she said, her voice rising. 'I know thou are there.' She paused. 'I can get a doctor.' Still there was no reply and she stood pondering what else to say.

'I will let thee out in the morning. In the meantime, it is best if thou stay. I will not tell anyone. Thou hast my word.'

Pearl placed her hands on her small waist so they would not shake and waited for some sound from below. None came. Finally, she said, 'Good,' as if they had reached some mutual understanding.

Some ten minutes later, she was sitting on a stool in the hallway facing the cellar door, her troubled thoughts on the man's possible injuries. Was he unconscious? Was his life ebbing away because she refused to open the door? The image of a Negro in death throes flashed in her thoughts, forcing her to pace nervously between the hallway and the parlor. Should she not open the door? She hesitated. Was he dangerous?

It didn't matter – she couldn't just let him die. She thought of her mother ministering to the criminally insane in the asylums of New York City. Pearl took a deep breath and moved into the hallway again. She stopped. Her lip was trembling and she touched it with her fingertips. No. She couldn't. She didn't possess her mother's courage.

'I am trying to help.'

She waited a long time, but no answer came.

'If thou cannot talk – make noise.'

Pearl was turning away when she heard what she thought was a muffled banging from below. She hesitated, then with a hand that was shaking so hard she had to hold it by the wrist to steady it, she unlocked the cellar door.

He was hiding and shivering from the early April cold and his wet clothes, his throat burning from the stove-smoke, his tearing eyes searching nervously for whoever had come down the steps moments before. He knew Negroes who'd been taken by mobs. It wasn't going to happen to him. Not while he could still fight. He hefted the sap in his hand. Some comfort. But not much. It would only work if he could get close. Suddenly he felt the dizziness coming over him and he clamped his eyes shut and clutched his head in both hands to clear it. He had to clear it. Either that or he was going to get caught. Then for a fleeting moment he saw the black woman's face.

'Go away,' he muttered under his breath.

He was seeing her more and more, and it was beginning to bother him. The first time – five years ago – he'd been lying unconscious in a ring after a fight in St Louis. Caught with a sucker punch, he'd hit the canvas hard and as he lay there, he remembered, she'd just popped into his thoughts how-do-you-do-like – looking smug and righteous, as if she belonged there. She never said anything, just stared at him as though he were some pitiful creature.

He hadn't seen her again for maybe a year; then he'd see her off and on. But lately it had been happening regularly. Whenever he was tired or badly winded, or had gotten tagged on the button.

He blinked his eyes hard. She was gone. The dizziness gone as well. His mind leaped back to the person who'd come down the cellar steps moments before.

Except for the weak glow from the stove, there was no light in the cellar. Whoever it was, they were walking around in the dark without so much as a candle. He figured they had a gun. Even so, they were stupid.

Suddenly the fire flared and the figure whirled toward him. He ducked, kicking himself for having started the stove, but his clothes were soaked and he was freezing, having run a mile or so in a river to escape the town dogs. On top of that, he had no other way to cook the chicken.

'Are thou hurt badly?'

He jumped: a woman's voice. Stunned, he let her pass by his hiding place, circle the stove and move away. She was at the other end of the room now – walking in a halting way, as if her eyes hadn't adjusted to the dark.

'I will help thee.'

He bit at his lip. The fact that it was a woman didn't make a whole lot of difference; she could still shoot him. Nevertheless, it bothered him. He'd never hit one before. He guessed the distance to the stairs – figuring he could make it in six strides – then forced himself to stop. She'd see him as soon as he stood and start firing; then he'd be running again . . . or dead. Neither possibility appealed much. Wait, he told himself. She'd give up and go back upstairs.

He shook his head hard. It was dangerous when a man started telling himself lies. Lightning hadn't killed and plucked the chicken, stuck it on the metal rod, and then started the stove; no, she knew he was here. And from the way she was doggedly searching she appeared loony enough to keep at it.

'Can thou groan?' She paused. 'If thou will groan, I will find thee.'

He ducked into a tighter ball, feeling stiff and far older than his thirty-four years, then he felt the dizziness coming on him again, and the face of the old Negro woman was swimming rapidly out of the shadows at him.

'I'm no criminal,' he said as if the black woman had accused him of something.

The word bumped around in his head. He didn't like the sound of it. He stole things, but he wasn't a criminal. Not in the regular sense. He had a long list of good reasons for everything he'd ever done. And even if he hadn't covered them all, there was nothing he could do about it.

The old woman disappeared again, taking the dizziness with her. He waited for his thoughts to straighten out. He was feeling better. But the word – criminal – was on his mind and making him feel shabby. It had to be because of this woman down here thinking he was hurt and trying to help, while he was waiting to crack her skull. It didn't seem fair.

He started to stand, then stopped, getting a quick grip on himself. Maybe she wasn't trying to help. Maybe she was trying to lure him out so the mob could get at him.

'Sir.'

She sounded white and sincere.

'Can thou hear me?'

He let out the air he was holding. It was no use. She wasn't going to quit until she found him. And things might go better, he figured, if he just gave himself up. Perhaps he could convince her he hadn't done anything wrong. It was a chance – and he didn't have many left. If she got scared and went back upstairs without finding him, knowing that he was down here, she'd surely set the mob on him. He might be able to convince her he was wrongly accused.

When she turned away, he started to tiptoe to a barrel in front of the stove, stepping as quietly as he could so she wouldn't hear. But he dragged his right foot slightly, the way he did sometimes after one of his spells, not much, but still it scraped across the cellar floor.

'Sir?' Her voice quivered in the darkness.

Ears like a damn bat, he thought. He sat on the barrel and tried to look nonchalant; listening to her rapid breathing and knowing she was badly scared. But scared or not, she was scurrying toward him now like a dog after a cat.

He cleared his throat and started easy-whistling to warn her. She stopped moving and he stopped whistling, the notes drifting away ghostlike in the darkness. He squirmed. She was no more than ten feet away, with a clear line of sight, but watching her turning her head back and forth – nervously trying to catch sounds in the air – he knew she hadn't seen him yet.

'I have come to help thee.'

He braced. 'Pipe needs fixing,' he said, as friendly as he could, clamping his eyes shut and praying she was a bad shot. Seconds ticked by. He peeked at her.

She'd hopped back and was staring open-mouthed at him, looking small and badly frightened. Then she took a breath as if she might be drowning in the shadows.

'How badly are thou hurt?' she asked.

'I'm not, ma'am. Just cold.'

She paused. 'Thou are not hurt?'

'No, ma'am.'

'Thou signaled thou were.' There was the slightest change in her tone.

'No, I didn't.'

'Yes, thou did,' she said quickly, some of the nervous tension breaking through her voice. 'I said make noise if thou are hurt and cannot talk – and thou hit something.'

He was surprised. She seemed less concerned about standing in a dark cellar a few feet away from a stranger – a half-drowned Negro who'd just broken into her house to escape a mob – than whether or not he'd humbugged her into coming down the stairs.

He hadn't tricked her. The last thing he wanted was a woman down here arguing with him while the whole town was hunting him.

'Ma'am, I didn't signal anything.'

'Yes, I heard thee.'

He shook his head and started to reply, then decided it was best to simply ignore her. He glanced at her hands. Empty. No pistol. It must be in her pocket. He was surprised she wasn't waving it around, threatening him.

Since she was agitated about the so-called 'signal' that had caused her to come down, he picked up a hammer and banged the stove pipe a couple of times. She jumped as if she herself had been struck.

'There's your signal,' he said, forcing a smile. 'All I was doing was trying to get this damn thing to stop smoking.'

When she finally got some control over herself, she said, 'Please do not swear.'

He stared at her, the smile barely holding, his teeth chattering, then pointed the handle of the hammer at the old stove. 'When was the last time you had this contraption fixed?'

'Never mind. What are thou doing down here?'

It was a tough question.

'Sir?' her voice tremulous.

He paused. 'Fixing dinner.'

The absurdity of his reply stopped Pearl for a moment and she clasped her hands behind her so he wouldn't see them shaking. Her face and clothes were badly smudged with cellar dust.

'Dinner?' She smelled roasting meat for the first time through the smoke, and realized that it had been animal blood on the floor upstairs. He really wasn't hurt.

'Dinner,' he repeated.

'Chicken?'

'Yes, ma'am.'

She got a funny look on her face. 'What kind?'

'Hen.'

'But what kind?'

'I don't know.' The smile was fading. He crossed his arms and rubbed his hands up and down them – hard – then gripped himself, trying to conserve what little body heat he had left.

'Surely you know one from another.'

'Red feathers, ma'am,' he said, shrugging his shoulders and glancing at the pile of them near his feet. 'That's all I know.'

'Rhode Island Red,' she mumbled. Then the tension building inside her released in a sudden flood of words. 'Thou had no right to kill my hen – no right to break into my house.' She stopped, grappling for words to express her emotions. 'Thou – thou ought to be ashamed.' She said the last as if it was the worst thing on earth that could be said about a person.

He squirmed again. 'I got this chicken down the road.'

Her expression didn't change.

'Two farms away,' he lied.

She wasn't buying it. Slowly, he slipped the sap out. He didn't want to, but a nerve kept going off somewhere in his head, telling him it was the only way with this woman. Just a light tap. She'd wake up good as new.

'Those are my chickens.' She wasn't letting go.

He shrugged his shoulders beneath his wet shirt, the cold grabbing him again. She was a piece of something. Not much bigger than a Russian thistle, she'd come tripping down here, without so much as a match, to find somebody who'd broken into her house. And now, having found them, she was acting like a Texan at the Alamo. All because of a dead bird. She was a loony.

'Those are my chickens,' she repeated with growing firmness.

This wasn't going anywhere, he calculated. Somehow he had to distract her. He wanted her relaxed so he could get a good clean hit that would do the least damage to her.

'My name's The Prophet, ma'am. But I shortened it,' he added, fighting to keep his teeth from chattering, 'to just Prophet.' He sensed she wouldn't care for the whole of it: The Prophet of Doom – his ring name.

Her expression didn't change. Nor did she look the least distracted.

'Like the prophets in the Bible,' he offered.

For a while nothing much happened, then her stiff expression began to slowly change, the strained look in her eyes relaxing. At last he'd said something that had started her thinking. And when she thought, the whole process could be seen on her face. 'Are thou a minister?'

He shook his head no. She wasn't six feet away, but she continued to look like she was waiting for an answer. Again, he shook his head.

'Your name?'

'Pearl Eddy.'

'Nice.' He forced a smile. He'd get her to relax, then slap-bamm. She was bossy enough that he was feeling he could do it without regrets.

'Nice name,' he repeated for emphasis.

She didn't react and he sensed flattery wasn't going to work on her anytime soon.

'I do not understand thee,' she said.

'About?'

'Why thou, a minister, would steal my hen?'

Jessssssusssallllmighty . . . first she thought he'd tricked her. Now she thought he was a minister. She was definitely missing something vital in her head.

'Ma'am, it's just a chicken. From what I saw, there are fifty or sixty others.'

'That is hardly the point, Mr Prophet.'

'Yes, ma'am,' he said. He stood slowly, stretching out the stiffness in his shoulder joints and positioning himself so that he could move between her and the stairs in case she decided to run, but she hopped up quickly on to the second step. Nobody's fool.

'Just saying thou are sorry does not make up for what thou have done with my hen,' she said, backing up another step.

He shook his head and settled back down on the keg. It was as if he'd strangled her favorite aunt. It didn't much matter. She had him now. He might catch her before she reached the top but she'd be screaming murder all the way, and would surely shoot him. And if this was a trick, there'd be men at the top of the stairs. He thought of those dead Negroes again and shivered. Just sit, he told himself, slipping the sap back into his wet pocket.

'Ma'am, I'll pay for the hen.'

From the look on her face the offer hadn't appeased her much.

She was tapping her foot. 'I would expect that thou – a minister – would understand.'

He was suddenly very tired of this minister thing and he started to say so, then thought better of it. He didn't know why, he just figured it might be useful.

'Of course,' he said, in his best preacher voice. She didn't look impressed.

The fire cast a wavering glow over her and he thought she looked pretty, but he wasn't certain in the shadows.

'Ma'am?'

'Yes?'

'Do you have any salt?'

She made an awkward little sound. 'I don't understand thee,

Mr Prophet. Thou dodge the law – break into my home – kill my hen – then ask for salt to season thy stolen food.'

She stumbled around on the stairs for a moment before starting up, taking the steps in a careful stride that caught his eye. He stood and she heard or sensed him, and whirled back. 'Stay where thou are.'

He could see she was trembling like a snared sparrow.

'Ma'am, you've nothing to fear from me. I've done nothing but hide myself from a mob.'

The latter statement was another lie. He'd tried to pick an old man's pocket and been caught. Three men had jumped him. He'd handled them easily enough with the sap, but getting out of town had proven more difficult; the crowd had chased him through yards, up alleys and over fences, before he'd lost them by hiding under a pile of corrugated iron. But then a dog had dug him out, raising a ruckus in the process. After that, he'd run hard down a river and across the fields until he escaped by slipping in here at this lonely farmhouse.

'It is not my place to judge thee.' She was halfway up the stairs. 'Just stay where thou are.'

He watched her climbing, calculating the odds she wouldn't get the mob. Not good. His impulse was to move at once, to rush up the stairs to freedom, but he resisted it. He wouldn't last out in the open. Not with the dogs. He had to be certain the crowd was gone. He continued watching her, again noticing her gait: a careful, methodical way of moving that seemed awkward and unsure.

When she was near the top, he called up, 'If you –'

She looked down at him.

'Turn me in,' he said weakly.

'I gave thee my word.'

'But if you change your mind, ma'am – I'd be obliged if it was the sheriff.' In the hands of the sheriff, he might have a chance.

'I gave thee my word.'

Minutes later, she was back on the stairs, taking her ponderous steps and gripping the banister with one hand as if she might fall a thousand feet if she let go, a tray balanced in her other hand.

She set it down on the keg and stood without saying anything. Generous portions of bread and butter, a glass of milk, pitcher of water, a slice of apple pie and salt. It looked wonderful. But even better were the two blankets she carried under one arm.

'Thank you, ma'am,' he said, hurriedly stepping behind a pile of boxes and undressing, wrapping one blanket around his waist and pulling the other across his shoulders. They were badly worn. Clean-smelling and neatly patched, but worn. They felt wonderful against his chilled skin.

'Thank you,' he said again. He was feeling embarrassed standing in front of this tiny woman like some African chieftain in blankets. But she didn't seem to notice, or care. She was still hitched up over the dead hen, he guessed.

'Thou are welcome,' she said, a cool sound in her voice.

He returned to the meal. He'd eat it – then if things were still quiet, he'd give her a tap on the noodle and be on his way. If he could make the railroad, he might escape. He looked at her again. She was small but stood up proud. Even so, it wouldn't take much to knock her out.

'I'm no criminal, ma'am,' he offered, suddenly feeling the need to explain himself. 'Just a preacher running for my life.'

'Though thou stole my hen, I did not say thou were a criminal,' she said quietly from the shadows.

She kept a bead on the truth, he thought, and she wasn't going to let go of her damn bird without a struggle. He'd seen bulldogs with less determination.

He started to carve the chicken, then stopped and held up the knife she'd brought him: it was large and razor-sharp. The kind butchers used on beef carcasses. The kind a person might use if they wanted to slit someone's throat. She was loopy. Or . . . His heart sped some. Either that, or she was trying to plant a weapon on him. It didn't matter, he told himself. The mob would do what they had a mind to do.

She wasn't much on small talk and minutes later the quiet started bothering him.

'Married, ma'am?'

'Yes.'

He wondered where her husband was. Maybe upstairs waiting.

'Quaker?'

'Yes.'

He nodded, watching her between gulps of food. 'Negro,' he said, as if she might not be able to tell. 'Some men and I disagreed over money and they attacked me. Them being white – I ran.' He lowered his head and tried to look repentant. 'I should not have.'

She didn't say anything.

He sat eating and perfecting his tale in his head.

'We argued over church money.' He certainly wasn't going to confess that he'd tried to steal a wallet. He studied her out of the side of his eye, uncertain as to whether or not she believed him. 'That's the truth.'

'I was told that thou robbed a man – beating him and his sons.'

'I am afraid I raised my hands in anger, Mrs Eddy.' He lowered his head and folded the offending objects together at his waist for effect.

'That the men are injured,' she continued.

Things were getting tight. He bit at the inside of his lip. Then he used the one and only biblical line he knew: 'Wait upon the Lord, and He will strengthen thee.' Fortunately, it seemed to fit.

She mulled this over for a while before she said, 'Thou are a minister. I believe thee.'

He smiled, then squirmed inside, feeling something like guilt. Maybe because she seemed ready to swallow everything he fed her. He shrugged it off. Let her believe what she wanted. If she wanted to believe he was the Holy Ghost, it was all right with him. She had the gun. All he wanted was out of this town.

'I didn't take a penny, Mrs Eddy,' he continued. That was the truth. But only because the fat man had caught him. 'Your husband upstairs?'

21

'No. He is dead.'

That surprised him. Not that her husband was dead, but that she hadn't concocted a tale about one lurking upstairs, waiting to pounce on him. He returned to listening for the mob. Nothing.

He spread butter on a slice of bread, then glanced at her. The way she stood – staring off into the shadows, her head canted slightly – seemed peculiar and he studied her more closely. She was small and youthful-looking, her brown hair done up in a neat bun, her skin the color of flour dumplings. While well made and of decent material, her long dress was a dull gray and lacking in style. And like the blankets, it, too, had seen better days. Still, with a little something – jewelry, or a touch of color on her cheeks, she might have been better than plain. He wondered again where she was hiding the pistol. It was bothering him.

'Mrs Eddy – do you have a gun?'

She turned toward him and stood without speaking.

'Being down here in the dark and all – I was just wondering,' he added, uncomfortable with the silence.

'I do not believe in guns.'

Something told him she wasn't lying. He let his breath out slowly. 'Yes. They're very dangerous,' he mumbled, knowing he had one in his traveling bag.

'I am here,' she continued in the same unhappy tone as earlier, 'because I thought thou were hurt.'

'I didn't trick you, ma'am,' he said, exasperated.

'I believe thou did – and thou a minister.'

She continued staring into the shadows. He went back to eating, sorry he'd asked about the gun. It just gave her another chance to lecture him.

'I will get the sheriff in the morning so thou can straighten this –'

'I'm leaving when I finish eating and my clothes dry.' He'd come to three conclusions. One: no one was upstairs. Two: there was no gun. And three: she wouldn't scream. She wasn't the type. Stubborn – but no screamer. And while he didn't know why, he

22

knew she hadn't called the law yet. He wasn't hanging around until she changed her mind.

'Thou cannot do that, Mr Prophet.'

'I'm going, Mrs Eddy,' he said, the food and drink giving him new resolve.

'No,' she said firmly. He noticed she had this way of pulling up her frame to maximum height whenever she got stiff over something. He figured she had some sand in her craw, but she controlled it well. That was part of what he sensed about her: she was always reining herself in like she was an unruly colt.

'Yes,' he said, just as firmly, not liking her bossy streak.

'They are still searching for thee.' She paused. 'Even if thou got away, it would not be right.' She said the words as if he'd be committing some awful crime by fleeing.

He didn't respond.

'That is not a proper way to live.'

He sat looking at her, convinced she was off in the head. 'Just my luck,' he mumbled. She was staring into the shadows in her queer way.

'Pardon?'

'Sweet like duck,' he said, pointing at the hen. Then he was agitated he'd dodged her and said: 'Mrs Eddy, don't get yourself worked up. You don't owe me. I don't owe you – excepting for this damn hen.'

'I asked thee not to swear,' she said, taking a step up the stairs. 'Thou being a man of God, I am surprised.'

'Yes, Mrs Eddy.'

'I do not believe in people being hurt or killed by other people.'

'That's noble.'

'Thou have a responsibility,' she continued, ignoring his remark, 'to thyself – and to me – to resolve this matter in the right way.'

He looked dumbstruck. 'To you?'

'Yes. I am involved in this. I hid thee.' She paused. 'I do not believe in breaking the law.'

He shook his head slowly, studying her through the shadows. She was standing and tapping her foot impatiently. He figured she was doing it to let him know she wasn't happy with him. It was annoying.

'Mrs Eddy, I'm leaving.'

She turned and darted up the stairs, gripping the banister with one hand, then stopped and looked down for a moment before stepping out and shutting the door behind her. He heard the lock turn. Then the chair slid back into place.

'Hey!'

'I will let thee out in the morning, Mr Prophet,' she said, her voice muffled. 'Whether thou choose to face thy accusers then, or run, is thy choice.' There was silence for a moment, then she continued, 'But tonight – I will not have thee harmed. I'm certain as a minister of the faith thou will do the right thing.'

'Mrs Eddy, you don't have any right to lock me up.'

'Oh yes I do – thou broke into my house.'

'You're crazy. I can tell things about people,' he yelled, 'and, Mrs Eddy, you aren't right in the head.'

'In the morning, Mr Prophet.' She paused. 'Good night.' Pearl Eddy leaned weakly against the door.

Prophet's clothes were hanging on the cellar line; his pants were closest to him, just in case she came back down to give him one more lecture. It wouldn't surprise him. He stretched out under the blankets on an old mattress, admiring a ring he'd lifted off a bedroom dresser the night before, simply by reaching in through an open window. Its red stone sparkled in the stove's wavering light. It might be a ruby. But he bet garnet. Then his thoughts were on the white woman again. There was no mistaking lunacy in man or beast. And she had it.

He shut his eyes and tried to sleep but was unable to shake the tenseness. Night had always been a breeder of unwanted thoughts for him. He jumped at a creaking sound in the floorboards overhead. Sweat was beading on his brow and he fought a sensation of panic. He held his breath: listening. Nothing. She'd kept her word. At least so far. He wondered why. It didn't matter. He was just damn glad. The men chasing him would likely kill a dog with more tenderness than a Negro.

He glanced around, suddenly feeling trapped. The room was filled with mounds of old stuff arranged in neat order. Empty boxes, broken chairs, a rusted tub and jars for canning. Not much else.

The tightness continued inside him. He had to get a grip. He'd had slow-moving dreams all his life, but now, trapped down here, they seemed to be grinding to a halt. That scared him. He climbed off the mattress, wrapping a blanket around his waist, and began to shadow-box in the darkness. Jabbing, feinting left, then right, throwing hard body hooks at invisible adversaries. He bobbed and weaved, covered up and fought out of desperate make-believe situations.

After some fifteen minutes, he started to wind badly and bent over, too fast, and quickly put his hands on his knees to catch himself. He could feel the blood and wooziness flooding into his head and he closed his eyes and locked his legs so he wouldn't fall, gripping harder with his hands. Then he saw the old black woman again, staring at him with her pitying look.

'I'm not muddleheaded,' he said loudly. 'I take my shots on top of the head: so fools bust their knuckles on it. But I'm not punchy.'

He started to straighten up but the giddiness was still with him and he stayed bent over, keeping his eyes closed and searching for the old woman. But he couldn't see her.

'If things get fuzzy – they clear,' he said quietly. 'And I move as fast as ever.' He paused. 'I can go forty rounds and take a man out with either hand.'

When the lightheadedness passed, he lay back down and tried to sleep. He felt better but the thought of the old woman was still pestering, so he jumped back up and shadow-boxed some more as if to show her he still had it, his hamlike fists flying through the air.

'I was never no talker. Maybe that's why I haven't had my shot yet,' he huffed, poking his jab at the dark air. 'But I'm coming up on it. I promise you, old nigger lady, I'm coming up on it. I'm listening to no one but me now.'

He stopped punching and looked around at the shadowy corners of the cellar as if he hoped to spot her watching him. She wasn't. He began to run in place, bringing his knees up high in a rapid sprint.

'All the time someone was promising me they were going to get me a fight with Paddy Ryan or Bubbles Davis or Joe Godfrey,' he said, panting and addressing the shadows. 'Just fight some no-name. Build up your reputation. Get you a shot.' He stopped talking and just ran. Then he said, 'All them years. Just gone.'

He was breathing hard now and he stopped running and bent over, carefully fighting the pains in his lower back, and tried to catch his breath.

'So I did, old lady. Only I never saw nothing in the newspapers about me. About how good I was. And I never got a fight with Ryan or Bubbles or nobody anybody ever heard of.' He stopped talking to let his breath catch up.

'But that doesn't make me a chump. I'm going into training, and I'm going to get a shot.' He straightened up and balled his heavy fists. 'I can stun an ox with these,' he said, speaking proudly into the darkness beyond the circle of stove light.

He lay back down on the mattress and stared at the ceiling, a slight tremor pulling the muscles taut around his mouth. 'No criminal and no chump,' he mumbled. The tremor passed. 'I take things, old lady, because nobody hires me to do nothing but fight. But even if they did, I wouldn't be their right kind of nigger. I'm no "Yes suh" and "No suh" boy.'

He stopped talking for a while and stared blindly at the shadows above. 'So get off my back,' he muttered.

Half an hour later, Prophet had been peering at the dark ceiling of the cellar for so long he was having a hard time focusing on it. The Negro woman was gone, but the old feelings were creeping up on him. They came whenever he spent time in a place. They'd come fast here. The disappearing woe, he called it.

Everything about him was made up. Birthday. Name. He'd changed it three times. It was like he'd just come to be one day. He didn't know much more than that. He hated that feeling of not knowing anything – feeling like he didn't even exist. He rubbed his eyes. Maybe he didn't. Maybe he was just somebody else's dream; maybe that old black woman's.

He sat up and roughly shoved the thought away. That was trash. He was no dream; he hurt too bad in places to be a dream. And he could remember things; he remembered a few of the folks who'd raised him for a while. Mostly he remembered moving on. But at least he remembered; and dreams don't remember anything. That thought made him feel better.

His eyes probed the darkness. He wondered what it was like living in one place, collecting junk, dust settling on you. The same house, same smells. Things just piling up. Not good. Choke a man under layers. The woman was wrong about staying. Moving kept things balanced.

He stared at the floorboards above him, cogitating what there might be worth taking up in the house. The thought did him good. Then he thought about getting his shot in the ring. That thought did him more good. It was what kept him going these days.

CHAPTER TWO

Pearl Eddy had worked late finishing the dress, then overslept, missing her morning meditation. That bothered her. She rarely missed. And the fact that she had, simply reinforced her feeling that things weren't going right.

She was hurrying through the sun-filled parlor, knowing the boys were going to be late for school and chiding herself, when she heard laughter coming from the kitchen and felt a surge of relief. Her oldest, Samuel, had gotten his brothers up. Such a responsible son. Her shoulders tightened. Too responsible. He had taken on too much after Matthew's death.

She forced her thoughts to the Negro. She would give him another chance to speak to the sheriff – would urge him to re-solve the matter properly. There was a possibility. He was a min-ister after all, though he seemed a little gone in the faith.

Pearl reached to touch the chair under the cellar doorknob: it wasn't there. She tried the handle: unlocked. Then she heard her six-year-old, Zacharias: 'Tell us about that tiger,' and she knew he was in the kitchen.

Prophet was cooking at the stove. 'Morning, Mrs Eddy,' he said over his shoulder as she came through the door. She sat with her boys at the table and didn't say a word, just began to tap the tips of her fingers on the hard surface. Prophet returned to his cook-ing, whistling as he worked. He was surprised that in the daylight she hadn't had a bad reaction to his face. Most people did. But she'd just looked at him as if everything about him was normal.

Samuel took sips of water from the glass he was holding and studied the Negro. He looked foolish in his red suspenders and maroon bow tie, flashy and out of place.

He guessed him at five foot ten and 165 pounds. Interestingly, his body didn't seem to fit together properly, as if he was made from parts of different people. Thick shoulders spread yokelike over a thin waist – as thin, Samuel thought, as his mother's own – and arms too long for his torso dangled at his sides. The hands were larger than they should have been. Mixed together, these anatomical bits and pieces made him seem powerful, and muscles like thick cords on wood and heavy bone added to this sensation.

From the back the rest of the man wasn't much. The strangest thing was that he was bald. Completely so. He didn't look particularly bad this way, just clean like a horse with a butched mane. Samuel figured him early thirties, close to his mother's age, though the Negro moved in some ways like an old man, limping slightly and seemingly stiff in his joints.

Then the man turned and Samuel was staring into the off-kilter face. Somebody had made a butchery of it. The nose had been pushed to the side and scar tissue blanketed his cheeks and webbed the corners of his eyes. One ear was almost gone, bitten or torn off, he suspected. It was a bothersome visage.

Without warning, the muscles of the man's face seemed to go rigid and Samuel watched in embarrassed fascination as he struggled to control the quivering around his mouth. The Negro turned away self-consciously and tried to hide the trembling under one of his huge hands. The boy also looked away so he wouldn't shame him by staring, squinting at the twins until they did the same. He felt sorry for him. But that didn't alter his other definite feelings about this man. And they weren't good feelings.

'Mr Prophet's an animal wrestler,' Zacharias said excitedly. 'That's why he looks the way he does.' The boy was small and freckled, his curly hair the color of caramel. His voice squeaked in a funny way.

The jerking movement had stopped now and Prophet lowered

29

his hand and smiled at Zacharias. The boy smiled back as if they were the best of friends and struggled to hold on to the red rooster that he'd been carrying around all morning.

Now as Zacharias passed by on his way to the sink, the bird took a calculated sideways peck at Prophet, but the man was ready and dodged. The three younger boys laughed. Prophet didn't see the humor. Nor did Samuel.

The creature was still eyeing him, as if cogitating some new plan for his destruction. He glared back, licking his lips in a simple gesture he hoped it would understand. It didn't seem the least intimidated.

Prophet looked around the room. Normal enough: a farmhouse kitchen, with an iron sink, plain white walls and hard, scrubbed floors. She kept a clean house. Almost too clean, he thought. He'd had a rough time trying to prepare the boys' breakfast – the cupboards were so bare. She was tight-fisted with the buck: short on salt, sugar, coffee and most other essentials.

'Mr Prophet is a minister,' she corrected. 'And thou are not supposed to have Hercules inside.'

Zacharias turned and stared hard at him. 'Thou said thou were an animal wrestler.' His small shoulders drooped some.

'Both,' Prophet mumbled lamely. It was going to do his heart good to even the score with her.

'Samuel,' she said.

Tall and thin, with shoulder-length black hair, the oldest had his mother's fine features and white skin. He was serious like her as well. Samuel was glancing sideways at him. Prophet had seen that same look ten thousand times before. Fear, distrust, dislike. It didn't matter. He'd be long gone before the lad was out of school.

Watching them moving out the door, Prophet didn't envy these children with their long hair, old men's clothes and large black hats. They had to stick out like tulips in rye. Red flags for every bully. Still, the twins – Joshua and Luke – looked like they could handle themselves: tanned and stout. Prophet had an eye for spotting fighters and these two appeared to be the material. They'd stopped and were taking one last look at him; he grinned at them, and they grinned back. Straightforward. No guile. He liked that.

Even Zacharias looked like a scrapper. But tough as he might be, Prophet sensed the little one missed his father badly. He'd spent the morning trailing him around, hanging on to his hand and trying to crawl into his lap. Not even Prophet's frightening features discouraged him. After putting the bird out, Zacharias darted back and stopped in front of him.

'Will thou be here when I get home from school?'

'I've been tracking this runaway tiger.'

'Thou aren't an animal tracker.' Something in the boy's voice tugged at him.

'Zacharias,' his mother said softly.

The boy leaned over and whispered, 'Will thou be here? I need thee to do something for my pa.' He looked very serious.

'Samuel,' she said.

'Will thou?' the boy asked again, a small pleading sound in his voice.

'I'll see.' Prophet knew he wouldn't be staying – but for a reason he wasn't sure about, he didn't want to tell the boy.

Zacharias was watching him as he went out the door. Prophet waved goodbye. The boy pulled on his big black hat and again he mouthed the words: 'Will thou be here?'

Prophet sat motionless for a moment, his eyes on the boy, then he nodded, and Zacharias' face broke into a grin and he darted happily out the door. Prophet turned away, telling himself that he'd forget about it by supper.

He followed Pearl with his eyes as she walked to the kitchen sink and stood scraping burned toast into his used coffee grounds. He was surprised. He'd seen poor Negroes make burnt-toast coffee before, but never whites.

She was definitely stingy: sitting in this big house, keeping her cupboards thin, reusing coffee grinds. He guessed she wanted people to think she was poor. The rich were often like that.

'Nice boys, Mrs Eddy,' he said to break the uneasy silence.

She didn't respond.

Then the yard gate opened and shut and she said, 'I locked thee in the cellar.'

'And I got out, ma'am.'

'It does not matter.'

'That's how I saw it, Mrs Eddy.'

'I thought thou were going to run.'

'I was leaving,' he said, emphasizing 'leaving', 'when I ran into your oldest boy. I didn't want to scare him.'

'So thou told him lies instead.'

He shook his head, knowing from the night before that if she got wound up on a thing, there was no stopping her. He examined her more closely: small and delicate – but not dainty. Prettier than he'd thought.

'It'd go easier on them if they didn't have to wear those clothes.'

She didn't respond.

He took a sip of coffee, eyeing her over the cup. Still, she didn't react. That was OK. Silence was better than one of her lectures. He took another drink. Then he noticed that she was slowly pulling herself up straighter.

'Mr Prophet. Please do not worry about my children,' she said in a pleasant enough tone.

He eyed her cautiously.

'Thou are not supposed to be here – or have thou forgotten?' she continued, speaking carefully. 'Thou broke into my home, killed my hen, and involved me in thy unlawfulness.' Her volume was rising, the tone not as pleasant as before. 'Then thou lied to my children about thy acts and purposes.' She stopped and tapped the toe of her shoe.

There was no doubt about it: she was addled. 'Your way, Mrs Eddy,' he said, quickly resuming his meal and snatching glimpses of her between bites: pretty but dressed like she was leading a six-horse funeral. Too bad she was daft.

'I'm going to see the sheriff,' she said.

There she was, at it again. 'That would be a waste of time, Mrs Eddy. I'll be gone before you get back.'

'Fine – but it must be done.'

'No, it mustn't – but I don't think you see that.'

'No, I do not,' she said stiffly.

'Your choice, Mrs Eddy.' He pointed at a jar sitting on the kitchen counter. 'In the meantime, may I have some of that jelly?'

Prophet had always known that small things could change a person's life. And later he would remember that this jar of jelly had done just that. But he didn't know it now. The only thing he knew now was that Mrs Eddy was blind. Stone blind.

The shock of it caused him to sit open-mouthed and stare at her. Her eyes looked normal enough: a clear rinsed blue, like sky after rain. He studied them until she said, 'Mr Prophet?'

She was staring into an empty piece of air – holding the jar out a good six feet from where he sat.

Edward Johnson's law office was over Moyers' Café, and food odors were rising through the floorboards of the messy little room. Johnson was in a swivel chair behind his desk watching Pearl as she paced back and forth in front of the large window that faced Main Street. The tapping of her long, thin cane was soft on the dusty wooden floorboards.

'Edward, I have two problems.'

'Yes?'

'The bank is threatening to call my mortgage if I don't pay some equipment loans that Matthew took.'

He watched her for a while, waiting for her to continue. When she didn't he said, 'And you don't have the money?'

'Half.'

He continued to watch her walking around the office, her face drawn and lips moving silently. He'd never seen her like this before. She turned quickly in his direction.

'I have my seamstressing, the gardens, the new pullets.'

Johnson ran his hands through his hair. 'How long to raise the rest?'

'Six months.'

'Six months,' he repeated.

'Yes.'

'Long time.'

'Edward, I can't lose the farm.'

Again he was surprised by the desperate sound in her voice. Then he thought about her boys and her blindness and, as the father of eight kids, he understood. 'Of course not, Pearl.' He did some quick calculating. 'Let me talk to Snipes. I'll tell him you'll pay half now – and half in six months. He'll accept that.'

'Are thou certain?'

'Land values are down. The bank wants your mortgage money each month. Not farm your place.' Edward laughed. 'Snipes is no farmer.'

Pearl didn't laugh but the lines around her eyes relaxed some. 'I will bring the money to him.'

'Hold it until I work out the details.'

She nodded.

'And the second problem?'

'There's a man hiding in my home.'

Some fifteen minutes later, Pearl was done explaining about Prophet and the mob and the dead chicken.

'He'll run,' the attorney said.

'He is a religious man, Edward.'

He shook his head. 'Preacher or parrot – he won't stay. But I'll talk to the sheriff.'

He locked his fingers together behind his head and leaned back in the chair, stretching his long legs and wishing she'd leave so he could prepare for court.

'Anything else, Pearl?'

She wasn't hearing him. She'd stopped in front of the window and stood listening to the sounds of cat-calls and hollering rising from the street below.

'Edward?'

Johnson was tall, about six foot five, lean and strong, with a pleasant face and thick glasses that belied a toughness. Forty years old, he still retained a look of vigor and youth. He'd been the Eddys' attorney since they'd arrived in Liberty.

'Not the Negro,' he assured her, looking down into the street. 'Just a bunch of bums ragging an oriental family.'

'Orientals?'

Johnson cleaned his glasses on the corner of his coat. 'Came to claim some fellow's homestead. He'd made a deal with them: a quarter section he owned in Liberty for five years of the family's labor in Hawaii. Left it in his will. Unfortunately, the land was declared abandoned years ago. But the oriental woman won't believe it. Judge Wilkins and I showed her the records, but she still won't believe it. She just squatted her family down in front of the hotel.' He put his glasses back on his prominent nose. 'Doesn't much matter,' he continued, returning to his desk and stuffing papers into a satchel.

'What doesn't matter?'

'About the land. Orientals can't legally own it anyhow. Even if they could, nobody would sell them anything. They can't even buy food. And those hecklers would drive them crazy.'

Pearl stared down at the street as if she might actually be able to see them. 'How long have they been there?'

Johnson was signing something. 'Tuesday's train.'

'They haven't eaten in two days?'

Johnson didn't respond, studying the paper he'd just signed.

'Edward?'

'Sorry, Pearl.'

'They haven't eaten in two days?' she repeated.

'The judge and I dropped off milk, bread and eggs last evening.'

The cat-calls increased.

'We'll see they get headed wherever they want to go.' He glanced at her. 'Pearl.'

35

She didn't respond.

'Pearl?'

'Edward?'

'Don't get involved.'

She nodded.

He glanced at his watch. 'Court opens in fifteen minutes.'

She was listening to the sounds on the street again.

'Pearl.'

'I'm sorry. What did thou say?'

'I said stay away from the orientals. People are already worked up over them.' He was loading things into his satchel. 'And court is opening.'

Pearl looked suddenly stunned by some unseen blow, then she was moving toward the door, her cane tapping fast. Johnson grabbed quickly at her elbow, guiding her through the maze of papers stacked in little piles on the floor.

'Thou will remember to speak to Mr Snipes?'

'I've written it down.'

Nine-year-old Chrissy James was wrapped in a blanket and resting in her father's arms, rhythmically opening and shutting her mouth like a baby bird begging for food, pulling hard for each breath. Her father, Simon, stroked her thin black hair and said something soft to her and she rolled her long, narrow head hard against his chest, seemingly unable to control the movement. Her eyes gazed up at him in an unfocused way, then she began to drool and prattle in the morning sunlight, blue veins bright under the white skin of her temple.

Simon pulled out a handkerchief and wiped her mouth; then he looked away to Main Street and the dusty little campsite in front of the hotel, noticing Pearl Eddy coming down the stairs from the county attorney's office and tapping her way quickly along the sidewalk to her buggy.

Chrissy's brother, Hector, sixteen and strong-looking, with a badly poxed face, the youngest of Simon's three boys, was sitting close beside his father, holding Chrissy's toys. He made a funny piglike noise with his nose and waited while his sister turned her head toward him in her lunging way. He grinned. 'Hector pig. Hector pig,' he said, continuing to grin, and starting one of her little cotton figures dancing whimsically before her.

Simon glanced at Hector's play and absentmindedly reached a hand and patted Chrissy's head, then went back to staring at the Quaker woman, squinting his eyes against the morning sun and watching as she climbed hurriedly into her buggy and let the old horse start on his own down the street.

He pursed his lips and thought a moment, an idea not quite yet formed in his mind, then he looked back at the little camp in the road. There was a small group of rough-looking men sitting in chairs behind them. Friends of Simon James.

Simon and his boys had been stealing for the past two hours. Not for gain. Simply to 'encourage' the Johnnie-Johns – as orientals were known in these parts – to leave town. Half a bag of rice, a pair of sandals, a tattered parasol, all snatched from the edge of the little makeshift campsite whenever the deputy wasn't looking.

Now the Johnnie-Johns' hog was feeding on chunks of bread they'd tossed into the street from their seats on the sidewalk.

'Come on, pig,' Penny James hissed.

Twenty-six and the oldest of the James boys, Penny was average in height and weight, but broad-chested and bull-strong. His normally ordinary-looking face was lumpy and bruised this morning, one eye swollen shut and his lips puffed and split. He squinted his good eye and tossed another piece of bread.

Straining against its rope, the sow stretched hard for the tidbit. 'Pull, you stupid hog,' Penny urged.

She was a sorry-looking beast: runted, sway-backed and covered with coarse black hair. Didn't matter. They wanted her.

But there was one problem: a little oriental girl of five or six was hanging over the sow's back, watching them and chewing hungrily on each piece of bread they tossed. She darted after this new morsel like it was gold.

'Damn Chinee suckling,' Simon James muttered.

One of the men behind Simon moved up close and whispered in his ear, 'Why don't we just take her for a little ride somewhere?'

Simon shook his head. 'I got no urge to get hung on account of some Chinee brat.'

Dusting the bread off, the little girl shared half with the old sow, then she went back to her contented wallowing on the animal's back.

'Get,' Simon snapped at her, spittle flying through a gap in his teeth. She laughed, thinking he was playing. He was tired from having stayed up half the night chasing a Negro who'd tried to pick his pocket. The colored had jumped his boys with a black-jack and fought like a doped man, then turned tail and run.

Simon continued thinking about the Quaker woman, watching her buggy moving down Main Street. Something about seeing her at the lawyer's office had triggered a thought in his head and he sat connecting bits and pieces in his mind. Then he nodded as the conclusion fell into place and turned to the men behind him.

'That's what happened to our nigger friend,' he said, pointing at Pearl Eddy.

'What?' one of them asked.

'We thought we lost him on the prairie. We didn't. She was hiding him. That's why she wouldn't let us search her house. He was in there. Snug and cozy.'

'How you know that?'

'He's probably still there,' Simon said, ignoring the question. 'We should think some about that.' He rolled his shoulders and moaned. The Fraternity should have fixed the woman years ago. He would have let them if it hadn't been for Chrissy. Regardless, they could pick up the Negro.

Ugly in face, with fifty-six years of a well-dug-in smell about him, Simon James had the meaty body of one who couldn't resist his impulses in any form. In youth he'd been a merchant seaman traveling to foreign ports. It was in one such port, São Paulo of Brazil, that he had gotten the idea for his Amazing World Wonders. There he had seen a similar affair that purported to show customers the strange oddities and horrors of the Amazon.

Simon had broadened his exhibits to include specimens from many continents, and each summer and fall he toured his tent show through the small towns of Kansas and Oklahoma, following the Chautauqua cultural tours to take advantage of small-town America's thirst for knowledge.

For two years he and his wife, Angela, a girl of little more than sixteen, had collected freaks and wild beasts to exhibit. And while his phoney shrunken heads, animal skins, a dead elephant fetus and other grotesques had not made him rich, they made him a living. Angela had run off somewhere near Tulsa, Oklahoma, after Chrissy. Now his boys helped run the show. They were on the road half the year, but Liberty was home. And they weren't about to have it infected by Chinamen.

He glanced across the street at Frank Willard, the deputy. The man had been sitting in a chair watching the crowd all day and now looked half-asleep.

'Hurry up,' Penny snapped.

'Hold on,' Mike James muttered. Simon's middle boy – twenty-two, big and strong, well over 250 pounds – Mike was sliding his large body forward, shoving a long stick toward the pig and the girl, a double-bladed knife lashed to its end.

He stretched his arm and the stick through the bundles, slipping the blade under the pig's halter. Carefully, he began to saw. The animal was stretching to reach the bread, supplying the right tension to the rope, but the knife turned under the pressure. He tried again. But again it slipped.

Then suddenly Penny was beside him. 'Give it to me.'

'We ain't going to cut her loose,' Mike hissed.

'Fine,' Penny said. He seemed to hesitate for a moment, gathering himself, then thrust the pole forward with a hard lunge, the blade disappearing in the pig's neck, the blow knocking it and the child to the ground. Then the little beast was up and squealing, rushing round and round with the spear still stuck in it, blood

39

spraying over everything. Penny was laughing in a crazy way and Chrissy was babbling and trying to clap her hands at the fine mist.

Then suddenly an oriental girl of fourteen or fifteen was standing over them and the men tensed, expecting her to scream or strike. But she didn't. She just whirled and glared at a place they couldn't see among the large canvas bundles, pointing at this spot and yelling, then kicking dirt.

Penny rose up on his arms and tried to see what she was hollering at, but couldn't. Then the screaming girl was joined by a worn-down oriental woman who was talking sharply and pulling her away by the arm. After she got her from the place, the woman shuffled back and bowed at the mysterious spot a couple of times.

The old pig was down on its side now, its legs twitching, the little girl crying and holding one of its hooves as if trying to stop the terrible quivering. But it would not stop.

Safely on the sidewalk, Penny stood on his tiptoes attempting to see into the place among the bundles. He couldn't. Then the Jameses were hurrying away.

CHAPTER THREE

Pearl let her horse, Jack, slip into a steady single-foot on the road west of town, reining him in whenever he broke into a trot. It was a habit with her to refuse to draw attention by scurrying down the road in her buggy. As a result when Jack finally turned into the farmyard she was better than thirty minutes late for Mother Rose Sherman's fitting.

Sixty and a wealthy widow, Rose Sherman was a Liberty social pillar. If Rose was for you, few were against you. The reverse was equally true. Peal tensed at the unpleasant thought, her mind grappling with her money fears again. She tied Jack to the front fence, tapping up the path to the door.

'Rose?' She tried to sound a cheerful note she didn't feel. No answer. Her heart beat a little faster. Rose hadn't waited. She'd come promptly at nine, and then not finding Pearl at home, she must have huffed back into her buggy and headed for town.

Pearl sat on the steps and tried to collect herself, the sunlight warm against her, the morning quiet. Then a grackle in the large elm on the side of the house began its rasping 'chack-chack' call, the sound as disconcerting as her thoughts. She waited for the bird to depart and the spring air to calm her. Neither happened. 'Thou cannot sit idling – do what thou has to do,' she chided herself, knowing those were her dead mother's words.

Pearl's thoughts were drawn to the woman. She had never wavered during her life – not during good times nor bad. She had always known her duty and done it. Pearl straightened the fabric of her long dress, then her mother's admonition against idling was back in her thoughts and she forced herself to stand. Pearl knew she would have faced these problems head-on. Without whimpering. That thought made her feel better. Not great, but better. She opened the front door and heard laughter.

'Hello?' she called.

'Oh, there you are, dear.'

It was Rose Sherman's voice, and she sounded happy.

'I love it.'

'Mother Sherman?'

'Jerome says my new dress fits exquisitely,' she bubbled. 'And having worked in Paris,' she paused, glancing admiringly at the man, 'it has the perfect – what did you call it, Jerome?'

'Silhouette.' The accent sounded almost French.

'That's right, silhouette.'

'Who?'

'Jerrroome,' the voice with the phoney French accent offered. Then quickly, 'Your assistant.'

'My assistant?'

'I weeell explain laaa-tur.'

'Where have you been hiding him?'

'In the cellar,' Pearl said firmly, facing in Prophet's direction.

Rose laughed. 'Well, he's certainly a big surprise.'

'Yes. He is that.'

'Goood morning, Madame Eddieee.'

Even with the bad accent, the voice was unmistakably Prophet's. Pearl didn't move. He had not run. Worse, he was in her house, lying and pretending to fit her best client. She grappled with the mix of fear and anger swirling inside her.

'I love it,' Rose gushed.

'I'm glad,' Pearl ventured. 'As for Jerome, he surprised me by arriving late last night,' she said, turning to glare in the direction she'd last heard the voice. 'But he'll soon be leaving – won't thee, Jerome?'

42

'Aaaah, Madame. Weee can disscuss that laay-tuurrr.'

Pearl was tapping her foot, a dour expression on her face.

'Ohhh, Pearl, we can't lose him. The two of you must create a dozen – no, two dozen – outfits for me.'

Pearl was stunned. Two dozen outfits. The possibility in the face of her financial need was wonderfully tempting. It would not only pay the loan on the equipment, it would clear her other debts. Her heart was beating faster. She spent a moment calculating other uses for the money. Then she pulled herself up straighter. No. The man had tricked Rose. He was no more a French designer than she was. She couldn't do it. She would let Rose down slowly.

'That is always a possibility. But for now, let us finish this one.'

'Finish? It's finished, my dear. Isn't that right, Jerome?'

'But of course,' he said grandly.

'I thought we might add a sash – something in a soft green perhaps,' Pearl offered.

'I told Jerome we'd discussed that,' Mother Sherman said, 'but he suggested red.'

'Oh?' Pearl tried to locate where Prophet was standing. But he was very quiet.

'See what you think,' Mother Sherman offered, standing with her heavy arms raised like a large bird in pre-flight, beaming at Prophet.

Dressed in a collarless white shirt, bright green suspenders bracing his black slacks, a magenta-colored silk scarf around his neck, he was standing and cupping his chin: contemplating his creation, seemingly determined not to look at Pearl.

'Here I am, honey,' Mother Sherman beamed at Pearl.

Pearl hesitated and then walked over and touched the satin sash, visualizing it with the tips of her fingers. She felt the small stitches in the material. She was surprised: he'd actually attached it to the dress. The work was not bad either.

'Isn't it lovely?'

She couldn't lie. 'It is nice.' Pearl backed up a step, her hands

43

trembling with agitation. 'Mr Prophet, may I see thee in the kitchen, please?'

'Prophet?' Mrs Sherman sounded surprised.

'Jerrrome Prophetttt,' he said quickly. 'Creole – New Orleans.'

The smile returned to Rose Sherman's large and powdery face.

'What are thou doing?' Pearl snapped as soon as she'd shut the kitchen door. Then just as quickly, he saw her catching up her anger and boxing it away again. 'That is my best customer. I will not let thee toy with her. And thou hast no business –'

'I'm not toying, Mrs Eddy,' he interrupted, his voice low. 'That old lady was hammering on your front door.'

'Thou had no business opening it,' she said quickly. 'Thou do not belong here.'

He looked surprised. 'At breakfast you were telling me to stay so you could patch things up with the law.'

'Be that as it may,' she said, straightening her long skirt, 'thou should not have opened my front door, and then assumed a false relationship with me, involving me in thy trickery and lies. What kind of a minister are thou – tricking people?'

'Mrs Eddy. I didn't open your door. That woman walked into the kitchen where I was having coffee.' He sounded indignant. 'What was I supposed to do: tell her I'd just broken in and was finishing breakfast?'

'At least it would have been the truth.'

Both of them stood, uncertain of what to say. Pearl was upset at herself for losing her temper; Prophet mad that she kept ruining his plans. He watched her struggling with her anger. Then he turned and walked quietly across the kitchen, putting the silver pill box that he'd stolen from Rose Sherman into his traveling bag.

'Where are you?' Pearl called.

'Putting my thimble away,' he lied.

'Thy thimble?'

44

'Yes.'

She thought about this. 'Where did thou learn to sew?'

Prophet hesitated. He had taught himself as a kid, so that he could make clothes for himself. But that didn't sound good enough. He cleared his throat. 'I sewed robes for the choir,' he said, sounding ministerial once again. 'And clothes for the poor,' he added for extra effect.

This last part of the lie put an immediate brake on her tongue, and he could see her scurrying around in her head catching up the remnants of her anger. It looked like an opening. He stepped closer. She was breathing hard.

'I was just keeping her from getting that mob after me again.' Then in a conspiratorial tone, he said, 'Mrs Eddy. Can't we forget our differences? I didn't have many choices – I just took the one that would work best for both of us.'

'I do not view it that way, Mr Prophet. Thou are a bold man.' She turned to open the hall door. He quickly put a hand on it.

'Don't you see?'

'See what?' Her tone was cool.

'Opportunity.'

'What are thou talking about?'

'That woman thinks I'm a French designer. She'll tell others. Mrs Eddy, we can raise prices.' He was beginning to pace the room in his enthusiasm. Pearl was staring blindly in his direction, and for a fleeting moment, he thought he saw something deep in her blue eyes that looked like interest. Then she shook her head hard, as if denying something.

'Just understand: I will not participate in thy lies. Thou are in trouble with the law. I have spoken to the county attorney and he will bring the sheriff as soon as he returns. Thou can then straighten out thy legal problems and leave.'

'Great, Mrs Eddy,' he mumbled. 'I hold on to your best client – I create the business opportunity of your lifetime.' He stopped and looked at the old paint and the cracked window. 'And from the looks of things around here, you could use it – and you repay me by running me into the sheriff.'

'We just believe different things, that is all.'

'We surely do, Mrs Eddy . . . and I'm thinking we should keep it that way.' His voice was rising.

'Please lower thy voice,' she said firmly. 'I am sorry thou feel like that – but that is thy choice.'

Prophet watched her for a moment, then turned and started for the back door. 'I'll be going now before your righteous living gets me put in jail.' He stopped and looked back at her. 'I'll send money for that hen,' he snapped.

'Good,' she said coolly. 'Do thou need to borrow postage?'

He flashed angrily. 'I'll buy my own.'

'Fine,' she muttered.

He stepped out into the sunlight and pulled the back door shut with a hard yank that shook the kitchen and made Pearl wince as the dishes rattled.

Five hours later, it smelled of rain and evening was casting shadows off the houses and on to the dirt of Main Street, when Pearl and her son Samuel came around the corner from Lincoln Avenue in the buggy, headed for town. Samuel was quietly urging Jack to pick up speed, glancing at his mother to see if she'd noticed. She had.

'Samuel.'

He pulled the horse into a walk. 'Is that Negro gone?'

'Yes.'

Pearl was holding a large cooking kettle on her lap, still dressed in her gray suit, a shawl across her small shoulders, a plain black bonnet covering her head.

'How long have thou known him?'

'Since last night.'

'Is he really a minister?'

'He says.'

'But thee doesn't know.'

46

'Thou means, do I have proof?'

'Yes.'

'No.' She waited a moment. 'But I have his word.'

They rode in silence for a while. Samuel was building up arguments against the man, convinced he was a crook.

'Why was he at our house?'

'He had a difficulty with the law.'

'Criminal,' he said.

'Just a problem.'

'I saw him searching over the parlor desk this morning.'

'I am sure he was just curious.'

'Looked more than curious to me.' He waited a moment, then asked, 'What kind of problem?'

'He was accused of robbery.'

That did it. 'He's bad.'

'Thou thinks he is bad. There is a difference.'

Before he could respond, a strange sound reached his ears. Samuel stopped talking and reined Jack in, staring down Main Street at a crowd in front of the hotel. From a distance the people sounded mad about something. His mother felt along the buggy seat.

'Thy hat.'

He didn't move.

'Samuel. Thy hat.'

He put it on, then chose a hitching post, watching the crowd as he secured Jack.

Samuel was a head taller than his mother, the result of recent growth that showed in the ill-fit of his dark clothes. But he wasn't worrying about his clothes. He was trudging reluctantly forward, carrying the heavy pot, his mother's hand on his arm, his eyes fixed on the men in the road.

Upon seeing them approaching, the crowd opened like the maw of some creature, and directly in front of them, kneeling before a small stove, was a little oriental woman. Samuel made straight for her.

The noise of the crowd was increasing. He'd seen most of the men before: idlers and drunks who hung around the saloons and stables; and he smelled alcohol and the bitter odor of old urine in clothes. Somebody grabbed at his hat, and he dodged, yanking his mother roughly along.

'Crowded,' he yelled, not wanting to alarm her.

Pearl knew that Samuel was talking to her but she was busy arguing with herself about why she was here. The county attorney, Edward Johnson, had warned her away; and she knew instinctively that he was right.

She had no call getting mixed up with these people. It wouldn't go down well in town. She'd taken enough of a chance with the Negro. She lifted her chin. She would do what she'd come to do, then be done with it.

Then suddenly, Penny James – a figure of considerable menace – was standing before them, his right eye an ugly purple.

'Where you going, boy?'

Samuel stopped abruptly and gasped for breath to answer, but before he could, his mother said, 'We are simply bringing the evening meal to this family. Then we will be on our way.'

Penny ignored her. 'Boy. I asked where you were going.'

Samuel stood fighting the quivering in his legs.

'Samuel,' Pearl said, her voice unchanged.

Samuel didn't move.

'Let us through, please,' she said, putting her hand out as if she might be able to part the seas.

Prophet heard a commotion in the street and looked out the dirty window of the 'colored section' of the railroad depot. He'd been hiding inside this dusty room for the past few hours, sitting quietly in a shadowy corner with a hat pulled low around his head, trying to look asleep. He didn't need anybody seeing him. As soon as the next train arrived, he was out of here. That's all he wanted. Then he spotted the Quaker woman and her boy.

They were a matched pair. Excepting right now the boy looked sick, while Mrs Eddy looked well enough. He shook his head, wondering what the heck she was doing in the middle of this mess. She was definitely loony. If last night was any indication, he figured she must get herself involved in dumb stuff on a regular basis.

He was starting to sit back down when he saw one of the men he'd fought in the saloon step in front of the woman. The man had all the markings of a bully. Still, it wasn't his business.

He watched a moment longer, then returned to his seat on the floor. The last thing he needed was trouble with that crowd again. He'd always figured he was lucky. But escaping the same mob twice was pushing a body's blessings. He sat and pulled his knees up to his chin and thought about things. Nothing in particular. Fights and stuff. Then the crowd was roaring louder and he swore and took another peek.

Pearl Eddy had her hand out in front of her and was moving stubbornly forward. Prophet scratched his good ear. This affair wasn't headed anywhere useful. Then the man grabbed her hand and shoved it down between his legs, howling with pretended pleasure.

Prophet felt something rising in his throat but he swallowed it down and headed for his corner. It was the smart thing to do. Under different circumstances, he might have told the man to leave her alone. But the circumstances weren't different. The crowd outside had wanted to lynch him the night before and he doubted that their sentiments had changed much.

There was no question the woman had saved him. He owed her for that. He just didn't figure he owed her his life. And going out into that street might add up to something like that. Nope. He didn't owe her that much. Her messes were her messes. The crowd roared again and Prophet took to humming quietly to shut the sound out.

There are times a person wants to scream and they can't and this was one of those times for Samuel Eddy. He tried. But nothing would come out. Absolutely nothing. Nor could he get his arms to move so that he could swing at Penny. Things on his body didn't seem to be working right. Then the Negro was suddenly there and pulling Pearl Eddy's hand away. Caught off balance, Penny fell hard on to the seat of his pants, the crowd roaring.

Momentarily surprised, Penny sat staring up at him, then a look of recognition came over his face. 'Well, look whose nigger we got here.'

He started up out of the dirt at Prophet, the Negro waiting until he was halfway up before he put a large hand on his head and pushed him back down. The crowd was quiet now.

'Don't get up fast like that again,' Prophet warned. 'Or I'll get the wrong idea.'

Pearl recognized the voice. 'Mr Prophet,' she said over the noise. 'Calm thyself.'

He got a funny look on his face. 'Me?' he complained. 'He's the fellow who grabbed you.'

Penny had taken the opportunity of Prophet's distraction to scramble to his feet and he was crouched and ready to fight. Prophet looked at him and shook his head as if he was tired. 'You don't want this,' he said in a cold voice. 'I guarantee – you don't want this.'

'Mr Prophet,' Pearl admonished.

'Beat him good. Beat that smart-talking nigger!' someone in the crowd yelled. Then Willard and two other deputies were wading through the men with their billy clubs out and Penny and Prophet and the rest of them were scrambling fast in different directions.

'I'll give it to them, Mrs Eddy,' Deputy Willard said, holding the heavy pot and nodding toward the oriental woman. 'I'm not supposed to let anyone near. You can see the trouble they've already caused.'

'These people didn't cause any trouble, Mr Willard.'

The man shrugged and turned toward the campsite.

Samuel couldn't stop shaking – couldn't stop thinking about what had happened. About what he, Samuel, hadn't done. Penny James might beat the stuffing out of him some dark night . . . but this other thing was gnawing like a rodent at his guts.

He tried to walk it off. Halfway down the street he noticed a small cluster of some of the town's more respectable citizens. They were watching and talking, and though he couldn't be sure, he got the uncomfortable sense they didn't approve of what they saw. His lip was trembling and he put a hand up to stop it, fighting off another wave of queasiness, then he looked past Deputy Willard to the orientals who'd caused it all. They weren't worth it. The woman was small like his mother, with short hair the color of roof-tar. She was dressed in baggy trousers he'd never seen a woman wear before, and a worn-out, green-colored jacket buttoned down both sides; squatting unladylike in front of her little stove, looking ready for bed.

But the thing that surprised him most was that she wasn't wearing any shoes. A grown woman: barefoot. Grown-ups in Liberty never went barefoot, unless maybe they were swimming. Their shoes might be near useless, but they wore them.

She looked indecent and he felt embarrassed for her, but she didn't seem to care: she was smiling and keeping up a steady stream of unintelligible conversation with two small girls of five or six. A third girl, closer to his age, was kneeling and hand-feeding grain to a bunch of hens, as if it was gold. Her head was down and he couldn't see much of her face.

Whenever he thought about Penny James the sickening feeling came back. So he listened to the woman's sing-song voice, trying to decipher what she was saying. He couldn't tell. She seemed happy. He wondered what about. They were no better than beggars, living in the dirt of Main Street. People yelled and gawked and wanted them out of town. It didn't make sense.

Trying to keep his mind off what had happened, he scanned the rest of the encampment. Bundles of dirty canvas were stacked in a pile behind the family and there was a rickety-looking wooden handcart; on top was a small split-bamboo cage with a door in it. It was a strange-looking contraption. Beneath the cart hung a wire chicken pen. He wondered if they were show stock, the way the girl was caring for them. Probably not. He didn't figure these people had anything worth having.

He let his eyes drift over the camp again. There were two pigs: one was dead, stretched out on the cart wheel to cool. The other was a funny sway-backed creature, the hairiest pig he'd ever seen. Samuel was turning back to Deputy Willard when he noticed something else: a small movement among the bundles.

He tried to get a better look, standing on his toes. The woman and the little girls ignored him, as though used to the curiosity. The shadows of oncoming night were steeping Main Street in darkness, but Sam thought he could see something.

He inched closer, pushing against the rope. Nothing. Then he noticed the girl glaring at him, as if he had done something terribly wrong. She seemed to be challenging him to say something. Suddenly feeling rude he started to turn away, then he stopped and glanced back at her: small and graceful-looking, the soft contours of her body showing through her worn cotton blouse and pants, her thick black hair bobbed neatly above her shoulders. The eyes were dark and almond-shaped; the mouth full. She was barefoot as well, but didn't look bad like the woman. He watched her until he got uncomfortable again, then he turned and walked over to his mother.

'There's a lady, two little girls, and another girl about my age,' he said, explaining what he saw as he always did for her. Samuel looked for the girl again but she was kneeling behind one of the canvas bundles. 'They're poor – like pictures of Chinamen in books.'

'Chinese,' Pearl corrected.

'Chinese,' he repeated.

'And Mr Prophet?'

He could hear the concern in her voice. 'Last time I saw him he was running toward the river. Nobody was chasing him.'

She looked relieved.

'Good riddance if thou ask me,' Samuel continued.

Pearl didn't respond. Instead, she focused her thoughts back to the oriental woman. 'Has she taken the stew?'

Samuel was surprised that a refusal might even be a possibility. They'd risked their lives bringing it here.

'Not yet.'

Deputy Willard held the pot while the woman peered down into it, poking at the food with a wooden ladle. The deputy pointed toward them now, and Sam stood straighter as the woman turned and stared at his mother.

'She's looking at thee.'

Pearl's expression didn't change. After a moment, the woman bowed her head, grasping the pot's handles. Then her eyes returned to Pearl and she stood watching her for a while.

'Not very trusting.'

'Just concerned for her children.'

Samuel shook his head and took his mother by the arm, turning her toward the buggy. She was naive.

They were halfway back to the buggy when the little oriental woman suddenly hopped in front of them, looking hard at Pearl's face as if searching for something in it.

When he stopped, Pearl said, 'Samuel?'

'The woman,' he said uncomfortably.

Before Pearl could respond, the oriental woman said, 'We own land. Rikuchi. Here in this place. But they say we don't. They cheat us.'

Pearl shook her head. 'No. The men who told thee that are honest men. They did not cheat thee. Thy land was declared abandoned. I'm sorry.' Pearl waited a moment, then said, 'Samuel.'

He started to guide his mother around the little woman but she quickly hopped back in front of them in a determined way.

'I need you help. Fujin. Lady. No one help me.' She paused to study Pearl's face. 'Will you help? To you they listen.'

There was a strange pleading sound in the voice that Pearl intuitively understood and felt bad about. She listened for a

53

moment to the fast breathing of the woman, thinking again about Edward Johnson's warning, and concluding once more that he was right.

'I'm sorry,' she said softly. 'Judge Wilkins and Attorney Johnson have promised to help thee on thy way.'

'Everybody help us on our way. But no one help us.' The woman stopped talking and Samuel thought she might cry. But instead she repeated, 'We own land. Here.' She hesitated only a moment, then quickly asked again, 'Fujin, will you help? Please.'

Pearl had to take a deep breath before she could speak. 'No,' she said slowly, 'I cannot. I am sorry.'

Curious, Sam turned on the buggy seat and searched the camp-site disappearing in the distance behind them, trying to see the Chinese again. Darkness was closing hard, and he couldn't. He did see Simon and Penny James and some other men watching them from the shadows of a nearby side street and he squirmed. Then he glanced at his mother. She was sitting motionless, looking sick to her stomach, deep in what appeared to be troub-ling thoughts. Though surprised she'd done it, he was proud of her for turning the oriental woman away. They didn't need her problems.

'Are thou OK?'

She nodded but didn't look any better.

For the next two hours they delivered eggs, vegetables and garments to their customers in town. They also sold the first of their spring flowers. There were fewer of these than the year before, the flower part of the garden diminishing in vigor. This worried him. Not because of the money they lost, but simply because the garden had been his father's. He pictured the man, the familiar hurt filling his chest.

It seemed impossible that he was gone. Sam forced his thoughts back to their small but thriving business, glancing at the little ledger where he kept track of his mother's receipts and orders for things. While he and his brothers didn't care much for the work, he knew his father would have been proud. That made him feel better. He knew also that the townspeople respected his mother and her determination to take care of her family.

Samuel listened to the sound of thunder rolling across the prairie north of town. They were stopped at the house of old man McPherson. Jack began to sidestep nervously at the distant rumbling and Samuel talked quietly to him.

Then a bolt of lightning lit the sky, illuminating the little shanty house and the scrubby trees around them. He felt a cold swish of wind and shivered – hungry and tired of waiting for his mother to stop talking to Mr McPherson. He definitely wasn't interested in getting wet. He looked down at his worn-out shoes and pants that floated too high up his ankles, thinking about the oriental girl again. He tried to pull his pants down lower. They moved some but not much and his shoes were a mess; his little toe had broken through the leather on the right side.

'Mother?'

She didn't respond, just continued talking to the frail old man. He wondered if they were talking about Mrs McPherson – about what she'd done the month before.

He'd heard from Billy Jeffers that she'd gone into her barn and pulled a sack over her head, laid down, resting her head on a mound of sand; then stuck a pistol in her mouth and pulled the trigger. The sack had kept the splattering down and the sand had absorbed the blood. He shuddered. His mother had been coming each night since to visit with old man McPherson. Samuel didn't mind. He just wanted to beat the rain.

Jack was rolling the bit in his mouth, tired and hungry as well. The wind picked up, whipping at the canvas roof of the buggy. Sam buttoned his jacket against the chill, then worked at oc-cupying his mind. Once again he thought of his father and the muscles of his shoulders tightened, as if a cold hand from the shadows had grabbed him. The death still had an awful power over him. He guessed it always would. He wondered if old man McPherson felt the same way.

Then the rain hit, coming in from the north, riding on the wind, angling under the buggy top and striking his exposed legs. He peered through it until he made out his mother and the old man. Neither of them moved. They just stood carrying on their conversation as if it were a lovely night. Samuel shook his head.

Watching her getting soaked, he thought of how she was an odd mix of things: a puzzle. Sometimes he had a time of it trying to get her straight in his head – who she was and what she believed.

'Mother –' he hollered against the noise of the downpour.

His stomach grumbled. He wished she'd hurry, but knew she wouldn't. She had time for people like old man McPherson.

He studied her in the rain. She was a good listener. But she was also naive and believed too much of what everybody told her.

He stared down the darkened street at the rough-looking houses. They came here after their regular rounds to drop off extra eggs and vegetables to folks who couldn't buy. Again, Samuel didn't mind. It was just that he was always hungry by the time they made it. His pants were soaked from the knees down and he was beginning to shake with the cold. He wished she wasn't so mulish about things. Being Quaker in a mostly Methodist town was enough. The wind came down the darkened street again and the dripping trees sounded like they were talking.

Twenty minutes later, the rain had stopped but Samuel was still trembling from the cold as the buggy rounded the turn and headed toward the prairie road out of town. He noticed three men standing on a corner watching them and didn't like their looks, thinking for a second that they might have been ones he'd seen before around Simon James, but he wasn't certain and shrugged it off. His mother was still deep in troubled thought. She was also soaked: her hair hanging in damp strands, her woolen dress clinging to her.

'Thou need to dry off,' he suggested.

'Samuel,' she said softly. 'Thou are almost grown.'

He tensed.

'It is hard growing without thy father.' Her teeth chattered.

'It's fine enough,' he said, shifting on the seat.

'The world does not hold with much of what we hold with.'

'I don't care.'

She smiled but the smile was purely contemplative. Her face looked pale and chilled. And worried. He waited – but that was it. She'd said all she wanted to say: she had sent one of her silly messages. She kept a close understanding with him and his brothers, then every once in a while she'd interrupt it with something like this. At least she hadn't spoken about what had happened with Penny James. Regardless, he continued worrying over it. Half an hour later, he stopped Jack in the barn and crawled down and went and stood by the old horse's head.

'Mother.'

'Yes?'

'In town. I almost hit Penny James.' He was sweating now in the cool night air. Pigeons were moving in the rafters overhead.

She didn't say anything and he didn't feel like telling her the rest, but it was bothering him badly.

'I wanted to hurt him.'

She sat for a moment, then said, 'But thou did not.'

'But I wanted to.'

She was listening carefully.

'I wanted to,' he repeated.

'But thou resisted,' she said, as if he'd done a good thing.

He felt miserable. He'd resisted nothing. He had been afraid. That was the sum of it. She was simply being naive again. He had slunk away like a coward. The thought numbed him.

'Samuel, thou are old enough now to decide such things for thyself,' Pearl continued. 'Thou will have to decide many difficult

57

things. But thou must resist violence.' She hesitated, then quickly said, 'Thy father would want that.'

She gripped the front edge of the buggy seat hard with both her hands, thinking back to that night. To Matthew and what had happened. She was trembling in the barn's darkness when she heard Samuel talking and she forced herself to focus on the words.

'It was wrong to let him shame thee,' he mumbled.

'We shame only ourselves.' Samuel was standing at the side of the buggy now. She tensed her arm so that he wouldn't see her shaking, and held it out for him.

Her skin felt cool to Samuel, and she climbed down slower than usual. He wondered if she was sick. Then she oriented herself with her cane and started walking in her brisk way and he figured she wasn't. Something was just bothering her. She was silhouetted against the moonlight beyond the barn door, her back to him. He kicked at a stone near the carriage wheel. She was at the door now, tapping her long walking stick softly on the ground ahead of her.

'What kind of things?' he asked.

She stopped. 'Samuel?'

'Thou said I'd have to decide things – what things?'

She stood for a moment, then said: 'What thou will believe as a man.'

'I'll believe what I believe now,' he said quickly, his tone defensive as if someone was trying to take something precious from him.

She turned slowly and faced in his direction, then she pulled her shawl tighter over her shoulders and stood staring as if she might actually be able to see him. Finally she turned away and started toward the house. 'It is cool tonight – put the blanket on Jack.'

The first biting edge of the oncoming night was blowing over the road from the north when the men stepped out of the shadows around Prophet. Three in front, three behind. He glanced to his left and started to dive for the grass, then two guns cocked.

'Don't do it.' The man who spoke was tall and thick-looking in the half-light of early night. The voice was cold and calculating and Prophet guessed he'd pull the trigger. He relaxed his muscles.

'Take it easy, mister.' Prophet's voice was steady.

'Good advice. Where you headed?'

Prophet checked the faces of those standing around him, relieved that none of the Jameses were here. He didn't figure to last long around them.

Then somebody stepped up behind him and hit him hard on the back of the head, causing him to stumble forward, while another took a swing that he blocked easy enough. But he didn't see the right that dropped him into the muddy roadway.

'That's where a nigger ought to be – on his knees. Especially a nigger who fancies white women,' the tall man said.

Somebody kicked him hard in the back and drove him forward on to his hands, pain singing through his kidneys.

'That's enough,' the tall man said, squatting down in front of Prophet. 'Brutal and nasty, isn't it?'

'Let's finish the sonofabitch,' somebody said, shoving a pistol against the back of his skull.

'Hold on,' the tall man said quietly. 'This nigger has learned his lesson and is heading out of town. Right, boy?'

Prophet didn't say anything, figuring not much of anything he might say would matter with these men. They were going to either shoot him or let him go. Depending on how they felt – not because of anything he said. And he wasn't going to beg them. He didn't care much for begging.

The tall man stood back up. 'Yep. This nigger is heading for parts unknown. But if he ever comes back,' he paused, 'we'll just fix him the same way we're going to fix that woman. Real nice.' He placed the barrel of his revolver hard up against Prophet's head and pulled the trigger.

The concussion knocked Prophet cold, dropping his body flat on the ground. The men were laughing and heading back to their horses.

CHAPTER FOUR

The lawyer, Edward Johnson, was in the parlor with Joshua and Luke and Zacharias when Pearl walked in from the barn. The twins howled like attacking Indians, racing round the room, while Johnson sat on the sofa looking uncomfortable. Zacharias was in the rocker, holding a silver-framed photograph of his father.

'Boys,' Pearl said, brushing damp hair off her face.

'Looks like Jack took a detour upriver,' Johnson joked.

Pearl smiled, then her thoughts seemed to return to her troubles, and she stood spreading her wet shawl over the back of a chair, then unpinned her bonnet. The boys were panting and waiting for a signal that they could resume the battle.

'Excuse me, Edward,' she said, moving toward her bedroom.

'Can we, mother?' Joshua asked.

'Take a lantern and help Samuel with Jack.'

'Awwww, ma,' Joshua pleaded.

'Joshua,' Pearl said firmly, moving through the bedroom door. 'Thy brother has been working in the rain all evening. He is cold and tired.'

The twins trooped out the door but Zacharias continued to sit. Johnson glanced at him.

'I knew your father,' he said, reaching his hand out for the photograph.

The boy shook his head.

'I won't hurt it.'

Zacharias shook his head again. The two of them sat staring at one another.

'Promise,' Johnson tried again.

'No,' the boy said, looking away.

'Zacharias,' Pearl chided, coming back through the door a few minutes later. She'd changed into a black dress and a simple blue blouse with long sleeves. Like all her things, these had seen better days.

Johnson watched her a moment longer than perhaps was polite, then looked back at the boy who had conceded to turn the photograph slightly so that the man could see it; but he wasn't letting go.

'Your father was a good man,' the lawyer said.

Pearl smiled. 'Yes, he was, Edward. Thank thee.'

Zacharias looked at his mother. 'When did Mr Prophet say he'd be back?'

'I don't believe he will.'

'Yes. He'll be back.'

'I don't believe so, Zacharias. I think he just had other things that were very important. But thou stop pouting and go help thy brothers.'

The boy was shaking his head now. 'No. He'll be back. He promised.'

His tone of absolute certainty stopped her for a moment; she knew how much he missed his father. A fleeting look of sadness crossed her face, then she said, 'Hurry now and help thy brothers.'

She waited until Zacharias closed the back door, then turned in Johnson's direction.

'Edward?' her voice betraying her concerns.

'I spoke to Snipes.'

'Yes?'

'He said it was irregular and that he'd have to check the bank's regulations. But that's just the way he is. He'll go along.'

'Should I bring the money in?'

'Let me work out an arrangement first. Snipes is wily.'

She sat looking down at her hands as if she might actually be able to see them. Then she sat up straighter and forced a smile. 'Thank thee, Edward Johnson. When my pullets begin to lay and my seamstressing expands – things will be fine.' She sounded distant.

Johnson walked to the window and stood looking out at the night.

'Coffee, Edward?'

'Yes.' He'd have a cup and then tell her the rest.

Prophet's ears were still ringing from the blast. He shook his head slowly back and forth but the ringing wouldn't quit. Then he stretched and felt the pain where he'd been kicked, and touched his cheek. He started to get mad, then shrugged it off. Hell, he told himself, weren't much more than he'd get in a good twenty-rounder.

He thought about what the men had said about him getting out of town. He didn't like being told things like that. Not by blacks or whites. It did something to his head. Always had. Still, it was probably pretty sound advice given the circumstances: figuring that if the Jameses had been the men who'd jumped him, he'd be dead now. Better to have your brains ringing than splattered over the road.

He stopped and stood thinking about the woman and the man's threat against her. He wondered if it was just talk. Maybe. Something was stirring slowly inside him. He didn't like threats. Never had.

He wiped an arm across his damp forehead, marveling at what he could still see in the surrounding darkness. So this was what folks in eastern Kansas called the tallgrass. He shook his head. Massive walls of plants – sunflowers, coneflowers, wildgrape, needlegrass, goldenrods and hundreds more he didn't know – lined the muddy roadway so thick that a man would have to cut his way through. All of it was over his head, some of it twelve feet high. But not one tree.

He shivered against the cool night air, his head aching, his ears still ringing, then he reached a hand and rubbed his neck, tipping his head back. A thick black vault of prairie sky floated overhead, strewn with a spray of spring stars; and sandwiched between it and these plants, he was feeling as if he wasn't worth much. He wondered why the woman chose to live out here in this forsaken place. His thoughts drifted again to what the tall man had said. Damn, he wished the ringing would quit.

Prophet shifted his heavy pack again, then he saw her. She seemed to be floating in the night sky a few yards ahead of him, staring down in her smug way. He'd seen her an hour before, after he woke up from the pistol blast. She'd taken the opportunity of his weakness to stare at him.

'I told you,' he hollered. 'All I need is a fight against somebody with a name.' He started walking again, looking down at the mud so he wouldn't see her.

A few minutes later, he took a peek. She was still there. Even he had to admit that she had a nice dignified-looking face, but that didn't give her the right to pester him. He looked quickly down at the roadway and tried thinking other thoughts. No luck. Once she locked on, she was hard to shake.

'I don't owe that white woman, and I didn't promise that boy anything. I just nodded my head so he'd go to school without bawling.' He trudged on through the mud. 'Anyhow, what's he want me to do for his pa? The man's dead; he's beyond doing anything for.' He jumped a puddle and tried whistling. No use. She was still there. 'I'm a fighter – no nursemaid. And that boy ain't going to die because I didn't hang around till he got out of school.'

He blew air hard out of his nose and began to jog and shadow-box his way down the road as if to prove his point. 'You want to worry about something – you worry about my shot. That's worth worrying about.' He grinned up at her. She wasn't grinning back; so he frowned and looked away, throwing hard, rapid punches at the towering walls of plants as if to keep them from swallowing

64

him. Still, he didn't like men pushing him around like he was a cow or something. Nor did he care much for the thought of the woman being hurt. It didn't seem right or fair. But even so, he determined to stay out of harm's way. This was one fight he was going to duck.

Some fifteen minutes later, he stopped and bent slowly over, his head throbbing, gasping for breath, and sensing she was still there. 'I'm not going back. I'm not. I only got a little while. Nigger lady, don't you see that?' He sat down hard in the muddy road and leaned back on his pack, exhausted. 'Don't you see?'

The garden was still dripping from the rain; it looked like a magical place in the prairie moonlight. The Eddy boys had not found their brother Samuel in the barn and they had come searching for him here.

They had been laughing and shoving each other into rain puddles moments before, but as they approached the fence they stopped talking. This had been their father's garden, the one exuberant passion that he had allowed himself in life – and he had shared it with them. Now, when they came to this place, they felt close to him.

Joshua led the way under the great arch of climbing roses – a profusion of red and coral blossoms that covered the garden gate. They stopped and stared as if seeing the place for the first time: an acre of land lovingly shaped by their father's hands, but now hopelessly overgrown and cluttered.

'Sam's not here,' Joshua whispered.

'Yes.' Luke pointed into the darkness ahead.

Their brother was standing inside a small picketed enclosure at the heart of the garden. Even with the moon above, the shadows here were deep, the night seemingly enveloping them like liquid. Their eyes fixed on Samuel, and beyond to the simple cross that marked their father's grave. They'd wanted a stone marker with their father's name and carvings of angels and some nice words on it, but their mother had forbidden it. They would mark his grave, she'd told them, with the simple sign of their Lord and nothing more. At least he was here with them. But still it bothered them.

The night air was chilly and Zacharias pulled in tightly against Luke. He was carrying Hercules, the rooster, under one arm, the old chicken clucking softly in the cool night air as though he found all of this worth serious contemplation.

The four of them stood a while in the shadowy silence before their father's grave, sharing something that they felt but had a hard time talking about. They came here almost every day, mostly at evening time after their chores were done. Alone or together, they watered and did little things with the plants to keep them growing.

But the only real work was on the vegetable garden, the money-making plants. Their mother agreed that the flowers were special, but practical considerations made them secondary. Only the gravesite was properly maintained.

Joshua broke the stillness. 'Sam – do thou remember much about dad?'

'Sure.'

'I get scared I'll forget him. What he looked like and how he talked. And the way I felt about him.'

'I just come here and talk to him when I feel like that,' Samuel said quietly.

'Does he answer thee?' Zacharias asked, glancing at the grave.

'I like to think so.'

'Like he used to do when we were working with him? Does he talk to thee like that?'

'No. Not like that.'

The boy looked sad.

His arm around his little brother's shoulder, Luke tipped his head back and stared up at the stars and the moon drifting peacefully through wisps of white clouds. 'Do thou think he's forgotten us?'

'No,' Samuel said quickly. 'He would never do that.'

Joshua looked sceptical. 'Thou said he wouldn't die.'

Samuel bit the side of his lip. 'I didn't think he would. But he hasn't forgotten us. He never will.'

'Why didn't they let us see him before he died? Or in the coffin,' Luke asked. 'I wanted to see him.'

'I don't know. It doesn't matter now,' Samuel said.

Zacharias was crying without sound. 'Mother says father is happy because he's with God.' He snuffed his nose. 'I don't think that's true. I don't think he could be happy without us.'

'Just talk to him,' Samuel reassured, putting a hand gently on his brother's head.

After a while, Joshua said, 'Mr Prophet is gone.'

'Good,' Samuel said.

'He's not gone,' Zacharias snapped in his high-pitched voice. 'He promised he'd do something for me.' He paused. 'And he will.'

'Thou are wasting thy time waiting for that Negro,' Samuel continued. 'He's of no account.'

'He wasn't so bad,' Luke said. Joshua nodded in agreement.

'He couldn't be trusted.'

'I don't believe that, Sammy,' Zacharias screeched angrily. 'I can trust things. Mother says that. And I trust Mr Prophet.'

Samuel didn't want to hurt his brother, so he stopped talking and stared at the moonlight that fell across his father's grave. He, too, wished she'd let them mark it. It seemed lost and lonely; just the earth and the cross.

The children were still outside and Edward Johnson was standing and looking out the parlor window. He turned, cup and saucer in his hand, and drank some coffee. It tasted weak and funny. Pearl was sitting in her chair working on a garment.

'Did thou happen to speak to the sheriff, Edward?'

He stood fingering the handle of the cup, then set it on the table. 'Yes.' She looked small and – with her blindness – hopelessly outmatched by all she faced. He picked up his hat. 'Yes, I did, Pearl.'

'And?'

'Simon claims the Negro tried to steal his wallet.'

'They argued over church money.'

Johnson raised his eyebrows. 'Discussing church funds doesn't sound much like Simon James.' He could tell from her expression that his remark had not changed her mind.

'Regardless. Everybody agrees that a fight started. And that the Negro got the best of it. Simon says he was high on opium from the Chinese.'

Pearl stuck her needle into the fabric and looked in his direction. 'He was not. And he is not a thief,' she said, matter-of-factly.

'Others think differently, I'm afraid, Pearl.'

'He is a Negro minister.'

Johnson shook his head in a way he wouldn't have if she could have seen him. 'Doesn't matter. Nobody was seriously hurt. And the sheriff isn't happy about the mob. He threatened to lock Simon up. Nobody is going to bother the Negro. Least not openly.'

Pearl turned her face up toward him with a funny little look of worry on it, mostly around the edges of her eyes and mouth, as if she were thinking about some distant thought that had nothing to do with what he'd just said. Then she seemed to focus her thoughts on the present again, and she smiled and said, 'Edward, I can't thank thee enough.'

Johnson didn't return her smile. He stood looking down at her and realized that along with being a good and hopeful woman, Pearl Eddy was badly scared. Deeply frightened of something. He had never seen her looking like this before; he had always thought of her as confident about life. She looked far from confident now. He walked to the window and stood staring out at the moonlight in the front elm. 'One other thing, Pearl.'

'Yes?'

'That Negro.' He paused and ran a finger around the inside of the brim of his hat. 'His name isn't Prophet. Least his real name isn't. It's Jerome Gilliam.'

She quit sewing for a moment, then she nodded and began

again. 'Yes. I've heard him use Jerome. I didn't know his last name.'

Johnson didn't continue for a time until Pearl turned her head up to him and said, 'Edward?'

'Mr Gilliam is not a preacher either.'

'No?' She looked uneasy, the same small lines showing around her eyes and mouth.

'He's a bareknuckle fighter. Or was until three years ago.'

Pearl pressed her lips together and sat contemplating this unpleasant news. Johnson let her. Sometimes, he knew, she didn't deal with reality the way she should. He wanted her to now.

'Prophet was his fighting name – Prophet of Doom.' He hesitated. 'Pearl, he killed another Negro in a fight in Missouri three years ago. The court called it manslaughter,' Johnson continued. 'Three years in jail.' He stopped talking and glanced around the room as if to see if there was someone listening. 'You are sure he's gone?'

'Yes. I'm sure.'

'If he comes back, you let me know.' He watched her a moment to see if what he'd said had registered. He wasn't certain. 'Pearl. Did you hear?'

He saw another trace of unhappiness around her eyes that lasted only a second. Then she nodded in agreement.

'Good.' He felt a little miffed that while he was the family attorney, this little widow oftentimes didn't listen to his advice. He was feeling this way at the moment and he turned back to the window and stuffed his badly blocked hat on to the top of his head and sank both hands into his pants pockets.

'I hear you delivered food to those Chinese.' He paused. 'And that the Negro got into a fight with Penny James.' He waited, then continued, 'Over you.'

'Yes.'

'I thought we agreed that you wouldn't get involved.'

'Yes,' she said quietly.

'Yes, we did,' he said, sounding like a troubled uncle. 'The whole town is talking about it, Pearl.'

'I didn't hold up the bank, Edward.'

'No, you didn't. But you've got a business and the boys. I wouldn't put my own children at risk for those people, Pearl, and I don't think you want to with yours either.' He paused. 'If you do, Pearl, it will come to no good end.'

The night was black now, the moon and stars gone behind a new front of dark clouds from the north. The boys were in bed. Pearl was trying not to let her emotions control her, but she wasn't getting far. Each time she'd believed in the Negro, he had deceived her. And now she'd come to learn the worst of it: manslaughter. The word made her shudder. Her mind flew to Matthew. She struggled against the painful memory and turned her body toward the parlor window, upset that her life was becoming a mare's nest of jumbled nerves and fears.

She forced her thoughts back to the Negro, gripping her hands, squeezing them as she often did when she was seeking inspiration or guidance. She tried to remember what he had said about being a preacher, but couldn't. He had not told her about the death, but there had been no reason for him to have done that. But they'd talked about him being a preacher and he had not mentioned he was a fighter.

Suddenly a thought flashed into her mind: he could still be a minister. Perhaps the death or prison had awakened his spirit and he had turned to the Lord. It wouldn't be the first sinner's redemption. History was filled with sinners turned saints. Far greater sinners than Mr Prophet. She shifted awkwardly in her chair. Still, she knew, he had not forsaken violence.

Nevertheless. Her spirits rose. Then she heard someone riding hard down the road and turning in at the farm. Moments later, they were banging on the front door.

Pearl pulled it open and felt the cold night air hit her. 'Yes?'

'Doc Trotter needs you.' Hector James sounded scared.

*

70

The men looked badly shaken when Hector led Pearl into Dr Smith Trotter's small office on Elm Street. Simon James and Trotter were trying to restrain Chrissy on a small cot in the center of the room, the girl's eyes rolling to white in her panicked struggle for air, while Penny and Mike looked on helplessly. The room was hot and moist and filled with the awful shrieking of a kettle at full boil.

'She's not settling down,' Trotter said over the noise. 'The steam isn't working.'

A tall, thin man in his sixties, the doctor turned toward Pearl, momentarily releasing his grip on the girl. It was long enough for her to lunge from the cot and scurry crablike to a corner of the room in her desperate search for air.

'Take the pot off,' Pearl said.

'That's how we've always done it,' Simon snapped.

Trotter pulled the pot from the stove and a silence fell over the room, broken only by Chrissy's gasps; the sound wet and thick as she sucked each breath down her swollen, mucus-covered throat.

'Gawddamnit, Trotter, she's no doctor!'

Pearl was bent over a large cloth bag that she'd brought with her, removing various things and setting them to one side on the examining table. Simon looked like he might explode. Then Hector said, 'Come on, pa. She's helped Chrissy before.'

'Sit,' the doctor said, as if they were schoolchildren.

'The girl's rapid panting suddenly seemed to increase and Simon stood back up. 'She can't breathe without the steam!'

Pearl had been through more than a dozen of Chrissy's worst attacks, using her knowledge of asthma gained helping her father survive similar attacks; she knew how frightening it was to watch someone you loved strangling, so she ignored Simon's ranting, humming loudly as she continued removing things from her bag. Chrissy was watching her now. Pearl handed the doctor a small vial.

'Eucalyptus oil. Put a dozen drops into the pot and bring it back to a boil – then give it to me.'

Pearl went back to humming and looking through her bag while the doctor went for a blanket.

'Hello, Chrissy,' Pearl called to the girl. 'I'll be with thee in a moment.' She paused. 'Hector?'

The boy hopped up, nervously watching his sister who had begun thrashing wildly around on the floor again, gasping for air as if each gasp would surely be her last.

'Chrissy,' Pearl called, still sounding like she was out for a Sunday stroll. 'Thou knows that does not help thee. Remember to put thy hand on thy stomach and fill it up with air. Remember how we do it?'

'She isn't smart enough – so quit tormenting her,' Simon yelled.

'She is smarter than thou may believe.'

The girl didn't put her hand on her stomach, but she had stopped thrashing and was staring at the woman again.

'Hector?'

'Yes, Mrs Eddy?' Hector said.

Pearl handed him some dried mullein leaves. 'Roll me a cigarette from this.'

'What?' Hector asked.

'Do thou smoke?'

'Yes.'

'Then make a cigarette from this as thou would from tobacco.'

The boy walked out of the room, mullein plant in hand, shaking his head.

'Gawddamnit – I'm not going to just sit here while my little girl chokes to death!' Simon yelled. Mike James restrained him. Penny kept his eyes locked on Pearl.

She was kneeling now in front of Chrissy, the girl drenched in sweat and staring wild-eyed at the floor, slobbering and fighting desperately hard for air. 'Chrissy,' Pearl said softly. 'Chrissy. Thou need to help me.' Pearl reached out and stroked her hair.

Chrissy James raised her head slowly, trying to hold it upright to look at Pearl. Pearl put her hands on both of the child's cheeks and helped her, smiling into her dark eyes. Suddenly the girl reached out, as if grabbing for a log in the middle of a sea, clinging to Pearl. The kettle was screeching again.

Pearl sat down beside the girl and pulled a blanket over their heads, the doctor slipping the steaming pot under the edge.

'Is Chrissy going to live?' Simon was near tears. 'She's no damn doctor.' He was struggling hard to stand again.

'Pa, let her.' Mike said. 'For Chrissy.'

'I got it,' Hector said, rushing back into the room.

'Light it,' Pearl said, sticking a hand out from under the blanket.

Hector made the mistake of inhaling a large gulp of smoke and he began a wild coughing spree, bending and placing his hands on his knees. When he got control of himself, he knelt and put the cigarette into Pearl's outstretched hand. It disappeared under the blanket and soon Chrissy and Pearl were coughing just as hard, the woman talking quietly between gasps.

Fifteen minutes later, it was over. Pearl raised the blanket and leaned back weakly against the wall, her legs straight out in front of her, Chrissy clinging to her. The two of them looked awful: their eyes bloodshot and streaming badly, mucus draining from their nostrils. But Chrissy had survived.

Simon approached and Pearl helped him take his daughter, the girl reaching a hand back to her.

'Thou needs rest, Chrissy.'

The girl mumbled something and then reached back for her again, but Simon was moving her toward the door.

'It's thy cat, Mr James,' Pearl called after him, bending over a basin that Trotter held and losing her dinner.

He ignored her.

'Mr James. It's thy cat.'

'You're no damned doctor,' Simon snapped.

'Chrissy's attacks come from thy cat,' she persisted, wiping her face with a wet cloth.

'Simon,' Trotter added, 'she's probably right.'

'I thought you didn't know nothing about it.'

Trotter shook his head at the man's comment, watching Simon as he stopped to talk quietly with a rough-looking man at the office door.

'We've been lucky so far,' Pearl continued, sniffing and wiping her eyes on a towel. 'But one of these times we may not.'

The James boys were following their father and the other man out of the door of the doctor's office. Hector stopped and turned back and looked at Pearl.

'Thanks.'

'Thou are welcome, Hector.'

Mike James nodded in agreement with his younger brother, then Penny pushed him out of the office. Looking mad, Penny glared back at Pearl and said, 'I'm not done with your nigger.'

Penny caught up with his father and Chrissy at the Reliable Livery. The other man was gone. Simon was standing near the stable door under the yellow light of a kerosene lantern, deep in thought.

'Did they get him?'

Simon shook his head. 'Nope. But he's there. Mark my words, he's there. That woman is hiding that nigger.' Simon glanced at Penny. 'You got any paper on you?'

Penny shook his head, still fuming over the Quaker woman.

'Get me some,' Simon ordered, continuing to look like he was thinking hard about something.

Penny reached up and pulled a poster down from the livery stable wall. 'Here.'

'No,' Simon said, handing him a pencil. 'You write.'

Penny took the pencil and sat down on a bench next to the building. 'Write what?'

Simon adjusted the shawl over Chrissy and began to pace up and down the wooden sidewalk. 'One blanket,' he said. 'Write that down. One blanket. Then: twelve drops of eucalyptus oil.' He thought for a moment. 'Put the drops in boiling water.

74

Muellin cigarette.' He squinted his eyes. 'Plain old dried muellin plant.'

Penny was grinning.

The burning sensation in her eyes and throat had lingered all night, waking her well before she wanted. She sat up in bed, groggy and tired, and thought about the things that were bothering her. About Lillian. Her many problems. The orientals. Matthew. Her boys. And finally about Jerome Gilliam. Manslaughter. She shuddered as she had the night before.

Pearl closed her eyes, trying hard to recall the good feelings she'd gotten when she chanced upon the idea of his redemption. She couldn't. And certain unsettling doubts about him – as a minister and as an example for Zacharias – kept coming back to her. She knew how easily influenced her youngest would be by a man he admired. And Mr Gilliam was the first man he'd admired since his father's death. It was best that he was gone.

The house felt unusually cool as Pearl moved toward the kitchen. Then she heard Hercules. 'Zacharias. Is thy rooster inside?'

A strange scraping noise was drifting down the hall. She stopped and listened until she heard a voice, straining hard.

'Hit it.'

'Mr Gilliam?'

The three younger Eddy boys were helping Prophet take the back door off its hinges when Pearl came into the kitchen. Samuel was standing off to the side, watching and looking miffed.

'I told thee he would be back,' Zacharias beamed.

Prophet, momentarily surprised that she knew his last name, muttered a weak, 'Morning, Mrs Eddy.'

'Thou have returned.'

Zacharias gazed admiringly at the man, nodding in agreement with his mother's observation.

'Paying for that hen, Mrs Eddy,' he lied, still angry that the Negro woman had gotten him back in this mess. 'Door doesn't close right.' He returned quickly to the hinge, glancing at her periodically. The children were still in their places, but they were watching her as well. All but Zacharias, who seemed hypnotized by the Negro.

'Boys, please feed and water the chickens.'

'It's only half off, Mrs Eddy,' Prophet said, forcing a smile and straining to hold the door himself. The three boys halted and looked at their mother. Samuel turned and walked outside.

'Help Mr Gilliam,' she relented.

Prophet and the boys resumed their efforts to free the hinge. Then suddenly, as if coming to the old door's rescue, Hercules took a hawklike leap at Prophet's ankles, the man hopping wildly to avoid the bird's spurs.

'Call him off, Mrs Eddy!' He was trembling as if the bird were a five-hundred-pound lion.

Pearl stooped and made some clicking sounds and Hercules broke off the attack and strode over to her. She picked him up and stroked the feathers on his neck, 'Good bird,' she said gently.

'Dumb bird, Mrs Eddy,' he said. 'Attacked me three times this morning.'

'He is not dumb, Mr Gilliam.'

'Maybe not, but he's trailing behind smart,' he muttered. Minutes later, the door was off its hinges and the boys were heading outside.

Pearl waited until they were gone, then said, 'Mr Gilliam. What do thou think thou are doing?' Agitation rose in her voice.

'I told you, Mrs Eddy, paying for the hen.' He picked up a wood plane and began stroking the tool gracefully over the door edge, wood curls falling. Hercules canted his head and eyed the mess on the floor, struggling to get down to investigate. Pearl held him.

'Thou lied to me again.'

'Mrs Eddy?'

'Thou lied to me.'

'About?' he frowned.

76

'Many things.'

'Like?'

'Thy name for one. Thou said it was Prophet.'

'That's right.'

'It is Jerome Gilliam.'

'Once – but not now. It's Prophet, Mrs Eddy, just plain Prophet.'

'Not just plain Prophet,' she said quickly.

He stopped and looked up at her, sensing she knew still more. How much more he didn't know. He watched her a moment longer, then went back to working.

'Is that not correct?'

'You're the one talking, Mrs Eddy.'

'The Prophet of Doom – I believe is thy entire name.'

He straightened up slowly. 'My, my,' he said, after recovering from his surprise. 'Along with being righteous, Mrs Eddy, you're a regular detective.'

'Storytellers usually get caught, Mr Gilliam.'

He went back to planing the door edge. 'Don't recall I told you stories.' That was a lie and made him edgy, which was unusual.

'Oh, yes thou did. Thou let me believe thy name had some religious meaning.'

'You were the one doing all the talking, ma'am. If I'd waited long enough you'd have named me Pope.'

She pulled herself up straighter. 'Silence that deceives is the same as lying.'

He shook his head as if she was loony, wondering how much she actually knew.

'Suppose the sheriff told you I boxed, Mrs Eddy.'

'Not the sheriff.'

He hesitated, guessing she knew most of it. If he was to have any chance of finding her money, he'd better come clean. She had to have a bundle somewhere. She was standing and looking innocent, as if she was teaching Sunday school. Crafty like a fox, he figured.

'Something else you should know, Mrs Eddy,' he muttered, trying to sound repentant. 'Three years ago,' he paused, 'I killed a Negro in a fight. I served my time in prison. I just thought you should know.' He lowered his eyes, then remembered she was blind and looked to see if she'd bought it.

'You killed a human being,' she corrected.

Damn, she was an irritant – straightening out every little sentence. He didn't say anything, his thoughts drifting back three years. The man and two others had jumped him in a Texarkana alley one night and tried to slit his throat. He'd never known why – knew only that he'd pulled a board off a fence and crushed the slasher's head. He wasn't sorry, but he wasn't telling her.

'Have thou sought forgiveness?'

'They tried to kill me, Mrs Eddy.'

'It does not matter, Mr Gilliam. Thou must seek forgiveness so thou can have peace.'

At last, he thought, something that sounded like sympathy. But even so it had the smell of one of her lectures.

'I am sorry thou believe in violence. That thou deceive. But the Lord will forgive even thee, Mr Gilliam.'

The lines of a new frown formed on his face.

She continued tapping her foot on the floor.

'Mrs Eddy. That's annoying.'

'No more than thy deceits.'

'Ma'am, I came back to pay for the hen,' he muttered, exasperated. 'Nothing more. I'll fix this door, then be on my way.' He paused. 'I pay my debts.' He squirmed; he'd just told her two new lies. She was getting to him. Do what the kid wanted done, he told himself, find the money, then hit the road. Not much time. Every man, he knew, had just so much time on this earth to get his things done.

'Fine,' she said. 'I expect no violence while thou are here.'

They didn't say anything else for a while. She just stood holding the rooster while he worked on the door. When she finally set the bird down it began to scratch in the wood curls. Prophet watched it until he was convinced it had no designs on him, then he scanned the room again. Women mostly kept their money somewhere in the kitchen. But he'd been over this one three times. She definitely wasn't most women. He looked past her into the parlor. Must be in there.

'The county attorney, Edward Johnson, spoke to the sheriff on thy behalf.'

He didn't respond.

'Everything is settled, Mr Gilliam. Thou do not have to sneak around like a common criminal, telling tales and such.'

He felt hot on the back of his neck but he just went back to working. He'd find a way into the parlor, he promised himself. He wondered how much she had stashed. She obviously wasn't spending it on anything.

'No one will arrest thee. Those men will leave thee alone.'

He didn't reply.

'Did thou hear, Mr Gilliam?'

'My name's Prophet, Mrs Eddy.'

'I did it to clear my name,' she said, ignoring him, 'as well as thine. Whatever thy name is.'

'That's nice.'

She turned and stared in his direction until he got an uncomfortable feeling.

'Did thou find religion in prison?' There was a funny sound in her voice.

He started to tell her no, then something in her look caused him to reconsider. This thing about religion seemed tremendously important to her, and an opportunity for him. 'Yes, Mrs Eddy,' he lied.

'And that is where thou became a minister?'

He didn't even hesitate: 'Yes.'

CHAPTER FIVE

The hour was late and Prophet was standing in a deep pile of fresh wood shavings, bent over a workbench in the tool shed, squinting hard under the harsh light of a kerosene lantern. He swore softly under his breath. This was his fifteenth attempt and he was ready to call it quits. If he didn't get it done this time, he promised himself, he was going to pack up and hit the road. He was beyond caring about the old black woman's woeful stares or what the boy thought about him. And he figured the men on the road were just all talk about bothering this woman.

He straightened up and rolled his shoulders to stop their aching; his lower legs were hurting as well, and his hands were tired from six hours of using the wood chisel and the hammer. Then he heard sounds coming toward the room from the direction of the barn and tensed.

'Zacharias,' Pearl called, her voice sounding nervous.

'Shhhh,' he hissed out the open door, glancing sideways at the boy sleeping on a pile of grain sacks.

Zacharias had given him clear instructions about what he wanted done, then had watched him work for a time, chattering in his screechy voice about different things, as if the two of them were old friends, then dropped off to sleep seemingly confident the man was going to produce exactly what he'd asked for. Prophet wasn't feeling the same confidence right now.

He'd cut pieces of two-by-sixteen pine planking he'd found behind the barn, planed each piece down to a smooth, fresh surface, then gone at it with chisel and hammer. At first his mistakes had been made early, and he'd toss the ruined boards aside with little concern. But then as he got better at it, his mistakes were being made later and later into the work . . . costing him time. This current piece was mistake-free and almost done.

He wiped his forehead with a rag and fought a slight trembling of the muscles around his mouth, as Pearl tapped her way into the room. She looked worried, and Prophet realized he'd lost track of the time and that it was late.

'He's asleep on the oat sacks in the corner, ma'am,' he whispered. He watched as she worked her way around the table, feeling with her hand for the boy. She looked agitated. 'To your left,' he guided. 'Didn't you know he was here?'

'He climbed out a window,' she said coolly.

Prophet grinned at the little boy; he was indeed a scrapper.

The night was chilly. She felt Zacharias' forehead and then Prophet's jacket that had been laid over him for warmth, nodding at his consideration, then she turned and tapped her way back to the workbench. She didn't look agitated any longer, just distant and reserved.

She pulled herself up some and said, 'Mr Prophet. Thou know how impressionable Zacharias is.'

'Yes, ma'am. He's just a boy.'

'Yes. But, also, he thinks a great deal of thee.'

Prophet didn't respond. He just looked uncomfortable and went back to working on the wooden plank.

'I would not want him to get ideas about certain things.'

'No, ma'am,' he mumbled.

'About violence and swearing and things like that.' She paused. 'Thou understands.'

'Yes, Mrs Eddy.'

'Then thou will avoid these things?'

'I plan on moving on, ma'am. But as long as I'm here you can count on me.'

She smiled. 'Thank thee, Mr Prophet.' She pulled her shawl

tighter around her shoulders. 'What does he have thee working on?'

He stiffened. 'Why would you think he has me working on anything?' he asked, wondering if he should give away the boy's secret.

'Mr Prophet. Deceit is one of the things I would like thee to avoid.'

'I didn't deceive you, Mrs Eddy,' he said quickly. 'I just wondered why you'd think he had me working on anything. That's all.'

'Because I know Zacharias, Mr Prophet.' She paused. 'And because he told me that thou had promised to do something for him.'

'Yes, ma'am,' he said. 'Sign for the garden.'

She sniffed the air. 'I don't smell paint.'

'He wanted it chiseled.'

'May I read it?'

He started to say no, then shrugged. She'd read it soon enough anyhow. 'It's your garden.' He held the board toward her outstretched hand; moving it forward slowly until the wood just met the tips of her fingers.

She moved them probingly over the grooves of the freshly carved letters. Watching her sightless blue eyes and seeing her lips silently forming each letter, he got a feeling for her blindness that he hadn't had before . . . something of the helplessness and isolation. When she finished reading, she looked upset.

'Something wrong with it, Mrs Eddy?'

She didn't answer him. He turned the sign and checked each letter against the ones he'd made Zacharias write out for him on a piece of paper. They were all there. And in the right order. He couldn't figure what was bothering her.

THIS IS OUR FATHER'S GRAVE
MATTHEW EDDY
1861 TO

Nope. No mistakes that he could see. But she was biting at her lower lip and still looking upset about something.

'I told the children they could not mark their father's grave with anything but a cross,' she said quietly. Almost to herself, he thought.

Prophet just listened.

'It bothered him,' she said absently.

'I guess.' He cleared his throat. 'It isn't much of a thing, Mrs Eddy.'

'What is that, Mr Prophet?'

'The sign. It's not much of a thing – if the boy wants it.'

'We don't believe in the decoration of graves. We are dust at the beginning, Mr Prophet, and we return to dust.' She paused. 'My husband is with God. That's enough.'

'Maybe not for your boys.'

'Put it outside the garden, Mr Prophet,' she said, turning away.

'It won't be right.'

She turned back. 'Sir?'

'If I put it outside the garden fence, Mrs Eddy, it won't identify the grave. Not the way the boy wants.'

She stood and thought about this for a few moments, then said, 'Outside, Mr Prophet.'

He shook his head and wondered if it was her blindness that made her so rigid about things. Maybe. Regardless, he'd worked long and hard on this sign. And the boy wanted it on his father's grave.

'It's just a little thing,' he persisted.

He saw her skin turning crimson.

'We just believe certain things, Mr Prophet.'

'Your boys, Mrs Eddy? Or you?'

'We.'

'With due respect, I don't see it that way.'

'That is thy privilege. But the children are my responsibility.' She turned away again and went and gathered Zacharias up in her arms. She tripped over a piece of lumber and he caught her arm and guided her to the door. Zacharias was breathing softly in her arms. Prophet felt sorry for them both and wasn't certain why.

'You born blind, ma'am?'

'No. Samuel's birth. My eyesight just faded away,' she said in her matter-of-fact tone.

He watched her tapping her way out of the door with the sleeping boy in her arms and realized she'd never seen Zacharias' face. Never seen him smile or pout. Hadn't seen the twins either. This realization made him feel funny. He shrugged it off. It didn't give her any right to be stuffy about things.

'It isn't a big deal – the sign,' he called through the shadows after her.

'Outside the fence, Mr Prophet.'

'It won't work that way, Mrs Eddy,' he persisted.

She carried Zacharias toward the house without responding.

Prophet stood near the climbing rose at the gate of the garden early the next morning, watching Samuel pull weeds from around his father's grave. He glanced again at the sign he'd finished a few minutes earlier, nodding with satisfaction at the simple change he'd made and leaning the wooden plank and its heavy post and another thinner stake against the fence now, continuing to watch Samuel. The boy had stopped yanking weeds and was staring at the garden, unaware he was being watched.

'This place is pretty far gone.'

Samuel tensed, but didn't turn.

'Looks neglected,' Prophet continued.

'It wasn't neglected.'

'Looks it.'

'I thought thee were a minister – not a gardener.' The words were sharp in the still morning air.

'I don't know about plants. I just know neglect when I see it.'

The boy began pulling harder at the weeds. 'I told thee – we did not neglect it. We simply had no time.'

'Shame.' He paused. 'Want some help?'

'No.'

Prophet shrugged and picked up a shovel and surveyed an imaginary line between where he stood and the grave. Then he began to dig. Samuel watched him with a series of furtive glances, continuing his work on the weeds.

Fifteen minutes later, Prophet had finished setting the post and sign. He checked the angle of the plank face one last time, unable to contain another smile. Satisfied, he picked up the thin stake and walked under the roses and into the garden. Samuel whirled and angrily faced him.

'I told thee I didn't want thy help.'

'Wasn't coming to help you – though it looks like you could use a hand,' Prophet said, looking around at the heavy overgrowth. 'Shame,' he said again.'

Samuel stared at him for a moment. 'I don't know what thee are up to, but I know it's not good.' He hesitated. 'And thou should not be here.'

'It's just an old overgrown garden,' Prophet said, sounding innocent.

'I don't mean the garden – and thou knows that.'

Prophet bent over and examined a number of large rocks that lined the path where he stood, selecting a heavy one with a flat side. Straightening up and stretching out the stiffness in his lower back, he again eyed the sign and the grave, surveying an imaginary line between the two; then he carefully placed the point of the thin stake on the ground next to the little graveyard fence. Satisfied with its position, he pounded it deep into the earth with the rock, his powerful arm slamming the stone down hard like some mechanical tool. Even Samuel watched this display of strength and was impressed.

Prophet put the rock back where he'd gotten it and studied the plants again. 'It's a shame, letting it go like this,' he said again. 'With some hard work, it could be put right.' He stopped, realizing the boy wasn't listening. Instead, Samuel was squinting his eyes against the morning sun and reading the sign.

'Zacharias wanted it.'

Samuel didn't say anything, he just turned and picked up a board lying in the dirt next to him. From the way he was shielding it with his body, Prophet thought he knew what it was.

'What you got there?'

'None of thy business.'

Prophet stepped over and put a hand on the boy's shoulder. 'Let me see it.'

Samuel looked at him a moment, then turned the board over. The crude sign had been painted with red paint.

'Can't read without my glasses,' Prophet lied. 'What's it say?'

Samuel hesitated.

'Read it,' Prophet said more firmly.

'Nigger Town.'

'Where was it?'

'The front porch.' Samuel turned and started toward the place behind the barn where the Eddys burned their trash. He stopped and looked back. 'Thou should not be here,' he said.

Prophet ignored him. Still, he was certain the boy was right. And as soon as he found her money, he'd be gone. The sooner the better. He bent at the waist and slowly stretched out the pain in his lower back again, finally straightening up and admiring the large arrow that he had chiseled into the wood at the bottom of the sign. He had carefully painted it bright yellow and was angled so that the arrow's tip pointed directly at the yellow stake beside the grave of Matthew Eddy.

When Prophet shut the garden gate a few minutes later, he caught a glimpse of motion from the corner of his eye. The attacker was hidden behind the roses. He had the urge to make a break for it – but he fought the sensation. His best chance was to go slow. He probed the foliage again.

The leaves of the bush shook for a moment, then Hercules

strode forward, his beady eyes gleaming with a steely determination that made Prophet's legs weak.

'CCLLUUUUUUcckkk.'

The bird took another step.

'You do anything, dammnnnnit,' Prophet stammered, 'anything at all, and you're going into Sunday's stew! I promise.'

Hercules stopped and cocked his head as if considering the seriousness of the threat.

'CCLLUUUUUUUcckkk.'

'That's right, you coward, just think about it. You and the potatoes and the hot water.' Though Prophet had faced hundreds of men in and out of the ring, something about this crazed rooster sent chills down his back. 'Just keep thinking.'

The sound of Prophet's voice seemed to irritate the bird, his red hackles rising in the morning sunlight.

'Don't you dare!'

Prophet and Hercules were both professional fighters. The difference was that Prophet knew it, and only did it for money or a shot at the title. But Hercules seemed to think his was a nobler calling, some sort of strange blood vendetta involving the man.

The bird was standing a couple of yards away, glaring. Then, slowly, it tipped its head forward, stretching its neck out and spreading its wings like a swooping hawk. It held this awkward pose for a moment, teetering; then suddenly it was scurrying forward ready to exact some weird sort of chicken justice.

'Stop right there!' Prophet hollered. 'If you do this,' he yelled, raising the shovel menacingly over his head, 'I'm going to finish your feathered butt once and for all!'

The bird slid to an awkward halt – but his head and wings remained in the attack position, his hackles flaring wildly.

'Oh, Mr Prophet,' Pearl called from somewhere behind him.

'Call your bird off, Mrs Eddy. Call him off before I kill him!'

'Mr Prophet, thou hast already killed one of my chickens. And we spoke about violence.'

'He started it,' Prophet snapped, pointing the shovel at the bird. Hercules was beginning his mad charge again.

'Thou must have annoyed him.'

'Annoyed him?' His voice was incredulous. 'He attacks me every time he gets a chance.'

'Please do not exaggerate.' Pearl tapped her cane past him.

'He's crazy, Mrs Eddy.'

'Perhaps he senses thee wishes him ill,' she speculated.

'He's got that straight.'

She bent and clucked her tongue softly and Hercules slowly straightened up, then shook his feathers as if he had suffered a great indignity at the man's hands. He strode over to Pearl's waiting arms.

'Good bird,' she said softly. 'All thy need do is to tell him thou like him. Like all of God's children, Mr Prophet, he responds to love.'

'I don't like him. And he hates me.'

'He doesn't hate thee. He is only a chicken.' She paused. 'And thou are a man,' she said, emphasizing the last word.

Prophet watched Pearl pull a small handful of grain from her pocket, letting Hercules peck from her hand. The rooster did this with great care and dignity. That's how, Prophet said to himself. She bribes the old murderer.

Pearl stood and held her hand out toward him. 'Just give him some food and get acquainted. I'm certain thee will get along fine.'

Prophet watched her as she walked toward her chicken pen, then he quickly looked back down at the rooster. He was pecking at a bug in the dirt. Slowly, Prophet squatted and cautiously held out his hand.

'Here,' he muttered. 'Dumb bird.'

The rooster stopped chasing the bug and looked up at him, and Prophet had the sinking feeling he could still see hatred in the beady eyes. Then the bird spied the outstretched hand and strode over boldly to investigate. He looked over and under the hand, not trusting the man, then ventured a careful peck. The thumps of the beak seemed harder in his palm than they had appeared with her, but they weren't hostile. So this was the key. They fed the old bird and he left them alone. Prophet reached out his free hand and cautiously stroked the fine red feathers on the rooster's neck.

'CCCLLUUUUcckk.'

The food gone, Prophet stood slowly, keeping a wary eye on the chicken. He was feeling better: in control and confident. 'Behave yourself, buzzard, and maybe there's more,' he said in the sweetest of dulcet tones. 'Or maybe I'll slit your gizzard. Understand? Of course not,' he continued, crooning gently and smiling down at the rooster who had returned to pecking the ground. 'All you know how to do is pound your ugly mug into the dirt after a bug.' Satisfied that he had the bird's number, Prophet turned and studied the house.

It was a grand old structure with soaring gables and majestic lines. The back porch held up a dense mass of ancient wisteria which protruded out from the house like a pouting lip. In the summer it would shroud the porch in cool green shade. He wondered if Samuel was still inside. He wanted another look around the kitchen. Prophet started walking casually toward the house, dreaming about how much cash she had hidden away inside. He had taken three strides when Hercules exploded into him.

'Call him off!' he hollered, running hard for the porch, his right leg dragging slightly. The bird was making good time behind him.

The boy, Samuel, didn't know why he'd come out into the silent prairie night. He followed the darkened pathway to the huge barn, moving quietly toward the hen house. The air was still and cool, the vast black tent of night sky was strewn with a field of stars. He usually stopped and studied them, and thought about his father. But it was late and he was tired.

He listened. Nothing but the sound of Jack moving in his stall inside the barn. What had awakened him? He knew that he'd been dreaming about the Negro. About a mob lynching him. He felt somewhat guilty, remembering that he had yelled encouragement.

He glanced back at the swell of prairie and the darkened house where his brothers and mother slept, then out across the gardens and beyond to the tallgrass prairie that shouldered the edge of the fields. The grasses were dead silent, swaying and nodding slowly in the night air. He turned in a circle, scanning the horizon for some sound or movement that would tell him what was bothering him.

Nothing. He knew the Negro was sleeping in the barn. Maybe he'd banged a door or dropped something, the sound carrying to the bedroom. He leaned close to the barn wall and tried to hear the man, but couldn't.

Something moved in the dirt near his bare feet and he tensed. It moved again and he knew the sound and knelt and picked up a fat Woodhouse toad, holding it close to his face.

'I surely didn't come out here because of thy ugly puss.'

A bright stitch of light darted to the earth in the eastern distance, and moments later the gentle rumble reached him. If it had been westerly, he might have paid attention, but he knew from his father that lightning appearing from any other direction meant a storm that would not reach the farm. He stroked the bony ridges on the toad's head, and thought about his father, the memories hurting. He forced himself to stop.

Yawning he bent and set the little beast free and started walking toward the house. Then he stopped. They were moving in the same place. He squinted as the moon slid behind a bank of clouds, seeing them clearly. He'd witnessed this strange occurrence a dozen times before and, each time, it had bothered him deep inside. It did now as well.

They were in the same old buffalo wallow a half mile south of the farm, moving slowly up and down in their strange way. What are they? he wondered.

Coyotes were yipping in the grasses to the west of him, forming up for the night's hunt. He ignored them and squinted hard at the three lanternlike lights moving in the wallow, being lowered and then raised up high. Always the same. He wondered if the towns-people were right: that these were ghost lanterns held by three men who had returned one night to the wallow to find their families massacred by the Sioux. His father hadn't believed that. He'd just thought the lights were caused by swamp gas from an old spring nearby. Samuel liked to think they were ghost lamps.

As he watched them moving slowly around, he could imagine the men stumbling in shock, their lanterns held high over their heads to view their dead loved ones. It made him want to go inside and hold his brothers and mother tight. It also made him want to cry. But he was fourteen, too old for crying. He whispered a prayer for them that his mother had taught him and turned and started walking back toward the house, careful to miss the toad.

Halfway there he stopped again and turned and studied the darkened barn, feeling something moving across his shoulders: a warning of sorts. About what, he had no idea. But he could feel it. And instinctively he knew the ghost lanterns had not awakened him. Whatever it had been – he sensed it was in the barn. He studied the open doorway waiting for the odd sensation to pass. When it didn't, he started slowly back toward the large structure, his hands trembling.

Carefully he moved into the blinding blackness of the build-ing's interior, standing dead still and feeling the warmth of Jack and the other animals. A pigeon fluttered in the rafters. There were no other sounds. But still the place was bothering him. Something was wrong. He waited for his eyes to adjust to the darkness.

Slowly the moon came out from behind a cloud, sending a ray of soft light down into the barn's interior from the hay loft. He froze. Then he began stumbling backwards, gasping for air he didn't need. He hadn't been dreaming. They'd hanged the Negro from the rafters.

Samuel whirled around and was about to cry out when someone grabbed him from behind, clapping a hand hard over his mouth.

'Hush,' the voice hissed in the darkness, then yanked him back into an empty stall. Samuel started to struggle to free himself when the Negro whispered, 'Be quiet.'

'I thought they'd hanged thee,' Samuel said, shaking so badly he could barely talk.

The Negro shook his head.

'Who then?' Samuel stammered, pointing up at the rafters. 'They hung somebody.' He could see the awful figure swaying gently in the moon's weak light.

'Straw man,' Prophet said. 'You see any of them?'

Samuel let the relief he felt flood through him, then he shook his head.

'Let's wait a while longer.'

'Would they have hung thee?'

'Maybe.'

Samuel continued to stare at his face. When he didn't stop, Prophet got annoyed and asked, 'What?'

Samuel looked away. 'Nothing.'

Prophet had burned the Negro straw man on the Eddys' trash pile early that morning and now was squatting in the bright afternoon sunlight two stories above the earth, surveying the shingles of the roof, when little Zacharias appeared below. The boy had liked the sign and the yellow stake and had followed Prophet closely throughout the morning, keeping up his constant chatter as if he were catching up on a lot of things that he'd wanted to say to someone for a long time. Prophet figured that someone was his pa, so he let him talk. Now the boy squinted at him as if he were a hero of sorts. While glad he liked the sign, all of this attention made him uncomfortable.

'Can I come up?' Zacharias hollered.

'Nope – too high.'

'Then thou must come down to lunch. Mother says to do so now.'

'That so?' he said nonchalantly.

He was tired of her orders. Prophet pulled off his black bowler and carefully wiped the inside band with his handkerchief. He pulled a forearm across his brow, then took another look around. He'd been doing this periodically since he'd crawled up on the roof; each time the same sense of awe returned.

The grasses surrounding the farm were even more amazing when viewed from the vantage point of the roof, stretching in undulating waves to the far horizons. The fields hadn't been worked for almost two years and had returned to prairie, leaving the farmyard walled off on all sides by the towering plants. How this woman could live out here escaped him completely. He spat defiantly, then looked back down at the broken shingles and ripped tar paper on the roof. There had to be leaks in the attic, he figured.

'Zach,' he called down, 'ask your mother if she has shingles.'

The boy disappeared, returning a few moments later. 'She says to tell thee: come to lunch. We're waiting on thee.'

'Does she have shingles?'

The boy dutifully disappeared again, then reappeared moments later. 'No.'

'Tell your mother I'll eat later. On the porch.'

The little boy looked up at him like he'd just burned a stack of Bibles, hesitating until Prophet said, 'Go on.' Then he darted back inside the house. Prophet spat again. He'd eat where and when he wanted. He pushed the bowler down harder on his head. He didn't work for her. And he wasn't going to be bossed any more. He took a deep breath, feeling better at having finally declared his independence from this small woman.

He scanned the roof again and shook his head. The closer he looked, the more he saw that the grand old house was in sorry shape. She was tighter with her cash than he'd first suspected. He stood and stretched. She must have a bundle secreted somewhere.

When he stopped stretching and glanced down, she was staring up. 'Mr Prophet. We are waiting for thee.' She was still acting coolly toward him.

'I'll eat later.'

'Thou will eat now.' She disappeared into the house.

'Hey, Mrs Eddy!' He waited a moment. But if she heard him, she wasn't coming back outside. He kicked at a piece of loose shingle, slipped and almost fell. 'Damn,' he mumbled. Then he shrugged and started slowly down. It wasn't worth fighting over – he was hungry and she was just mean enough to not let him eat if he didn't do it now.

He took his time washing up on the porch. Even so, they were still waiting for him, seated quietly around the kitchen table, their hands folded neatly in their laps, looking like mourners, Pearl at the head of the table. Zacharias was missing. The room was quiet and he felt awkward as he took the empty chair opposite her. She sat staring in her blind way. He wondered if she could see anything at all – shadows and such. Her eyes were normal enough looking. It was too bad.

Then Zacharias returned carrying what looked like part of King Solomon's treasure. Prophet's breath caught. It had been worth the wait. The little boy struggled into his chair and leaned over to him.

'This is my pa,' he said in solemn tones.

Prophet couldn't get his eyes off the silver frame. He'd been right: there were treasures in this house. This was proof positive.

'Zacharias,' she said firmly.

'Mother, my shoes are hurting again,' Luke complained.

'Mine too,' Joshua said.

'This is not the proper time.'

Ignoring Samuel's glare, Zacharias again mouthed the words, 'This is my pa.'

94

Prophet put his finger to his lips, then he held out a hand for the magnificent frame. Solid silver and worth a fortune.

Zacharias looked ready to burst with pride. Prophet pretended to admire the pleasant-looking, square-jawed man in the photograph, while casually gauging the weight and quality of the silver; he didn't know the ounces, only that it was top grade.

'Where do you keep this?'

'Where it's safe,' Samuel interrupted, holding his hand out for the frame.

'I hope so,' he smiled.

'Samuel, Mr Prophet and Zacharias. Please.'

The three boys looked straight ahead, while their older brother disappeared with the frame. Prophet forced himself to stop thinking about it and instead thought about the boys' shoes, pretending to drop his napkin and peering quickly under the table. They were wearing high-buttons.

Zacharias' right sole was hanging loose, while the toes on Joshua's looked ready to burst. The laces on all three pairs were spliced with knots, the leather split and hard. No wonder they hurt. He was shaking his head and setting up when he noticed her shoes sticking out from under the edge of the long gray dress: as badly worn as the boys'.

He couldn't figure it. Maybe she was a miser. He'd heard of people who couldn't bear to part with their money. He took a deep breath and resumed listening to the parlor clock. 'Need shingles, Mrs Eddy.'

The boys giggled.

'Children,' she said solemnly.

He didn't say anything for a while after that – unable to tell what was so funny and not wanting to trigger another round of merriment. But then he was growing hungry and nobody was doing anything, so he cleared his throat and said, 'Mrs Eddy. Shall I speak over the food?'

'If thou are moved to, Mr Prophet, please do. Otherwise it is not necessary.'

'No, ma'am,' he said quickly.

A minute later, she picked up her fork and started. The boys followed. The silence followed as well. He didn't like it.

'Buy shingles – I'll patch the roof, Mrs Eddy,' he said between bites.

'I do not have the money.'

He stopped and studied her face. Her expression remained serene. Nevertheless, he was certain she'd just told a lie. He'd seen the silver frame. It was worth a small fortune. She had to have money. He didn't care for the thought of her telling tales, still, he knew people would do strange things over money. Lying was just one of a long list.

'That's OK. Other things need fixing,' he said, playing along.

'Thou have done enough, Mr Prophet. I consider the hen paid for.'

'Fine, Mrs Eddy.' He wasn't going to beg her for work.

They went back to their respective silences. He focused on where he'd head next. Minnesota. Name fighters, he'd heard, trained in the woods up there. As he was mulling this over, the idea came to him suddenly and fully formed: he'd catch on as a sparring partner at one of the camps. His heart beat a little harder. It was a sweet idea. It didn't matter what they paid him. They could even charge him. But when he got in the ring with one of those fighters he'd knock the stuffing out of him. They'd have to pull him off. They'd see how good he was. He was smiling.

Prophet was so wrapped up in his new scheme that he just blurted the words out, 'Be on my way this evening.'

Zacharias looked stunned. 'We were going to talk some more,' he said quietly.

'After lunch,' Prophet said quickly.

'Never mind.' Zacharias stood and ran out the back door.

'Zacharias,' Pearl called. He didn't return.

'He just wants thee to stay,' Joshua said. 'Maybe thou should.'

'Thou could help us make a sod fort behind the barn,' Luke added, hopefully.

'Boys. Mr Gilliam has things he must do. So do all of thee.'

'Prophet,' he corrected.

She hesitated, then said, 'Mr Prophet.'

Then the back door slammed hard again and Zacharias ran panting back into the room.

'There's people coming down the road!'

'Please go to the cellar, Mr Prophet,' she said.

'He's not our problem,' Samuel objected.

'Samuel,' she said firmly. 'Lock Mr Prophet in the cellar.'

'I can't.'

'Why?'

'He's gone.'

Pearl Eddy opened the front door and listened anxiously to the crowd milling around the front yard, and someone walking across her porch. Reflexively, she raised a hand and touched the high collar of her blouse. 'Yes?'

There was no response until Samuel said, 'It's the woman.'

'The woman?'

'The Chinese one.'

Pearl forced a smile and nodded. Though relieved the mob hadn't come for the Negro, she was uncomfortable facing this woman again.

'Hello,' she said.

The woman didn't respond; she just stood looking at Pearl's face in the same curious way she had the evening in front of the hotel. It was obvious she was as surprised as Pearl that she'd chanced upon her here on this lonely road.

'I'm sorry,' Pearl continued, 'but I cannot help.' The words seemed to take something out of her and she sucked in a deep breath, letting it out slowly.

'Mizu. Water. That is all I want from you.' She held a large ceramic jar in her arms like a heavy baby. 'The town help us on our way,' she said, her eyes fixed on Pearl's face.

97

Watching his mother, Samuel began to worry that she might get involved. That's all they needed. They already had the Negro hiding somewhere out back. They didn't need this Asian family. He looked past the woman at the girl standing behind the old cart, holding her little brother gracefully on her hip; watching her until he heard his mother's voice.

'Where?'

'Out of town.'

'There's just prairie.'

'To rikuchi. To my land.'

Pearl looked surprised. 'Thou do not have any land.'

'They ask me where we want to go. I say: to my land.'

'I'll get the water,' Samuel offered, reaching quickly for the jar.

'Yes,' Pearl said absently. Finally she collected herself and turned toward her boys. 'Joshua and Luke, gather all the eggs thou can find.' She paused. 'And bring that sack of potatoes off the back porch.'

The boys darted away through the house.

'Thy land doesn't exist,' Pearl said again.

The woman just stood staring into her face as if she were disappointed with her. Pearl cleared her throat. 'The men – the judge and Attorney Johnson – they did not steal thy land. They are honest men.' She paused. 'And they say that thy land has been lost.'

'No lost. We going to it. To rikuchi.'

'But it doesn't exist.'

The woman got a funny expression on her face. 'Land always exists.'

'Yes, but the county took it,' Pearl explained. 'For back taxes.'

The woman shrugged her shoulders and took the jar of water from Samuel. Small though she was, she held it without any apparent strain. 'It not matter. These men take us to it.'

The woman turned away and Pearl could hear her moving down the steps. 'Thy land is gone,' Pearl repeated firmly. 'All these men are going to do is leave thee and thy children out on the prairie.'

The woman smiled. 'Land is never gone.'

'It is gone,' Pearl said, sounding frustrated. 'I would help thee if I thought I could. I would.' She hesitated a moment. The words seemed to stick in her throat and she had to force them out. 'But I cannot.'

The woman studied Pearl's face for a moment longer, then she blew out her nose in a disdainful way and continued down the steps. 'Land never gone,' she said over her shoulder. The twins followed with the eggs and the sack of potatoes. The crowd cheered as the woman approached, the noise festive-sounding.

Pearl started to take a step out on to the porch, then stopped herself and leaned into the side of the door as if she needed support. Samuel watched her, concerned that she might fall. Then she pushed away and walked quickly toward her bedroom.

Pearl was still feeling sick over the orientals when later that same evening she opened her front door to the sound of knocking and was immediately covered by a wave of heavy perfume.

'Rose?'

'Shhhhh,' the woman cautioned.

Sheriff Haines, a well-used barrel of a man with a kindly face and prematurely white hair, was standing beside her. He tipped his head and said, 'Mrs Eddy.'

'Sheriff?'

'Is he still here?' Rose whispered.

'Who?'

'That Negro. I knew he was lying.'

'Rose?'

The sheriff was looking beyond Pearl into the shadows of the parlor.

'Pearl,' Rose hissed, 'just listen. He's a thief. His name isn't Jerome Prophet. And he's no French designer.' Rose stepped closer and took hold of Pearl's hand as if the news she was about to impart might cause instant paralysis. 'Worse: he's a killer. If he's harmed you or the boys!'

'Rose. We have not been harmed.' She looked suddenly embarrassed. 'He just stretches the truth.' Pearl turned in the sheriff's direction. 'Edward Johnson and thee spoke about him.'

'He said the Negro broke into your house but you didn't want him arrested.'

Rose Sherman looked back and forth from the sheriff to Pearl, raising a hand to the heavy strand of necklace around her throat. 'Pearl Eddy! You let a killer touch me – but didn't want him arrested!' She patted her powdered face with a lace handkerchief.

'Rose. The death was accidental.' Pearl gripped her hands together. 'But thou are right. I should have told thee he was not my assistant.'

Rose made a little hhrrrmmmping sound deep in her fleshy throat and looked indignant.

'Mrs Eddy. The Negro isn't holding you against your will?'

'He is not a dangerous man, sheriff –'

'I beg to differ,' Rose cut in. 'My pill box. That man stole it.'

'That is not true, Rose,' Pearl said, her voice barely audible.

'Pearl Eddy!' Rose snapped, pursing her lips, then spluttering. 'How dare you call me a liar!'

'I am not. But Mr Prophet is not a thief.'

The sheriff cleared his throat. 'Is he here?'

'Yes, sir.' Prophet's voice came from the shadows of the hallway where he had been listening, Zacharias clinging to his hand. Samuel was standing behind him, looking pleased.

Sheriff Haines took a small step back when he saw Prophet's face. He studied him carefully, uncertain what he'd bitten off. 'Let's talk out on the walkway,' he said, his hand on his pistol grip.

Prophet put Zacharias' hand into Samuel's, then walked with the man down to the waiting deputies, one of them immediately beginning to pat down his clothes.

'Why are they doing that to him?' Zacharias sniffed.

'Mr Prophet has been wrongly accused of a crime,' Pearl said.

'He didn't do it,' Zacharias yelled.

'Zach, be quiet,' Samuel snapped. 'Mother . . . thou are being foolish.'

Mrs Sherman turned to face the boy. 'Samuel Eddy – what do you know about this Negro?'

He looked down at his feet.

It was Pearl who finally broke the uncomfortable silence.

'Samuel. Tell Mrs Sherman the facts thou possess to condemn this man. To have him arrested.' She paused, gathering up her anger, then said in a soft voice, 'Go ahead, son.'

Samuel looked sick, glancing from his mother to the woman. Finally, he said, 'I just have a feeling about him. That's all.' His face had turned red and he spun on his heel and walked quickly back into the house.

At least one Eddy has some sense,' Mrs Sherman grumbled.

Pearl tensed but did not respond. Then the sheriff, Prophet and Deputy Willard were on the porch.

'Have you arrested him?' Rose asked.

Zacharias was crying without sound, when he darted forward and began to kick at the sheriff's ankles.

'Thou leave him alone! He's no crook!'

'Zacharias!' Pearl said.

Prophet grabbed him up in his arms. 'Zach. You settle down. There are times to fight. Times not to.'

Pearl tensed. 'There is no right time for violence, Mr Prophet.'

He couldn't believe it. Even here, in the middle of this mess.

Rose looked huffy again. 'This family is disgraceful.'

Pearl began to pull herself up to her full height. She was trying – as she had with the orientals – to avoid trouble, to stay out of harm's way, but Rose was making it extremely difficult.

'We're just going to check his belongings,' the sheriff said to Zacharias. 'No need to get riled.'

'He didn't take nothing,' the boy shot back angrily. 'Mrs Sherman just doesn't like him.'

'Zacharias, thou will not speak to thy elders in that tone,' Pearl said quietly. 'Apologize to Mrs Sherman.'

The boy just glared at the woman.

Rose ignored him.

'Zacharias,' Pearl said again. Louder this time.

Still the boy didn't budge.

'Zach,' Prophet said.

The boy looked at the Negro for a moment, then said, 'Sorry.'

Rose Sherman hhrrrrumphed.

After the men and boys had disappeared into the house, Pearl turned toward the woman. 'Rose. I should have told thee he was not my assistant. But to accuse him of stealing thy pill box is also wrong.'

'Pearl Eddy. You can shelter a murderer with your children if you wish. But I will not give him comfort. You can see the ill effects. That young one is growing violent.'

Pearl crossed her arms and began to tap her foot.

A few minutes later, the men returned.

'Where is it?' Rose demanded.

'It wasn't there.'

Rose Sherman looked indignant. 'He's obviously hidden it.'

'Maybe. But I can't arrest him on maybes.'

'You have my word,' Rose snapped.

'But you didn't actually see him steal it.'

'That's beside the point, he's a murderer and a liar.'

'Rose,' Pearl interrupted, her voice full and firm. 'Mr Prophet stole nothing. He is a minister.' She paused. 'And a good man.'

Prophet turned and studied the side of Pearl's flushed face, peering at her as if she had suddenly risen to a new level of daftness. No one had ever taken his part before. And, strangely, he didn't like it now that it had happened.

He swallowed hard, trying to toss off the queasy feelings. It didn't matter, he told himself. It didn't matter at all. However this mess turned out, it was her own fault. All her own fault. She should have figured him out by now. Most folks saw right through him. Anybody with half a brain. Her oldest boy had. But no. She pretended that he was something good and grand. He wasn't. And she didn't have any right saying he was.

He felt better now having chalked the outcome of this matter up to her. He watched as she grasped her hands behind her back to keep them from trembling, noticing she looked suddenly exhausted, and for a moment it seemed that her fight had drained away. He hoped so. For a woman who didn't like fighting, she sure had a knack for it.

He was waiting for her to turn and go back into the house when, in a quiet voice, she said, 'Mrs Sherman is mistaken. Mr Prophet stole nothing.' She hesitated, drawing a deep breath. 'And I doubt that there is a law about impersonating a French designer.'

'That's right!' Zacharias yelled.

'Zacharias,' she said. The twins put their arms around their little brother, restraining him.

The sheriff watched the boy for a moment to make certain he wasn't going to be attacked again, then looked at Prophet. 'You keep your skirts clean. Hear me?' Prophet nodded and went back to staring at Pearl Eddy.

Rose Sherman looked stunned. 'He's still a vagrant.'

The sheriff looked at him. 'How much money do you have on you?'

Suddenly Prophet's face went rigid, the tremor catching him as it always did, by surprise. He turned his head, self-consciously trying to hide his mouth under his large hand, pretending he was yawning. 'Dollarrr maybeee,' he said, fighting for control of his muscles.

Rose and the sheriff and all the children watched him, mesmerized by the strange seizure. When it was over, Prophet looked embarrassed.

'You OK?' the lawman asked.

He nodded awkwardly.

'How much money you got?'

'About a dollar.'

The sheriff looked disappointed. It was clear he had no interest in arresting this man. 'Law says you need ten dollars.'

Rose Sherman beamed. Then Pearl started her foot-tapping again and Prophet knew she was prepared for round two. Like all good fighters, she could take a punch and get up. He shook his head, wishing she'd just quit. Though loony, he didn't like her taking a beating on his account.

'I'll just be moving on.'

Zacharias started to cry.

'No. He's a vagrant and I demand his arrest.'

Sheriff Haines frowned. 'Let the man leave town, Rose.'

'You arrest him,' she said, a warning in her voice. 'I'll not be humiliated by the likes of a thieving murderer. I don't care what Mrs Eddy's odd feelings are toward this Negro,' she hissed, the words carrying an unseemly implication. 'That's something she will have to answer for.'

The sheriff looked at Prophet. 'Get your bag.'

Zacharias was sobbing loudly now.

Prophet had started for the hallway when he heard Pearl's voice. 'Stay where thou are, please.'

Her hands were on her small hips and she looked ready for some action that he was certain would be unwise. She was definitely deficient, casting everything – her livelihood, her good name – away like this.

Pearl turned slowly toward Rose Sherman. Prophet could see she was shaking. 'Do thou mean that thou would have a man arrested because he has no money?'

'Absolutely,' the woman replied, tossing her gray-haired head.

'Rose. Thou are too good a person.'

'Apparently not as good as you,' she said, insinuating something else again.

Pearl's voice was barely more than a whisper when she finally spoke. 'Will thee truly harm this man by throwing him in jail, simply because he is poor?'

'I have every intention of doing just that, Pearl Eddy.'

Pearl waited before she finally spoke. Snippets of Edward Johnson's warning about getting involved, of Mr Snipes' letter and Lillian's threat flashed through her thoughts. But these things could not stop her rising anger. 'Then, Rose, we can no longer be friends.'

Prophet closed his eyes and shook his head.

'There's no question of that!' Rose Sherman snapped.

Pearl nodded. 'I simply wanted thee to understand.' Her voice trailed away uncertainly.

Then she turned quickly toward the sheriff, her eyes shining with a strange expression, and Prophet knew that she was about to cry. He had the urge to grab her by the shoulders and shake her and tell her to stop.

'A man is not a vagrant if he is working – is that correct?'

'Yes.'

'Then, sheriff, Mr Prophet is not a vagrant. He has been working for me. And I will vouch for him while he is in town.' She pulled herself up straight again, seemingly having regained her strength. 'Is there anything else?'

Rose Sherman looked stunned for a moment, then she started off the porch. Halfway down the stairs, she turned and gave Pearl a cold, penetrating stare. 'Pearl Eddy, you are behaving disgracefully – and you will account for it!'

'Goodbye, Rose,' Pearl said, very quietly.

'I don't need your do-gooding.' Prophet turned from where Pearl sat shelling peas on the back porch and placed his hands on the railing, staring out across the backyard. 'You don't owe me. And I don't owe you.' He was breathing hard, uncertain why he felt so angry.

'As a minister, thou should understand.'

She sounded OK but he could tell she was worried. He figured she ought to be. He whirled toward her. She hadn't said much up to this point and looking at her now – rocking slowly and steadily snapping peas into a large pot on her lap – it didn't look as if she was going to say anything more. There was a faraway cast to her eyes, as if she might be remembering other times. Better times.

'Well, I don't,' he snapped.

Pearl stood up and started for the kitchen door.

'Do you understand what I've been saying?' he called.

She stood thinking for a few moments. 'Only that thou does not understand.'

'What's that mean?'

'Thou thinks I did what I did for thee.'

'And you didn't?'

'No.'

'Why then, Mrs Eddy?'

'For me.'

Prophet frowned.

She stood resting the pot on her small hip, brushing a strand of hair away from her face with a frustrated wave of her hand, as if she had no time for this. 'Thou were innocent. Therefore, it was not only right – it was my responsibility.' She started for the kitchen.

'That's crazy – your responsibility.'

She stared at him. 'Mr Prophet, whether thou like it or not we each have a responsibility to profess the truth in this life.' She turned and disappeared into the kitchen.

Pearl set the pot down on the kitchen table and stood with her hands gripping its rim, her body trembling as the words came battering back at her: 'my responsibility'. What did that mean? The Negro? But not the orientals? What about her boys and the damage she had done to them?

The longer she thought about it, the more she began to sense that she hadn't been honest. The realization caused her chest to hurt. Not honest with herself or the Negro. She hadn't stood up for the man just because she believed he was innocent. She believed that, but she also knew she'd stood up for him because she'd lost her temper at Rose Sherman.

Wrath, she knew, had dictated her righteous sense of responsibility. And because she hadn't been angry enough, she'd let the likes of Penny James drive the orientals on to the prairies. She bit hard on her lower lip and slowly began to twist her head back and forth, crying without sound. She had put her boys at risk because of her wrath. She had saved the Negro because of it. She had abandoned the orientals for lack of it. She moaned deep inside. Her entire life seemed inextricably tied to it. And she had no idea how to deal with it.

Prophet watched the empty doorway for a long while, listening to the sounds of her in the kitchen. Then he turned and leaned hard against the railing, staring at the backyard as it faded in the weakening twilight. The words returned: 'Thou were innocent.' He waited for the muscles around his mouth to stop twitching.

Then he started to follow her into the house, but stopped, uncertain what he would say. It didn't matter.

'I apologize, Rose,' Pearl mumbled, perspiration beading slightly on her brow. 'I was wrong. Wrong about the Negro. Wrong not to tell thee. Wrong about the fact that he stole from thee. I'm certain he did.' She paused. 'Yes. I'm certain.'

Rose Sherman formed a satisfied-looking smile across her powdery face, but didn't respond.

Pearl continued quickly. 'But he is a French designer. He has created for the royalty of Europe. And he made these patterns for thee,' she lied, holding out a box filled with dress designs. Pearl set the box down on the floor and rubbed her hands together, trying to dry her sweating palms.

Rose's eyebrows lifted in an expression of half-interest, then she yawned in Pearl's face.

'All I have to-to-to do,' Pearl stammered, 'is to sew them up for thee. And thou will have two dozen of Europe's most beautiful dresses.'

*

Pearl sat bolt upright in the darkness of her bedroom and let out a little yelp. She was shaking hard and listening as if the devil himself were lurking in the shadows. She had been tempted. She was certain of it. The Antichrist had realized her vulnerability. And he had tempted her. She shuddered again.

She remembered snatches of the awful dream: she'd lied in an attempt to sell Rose Sherman two dozen dresses. Pearl bent forward, moaning and clasping her head in her hands as if it might explode. She was losing herself and what she believed in, driven by wrath and her mad pursuit of money.

She shoved her legs over the edge of the bed and stood up and began to slowly pace the darkened room.

Samuel was on the back porch trying to repair his brothers' tattered shoes, the sun just topping the barn, when Pearl came and stood in the doorway. She looked worn out, deep circles under her eyes. He waited for her to say something, but she just stood staring blindly in the direction of the barn as if listening to some sound that he couldn't hear.

The Negro had packed his bag earlier, heading west down the prairie road toward the railroad tracks, Zacharias crying after him until the twins had caught up with their brother and held him back. Samuel had watched the three of them shouting goodbye to the man. He was glad he was finally gone. He looked up at his mother again.

'Are thou ill?' he asked.

'No,' she said, her voice sounding far away.

'Do thou want something to eat?'

'No.'

Neither of them spoke for a while, then Pearl said, 'Samuel. Take Jack into town and bring the sheriff, Judge Wilkins and Attorney Johnson out.'

'Why?'

'Just do what I ask, please.'

CHAPTER SIX

The day's light was fading across the prairie, shading the grasses pink; the bird sounds dying in the evening breeze. Moving slowly in the sands of the cross prairie road, the Eddy buggy was headed back toward the farm, a crowd following behind. Edward Johnson and Judge Hyram Wilkins, a smaller, older man, walked alongside, leading their saddle horses.

'They'll stay at my home,' Pearl said firmly. She was seated beside Samuel, the boy guiding Jack down the deeply rutted road. Small groups of townspeople were waiting in buggies or on horseback along the route, watching them, no one saying anything. Then Samuel saw Rose Sherman and some women in her large double-traced carriage, the ladies stopping to stare as the buggy passed. Something in their collective look made him want to crawl under the seat.

He turned away, glancing past his mother at Johnson and the judge. Both had been his father's friends and he knew they had his mother's interests at heart. Samuel also knew that what his mother was doing was a decent thing. But foolhardy. Nobody wanted these people around. Nobody trusted them. And the last thing they needed was to get involved with them. People thought Quakers were strange enough as it was.

'Pearl, it's just not smart,' Judge Wilkins said in a solicitous way. The judge was small and thin, and wore a long, heavy raccoon coat. He wore it all year long. Past eighty, he was puffing hard to keep up.

'Sam, slow that horse before I drop dead in the road,' he snapped. He wasn't used to people not catering to him.

'Pearl. The judge is right – this isn't a good idea,' Johnson continued.

A crowd of men and boys was trailing a dozen yards behind the buggy, kept back by Sheriff Haines and his two deputies. More folks were riding up to stare at them. The mood was festive but Samuel didn't feel anything but embarrassed. All his life his mother had told him to not draw attention to himself. Now they were leading a parade of misfits down the road.

'It is a far better idea than that law,' Pearl insisted, turning in the seat toward where she had last heard the judge. 'Thou are certain it is still on the books?'

'Pearl Eddy. This is the third time.' He opened a small book and pushed a pair of metal-rimmed glasses up on the bridge of his nose. 'No persons of color shall be on the streets of Liberty after sunset, unless in the employ of Caucasian residents and on a specific errand for said Caucasians.' He pulled his glasses off and looked up at her. 'It's just rarely enforced.'

'Outrageous,' she muttered.

'It's a silly law,' he continued, 'but folks signed the complaint so I had to enforce it.' He paused. 'And Pearl, these are your neighbors.'

She didn't respond.

Edward Johnson reached a hand up and touched her forearm. She stiffened and he quickly withdrew it. 'They can camp on the edge of town, while we raise money for their passage home.'

'The woman does not want to leave, Edward. Thou heard her. And there are little children. They do not have proper things to camp out on the plains.'

'They'll be fine for another night or two.'

'She does not want to leave,' Pearl repeated slowly.

'Not now – but in a few days, she'll see that this isn't going to work.'

Samuel knew that Johnson and the judge were going to lose this argument, and he figured they knew it too, so he quit listening and turned and looked over his shoulder at the procession following the buggy.

He shook his head: Liberty's worst and all of them headed to their house. He could see Hector, the youngest of the James boys, and a couple of his rough cronies walking along the roadway, carrying rocks and glaring. The sheriff and his deputies were keeping order, but the sheriff wasn't going to live with them.

He looked away to the Chinese family struggling behind the buggy. All their belongings had been loaded on to the rickety old handcart and this was being pushed by the mother and the older girl, the two smaller children holding the woman's baggy pants, as if they'd be murdered if they let go. The baby was in harness on the woman's back, drooling, while the hairy pig trotted alongside, still tied to the axle. Every once in a while, the little animal would dig his feet in, forcing the women to pull him like a plow.

They'd found them squatted down in a flimsy tent in the middle of the sandhills five miles west of town. They had a little water and food, but no prospects. They looked even worse than when he'd first seen them squatted in Main Street. After an hour or so of talking, his mother had convinced the oriental woman to come back to their farm. Samuel didn't know how. She was just a good talker. And she was stubborn. He looked back over his shoulder again at the little oriental woman.

She seemed determined to keep smiling; her expression was in sharp contrast to the anger of the girl struggling beside her. The teenager appeared ready to turn and fight at any moment.

She had a nice look to her face, and this surprised him. In photographs of Chinese he'd seen, they looked starved and shriveled or short and squat-bodied like dirty jelly jars – or like painted dolls. She wasn't like that. She was healthy-looking.

'Pearl, you don't need this problem,' Judge Wilkins huffed.

Samuel didn't listen for the answer: he knew his mother. He continued watching the girl. Then suddenly she looked up into his face, her eyes flashing, and he quickly shifted his gaze to the top of the bundles, stopping at the strange little bamboo cage.

It was an odd contraption, four feet tall and some three square, secured to the cart by leather thongs. While he couldn't see what it was, he could make out a shadowy form through the cage's thin slats. Then, to his surprise, the girl lifted her head and yelled at the cage. The woman spoke sharply and the girl stopped yelling.

Puzzled anew, Samuel studied the container a while longer, wondering what was inside. Whatever it was it angered the girl. These were strange people.

Furtively, he studied her a while longer, then glanced at his mother. She was sitting very straight with her arms across her breast, gazing in her sightless way over Jack's head. The judge and Mr Johnson had stopped and stood now watching the buggy. Samuel took a good grip on Jack's reins, as if what he was about to say would cause the old horse to lunge down the road.

'Thou tell us to avoid ill-considered things,' he said.

Pearl didn't respond.

'Judge Wilkins and Mr Johnson say this is ill-considered.'

'They have no place to stay. Nothing to eat.'

'Thou told the Negro we can't repair our roof.' He paused. 'We've got Zacharias and Joshua and Luke. I'm worried about them – not these strangers.'

She waited a moment before she spoke. 'I will decide this matter.' She stopped talking and put her hands in her lap, rubbing them slowly together.

'We cannot do it.'

'Thou are not my husband. Thou are my son.'

Samuel's face reddened and he shook his head obstinately; then he turned back just as a tomato arched through the air, coming fast at the girl from the tallgrasses off to his right. He started to yell, but there was no chance.

He hadn't seen the thrower, just caught a glimpse of the tomato as it sailed over the main body of the crowd and splattered against the back of the girl's head. He winced. But then his anguish turned to surprise. It was as if the tomato had not even touched her. She didn't flinch or react in any way, she just continued to shove the little cart, staring straight ahead as if glaring at some invisible enemy, tomato dripping from her hair. The crowd roared its triumphant approval. Jack picked up his pace.

'I'm going to help with the cart,' he hollered over the yelling. Pearl nodded and took the reins.

Prophet had been searching frantically for almost an hour. Instinctively he sensed time running out. From long experience, he knew it was never safe inside a house longer than thirty minutes.

He was on his knees in the bedroom – her room – running his hands expertly around the bottom of the dresser, hoping he'd find an envelope of money or bonds hidden there. Nothing. Absolutely nothing. Not even dust.

He rocked back on to his feet, too fast, and the old black woman popped into his mind like she'd been waiting for the chance, looking at him like he was doing something shameful.

He ignored her as long as he could, then said, 'You're no one to talk about shame. Sneaking around, peeking and sticking your nose into other people's doings.' He surveyed the room carefully one more time. 'Like now. You don't belong in here. At least I worked for the woman.' He let his eyes roam again. Sometimes it was the best way to discover hiding places.

The bedroom was plain and neat, and empty of anything valuable. Plain and neat like the woman herself. Barren of anything soft. A four-poster bed stood against the far wall. The floors were hard-swept wood. A white porcelain bowl and pitcher sat on the bedside table. Practical. Like the woman. He could almost feel her in this room. He squirmed at the thought, then the muscles around his mouth began to twitch and he knew the old Negro woman had gotten to him.

'I worked for this woman,' he explained. 'But she never paid me a dime. And I need money to get to Minnesota.'

Still not able to figure where she kept her valuables, he ran his hand over his smooth head, his eyes coming to rest on a neatly sewn sampler hanging on a sidewall. 'Charity', it read. That's all he wanted. But he sensed he wasn't going to find any – not in this woman's house.

After pretending to leave earlier that day, Prophet had simply slipped back and hidden in the gully down the road, watching until he'd seen the Eddys leave in their buggy. He thought about Zacharias, remembering how the boy had attacked the sheriff, and didn't like the feeling in his gut. He shrugged it off. It was high time the boy learned some hard facts about life. He shouldn't be trotting around believing in every Tom, Dick and Harry who dropped out of the sky. This thought – that he was teaching the boy a valuable lesson about life – made him feel better. Not great. But better.

As soon as he'd seen Mrs Eddy and Samuel leave the farm in their buggy, he'd let himself into the house. He'd been over every inch of it, hunting for money, silverware, jewelry: anything of value. He hadn't found a thing. Not a spare dime. It was the most barren house he'd ever laid eyes on. Even poor Negroes had a few prize possessions. But not this woman. It was crazy. Nor could he find where the boy had hidden the silver frame.

The only things of worth were the books on the shelves. Dozens of them. For a blind woman she surely liked books. But he couldn't cart them off across the prairie. He shook his head. Even her thimbles were brass, when silver and gold were all the rage. He scratched behind his ear. There simply wasn't anything worth stealing.

But that wasn't possible. He hurried into the parlor. It had to be a trick. She had to have valuables somewhere. She had the silver frame. He froze. Off in the distance, he heard a faint sound that was oddly familiar. He listened harder. Yes. The noise of a crowd . . . and it was growing louder. Damn this place. Two in two days. For a lonely road, this one was getting a lot of traffic.

He was starting for the door when he caught a glimpse of it: a corner of the silver frame sticking out from behind a sofa pillow.

He hated to do it. He liked the boys and this was their father. But he also hated the thought of not making it to Minnesota. When he made it big in the ring, he promised, he'd make it up to them. Buy them a dozen frames. He stared at the photograph, thinking about Zacharias.

He didn't know how long he'd stood there thinking before he grabbed the frame and started to remove the photograph. He'd leave it on the table. He was certain they had others – but he'd do it anyway. He stopped and listened again, then he ran to the window, his right leg dragging badly now.

While he had been daydreaming, the noise had grown significantly louder and he could see dust rising a few hundred yards down the road. They were coming fast. And he wasn't waiting around until they arrived. He went out through the kitchen.

Half a mile from the house, Joshua, Luke and Zacharias darted out of the weeds and up alongside the buggy, as if Geronimo was no more than a step behind. Their clothes were dirty and the twins looked as though they'd been fighting.

Samuel raised his eyebrows at them and Joshua turned and pointed at a cluster of boys at the side of the road. Hector jabbed his middle finger into the air. It had started.

The road was steeper here and the two women were having a hard time getting the cart to roll. They looked badly winded, and Samuel realized he had set too fast a pace.

'Josh and Luke, get Zach into the buggy,' he hollered, 'and take over from mother!' He trotted back to the cart.

Pearl patted Josh's arm, a slight smile set firmly on her face, looking to all who saw her as though she were at a Sunday meeting.

'Take Jack in through the back,' Samuel called. 'And when we get inside, get the barn door and shutters closed down fast.'

'No,' Pearl said. 'We will not barricade ourselves inside. These are our neighbors.'

Samuel looked at his brothers and shook his head. The

Chinese woman was smiling and nodding vigorously at him as he grabbed the cart's handle. He wondered what she found to be so happy about. They'd be lucky if they didn't get stoned. He returned her smile with a weak one of his own, then started shoving. The crowd let out a roar as the rickety contraption moved forward. Samuel struggled to squeeze between the woman and the girl. The woman gave way for him, but the girl wasn't budging.

'I need room,' he hissed. She ignored him.

He started to say something more, then figured she wouldn't understand anyway, so instead he pressed his shoulder against hers and began to apply steady pressure. He could feel her shoving back. She was strong. He pushed harder. She did the same. Then suddenly the cart and its towering cargo was surging forward.

The westbound was slowing as it climbed the hill. He waited for the brakeman to pull his head in the window, a cold wind blowing from the south. Having pre-selected the car he wanted, he went for it without hesitation, throwing his bag in, then lunging.

Inside he checked his clothes for tears. He was a mess but there wasn't much he could do about it now. He looked around, poking bags of grain – better than he'd hoped.

The train was rocking steadily now and picking up speed – they hadn't spotted him. He glanced through the open door into the evening light settling over the town. It wasn't a bad-looking place, situated between two creeks, wide streets lined with pleasant houses and tall trees. Fact it was nice. It just wasn't for him. The only place for him, he figured, was the ring. If the woman had shown interest in his ideas about the dresses, then maybe. But she hadn't.

He shadow-boxed a few minutes to get over these feelings, moving his hands fast, jabbing expertly, then driving a few hard punches into the sacks of grain.

Afterwards, he sat on the bags, his thoughts drifting back to

Pearl Eddy. Crazy, yes. But she'd kept her word. He'd give her that. She'd saved him from the mob. Then from the old woman and the sheriff. But she couldn't save him from herself. She had too much holiness to go around.

He opened his travelling bag and pulled out the silver frame, examining it closely. It was beautiful. He was sorry he'd had to take the photograph, but he'd had no choice. Anyway, he was certain they had others. He ran his fingers over the smooth, cold metal. Truly a masterpiece. Moments later, as he was putting the frame away, his fingers felt something, a bulge of sorts: something under the cloth behind the photograph. He unsnapped the back and sucked in his breath and held it. He felt like he could go without breathing for a long time.

He'd been right all along. She had money hidden away . . . and he'd just found some. Slowly, he forced his trembling hands to count it out: 250 dollars. He smiled. Then his gaze fell on the man's face and he squirmed. He and Zacharias had the same eyes. Prophet turned the picture over.

'Thank you – thank you,' the oriental woman said, smiling and nodding her head up and down, gooselike, her two young daughters still clinging to her legs. They looked frightened.

'Everything is OK,' Samuel grinned, trying to reassure them. They hid from him behind their mother's legs. Amazingly, the baby had slept through everything.

'Thank you – thank you, boy,' the woman said again.

Samuel smiled at her. 'Thou are welcome,' he said, breathing hard and glancing at the girl. She was standing next to the cart and catching her breath as well, studiously ignoring him. Tomato still dripped from her hair. Samuel put his hands in his pockets and wiggled his pants down so they covered more of his ankles, then he rolled his right shoe over so she couldn't see his little toe through the break in the leather. But she wasn't watching.

They had just entered the barn and Samuel could hear the

117

sheriff ordering the crowd off their property. He walked outside and dunked a rag in the rain barrel and returned. He held it for a minute, his hands trembling, then walked over and offered it to the girl. She didn't even look at it. She just turned and walked away into the barn's shadows. His face was hot from the embarrassment and he quickly laid the rag on the wheel of the handcart, as if he had no idea why he was carrying it.

That was when Samuel first heard it: a series of rapid tappings from inside the little cage. He stopped and listened. Yes – there it was again. It sounded like a woodpecker knocking impatiently against a tree limb. Seemingly in response, the girl yelled something harsh and spat at the cage. Samuel hopped back reflexively, shocked at her fierceness.

The woman barked a few coarse-sounding words of her own and the girl turned and began to untie the bundles on the cart. The woman continued to stare at her, the impatient tapping continuing, until the girl relented and hopped up on the cart and unlatched the small door to the cage. Finished, she jumped back to the ground and returned to the bundles.

Samuel couldn't take his eyes from the tiny door. His mother and brothers were coming toward him.

'Samuel.'

'One moment.'

Pearl stopped beside him. 'What is it?'

'Just something odd inside a little cage on the cart.'

'What kind of odd?'

The sound of the boys' breath being sucked in was loud in the barn. They stood trembling. Something had shoved the little door open from the inside.

'Boys?'

'Just a moment, mother,' Samuel answered, his eyes glued on the shadowy opening.

The oriental woman was keeping up a stream of what sounded to Samuel like apologies. His eyes moved slowly over the dark figure inside the cage and he quickly changed his assessment: it wasn't a cage at all, it was more like a tiny throne room of varnished bamboo, complete with a high-backed chair padded in a rich green velvet-like material.

'Samuel.'

He continued staring at the strange sight. 'There's a little oriental man,' he said, his voice reflecting his confusion. 'He's sitting in a tiny bamboo room that rides on top of the cart.'

'Who is he?'

'I don't know.'

Samuel's gaze still hadn't moved off the man. He was maybe in his seventies, small and trim-looking, but not frail or weak. Nor did he look sick or so old that he couldn't have helped with the cart. But from the way he sat staring haughtily over the heads of everyone in the barn, he looked as if work of any kind was beneath his dignity.

He reminded Samuel of a little king, arrogant in his beautiful mahogany chair, wrapped in fine red robes of silk, gazing out imperiously with his small dark eyes as if none of the rest of them existed. Samuel studied his face closely. The skin was oily and deeply lined, appearing monkeylike in some respects, but the fierce face commanded attention and respect. His silver-colored hair was pulled back into a bun that would have looked feminine on most men. It didn't on him.

The woman hurriedly shoved the small cart deeper into the barn, the tiny man swaying expertly with the movements of the wheels and the woman's shoving. Samuel wondered how many hundreds of miles they'd pushed him over the years. No wonder the girl didn't like him.

With the cart in a quiet corner of the barn, the woman barked another order at the girl. It had no effect on her.

Suddenly the old man rapped a bamboo staff he was holding hard against the cage and the girl moved, retrieving a small stool from the cart. Then with a movement so fast and ominous that it caused Samuel and his brothers to hop backwards, the old man leaped from his chair, grunting and brandishing the bamboo rod in his hands. He stood bent-kneed, his sandaled feet spread wide, a fierce scowl across his face.

In the lantern light, his skin glistened as if waxed. He looked ready for mortal combat. Prepared for any adversary. Then, with his banty, roosterlike legs still bent, he took a great exaggerated high step on the cart-top, turning for the first time to glare at the boys.

They held their collective breath.

'I wish Mr Prophet was here,' Zacharias whispered.

'Samuel – what is going on?' Pearl demanded.

'It's the old man,' he whispered.

'Yes?'

'He looks dangerous.'

'Samuel, don't be silly. These people are our guests. I want to meet them.'

'In a moment,' he hissed.

As if their voices had triggered it, the woman and the two small girls bent over at the waist. The girl didn't move until the woman grabbed her arm and yanked her forward. Even so, her bow was not obedient.

When the old man finally reached the ground in his funny half-squatting way, the woman and the two little girls scurried ahead of him, rolling out a large reed mat. Then with deliberate and posturing movements, he settled himself into a cross-legged position, his back to them, staff across his knees.

'Samuel,' Pearl said.

He didn't respond. He was studying the back of the tiny man sitting in the darker shadows.

'Samuel,' she said again.

The tone of her voice caused him to sense that she had something serious on her mind. 'Yes?'

'I want thee to collect as many eggs as thou can find.' She paused. 'Then cull two pullets and get them ready.'

Samuel looked stunned. 'Kill them?'

'Yes.'

Slowly his expression changed from surprise to anger, the skin on his neck reddening. 'They are for our egg business,' he said firmly.

'It will not harm us to cull two of the least likely layers.'

'We've already culled them.'

'We do not have enough for dinner,' she continued quietly.

'I told thee that we couldn't care for them,' he said, his voice rising.

The younger boys looked shocked, their eyes on their mother's face. She stood motionless for a moment, then reached out, searching with her hand until she found him, putting it softly on his shoulder. 'And I told thee that thou were my son – not my husband. Do thou remember?'

Samuel looked off into the shadowy rafters of the barn. 'Yes. But I do not agree with what thee are doing.'

'Perhaps. But I still have asked thee to do it.'

Samuel started toward the barn door.

'Hello?' The voice was high-pitched.

Samuel turned to see the oriental woman struggling to hold a dead pig up by its hind feet. The two little girls were crying again and reaching out to touch the carcass.

'Hello, boy,' the woman said in an oddly cadenced voice. She was smiling against the strain of holding up the dead animal. Then she shoved it out toward him. The girls screamed.

'Samuel?'

When he spoke, Samuel's voice sounded cool. 'The woman wants me to take her dead pig.'

'Here, boy,' the woman coaxed.

Samuel scrunched up his face and didn't move. The woman struggled forward.

'Cook pig,' she offered.

Pearl nodded in the woman's direction. 'Yes. Thank thee,' she said smiling. The woman smiled back.

'Samuel, take the pig, please.'

He looked as stunned by this directive as he had been by the order to kill the pullets. 'It has been hanging on the side of their cart.'

'Gutted and bled?'

'Yes.'

'Then she was cooling the carcass.'

'There's no telling what it died from,' he protested. 'It's got stiff black hair all over it.'

'Samuel. We know how to clean pigs.'

'Yes. But we don't know the meat is good.'

'I'm certain it is.'

'No rot.' The woman was smiling and nodding vigorously.

'Thank thee – that's very generous,' Pearl said.

Samuel still hadn't moved. He was trying to think of another argument when he noticed the girl watching him with a sullen look. He felt suddenly uncomfortable. 'Josh and Luke, get a fire going,' he said, grabbing the pig's hind legs, then glancing back at the girl. 'We'll burn the hair off.' She was moving forward and he thought for a moment that she was coming to help, but she turned and collected the crying children. He noticed that her hair looked damp and that the tomato was gone. He looked but couldn't see the rag. He felt suddenly warm all over.

CHAPTER SEVEN

Prophet stood listening to the night, making certain things were still right, then he stepped back to the saloon wall and nonchalantly leaned against it, his head positioned so he could see the pigeon through the window. The man was at the blackjack table.

Prophet watched him a while before turning back to the street and pulling his collar up. He blew into his hands, then smiled as a calico cat moved down the sidewalk. Omen of good luck. He'd won a lot of money on calico cats. Two hundred dollars once. He'd bet a gambler in New Orleans two hundred that he couldn't find a male calico cat. He'd given him thirty days. Prophet laughed. He could have given him a year. Two years. Two thousand years. He'd still won. It was a sure thing: calico cats were never males. Always females. He didn't know why. It was just so. One of those freaky things.

He stooped and clucked softly. 'Here, cat. Good cat,' he cooed. But she ignored him and kept walking, furling and unfurling her tail. Then she turned in at the bright light of the doorway. It was cold and would get colder. He was glad the cat had a place to sleep.

He thought about the Eddys but it made him uncomfortable so he quit. He was a hundred miles from Liberty in a town he didn't know the name of and didn't care to know. And he wasn't looking back. All he wanted was to pick up some extra money. Then start for Minnesota.

He squatted on his haunches and leaned against the wall, thinking about boxing and his plan. It was perfection. Simple. Clean. And it was going to work. There were few sure bets in this life. Calico cats were one. And this was another. He whistled softly and tried to look like part of the local scenery. It wasn't hard.

The moon was rising like a big yellow plate over the town's church steeple, lighting the roadway and casting both sidewalks in darkness. It was the perfect set-up. Then he heard the old man cussing the woman again and let his eyes drift across the street. It took a while to spot him. He was in the same place. On the bench in front of the dry goods store.

He'd noticed him an hour ago; just sitting there and pulling on a wine bottle. Maybe in his sixties, thin and poorly dressed and, from the look of his hollow cheeks, poorly fed. Prophet knew all this because he had checked him out very carefully before he'd started his work; done it just to make certain he wouldn't be performing his artistry in front of some deputy sheriff.

He wouldn't. Nobody could fake that mixture of smell, age and drunkenness. Something about the old man's looks bothered Prophet. Men like him always did. They made him think about the future – about things he didn't want to think about.

Prophet cleared his mind of distractions, dismissing the old man. He was a bum. Nothing more. And an unpleasant one at that. He'd muttered 'nigger' when Prophet had walked by him the first time. If the old man knew what Prophet was up to, he didn't look capable of doing much about it.

Prophet slid his back up the wall and looked in the window again. He'd picked the man carefully. He was maybe fifties. Loose but not drunk. Therefore no one else would likely get the same idea. Prophet didn't want a party. He continued going over the checklist in his head. The man was stout, out of shape: therefore little resistance. Not a cripple: so nobody would be coming to collect him or be watching out for him. He'd won some money on the tables and lost some. He wasn't flashing a lot of cash that would attract attention. He was a loner. And he didn't look like a cry-baby who'd start yelling if somebody said boo. And Prophet planned on saying 'boo'.

He turned his back against a chill wind. Normally he didn't like working this way. It was a little too risky. But not as risky as a Negro sneaking through a strange town in the dark looking for a house to break into. If you didn't prepare properly before a burglary you never knew when you might walk into the muzzle of a dog or a shotgun. Both could hurt.

'Damn,' he muttered. His guess had been that the man would turn right when he came out of the saloon. He'd guessed wrong and was now sprinting hard around the back of the building, leaping over trash cans and running for all he was worth to make it just as the man was stepping down the steps into the alley.

The result of this frantic effort was that Prophet collided with the man harder than he had intended, knocking him sprawling into the dirt and leaving him stunned and gasping for breath. Worse, Prophet was breathing hard himself and began to feel his head spinning. Fortunately his head cleared before the man got to his feet and Prophet was smothering him with assistance. He shoved his arms around the man and bodily lifted him off the ground, slipping a hand into the pocket where he'd seen the money going. Coins! Damn! They made a noise.

Prophet started talking loudly to cover the sound of metal clicking against metal. 'Oh, mister, I'm sorry. I was running after my mule.' He began to pat the man's clothes down hard. 'Are you hurt? Ohh, I hope not.'

Prophet's routine gave the pigeon the confidence he wanted him to have, and the man stood and angrily shoved him away. 'You colored bastard! I ought to give you a good –'

The man had just gotten a look at Prophet's face in the soft moonlight and he gasped for air again. But this time not because he needed it. Prophet gave him a hard look. And suddenly the man was stammering and ready to wet himself. Prophet calculated the tension until he thought the man might break and run or start hollering. It was time to let him off the hook.

'I'm sorry, suh, I truly am.'

The man smiled with enormous relief. 'No one is mad at you, son,' he said in a shaky voice and started backing away up the street. 'Think nothing of it. Accidents happen.'

'Yes. I'll be more careful.' Prophet figured by the time the man's heart stopped pumping and his hands quit shaking it would be next week.

He stepped into the shadows and counted the money. Sixty-two dollars. He hadn't taken it all. He was too seasoned for that. Maybe half. Maybe less than half. Even shaken up, the man would know if all of his money was missing. Nope. That was an invitation to a hanging.

He smiled and started toward the saloon he'd seen on the other side of town, then he stopped and looked at the old man sitting on the bench. He was arguing with the invisible woman again. Calling her names and cussing. Prophet crossed the street.

'Hello.'

No response came from him, but when he saw Prophet's face in the moonlight he raised his free hand to his mouth as if he was in sudden pain.

'Nothing to be scared of,' Prophet muttered. Then the man was rising unsteadily, changing his grip on the bottle as if he planned to use it as a weapon.

'Hold on,' Prophet protested, putting a hand on the man's thin shoulder and setting him back down. 'No cause to rile.'

'Fffnnn-off. If it's a fight you want, I can handle you. You little shit!'

Prophet had to keep himself from laughing. 'I'm sure you could.' He turned his back on the old man. 'It's going to get cold.'

'Leave me alone – you ain't my gawddamnn nurse,' the man mumbled. Prophet figured with no money he'd pass out and lie outside like a dog tonight. That brought the things that scared him flooding back into his head.

He reached his hand into a pocket and pulled out a five-dollar gold piece and some smaller coins, turning away so the old man wouldn't see him. As he turned back he faked a stumble and spilled the coins over the sidewalk. The old man watched but didn't move.

'Damnit,' Prophet muttered, stooping and picking the coins up. All but the five-dollar half eagle which he shoved under the bench. Finished, he stood and stretched the pain out of his lower back.

'Night, old man.'

The drunk didn't respond, just continued eyeing him. Prophet whistled his way up the sidewalk, smiling when he heard the faint cackling behind him.

Prophet was feeling good. He had two pockets full of money and he was heading north to take his shot. He checked to make certain that Mrs Eddy's money was separated from the coins, determined to put hers to good use on the road to a shot at a title.

That way it was sort of like she'd invested in him. Again, he told himself he'd pay her and the boys back after he won. Ten times over. He figured if they knew that, they'd be excited. At least the boys would. He smiled and walked on, his right foot dragging softly over the wooden sidewalks.

There was brisk activity in the barn following the meal of pork and fried vegetables that Pearl had made. They had all enjoyed it . . . all but the old man who continued to sit in the shadows with his back to everyone. It was late evening now and the Chinese girl was unloading the family's parcels, the mother setting up her charcoal stove, the baby bellowing and the two little girls darting through the barn, chased by the three younger Eddy boys. Pearl was standing before the woman, a shawl across her shoulders. She hadn't said anything in a while, she just stood there letting the family get settled, her three younger boys, sweating and panting, lined up beside her while the two little girls talked to their mother.

Samuel was oiling the hinge on the buggy door and watching.

He had oiled the same hinge three times. He wasn't certain what he was feeling, he was just worried about his mother's decision to bring these people here. It wasn't going to turn out well, he figured. He was certain it would bring the town down on their heads. Joshua and Luke had already had one run-in with Hector James and his friends. And he knew more were going to follow. The Negro had started it by causing Penny James to fall. But his mother had capped it off bringing these people here.

He stood up straighter. Even though his mother didn't want him to, it was his job to help protect the family as much as hers. His father would want that. He felt hot – even if he was a coward. Maybe it was a good thing he was a Quaker. Maybe that way nobody would ever find out about him.

The thought bothered him and he glanced at his mother. She was standing in her still way, as if she might stand like that forever. He knew she did what she thought was right. Just sometimes she went too far. And this was one of those times.

She turned towards him. 'Samuel?'

He joined her and she put a hand on his shoulder and smiled, turning back toward the woman and the girls.

'Hello?' she called politely.

The woman looked toward them. The mother and the little girls were grinning, the older girl was glaring. She had a good case of something.

The orientals had been so hungry that Pearl had not made any introductions earlier. She was about to remedy that, Samuel knew, and he felt uneasy.

'My name is Pearl Eddy – and these are my four boys: Samuel,' she put both hands on Samuel's shoulders, a smile on her face, 'and Joshua,' she said, running her hands over Joshua's head, her fingers passing lightly over his cheeks. She brought her fingers back and touched gently at the scrape on his skin and he winced. The smile left her face for a moment, then she continued on, introducing Luke and Zacharias. Samuel knew she had spotted the bruise. Joshua looked sick.

All the time Pearl was speaking, the oriental woman watched her attentively, grinning and nodding vigorously. She seemed to understand English well enough, Samuel thought. That was something anyhow. The two little girls, and even the baby, paid attention. But not the older girl, who was poking at the ground with a stick. And certainly not the old man.

Samuel had noticed that once she got him seated on his mat, the oriental woman ignored the old man, as though well used to his ways. He just sat, his back to them, staring at a corner of the barn, all this beneath him.

Samuel looked back at the girl. She was kneeling now beside her mother, unpacking things from a large cloth bag, the familiar scowl on her face. He looked over the whole lot of them and shook his head – these were the people that he and his brothers were going to get trashed over. They didn't look worth it.

'So nice,' the oriental woman said, standing up quickly and bowing slightly at the waist. 'So nice to meet you,' she said in her awkward cadence, smiling enthusiastically.

'Boys,' Pearl said quietly.

'Pleased to meet thee, ma'am,' the boys said in unison.

The woman said something Samuel couldn't understand and the little girls came over to her, the taller of the two carrying the baby. While dirty, he at least looked chubby. From the thin look of the little girls and the rest of them, they were keeping the baby fed while they were on half-rations. That, at least, accounted for the rude way they'd wolfed their food. Both girls looked drawn and they were dressed in shabby pajamalike clothes. Samuel felt bad for them.

He looked away to the older girl. She continued to unpack things from the bag, ignoring the introduction; although he thought he'd seen her glance in his direction when his mother had said his name. But he wasn't certain.

The smile left the woman's face and she spoke stiffly to the girl. Reluctantly, the scowl still on her face, she stood. She would do what the woman demanded, but not happily. The smile reappeared on the woman's face.

'Samuel, take me to them.'

This was the part he hated. It always embarrassed him, but this time – with the girl – it would be even worse. But there was no escaping it. He took his mother's arm and guided her forward, stopping in front of the woman.

'May I touch thy face?' Pearl asked.

'Yes, yes.' The woman nodded enthusiastically, sticking her head forward. She looked serious, as if this were a tremendous honor.

At least she was good-natured, Samuel thought, as he guided his mother. Suddenly, the woman reached up and took Pearl's hands and brought them quickly to her face as if she were being blessed by the Pope.

Pearl's fingertips moved carefully over her smooth features, across the round and pudgy cheeks, the heavy lips, the curve of flat nose. She was no beauty, Samuel thought, she just had a pleasant face that had a certain strength to it.

'Eiko,' the woman beamed.

'Eiko,' Pearl repeated.

Pearl was concentrating hard, her expression focused. The woman frowned momentarily, as if this were a very solemn occasion. Then, after Pearl had finished examining every bit of the woman's visage, she brought her fingers back to the mouth. The woman smiled and Pearl slowly traced her lips with the tips of her fingers. Then the woman touched her fingers to Pearl's lips, and she too smiled. Then Eiko's eyes began to stream through her smile. Then Pearl's eyes were streaming as well. Samuel didn't understand.

The two little girls giggled and squirmed but seemed to enjoy having Pearl touch them. Samuel watched as his mother's fingers moved through their snarled and dirty hair, over the grimy little cheeks. He knew that she was cataloging everything, missing nothing. Not the hollowness of their cheeks. Not the dirt. Nothing. Her hands went back a couple of times to their hair. He didn't need to look at her face to know that bothered her. She was big on cleanliness. She took a deep breath. One of the little girls was tall and narrow-faced: Tamoko. Her sister, Isi, was small and narrow-boned with a bright oval face.

The baby, Ituro, sucked Pearl's fingers enthusiastically. She laughed and let him. Then she straightened up and waited. Samuel looked to see the older girl standing a few feet away, staring sullenly at the ground. The woman said something to her. Reluctantly she stepped forward and raised her head. Samuel started to say something to restrain his mother, but the oriental woman shook her head at him and nodded, and he brought his mother's hands to the girl's face. She frowned as the hands touched her, stiffening as if she deeply resented this.

'Fumiko,' the mother offered.

'Fumiko,' Pearl said, as if the name were a delicious taste to be savored. She held the young girl's head firmly between her hands for a long time, the way Samuel had seen the town's Baptist minister do at faith healings down by the creek. It made him uncomfortable and he wished his mother would let go. The girl gazed into the material of Pearl's dress, as if she, too, were blind. But she didn't try to pull away. Then Pearl's hands moved down and touched at the tattered fabric of the girl's clothing, moving expertly along her shoulders, down her arms. Samuel knew what she was doing: taking her full measure.

'Thou are a beautiful young woman, Fumiko,' Pearl said. Samuel felt embarrassed. Then the girl stepped back into line. She didn't look quite as angry.

'Thy father?' Pearl asked, waiting for the old man.

The woman giggled nervously. 'Father-in-the-law. Muneo Kishimoto,' she said with great dignity, as if the name might mean something to Pearl. 'My father-in-the-law,' she repeated.

Pearl reached her hands out, waiting for the old man. The woman shook her head hard. 'He will not allow you to touch him.'

'Of course,' Pearl said softly.

The old man barked something in his language.

The woman looked embarrassed.

From the shadows where the old man sat came an additional few sharp words, cutting through the air. The woman looked at him, then back at Pearl. She was plainly respectful of the old man but disturbed by what he had said. He barked at her again. She looked reluctantly at Pearl.

'He believes white people are inferior. I do not,' she said, clearly embarrassed.

Samuel looked at his mother. She turned in the direction of the grunt and said, 'It is a pleasure to meet thee, sir,' her voice friendly.

The old man didn't move or grunt again.

'Boys,' she said brightly.

'Good evening,' they said in rough unison.

In the kitchen, Pearl and Eiko were washing the last of the evening dishes. The children were playing in the backyard – all except for Fumiko and Samuel. They and the old man were still in the barn. Mr Kishimoto had not touched Pearl's meal, behaving as if it were carrion or poison. Eiko had scolded, but to no avail.

Pearl was bending over a large copper basin filled with soapy water, her sleeves rolled up. She held out a wet plate and Eiko took it and began to dry it with a towel.

'The judge will help thee start on the way to China.'

Eiko looked confused. 'China?'

'I thought thou might want to go back to thy country.'

'We are not Chinese.' She giggled. 'Nipponese – Japanese.'

Pearl smiled at the mistake. 'Then Japan. Or perhaps Hawaii.'

The woman looked suddenly serious. 'Here,' she said firmly, pointing at the floor with the dripping plate. 'We own land – deed.' She pulled a paper from a small cloth bundle that hung from a cord around her neck. Then she smiled again, nodding.

'Eiko, thy land no longer belongs to thee. It was lost to taxes.' Pearl tensed as she said the words, then shook it off. She wouldn't lose the house. She wouldn't, she assured herself.

The woman's smile seemed to freeze. She continued drying the plate for a moment longer than necessary. 'We stay. We farm.' She paused. 'For my children.'

The last words brought a feeling of sadness to Pearl.

'Thou would need money to do such a thing. A great amount of money. Enough for land, animals, equipment and seed. I know.'

The woman looked surprised. 'You are a farmer?'

'Not a good one,' Pearl laughed.

'I am a good one,' Eiko said, confidently.

'I'm certain thou are, but without money . . .'

'What is enough?' the woman interrupted.

Pearl shook her head. 'I don't know – hundreds of dollars.'

The woman shook her head, indicating she didn't have that much, then realized Pearl couldn't see her and said, 'No have.'

Pearl nodded.

Eiko watched her for a while, then suddenly her face brightened. 'Fumiko and I work for you – clean and cook until we have enough.'

'I do my own housework.'

'You are blind,' the woman said bluntly.

'I am able to work. But even if I wanted to, I could not pay thee.'

'I am a good worker,' she said with pride.

'I am certain,' Pearl said, submerging a dish into the sudsy water. They worked quietly for a while, each concentrating on her own thoughts. Then Pearl said, 'I will try and find thee a job in town. It will help until thou decide certain things.'

Eiko beamed. 'I work hard. We farm.'

Pearl smiled slowly and then reached out her dripping hands, waiting until Eiko grasped them in her own. She liked and understood this woman who had dug in her bare feet against the town's pushing – to make a place for her children. Pearl understood that. Moisture came to their eyes.

Then Zacharias darted past them into the parlor, the screen door banging behind him, and they let go of their hands and went back to the dishes, Eiko humming a happy little song in the quiet of the room.

Samuel was lying on his back – half under the buggy – applying grease to the axle of the carriage. He hadn't heard it squeaking, but it was wise to keep it greased. Every so often he would turn his head so that he could see the girl, Fumiko. She was busily rummaging through the various bags, pulling out matting and blankets for the night.

While he didn't like her any more than before, his first impression had been correct: she was better-looking than he thought oriental girls could be. In fact, she might be better-looking than a lot of girls in Liberty. Not that it mattered. She was too surly to be nice. She acted as though she was better than anybody else.

He crawled out from under the carriage and wiped his hands on a rag, then went over to the barn window and looked out toward the road. Empty. Deputy Willard was talking to a couple of men, but everyone else had gotten tired of the show and gone home. Thank goodness. He looked back and watched the girl again.

She was trying to manhandle a large canvas bundle down from the wooden cart, her grandfather sitting on his mat a few yards away, watching and doing nothing to help. He was the laziest man Samuel had ever seen. And while Samuel told himself he didn't care much for her, he nevertheless felt he should help since she was a girl. He pulled his pants lower and hurried across the stable, taking a path that brought him close by the man. As he passed, he thought for a moment that the fierce old man had moved slightly.

Samuel reached up and took hold of the bundle. The girl stopped and watched him for a moment, still looking angry, then together they pulled the heavy bundle to the ground.

'There,' Samuel said, dusting off his hands. He felt awkward standing there and not knowing what to say. 'Any more?'

She didn't respond, she just loosened the straps. But then, he figured, she probably didn't know how to speak English. He felt better, just having helped. He watched her for a few moments, then he started back toward the buggy.

He wasn't certain what happened next. He knew only that he had passed close by the old man again. The little man was sitting cross-legged, a shawl of some sort drawn over his thin shoulders, and looking half-asleep. But as Samuel was passing by, he suddenly let out a sharp yelp – Ei! – and swung his stick, catching Samuel across the ankles and dropping him in a heap. Then the old man hopped up in his half-squat, looking like he was going to wallop him again. Samuel rolled away, clutching at his head to keep it from getting split like a melon.

Satisfied, the old man sat on his mat again, settling down as if nothing had happened. Fumiko looked at Samuel for a moment, giving away nothing with her expression, then went back to the bundle she was working on.

Samuel was stunned, his eyes streaming from the pain and embarrassment. There were no broken bones, but the blow had numbed his lower legs. He struggled to his feet and glared across the shadows at the old man, starting to blurt something in his anger. Then he caught himself and turned and hobbled out.

The old man waited silently in the shadows for a few moments, then he stirred slightly, saying something in a childish-sounding falsetto to the girl. She grew red in the face and shook her head. The old man said it again. And made an odd little noise that might have been a laugh.

Pearl and Eiko continued to stand at the copper basin, washing and drying the remaining dishes, perfectly at ease with one another's company. Pearl could hear her youngest rummaging through the house, opening closets and moving books. He'd been doing it for the past fifteen minutes.

'Zacharias. What are thee doing?'

There was no response. Then she heard a door slam shut and the sound of running feet. 'Zacharias,' she called, raising her voice to the level she used to discipline.

Still no response came. Pearl waited, then straightened up and dried her hands on a towel. 'Zacharias?' she called one last time, then turned and walked into the darkened parlor. She stopped and listened. She could hear the soft sound of crying.

'Zacharias?'

'Father's gone,' the boy sobbed.

Later that night, Pearl sat facing Samuel in the small parlor. The Kishimoto family had settled down in the stable and Pearl's younger boys had been asleep for an hour. The house was unusually quiet, as if sensing the somberness of the moment.

Samuel was bent at the waist, working under lamplight at a long table. The only sound was that of his scissors as he cut blue cloth from a heavy bolt. Neither he nor his mother had spoken in a while when he finally cleared his throat, the noise loud in the stillness. Pearl brushed a strand of loose hair from her face. She looked worn and deeply worried.

'He did it,' Samuel repeated, for what was close to the hundredth time.

Pearl didn't respond but Samuel thought he'd seen her wince at his words. He didn't care. He had moved beyond anger to a kind of resolve; he was determined that if nothing else were accomplished this night, he would convince her once and for all that the Negro was a thief.

Finished cutting the cloth free of the bolt, Samuel took the pattern for a pair of children's pants that his mother had told him to use and pinned it into place on the fabric. He glanced at her in the hard yellow light as he worked, wondering what she was thinking. He hoped to Hades that she wasn't feeling sorry for the Negro again – but there was no telling with her.

Samuel doubled the blue material and quickly snipped around the pattern's edges with an experienced eye developed over four years of pattern-cutting. His father had cut them before that. But when Samuel had turned eleven, the task had been passed to him. He didn't mind. Normally he enjoyed being with his mother.

Normally. But on this night he had been working for the past hour cutting cloth to make new clothes for each of the oriental girls, without his mother having once said one word beyond indicating which patterns.

He rolled his shoulders to loosen them, then shook his head. Even now she was worrying about other people, when she should be worrying about how she was going to take care of her own family. While she didn't tell him anything about their finances, he could tell by watching her shop in town that they were having a hard time of it; they were barely able to keep the livestock fed and care for themselves. Just last month they had put Jack on a straight diet of oat hay, no longer buying the grain the old horse loved. He shook his head. She wasn't practical – not in business nor in other ways, the orientals and the Negro being examples.

'I knew he was a thief the moment I saw him. Thou remember my telling thee how he was looking over the desktop like a man searching a candy box for his favorite sweet.'

She was dressed in her long flannel nightgown, which fell in graceful folds down to her cloth slippers, her brown hair brushed out and hanging down around her shoulders. Her pretty face looked paler and more reserved than he had seen it since the day they buried his father. And she looked tired. He glanced at the clock standing in the corner: one o'clock – and felt the fatigue himself.

'Thank thee, Samuel,' she said in a soft voice that he had to strain to hear above the hiss of the lamp. 'Thou can put out the light and go to bed.' She paused. 'I feel like working some.'

There was a sad, lost sound in her voice that scared him and made him suddenly feel bad for what he had said. 'It's late,' he offered quietly. 'Thou should get some sleep as well.'

Pearl smiled and nodded her head. 'In a little while.'

She began to sew. Samuel reached and turned the wick down into the kerosene until the flame sputtered out. Slowly his eyes adjusted to the dark and he stood watching her. She sat sewing inside a soft ray of moonlight from the window, looking like an apparition in the darkness. He shivered at the thought. He loved her and felt a surge of admiration for her. Naive or not, she was a deeply good person.

'I'm sorry,' he said, the apology seemingly fitting many things: his badgering attacks on the Negro, his protests over the orientals, the shared sadness they felt over the loss of the photograph . . . even their current circumstances. All of it.

She smiled again and continued to sew. 'Get thee to bed,' she said, softly. Samuel watched her a moment longer, then left, quietly shutting the door behind him to keep the room from getting drafty. When she was certain he was gone, Pearl stopped sewing and sat thinking. She sat long enough for the moon's light to move off her and on to the work table. She was breathing hard, in short little gasps, as if she might be drowning in the air. She felt a knifing pain in her chest as though her heart were breaking up inside her.

She began to shake her head back and forth, slowly at first, then increasing the force of the shake until her hair was flying over her thin shoulders. Then she collapsed in sobs in the chair. It was gone. The money was gone. And while she had fought the thought for most of the night, she knew that Samuel was right. Jerome Prophet had stolen it.

She bit at her lower lip until she tasted blood, fighting off the tears and a rising anger. She was swamped by the sensation that she was losing everything she'd been trying so desperately to hold on to for the boys: their home, a decent living, a future. All of it was slipping through her fingers. And it was all happening because of her own acts. She shook hard, trying to calm herself. She had sheltered the man and defended him. A shudder went through her as if an invisible hand was shaking her.

The house would be auctioned now. As soon as he learned that she had no money, Mr Snipes would proceed with the foreclosure. She didn't blame him. He had no choice. He had already given her one extension.

She felt her heart contract, her breath quickening. Where would they go? This had been their home for sixteen years, the only home her boys had ever known. They'd all been born in the big bedroom, and Matthew was buried here. This last thought was the worst. They could find another house, even if it was poorer and smaller. But how could she ask the boys to leave their father? Would strangers care for his grave? Would they even allow it to remain in the garden, or would they have his casket dug up one night and buried somewhere else?

Could she hold the family together now? Or would Lillian make good on her threat? Her hands were trembling hard and she clutched them together in a tight ball. She was heaving for breath, panic overtaking her once more. Then she stopped and sat up straight in her chair, a deep anger – stronger than she had ever felt in her life – seizing her, shoving the panic aside.

'How could thee?' she snapped. 'I believed in thee, I sheltered thee, I gave thee food and my protection.' She fought down the angry sobs welling up inside her breast. Never in her life had she felt so betrayed.

She struggled against the anger, desperately seeking some sense of inner peace. It was no use. She sagged back into the chair. 'Jerome Prophet – how could thee?' she cried.

It was shocking but undeniable. They were right there in his hand, his eyes glued to them under the harsh lantern light. After a moment of seemingly casual contemplation, Prophet leaned forward in his chair and slowly folded the cards together, holding them in the palm of one hand, trying hard to look nonchalant and hopefully a bit disappointed.

Four other men were seated around the table watching while he laid the cards face-down on the worn felt surface, far enough out in front of him so there was a clear sense he felt they simply weren't worth protecting. Then he tipped back in his chair, glancing over his shoulder toward the bar.

'What you looking for – a hot cow turd to keep that bald head of yours warm?' the dealer asked. The man squinted at Prophet for a second longer and then said, 'Gawd you're ugly.' That was maybe the twelfth time he'd said it. There was no humor in the voice, but Prophet smiled anyway. The last thing he wanted was trouble. Not with the cards he had.

'That's what I'm doing. Looking for a hot cow plop,' he joked. 'I always try to wear one to bed.' He waited a moment, still looking over his shoulder. 'Actually,' he said, 'I'm looking to buy a beer. Nothing else is going right. May as well have a cold beer.'

Prophet calculated the man wasn't much more than a drifter. He certainly wasn't any gambler. He'd lost almost as much as he had. The difference was, the dealer was getting disagreeable over his misfortune.

Prophet glanced at the ferret-faced man to his left. He had nervous eyes and they kept jumping to Prophet's cards. Prophet yawned. The little weasel, he thought, must have something, or thinks he does.

The other two players just looked tired. The man on the dealer's right looked to be in his fifties, balding and stout, dressed in a worn-out business suit. Prophet figured he was a drummer on the road. There was a bulge under his vest. He was packing.

The dealer was wearing a little side pistol and Prophet would have been surprised if the weasel wasn't carrying. Friendly little trio. Only the young farmer to his right looked like he wasn't in the Mexican militia. Prophet was clean as well.

The dealer straightened a stack of coins in front of him, creating a sound of metallic clicks as he let them drop back into place on the table.

Prophet could hear a dog barking somewhere out back, then scratching at the rear door of the saloon. He reached and picked up his cards as if he'd just remembered they were his, trying to shift the focus back on to the game. He was holding four kings. The first time he'd ever drawn four honest kings in his life. The sight made him want to suck in a deep breath. He didn't do it.

'Forget the beer. This place don't serve niggers.'

The words drifted over the table like a bad smell. Prophet felt the muscles across his shoulders and neck bunching. Instinctively, he calculated the distance between himself and the man, guessing at his weight, then casually checking to see that there was enough of a clear path to the back door. Hopefully it would be unlocked.

He cleared his throat and refolded his cards, laying them back down on the table and looking up at the man. 'That's a hell of a smart rule,' he grinned. He wanted this hand bad.

Nobody moved or spoke for a moment, then somebody near the bar laughed and the others joined in. Even the dealer laughed, nodding toward him. 'Smart nigger.'

'We going to play this hand?' the weasel moaned.

'Five-dollar anny?' Prophet suggested, putting his bet forward to get the game moving.

'Ten,' the dealer snapped.

'Ten the man says,' Prophet smiled, adding the additional money.

The betting went round the table three times and each time Prophet jumped the pot until there was more than a hundred in it, he figured. He was ignoring everything now but the game. He glanced briefly into the dealer's eyes. He looked too ready for trouble. So he returned to his calculations of distances, weights, angles and escape routes again. It was simple habit.

Then the man was reaching into his coat and Prophet was rising from his chair, until he saw the man's hand holding a roll of bills.

'I raise the smart aborigine $50,' he said, counting the money out. The saloon was quiet now. The drummer and the farmer went out with whimpers. The weasel stayed.

Prophet continued studying the dealer's face, deciding in the end that the man didn't have a hand – all he had, Prophet guessed, was a feeling that he could bluff a colored man out of a high-stakes game.

Then a strange thing happened. He had just reached into his pocket and grabbed Pearl Eddy's money – his hand and fifty dollars headed for the betting pile – when a voice exploded inside his head: 'Jerome Prophet – how could thee!' He froze. There was no mistaking it.

The Quaker woman had lectured him enough for him to recognize her voice when he heard it . . . and he'd heard it. There was no doubt in his mind. He glanced quickly around the room. She wasn't to be seen. He looked again. Nowhere.

He trembled as if he had been touched by a phantom, echoes of the voice still ringing inside his head as he lowered his hand and the money to the betting pile, then glanced over his shoulder, his eyes moving once more over the faces in the room. She wasn't there.

He had never been a believer in much beyond this life, but at this movement – in this dusty saloon a hundred miles from the town of Liberty – he knew he had heard Pearl Eddy admonish him when he touched her money, as if she'd been sitting right beside him. But she was nowhere to be seen.

Then someone grabbed his hand and Prophet turned, staring into the face of the dealer. The man had half-risen from his chair and was squeezing Prophet's hand, trying to force him to release the money into the pile.

'No,' Prophet said.

If he'd been sober or smart the dealer would have sensed something that wasn't safe in those eyes and that voice and backed away, but the alcohol had slowed his thinking. That, plus the fact that he outweighed Prophet by a hundred pounds and figured the Negro wouldn't want any part of him. Negroes had no guts, he told himself. Those were the reassuring thoughts going through his mind when he yelled, 'The hell!' and smashed Prophet's hand down on to the table.

Prophet had finally had enough. 'Let go of me,' he said in an icy voice.

'You weaseling buck.'

Prophet had been applying pressure against the man's hand in order to hold it above the table. Now he relaxed some and the man must have figured he'd won and that Prophet was going to drop the money. He wasn't.

In a moment so fast no one around the table knew exactly what had happened, Prophet jerked his hand free, dropped the money in his lap, then grabbed the dealer's hand before the man had time to react.

'Don't call me any more names,' he said. The man tried to pull away, his other hand prying at Prophet's huge fingers.

'You're breaking my hand!' he yelped.

While Prophet was slow to anger, he had arrived, his hand clamping harder on the dealer's. Then the man panicked and reached for his pistol. He never made it.

Prophet used the mental notes he had been making, bringing his left across the table in an arcing collision with the bearded face, the impact producing a popping sound – like a cork out of a bottle – then blood and a tooth were on the table. It was not a knockout punch, nor meant to be. He'd simply intended to slam a little sense into the man but perhaps, he figured, staring at the splattered blood and tooth, he had been too enthusiastic.

Stunned, the man was screaming and groping blindly for his pistol when Prophet cold-cocked him. No sooner had he accomplished this when he heard the voice again. 'Jerome Prophet.' That was all he heard, but it sounded like damnation. He froze, then slowly released the man's limp hand and stood, turning and staring past the crowd of men. They backed away. Sweat broke over his body. She wasn't here.

Was he going crazy? No. His imagination was just playing games. She'd gotten under his skin. That was all. Her bossiness knew no bounds. He picked up the money that had fallen from his lap, then looked across the table at the dealer slumped in his chair, drooling blood down his shirt front. The crowd was quiet.

He calculated he had about $35 in the pot in the center of the table. He looked around. Nobody seemed much interested in picking up where the dealer had left off.

'We'll play this one,' he said, looking at the weasel-faced man. 'Flip your cards.'

Prophet turned his kings, then nodded at the drummer. The man turned the dealer's hand: three queens. Prophet smiled. The little rodent still hadn't moved, a frightened expression fixed on his face.

'Turn them.'

The man complied, reaching a shaking hand and flipping his cards: a straight flush.

'Damn,' Prophet muttered and headed toward the door.

He stood in the deep shadows near the livery watching the saloon to see if anyone was going to follow him, his thoughts still on the crazy scream in his head. It had unnerved him in a way he definitely didn't like.

It was as if she'd been standing right behind his ear. Craziest of all, he'd never heard her yell before. Never heard her speak in more than a stiff tone.

He shivered in the cool night air and started walking toward the railroad tracks and the place where he'd hidden his bag and bedroll. Then he halted abruptly.

Someone had called to him from the darkness of an alley: a woman's voice. So she was here after all. Blind or not, she'd tracked him down, like a bloodhound. He could see the small shadowy shape approaching and felt himself getting angry. He was growing damn tired of her badgering.

'How the heck did you find me?'

'You just look like a man who could use a good time,' the prostitute said, stepping into the street light.

Prophet shook off his surprise. 'No thanks,' he said. He turned and started slowly for the railroad tracks, his thoughts on Pearl Eddy, his hand clutching the $250.

CHAPTER EIGHT

Samuel and his brothers were hauling hot water from the cauldron they had hung over a wood fire in the backyard, rushing the steaming buckets into the kitchen where their mother had ordered the copper tub placed after breakfast. Zacharias was holding Hercules under one arm and trailing along behind them, crying every once in a while over the loss of the picture. During the night he had cried himself to sleep, then woke every couple of hours sobbing that he would never see his father again.

Samuel smiled at him as he passed, wanting to cheer him up but knowing he was right. He himself had thought the photograph would always be among those things in his life that would last forever. It stunned him to think that it was gone. The moment he heard of the theft he knew it was the Negro and said so to his mother and brothers. But Zacharias refused to believe the man had done it. At least he had an excuse, Samuel thought. He was just a kid. He was feeling embarrassed and faintly annoyed as he entered the kitchen – he would like to have appeared above such child's work. But the girl seemed either not to notice or to care and he kept telling himself she wasn't worth being concerned about anyway. He'd thought about her last night.

He figured it was just that she was around his age and foreign. He was just curious. That was all. His mother was bent over the bath, testing the temperature of the water, Fumiko eyeing her cautiously.

He wanted to laugh. There would be no escape. He could have

warned them that after she'd run her fingers through Tamoko's and Isi's dirty hair, and touched their soiled clothing, they were headed for the tub. She was death to dirt. Therefore he hadn't been surprised by his mother's directive to set up the bath, even though it wasn't Sunday. But two things did surprise him.

The first was the three outfits lying on the table. She had to have sewn all night, though he couldn't tell it from her energetic movements and rapid talk.

The second surprise was that she had regained her normal bouncing spirit. The cloud from last night had disappeared as if the prairie sun had burned through. He was relieved.

Then his gut tightened: he knew what Zacharias was feeling. The thought of never being able to see the picture again, never to see his father's face, sucked the breath out of him. He shook the sensation off and watched as his mother left the kitchen heading for the parlor, talking happily over her head to Eiko who nodded enthusiastically.

Samuel lingered, pouring the last pail of water slowly, enjoying the chance to hear the happy talk, to observe the little girls' excitement over their new clothes, chattering in their rapid way. That was one of the good things about his mother: she could make any chore seem like a picnic. Except it wasn't working with the girl.

She was leaning against the counter with her arms over her breast, looking sullen. Even knowing his mother's great will and persuasive powers, he still wondered how she was going to get this girl into the bath. Then an interesting thing happened.

Fumiko glanced at the new outfit his mother had made for her, then quickly looked away, returning to stare balefully at the tub. But her eyes had betrayed a glimmer of interest. Before he could make much of this, his mother returned.

'Eiko?'

'Yes?'

Pearl was holding out a cotton dress and a pair of shoes. Samuel looked back down at the tub, fighting his feelings. It was a wonder they had anything, the way his mother gave everything away. She had maybe four dresses to her name and two pairs of shoes, and she was giving these away. He looked up. The woman was crying.

His mother looked equally touched, but when the woman reached out to take the dress, Pearl seemed to sense it and held up her own hand. 'Not until thou hast bathed.'

The woman started to protest.

'Not until thou hast bathed,' Pearl repeated firmly.

Amazingly, he thought, he'd caught a glimpse of Fumiko – apparently pleased that the tables had been turned on her mother – almost smiling.

'Certainly not until thou hast had thy bath,' Pearl said once more for emphasis, hanging the dress on the kitchen door. Then she picked the splashing Ituro from his bath in a smaller copper tub on the kitchen counter, turning toward the girl. Samuel smiled to himself – she had an exquisite sense of timing.

'Fumiko, please dry your brother while thy mother bathes.'

The girl stepped forward quickly, looking almost helpful, and certainly enjoying her mother's consternation, and wrapped the pudgy, dripping Ituro in a towel. Samuel guessed these people had been living in the middle of roads and barns so long they were out of the bathing habit.

'Thank thee,' Pearl said brightly. Then she turned back to-toward Eiko who continued to look like a cat cornered by dogs. 'The water is cooling.'

For the first time since he'd seen her, Fumiko was enjoying herself. She didn't smile, but he could tell. And it made him feel momentarily good. His mother had this way with people. Even if she was naive, she had this way.

'Samuel, put the blanket over the window – then thou and thy brothers start another kettle. I'll call when we are ready. We'll need three more tubs,' she said, calculating. 'Tamoko and Isi together . . . Fumiko . . . and Mr Kishimoto.'

Eiko drew her breath in hard with the sound of her father-in-law's name, while Fumiko clapped her hands together in glee.

'No. No wash Mr Kishimoto,' Eiko warned in a trembling voice.

Pearl laughed. 'I have no intention of washing Mr Kishimoto. He will have to do that himself. I will simply provide the facility to accomplish it.'

Fumiko was standing in a peculiar way now, feet together and bouncing up and down, her hands clasped together gleefully over her mouth as if she were attempting to contain a massive explosion of mirth.

'I don't tell him.' Eiko shook.

'I'll be happy to,' Pearl said, holding a bar of soap and a wash rag toward the woman, who still looked to be in a state of shock. 'Hurry,' she coaxed, while Samuel made a quick exit.

Later, Samuel was still grinning with the memory of what had happened. He was in the buggy waiting for his mother to finish her conversation with the widow Wendell. The two women were standing in the early twilight on the widow's front porch.

Then Jack stamped a foreleg and shook his head, trying to lose a horsefly. Samuel crawled down and chased it for him, then stood rubbing the old gray's forehead and remembering. And grinning again.

After the females had finished their baths, Pearl had marched out of the house, across the yard, and into the dim light of the barn, looking like she was heading to Sunday tea. Sam and his brothers trailed behind at a distance, knowing that if she caught them, she'd send them on some unpleasant errand. Eiko and the two smaller girls remained inside the house, as if seeking physical protection from the wrath of the old man's coming rage. But not Fumiko. She'd strolled along pretending she was on other business. Samuel had watched her, surprised at the freshness of her look.

He glanced back up now at his mother draped in her dull gray dress. She held a basket in her arms and was patiently listening to widow Wendell gabbing. He was filled with a sense of admiration for her. While she studiously avoided style herself, she had an uncanny sense of it for others. Blind she might be, but she could imagine what looked good. It was an amazing gift of sorts, though she'd have scoffed at that.

There was nothing dowdy about the clothes she made, her designs were always sophisticated and freshly modern. Never extravagant, her creations nevertheless had a pleasing flair and worked to the physical advantage of the wearer. They certainly did for Fumiko, he recalled. His eyes had moved slowly over the oriental girl as she hung back to look at the hollyhocks near the well.

Samuel scratched old Jack's ears. He'd been amazed at her appealing look when she was cleaned up; her cheeks smooth like polished stone, her eyes dark and deep. And equally amazed that his mother – blind and doing nothing but running her hands quickly over a face and body – could create so. She had stressed the oriental girl's height at the same time that she emphasized her strong shoulders. His mother's needlework had made her as pretty as any girl in Liberty.

'Come on, Sam,' Josh had complained.

At his brother's call, he'd turned toward the barn just as his mother said, 'Good morning, Mr Kishimoto.'

There was no reply. Nor did the old man move in any physical way.

Inside the barn, the boys' eyes slowly adjusted to the weak light. The old man had his beautiful red robe draped over his thin shoulders. Then, as if to underscore the fact that he didn't want to be disturbed, he had executed his amazing half-rise from his squatting position, rudely turning his back to Pearl, settling down cross-legged on the mat with little physical effort. He was certainly agile for an old man.

'I don't like him,' Luke had mumbled.

The others had nodded.

'Mr Kishimoto,' his mother had continued, 'my boys are preparing thy bath. Please follow me to the kitchen.' Pearl had turned as if there were no doubt that he would follow. She started tapping her cane back toward the barn door.

Halfway across the barn she had stopped and turned, listening for the old man. 'Mr Kishimoto. I know that thou understands English.'

Still, there was no reply.

'I assume thou hast not bathed in a period of time. I also assume from thy clothing and manner that thou are a man of education and refinement. Therefore it must be distasteful to thee to go without cleaning thyself.' She paused. 'Thy bath will be ready in ten minutes. All of the women and children will leave the house until thou are completed.'

No sound or movement stirred the cool air inside the barn.

'I will clean thy garments. If thou has replacements, fine. If not – I have a suitable robe for thee to wear until they are dry.'

'No.' The harsh word shot through the air like a bullet.

Then his mother was pulling herself up straight the way she did when she got heated over something, and she began tapping her foot, a small cloud of dust rising from the dirt.

It was at that moment – watching her stiff frame and that familiar tapping foot – that the boys had begun to sense that perhaps old Mr Kishimoto was in for a fight. Perhaps the old man somehow sensed this as well, because without moving a muscle anyone could see, he said, 'Put it in barn.' Then, as if to clearly show who was boss, he barked, 'Now!'

She'd nodded and said, 'Of course.' Then just as firmly, she added, 'It will now take longer than ten minutes.'

Samuel remembered Fumiko mumbling something in Japanese and looking shocked. They'd all been – but the boys knew their mother well enough to keep deathly still about it.

'Quiet,' he'd hissed. Too late.

'And thee children with the large ears, I want Jack's stall and corral cleaned before lunch. Also his water tank.'

Fumiko had started to walk away when his mother said, 'Fumiko, that includes thee, child.'

They'd moaned some but the punishment had been worth the spectacle. The girl had worked hard and done her share, ignoring the lot of them throughout the morning. But for some reason Samuel didn't understand, it didn't matter that she was rude. She just seemed to make the work go better. He guessed it was the novelty of it.

Now night had fallen over the town and Pearl was crawling back on to the buggy seat, Samuel guiding her with a hand. She looked tired. They had made their regular deliveries, but each had taken longer than normal, as Pearl had continued to seek employment for Eiko and Fumiko. So far, she'd found nothing. Not even a maybe.

She looked withdrawn and as close to being worried as she ever came, her expression one of deep contemplation. He wondered about her – how someone so naive about practical matters could be so constantly involved in hard thinking. It made no sense. She wasn't dumb. He shrugged and picked up Jack's reins, the old carriage horse automatically turning away from the hitching post toward home.

'Thee could use some dinner,' he said, trying to sound cheerful.

She sat straighter, as if she'd momentarily forgotten he was there, and placed her hands in her lap.

'First I want to speak with Mrs Randolph.'

Samuel's heart sank. He was hungry and while not as tired as she, still tired. He was thinking it would be another hour before they started home when she said, 'Drive me there. Then borrow a livery horse from Mr Syth and go home. I want thee to make certain that the Kishimotos and thy brothers have eaten.'

He started to say something about their not having enough but decided against it, she looked too worn. Jack, he knew, would bring her home whenever she gave him his head. He'd been doing that for more than twelve years, through fog and rain and snow.

Then Samuel began to feel bad about leaving her. He knew

how tired she was – always doing things for other people. He looked at her face again, at the profile even a son could admire; but in the waxing moonlight, she looked lost in a way that scared him.

'I don't mind waiting.'

She smiled. 'I thank thee. But thou needs to make certain the others have eaten.'

He hesitated, ready again to protest, but something in the lines around her eyes said it wouldn't be fair to continue arguing. 'Only if thou promises to hurry.'

'I promise.'

The bell in the steeple of the Methodist church was ringing nine when Pearl let Jack have his head. She was exhausted, having just left Sarah Randolph's with no more success than any other attempt to find the Kishimotos jobs. Everyone seemed to know she was looking for work for the women and everyone was at once very helpful and not helpful at all: offering up the names of neighbors and relatives who might need a cook or cleaning woman, but never needing one themselves.

She paid no attention to the horse as he threaded his way through the alleys and side streets of the livery and saloon district heading steadily toward Lincoln Avenue. The old animal would take Lincoln north until it ran into the road that cut west across the prairie. He would follow that for three miles, turning in at their gate.

If the boys didn't hear the buggy, Jack would gauge the door correctly and make his final turn into the barn. Amazingly, he rarely bumped the carriage into anything. Once inside, he would stand quietly until unharnessed. Familiar with all this, Pearl paid him no mind as they moved along.

Liberty was no more than 3,000 people and at this hour the streets were empty and quiet. But it wouldn't have mattered if she'd been in the middle of New York City, so deeply was Pearl submerged in her worries. So submerged that not even the whispering of the men on the sidewalk caught her attention. It was a small group and they seemed involved in some intense discussion that included her, one of the men pointing at the buggy. Then, after Jack had turned the corner, four of the men trailed in the direction she'd gone. The other three stood on the corner for a while, then turned and headed for the lighted doorway of the Chalice saloon.

Somewhere nearby a door slammed and a dog barked in response, but Pearl paid no mind to the disturbance, her thoughts on the missing money, her boys and her failure to find work for Eiko and her daughter. Nothing seemed to be going right. She tried to probe the silence of her mind, searching for the familiar inner peace. It didn't work. Her thoughts traveled back to the evening's efforts.

She'd made calls on six families, folks she knew used hired help. Their reactions had all been different, but surprisingly similar: each had seemed sympathetic to the plight of the woman and her children, but none was willing to do anything about it. What bothered her most were the lurid tales of Asians kidnapping children, poisoning employers, stealing fortunes, and selling teenage girls as slaves. Sarah Randolph had told her that they ground up children to make strange potions . . . and stole like Hindus.

She'd tried to argue, but the more she did the more exaggerated the stories became. She stretched her tired body on the buggy seat and shook her head, then breathed in deeply, trying to let the cool air of the plains clear her mind. Spring was coming hard on the land, and she could smell the weed growth by the side of the road. She heard an owl make a low pass over the roof of the buggy, its wings swishing in the night like those of an avenging spirit.

Jack's hoofbeats were steady and soothing. The old horse seemed to know that Pearl wouldn't want him rushing and he obligingly took his time heading out to the cross-prairie road. Pearl let her shoulders sag, feeling like crying but knowing that was wrong. She had to stand up to her troubles: a struggle in a good cause, she told herself, would turn out all right. And the

Kishimotos were a good cause. Every bit as good as holding on to the house.

Pearl's shoulders tensed again. She couldn't lose the house. Lillian would not take her boys from her. She had never considered her blindness much of a handicap. But always before, she'd had her parents or Matthew. Now she realized she wasn't as independent as she had often believed. This bothered her. She couldn't let her boys down.

Pearl forced herself to relax and leaned back on to the seat listening to the last faint sounds of the town slipping away behind her. Then, suddenly, Jack shied at something and Pearl gripped the side of the buggy, talking gently to him. Probably a possum scurrying on the side of the road, she thought, picking up the reins.

'Settle down,' she said softly. But the old horse wasn't going to settle down, and she sensed that he was about to break into a trot. She pulled him in, uncertain what had spooked him.

'Jack.'

The horse was turning his head to watch both sides of the road. Then he snorted, the buggy rounding the turn on to the cross-prairie road too quickly. The animal stepped hurriedly into a single-foot, causing the carriage to bounce over the ruts. Finally, the wheels straightened out and the buggy headed down the road, into the night and the tallgrass plains. But something was bothering the horse. She listened but couldn't hear anything unusual.

She knew the few lights of town were slowly being left behind, floating like a small island of stars on a great sea of black, as Matthew had once described it. Her thoughts drifted to him, then suddenly away: for a moment she had a passing sensation of unease, sensing something nearby that made her want to wrap her arms around herself.

Jack broke into a trot and Pearl reined him in, still uncertain what was bothering the animal. She sat with a good grip on the lines in case he suddenly got it into his head to bolt.

Without meaning to, Pearl was soon thinking about Matthew again. They had made this same ride together hundreds of times, Matthew talking about everything: plants, animals, the weather, politics, religion. She bit her lip, realizing – as she did a dozen times a day – how badly she missed him. She wondered whether the hurt would ever go.

Matthew had died a painful death. But he had never surrendered to the pain, never lost his dignity or serenity. Or his beliefs. She caught herself. His? Or simply hers? She shuddered at the possibility. Then she tensed, thinking she'd heard someone trip over a rock to the rear of the buggy.

'Hello?' she called.

No response. Jack was still nervous. Pearl listened hard again, sensing something nearby. 'Hello?' But there was no answer. She forced herself to relax, trying to decide what she was going to tell banker Snipes about the money. It would take a year to save the amount needed, and by that time she'd be facing new debts. The dark mood seemed to come over her like a wave out of the darkness. She struggled against it. She wouldn't give in. Wouldn't. God wasn't indifferent.

All she had to do was let the Spirit work. Her throat tightened. But what if this – the loss of the money, the loss of the house – was part of His plan for her? Could she surrender to that? She rubbed her face in her hands and felt the pressure and indecision snapping at her like some ravenous creature.

Pearl jumped as the buggy bounced over the center rise in the road, heading in a direction she sensed wasn't right.

'Jack – where are thou going? she called, trying to bring the animal back to where she believed the road ran. But, strangely, he did not respond.

Pearl braced her feet against the front of the buggy. 'Whoa, Jack,' she called firmly, pulling harder on the reins. But this didn't stop the horse, who continued moving in the new direction. Pearl was confused. In all these years, Jack had never made a wrong turn on the route home, and he had never failed to stop when reined in. She relaxed her grip on the leather lines for a moment, then pulled them back firmly. 'Jack, stop!' she called.

It had no effect. She couldn't believe it. She could hear that they were on a road, the wheels of the buggy turning in sandy ruts. But which road? And why had Jack turned? Was there fire ahead? She felt the panic rising in her throat and stopped it – the prairie grasses would be too green for fire for another month. She focused again on her problem.

There were a number of small roads that intersected the cross-prairie. Could the old horse have taken one by accident? Not by accident. Had something in his head snapped? She doubted it. He had been behaving normally enough and his hoofbeats sounded normal. It seemed impossible. Jack knew the road home even in a hard snow. Something would have to have prevented him from taking it. That last thought hit her like a physical blow.

Pearl's heart began to race. That was why he wasn't responding. That explained the noise she'd heard and the feeling she'd gotten: someone was leading him, holding the reins beneath the bit so that when she yanked, the horse didn't feel the pressure and didn't respond in any way.

She was certain of it; she could sense their presence and knew there was more than one. They were walking silently alongside the buggy. She sat up straighter. 'What do thou want?' There was no answer. 'Thou have no right to deter me.'

When Pearl felt the buggy start down the incline, she knew where they were taking her. They'd turned off the cross-prairie road on to the old south trail that dead-ended at Simpson's Creek. It was a lonely spot a good mile out of town, surrounded by cottonwood trees and sandhills and nothing else. The closest house was the Jacobs', two miles behind her. No one came here unless they wanted to load water or swim. Certainly no one would be coming at night. She fought a shiver.

'Ei-chinkchatchewy,' someone said in a sing-song falsetto that was a bad imitation of a Chinese accent. The others laughed. All the voices were male.

'If thou are trying to frighten me,' she said in a rush, 'it will not work.'

None of them responded, their silence unnerving her some. When Jack stopped and the quiet of the prairie fell down hard on the place. No one moved. Then Pearl sucked in a gulp of air.

'I expect thee to take me home now, gentlemen,' she stated matter-of-factly, as if this were a joke that she could put an end to simply by telling them to stop. But somewhere in a deep place inside her, she began to sense what they planned and understood they would not stop because she told them to. She fought her fear and then asked forgiveness for them, clasping her hands together to control her shaking.

She tried to escape by letting her thoughts travel back in time. She was walking down the hallway of her childhood home, climbing the stairs to her room and curling up on her bed – listening to the ticking of the mantel clock and the steady purring of her cat – forgetting this night and this cold place. These men. And what they were going to do.

But she couldn't. She was here in this desolate spot and she sensed them moving in on her, and there was nothing she could do about it but focus on the inner place in her mind.

Suddenly, her muscles contracted. Someone had climbed on to the seat beside her. She could hear breathing and smelled liquor and tobacco, then she felt a callous hand against her cheek. She reached to remove it, but the man grabbed her wrist hard, holding it pinned back against the seat while he ran his hand slowly down her front. Then someone else grabbed her left arm, holding her.

'Thou should be ashamed. Thou have mothers and sisters.' She was trembling, but also sensed a numbness spreading slowly through her until she no longer felt as if she were pinned against the seat while they pawed her. In her mind, she was standing away from all of this . . . would always be separate from it.

'If thou violate me, thou violate them.'

They were tugging at the bodice of her dress. She did not try to strike them. Even if she could have, she would not have struck in anger. Someone kissed her, hurting her mouth. They were ripping at her clothes now.

Then the flutelike notes of a meadow lark drifted through the darkness toward her. She focused her mind on the sound. It came again, sharp and clear through the shadows, its familiar call, 'seee youuu', strange-sounding in the quiet of the night.

In all her years on these prairies, she'd never heard one call after sundown. The muscles of her back tensed. They had been Matthew's favorite bird. He used to whistle their call when he was coming in from the fields. And she chose to believe that he was whistling again, trying to tell her he was with her, and would always be with her.

She was concentrating hard on this thought when suddenly the man to her right yelped like an injured dog and slumped into her lap.

'What the hell?' the man to her left said, his voice nervous. Then suddenly he let go of her as if she were leprous.

Pearl pressed her fingers against the neck of the unconscious man, feeling for his pulse. Strong. She used her free hand to search for his wound, eventually finding a large lump on the back of his skull.

As she was struggling to pull a blanket over him, fighting broke out behind the buggy. Somebody was yelling and she could hear moaning. 'Stop that!' she shouted, as if she were breaking up a fight among school boys. But this struggle was deadly serious and they did not stop, the blows coming faster and accompanied by groans. Then someone splashed through the creek. Jack bolted, dragging the buggy up to the wheel hubs into the water and then stopping.

Moments later, another man broke and ran, trying to escape through the grasses to the right of the wash, but she heard someone pursuing and then tackling him. 'Stop!' she yelled. Again, they paid her no mind.

Pearl Eddy wasn't certain what it was that led her to the

conclusion. It just seemed to suddenly be there in her mind and she was certain she was right. She turned in the direction of the struggle.

'Mr Prophet. Thou stop this second.'

The sounds of the fighting seemed to slow as if in response to her command, then resumed full force.

'Mr Prophet!'

'Can't.'

'Thou certainly can.'

'No,' the voice said, hoarse and winded.

'And why not?'

The fight continued for a moment, then the same voice said, gasping for breath, 'Because I'm not winning.'

'All of thee, stop!'

'Lord, why me?' she heard Prophet mutter.

Then someone groaned and seemingly let out their life's breath. The silence of the prairie seemed to flood in on the place and she shivered and clutched at the limp body beside her. 'Thou are violent. Thou seek trouble. Mr Prophet, how many men have thee hurt here?'

No response came to her.

'Hello?' she called, searching for Jack's reins but not finding them. The man on the seat moaned and she shook again in the cold night air. 'Hello?' she called once more.

When there was no answer, when the frigid prairie wind whipped down into the sandy gully bringing a deepening chill to her – a chill that would surely kill anyone lying hurt and unconscious on the cold ground for any time – she started to climb down into the creek water to search for the injured. Then she stopped.

The buggy had tipped with the weight of someone stepping up on the far running board. He was gasping and sounding as if he might expire at any moment. Light flurries of snow blew in from across the river and Pearl felt these tingling against her neck. Then abruptly the unconscious man was being pulled across the seat.

'No,' she pleaded. 'He'll die.'

The pulling stopped.

Moments later, the buggy swayed as the man stepped down into the stream. She heard him splashing through the water, then felt Jack turning back toward the shore.

'Are others hurt?'

There was a muffled answer but it was drowned in the noise of the stream.

'I could not hear thee.'

'No one's badly hurt,' Prophet said louder, still breathing in heaves. He paused. 'Too old to fight three-against-ones,' he said to himself.

Though the night was dark with snow clouds, he thought she had reacted in relief at the sound of his voice. But he wasn't certain. Nevertheless, he was positive she'd frowned at his remark about the fight. He started to respond but caught himself, knowing it would be useless.

He was bending and trying to catch his breath, the icy water of the creek swirling around his calves, and thinking about her lecturing him when he was getting the stuffing knocked out of him, and he started to laugh.

Pearl sat in the buggy with her hand on the shoulder of the unconscious man. 'Mr Prophet, I find no humor in thy violence.'

Prophet straightened up.

'None,' she continued.

He studied her through the dim shadows, the swirling stream beginning to numb his legs. She had covered herself but her clothes were badly damaged, and her hair was hanging in tangles. He shook his head. He knew what her fate would have been if he hadn't chanced upon the men and the carriage – he figured she did as well. But if she was even a tiny bit grateful, she was concealing it damn well. He ran his tongue over his split lip and kept turning the horse back to the edge of the creek.

'Are they conscious?'

He didn't respond.

'Mr Prophet?'

'Ran off.'

'What did thou do to this man?'

'Hit him with a sap.'

'I see,' she said disapprovingly.

What would she have had him do, he wondered, waltz with these characters? She had a warped outlook. He started to say so, then stopped. He didn't feel like another lecture.

'He'll come around.'

She didn't say anything, just sat staring forward into the night as if she were watching something in the darkness in front of the buggy. But he knew that was silly. She didn't look right.

After he'd led the horse back up the rise to the little road, Pearl got down from the buggy and stumbled off into the bushes. He could hear her retching in the darkness, then gagging hard. He didn't blame her. He went and wet a rag for her at the river.

She was shaking hard as if she was sick or freezing when, minutes later, he helped her back into the buggy. He glanced at her face in the moonlight. She looked ready to burst out crying. But then she pulled in a hard breath and seemed to stiffen up – seemingly more like herself again. He started to say something. But then he stopped. He didn't know what to say. All he could come up with was, 'You OK, Mrs Eddy?'

'Yes.'

Her voice sounded normal but he could see she was still trembling.

Some fifteen minutes later, she was looking better, and the man on the buggy seat was sitting up and trying to clear his head. He was young, most likely a drifter, with filthy clothes and hair. Prophet took all of this in, then grabbed the man's jacket lapels and yanked him out of the vehicle.

'Mr Prophet,' Pearl said sternly.

Prophet had an arm cocked. He held it.

'Mr Prophet,' she repeated.

'Fine,' he mumbled, lowering the arm. 'Let the law hang him for violating a white woman.'

The man began to blubber.

'I was not violated.'

'That's where it was headed,' Prophet snapped. 'Rape, plain and simple.' His eyes were locked on the man's terrified face.

'Please do not be vulgar. Or exaggerate, Mr Prophet.' She paused. 'What is thy name?' Pearl asked.

Prophet couldn't believe what he was hearing and looked at her sitting quietly in the shadows of the buggy seat. He'd never get her straight in his head.

They just stood there until Prophet shook the man again.

'Hank. Hank Meyers. I'm sorry,' the man moaned pitifully. 'I have a mother.'

Prophet yanked him close with a force that left no doubt he'd be harmed if he resisted. 'Then why'd you do it?'

'Man paid us.'

Prophet shook him hard. 'Who?'

'Mr Prophet,' she said in a soft voice.

'I never saw him. He paid my friend $50.' His eyes were pleading. 'Don't let them hang me.'

Prophet shook him again.

'Mr Prophet.'

'Bull,' Prophet said between clenched teeth, ignoring Pearl. He was seized with the desire to drive his fists into the man and no smack-bang act of repentance was going to change his mind.

'Don't let them hang me,' the man sniveled.

'No one is going to hang thee,' Pearl said quickly.

'Maybe thirty years,' Prophet snarled. 'I've been there in prison and it isn't pretty. You eat maggots –'

'Mr Prophet, are thou quite finished?'

He didn't say anything, just scowled at the man.

'Thank thee,' Pearl continued. 'Mr Meyers, have thou learned a lesson?'

'I swear I have.' He was crying.

'Then go and find God in thy heart.'

Prophet was staring in disbelief at Pearl Eddy.

'What can I do to repay you, ma'am?' Hank Meyers asked.

'Repay the Lord.'

'I promise.'

A minute later she sensed him still standing there.

'Thou may go.'

'I can't.'

'Why not?'

'The Negro won't let me.'

'Mr Prophet,' she said quietly.

Prophet stood for a moment holding on to the man's lapels and staring at her, not ready to let him go.

'Mr Prophet,' she said more firmly.

Reluctantly, he released the man's coat, shoving him away, and climbed up into the buggy.

CHAPTER NINE

It seemed to Prophet a strange thing to behold. He had knocked men cold, threatened them with death, beaten them into submission, but looking back at this man – standing in the road gazing after the buggy in a trancelike way – he realized he'd never brought another human being to this level. Never. Hank Meyers just stood there staring, his lips moving silently. Staring like he wanted to follow.

It was peculiar and unsettling in a way Prophet didn't fully comprehend, saying something about this tiny woman. Something he sensed but didn't understand and certainly didn't want any part of.

'You should have let me get it out of him – then we should have turned him in to the sheriff.'

'He renounced his sins.'

'You don't believe that.'

'I do. But even if I did not, I do not believe in violence. Thou should not either.' Almost as an afterthought, she said, 'As a minister.'

Prophet flinched. 'He knows who paid him.'

The snow was falling now. 'He said he did not.'

'That was a lie.'

'Mr Prophet. We witnessed his repentance.'

'That was a lie, too,' he said, marveling at her naivety.

Pearl pulled herself up straighter on the seat but didn't respond. She was trembling again.

He ran a hand over the top of his bare scalp to wipe the melting snow off, wondering why anyone would want to harm this tiny, gullible woman. She was a pain but didn't deserve harming. It didn't make sense.

For all anybody knew he'd left town. So why bother the woman? That old lady who'd tried to have him arrested might have stirred people up, but they'd just stopped doing business with Pearl Eddy. That would have been punishment enough. No. It had to be something else. Prophet gripped the reins and clucked the horse into a trot.

'Please slow down,' she said quietly.

He reined the horse back.

'Thou were headed to Minnesota.'

'Was.'

'And?'

He'd been asking himself this same question. He thought about the voice in the saloon. Then brushed it off. He should have just mailed the money and the photograph. But he hadn't. Whatever prompted him, he'd hopped a train back, built a fire by the side of the tracks and made a cup of coffee he didn't want, then started toward the farm . . . running into the buggy and the men. Had he found her by chance or, as she liked to calculate everything, by ordained providence? He wondered. Then he figured it was damn silly to think of God getting mixed up in this mess. She was just damn lucky he'd returned. But he knew she'd never see it that way.

'Mr Prophet?'

'It's still cold in Minnesota,' he lied. 'And I hate cold.' He pulled the collar of his coat up. 'And I hate owing – so I came back.' This was closer to the truth.

'The hen is paid for.'

'Not the hen.'

'What then?'

Prophet waited before he spoke, listening to the sound of the horse's hooves and watching the snow drifting down. 'What you said to that woman.'

'I told thee that I spoke for myself – because I knew thou were innocent.'

Prophet squirmed on the seat, then started whistling softly.

Pearl listened to the sound, wondering about the picture and the money. A sudden sense of shame came over her. This idea – that he was a thief – had pestered her often during the past two days and she had given in to it. And now she was filled with a sense of self-rebuke. She was becoming embittered and mean-spirited over her constant search for money. And it was wrong, very wrong. She had condemned a man in her heart who was obviously innocent – returning to repay what he mistakenly felt was a debt of honor.

'Thou owe me nothing.'

They rode for a while in silence, before Pearl continued, 'Thy pack is heavy.'

'I brought some things.'

'I'll not accept charity,' she said.

He fought down the exasperation he felt toward her stubbornness, then said, 'Me neither.'

She folded her hands in her lap but didn't respond.

'I've no place to stay and I don't like living on the road. You put me up. I'll kick in a few things – you do the cooking.' Prophet wondered what he was doing. All he'd originally planned was to slip the photograph and the money back inside the house, then be on his way again. 'It isn't charity,' he said sharply.

'Fine. As long as we have an understanding. About charity and violence.'

'Fine,' he snapped, clucking Jack into a single-foot just to annoy her.

'Mr Prophet. Please do not speed.'

He let the animal go for a few moments, then reined him in. He glanced at her and cleared his throat.

'Any chance you were in a town north of here last night – in a little saloon?'

'No.'

166

'Of course not,' he said, no more certain of what had happened than before. He clucked to the horse, momentarily forgetting she didn't like trotting.

'Mr Prophet,' she admonished.

The mystery was gone. Prophet stood open-mouthed and staring at the gaggle of orientals in the barn, a sudden, strange look in his eyes. They were the same ones he'd seen hunkered down on the street in town. He put his tongue between his teeth and bit down, as if trying to keep himself from saying something he knew he'd regret.

'These are the Kishimotos–'

Pearl was introducing him but Prophet wasn't paying any attention. He was just thinking these people were big trouble. Bigger trouble than any colored person could ever hope to be. The little oriental woman had hopped up and was grinning at him in a foolish way like they were long-lost cousins or something. He nodded back at her in reflex and then turned and started for the back porch, his large pack swung over his back. He definitely knew now why the men had been hired to harm her. He also knew she wasn't crazy: she was suicidal.

She was tapping along behind him in the darkness. It had stopped snowing but the night was still cold.

'Mr Prophet,' she called. He stopped and waited for her to catch up. 'Thou may use Zacharias' bedroom.'

'When's the funeral?'

'Mr Prophet?'

'When do you plan on having the burial for yourself and your boys?'

'I don't understand?'

He just shook his head. He was certain she didn't understand and he couldn't believe it. Couldn't believe a body that naive. Hell, most kids had more sense. 'I'll sleep in the cellar. Look better.'

'What does thou mean?'

'You don't need a Negro sleeping in your house,' he snapped, surprised at his own anger, 'and Chinamen in your barn.'

They walked on in silence until they reached the back steps. Prophet's mind was whirling. He wondered how she'd gotten this far in life without knowing any of the rules. She was lucky. But, he figured, it was just a matter of time until her luck fizzled.

He looked back toward the barn. One thing a Negro wouldn't want to be was a Chinaman. He didn't care if she called them Japanese or Jack-be-Nimbles; they were still Chinamen. Negroes could make it in this world if they knew the rules. Not Chinamen. He figured maybe that was where the saying: 'Not a Chinaman's chance in hell', came from.

It wasn't fair or foul. It was just the way things were. That's what bothered him most: this woman never saw things the way they were. She saw them her way. Period. And her way was usually wide of the mark.

She'd grasped the railing now and was slowly climbing the steps, as he followed. 'They had no place,' she said softly, as if she'd read his thoughts. She sounded tired.

He swung the pack off and looked up at her. 'They don't belong here.'

'That's not thy decision.'

'Still the right one.'

'They had no place,' she said again.

'They're the reason those men grabbed you.'

'Thou doesn't know that,' she said quietly.

'Yes, I do. You can't bring folks like them into a town like this.' He paused. 'They've got strange habits. They aren't really people.'

Moments before she had looked too exhausted to stand, but now she straightened ramrod stiff and Prophet could see the fight in her eyes. 'That is enough, Mr Prophet. Though thou may wish to believe differently,' she stammered, 'none are greatest in the kingdom of heaven.'

She turned and walked to the edge of the porch and stood facing the dark gardens, continuing to fight her emotions. 'We are all equal in the eyes of the Lord, Mr Prophet.'

'Not where I grew up.'

When she finally spoke, her voice was filled with an odd mixture of anger, frustration and fatigue. 'Do thou understand me?'

'I understand you've got trouble, Mrs Eddy.' He paused. 'You ought to cogitate on that.'

'Thank thee for thy concern,' she said, tapping her way into the house. 'I will bring thee blankets.' She hesitated. 'Thou remembers how to find the cellar?'

He didn't care for the way she'd asked that last part, but he shrugged it off and leaned against the railing of the porch. The boys' shoes were lined up on top. They were worse than he had thought. The soles were shot through and the topside leather was stiff and cracked from the winter.

He wondered if there was any tallow in the barn, then took a closer look and figured it wouldn't do much good. They were too far gone to salvage with a greasing. He picked up one of Samuel's, surprised he was still wearing high-tops, and set it on the porch beside his own. It was a size smaller.

Pearl was the first customer through the door of the First American Bank the next morning, tapping her way to the teller window and facing a young man who stood behind the bars still rubbing sleep from his eyes. Samuel was waiting for her in the buggy. There were five or six other customers and most were watching her. No one had said good morning, though most knew her.

'Mrs Eddy,' the teller said.

'I've come to–' she hesitated, then quickly said, 'borrow some money.' She had kept her low voice, as if she found the words embarrassing.

'Mr Snipes,' the teller called. 'Mrs Eddy wants to talk about a loan.'

'Next?'

Pearl didn't move out of the window.

'Step aside please, Mrs Eddy. Mr Snipes handles loans.'

Alfred Snipes' office was cramped and dusty and smelled of stale fish and other things that he fed to Queenie, his large gray cat. The animal was sitting on his messy desk now, Snipes petting it while his eyes moved over Pearl. He was busy taking a hungry survey of the contours of her body under her heavy gray dress. She was standing and holding her small purse and cane clutched together in both hands. She looked uncomfortable talking about borrowing.

Snipes continued to contemplate Pearl's figure with a half-smile behind his rimless glasses, his hand steadily stroking the back of the cat as if he might be stroking Pearl. He licked his lips, seemingly lost in a daydream. Small and thin, with a large nose that stuck out like a rock formation from his narrow face, Alfred Snipes had been a bachelor all his life. But that had not kept him from thinking hard and often about women and what it would be like to be with one. He stroked the cat faster.

'Mr Snipes?'

He sat up awkwardly, as if caught doing something he shouldn't have been. 'Well, yes. There's the possibility. But there is the matter of the equipment loans.' He stood and picked up the heavy cat, the animal struggling to free itself. 'I would have to come out and inspect the premises,' he said, looking out the window.

'Yes.'

Prophet was kneeling in the garden, listening to the screeching and chattering of a thousand nesting birds in the tallgrass that crowded around the edges of the cultivated land. He let his eyes roam slowly, studying the place. Mrs Eddy and Samuel had returned in the buggy from the direction of town a while ago. His gaze moved over the garden.

Two gardens, really. One, a rectangular three acres of carefully tended vegetables, the early spring growth marking the neatly ordered rows. The other, identical in shape but half the size, was filled with flowers of differing hues and forms. The dusting of snow from the night before was gone and the day promised to be warm. Prophet stretched a sore place between his shoulders. The fight had taken its toll, his hands and neck were stiff and there was a bruise on the side of his head. He was getting too old for it. That thought scared him. Too old to fight three men at once – but not to take his shot – he told himself quickly. He felt better and shrugged off the pain and looked around some more.

The flowering plants were nicely mixed with figs, peaches and pomegranates and the ground was covered with thyme, rosemary and boxwood. Around the edges were arbors for grapes, boysen-berries and raspberries. There was no question of the talent of the mind that had shaped all this. The garden had been cleverly designed to take advantage of layered plantings that filtered or captured the prairie light and warmth, depending on season and need.

Prophet balled a handful of rich loam in his hand, admiring the tattered remnants of the man's work. But talent didn't matter now. The garden was returning to nature: unruly and chaotic. Once the plants had been keeping happy company, but now they warred for crucial space and light, crowding and choking in a struggle to survive. To make matters worse, last year's growth had not been cleared and lay rotting in brown tangles everywhere. Nothing had been pruned.

Prophet was eyeing this when he heard shuffling on the garden path. He turned to see the oriental woman hurrying along carrying a basket, obviously intent on the early season produce. She stopped and grinned at him, raising both her arms and flexing like a circus strongman, then giggling. She'd done this same pantomime the night before when Pearl Eddy had intro-duced them.

It embarrassed him and he looked away. Then he heard the woman clucking her tongue in disapproval and he glanced back at her. She was frowning at the wild masses of flowers.

She clucked harder. 'No good,' she said.

He agreed.

'You strong man. We fix.' She paused and frowned again. 'Too nice. Too nice.'

He nodded at the last part – but had no interest in working with this little woman. He worked alone. He tossed the ball of dirt down and took a closer look at an old lilac near Matthew Eddy's grave. It was almost dead and under ordinary circumstances he wouldn't even try. But he knew it was a favorite with the boys, so he pulled out his pocket knife and selected one of the few remaining shoots that appeared to have some life left in it. He could feel the watchful eyes of the little oriental woman on him. He ignored her.

'Thou leave that plant alone.' The voice cut sharply through the morning air.

Prophet looked back over his shoulder at Samuel's angry face. The boy was outside the garden, his hands gripping the top rail of the fence.

'No,' Mrs Kishimoto chided. 'Let him cut.'

'It doesn't belong to either of thee and thou should leave it alone.'

'Samuel,' Pearl said in a firm voice. Earlier, Prophet had seen her tossing corn to the hens but he was surprised by her sudden appearance. She had a knack for being in places – at the right and wrong times.

'Mrs Kishimoto asked if she could pick greens,' she said. 'But even if she had not, she and Mr Prophet are guests and welcome in the garden.'

Samuel stood his ground for a moment, slinging his school books in their leather strap over one shoulder and staring sullenly at Prophet, then he started for the road in his long stride. 'Thy guests,' he said, loud enough to hear.

Pearl didn't respond until the boy was almost to the corner of the house. 'If thou wishes it: my guests. In my house. In my husband's garden. And thou will respect that.'

She stopped and Prophet knew from her expression she was hurting. For certain, she didn't accept much sass. But he could tell she viewed discipline as a responsibility – like sticking up for him with the old woman – rather than something enjoyable. And he could see from her trembling it took a certain toll on her.

Just when he thought she was done, she called, 'Samuel,' in a voice just loud enough to ensure the boy heard. She waited.

Samuel stopped, his back turned to her. 'Yes?'

'Do thou understand?'

The boy hesitated and Prophet wanted to crawl under the nearest bush. Even Mrs Kishimoto had turned away, politely pretending she couldn't hear a word. That surprised him. He'd have guessed she'd be ogling the whole thing like some country rube. But instead she was busying herself with garden matters.

'Yes.'

'Good. When thou get home from school, thou can assist Mrs Kishimoto. She has some ideas for the garden.'

The boy had started walking again.

'Samuel?'

'I heard thee.'

'Good.'

Prophet pretended to stare at the lilac bush. She didn't cut these boys much slack. He had started to return to the problem of the dying lilac when the back door of the house burst open and Zacharias popped out like a dark seed out of an overripe melon.

'Father's back! Father's back!' The boy was screaming and running toward his mother, his large black hat clutched in one hand. 'Father's picture is on the desk!'

Prophet busied himself with the bush, glancing out the side of his eye at Samuel; the boy glared in his direction. Then the garden gate opened and Zacharias jumped on to his back.

'Mr Prophet's back too!'

Prophet stood and spun in circles, the boy clinging to his neck and laughing, while Mrs Kishimoto grinned and clapped her hands. Prophet was careful not to look at Pearl.

'It's a miracle!' Zacharias yelled.

'Not a miracle – but certainly a wonder,' she said.

Something in her voice made Prophet spin harder, wishing he was anywhere but here.

Though she undoubtedly knew for certain that he had stolen and then returned the photo and the money, Pearl made no mention of it throughout the morning. He'd planned to be impudent if she braced him with it, but she hadn't and he doubted he could now because he'd been put off by how politely she was behaving.

He had, however, sensed an extra coolness about her. That was fine with him. He was in no mood for one of her lectures. He was working on resetting posts in the garden fence, the day warm to the point where he was sweating.

Mrs Kishimoto had been hanging clothes a few minutes before and she made a side trip to inspect his work, staring solemnly at the line of posts, nodding with satisfaction. It was easy to see she appreciated his labor. He liked that. But then she started teasing him again about his muscles and he retreated toward the barn to search for roofing nails.

The woman rejoined Mrs Eddy on the back porch where they were washing clothes in a big kettle. He could hear her talking fast and laughing. It was a pleasing sound. The little girls were playing with the baby in the dirt nearby.

Prophet stepped inside the barn and let his eyes adjust to the dim shadows. He could hear the old horse moving in his stall and pigeons in the cool darkness of the rafters. The place smelled of hay and oats and leather. He liked those things.

Moments later, he saw the teenage girl looking for something in one of the big canvas bundles the family used to transport their belongings. He'd met her the night before and nodded at her now. 'Looking for nails,' he said.

If she understood English, she made no attempt to respond. She just returned to her searching, the same sullen look on her face, snatching furtive glances at him as if she didn't trust him any more than the oldest Eddy boy.

Prophet ignored her, moving quickly toward some dusty shelves on the back wall where dirty jars and cans stood in rows. More than likely the nails he needed would be in one of them, he figured.

Prophet glanced briefly at the tiny old man, who was sitting cross-legged on a straw mat, his eyes closed. A beautiful red robe was draped across his thin shoulders. Prophet was tiptoeing quietly so he wouldn't disturb the man when somewhere outside he heard Hercules crow. He tensed and turned back to see if the rooster was following. That was what saved him.

The old man looked asleep, but Prophet caught a slight movement of his yellow hands. It telegraphed. He couldn't believe it. The little Chinaman had positioned his grip on the wooden staff. And Prophet knew instinctively what was coming.

Incredible as it seemed – even though he was expecting it – the blow took all of his agility and quickness to avoid. It came at him so fast that Prophet sensed rather than actually saw the swing slashing ankle-high. The back cut was just as quick and it, too, would have caught him had he not already leaped to safety. Then, with a final movement as rapidly deceptive as a magician's, the old man had the staff lying harmlessly in his lap.

'What the hell was that for?' Prophet hollered.

Kishimoto didn't move a muscle. Didn't even twitch. He looked like a sleeping lizard again – like he'd been asleep the entire morning. But Prophet figured he was squinting at him through his eyelashes. And he could tell something else. It wasn't a physical thing, but he was certain he saw it: the old man was stunned. Stunned that he'd missed at close range and with the advantage of surprise. It was apparent he wasn't used to missing. This made Prophet feel better. But even so, the attack confirmed what he already thought: these Chinamen were strange.

'Damn Chink,' he mumbled under his breath.

When he looked up, he saw the girl watching him. She was surprised as well. The old man, he figured, must have been a big ankle-slapper in the old country. And he had to admit: if he hadn't read the movement of the hands correctly, he'd have been nursing banged-up shins. But he had – and the crotchety old man was troubled by that fact. Prophet smiled.

He found the nails he wanted in an old coffee can, watching Kishimoto from the side of his eyes as he searched. This place was getting on his nerves. The Quaker woman was crazy enough to get them all killed; her son wanted him lynched; the rooster was determined to snuff him; and now this old man wanted to bust his legs with a damn stick.

He glared at Kishimoto. He'd had about enough. He would repair the roof, then be on his way. He started to walk way round the old man. Then he stopped. He'd be damned if he'd avoid a little Chinaman with a stick.

'You try that pole trick again – I'll break it over your head.'

The old man didn't respond.

'Understand? Comprende?'

Kishimoto looked dead.

'You've had fair warning,' Prophet said sternly.

He took his time moving by the little man, just to let him know he wasn't afraid of him or his stick. He was feeling good, certain the old man had learned who was fastest.

Prophet froze.

The noise was familiar and he was seized with the desire to flee, but before he could, he caught the full brunt of Hercules on his lower legs.

Prophet hollered, then broke for the door. The rooster was making good time behind him.

'Get him off – Get your damn bird off!'

'Mr Prophet. I've asked thee not to swear,' Pearl called from the porch.

'Call him off, Mrs Eddy, or I'll wring his neck!'

Prophet leaned against the wellhouse, his eyes fixed on old man Kishimoto. The little Japanese had been sitting next to the barn like a stone statuette for the past hour, close to the building but not touching it, as if simply using it to protect his backside from a surprise attack. 'Lunatic,' Prophet muttered.

The tiny man was cross-legged and stiff-backed on his little reed mat, his hands gripping his ever-present stick, his eyes closed. He looked like a desiccated lizard trying to ambush flies.

'Crackpot,' Prophet mumbled.

Pearl and the woman were in the kitchen cooking, the happy sounds of their voices drifting across the yard, while Hercules lounged in the shade of a large bush with his harem. Prophet shook his head. They were all crazy: from the woman to her chicken.

But he was crazier for having come back. He promised himself he'd remedy that after the evening meal. He straightened up and stretched, concerned that he was getting out of shape, then he heard a noise and turned to see Josh shoot through the garden hedge, running as if the devil was a half step behind and gaining.

'Josh?' Prophet called. The boy didn't break stride, disappearing around the corner of the house.

Prophet was just turning back when Luke broke through the leaves, emitting low cries of terror. He followed his brother, dodging Prophet's arms.

The bushes trembled again and Samuel's head appeared, followed by Zacharias', the boy clinging desperately to his brother's neck. Samuel tried to dodge around Prophet, but the man was having none of it. He grabbed Samuel by the shoulders and forced him to stop.

'Let go!'

'What's wrong?'

Samuel was just getting ready to answer when the bushes trembled yet again. The lad wasn't the ugliest white boy Prophet had ever seen, but he could have been runner-up, with dirty yellow hair and pocked skin. He was thick and coarse-looking, but he wasn't stupid. He came to a quick halt when he saw Prophet.

He was quickly joined by three other boys, all about sixteen and tough-looking. From their clothes Prophet guessed they were town kids.

'Help you boys?'

Caught off guard, Hector James, the yellow-haired boy, took a moment to reply. 'Watch who you're calling boy,' he snapped, trying to sound grown up. 'My brothers don't like niggers pushing me around.'

'Unless you've got proper business, son, you best get off the Eddy property.'

The boy looked at Samuel. 'We got business all right. But it can wait. Can't it, Sammy-girl?'

Samuel didn't say anything. Zacharias was sniffling.

'You brave boys run along now before you get in trouble.' Prophet took a step forward and the four of them hopped backwards as if they thought he might fly into them.

'Don't threaten me, nigger,' the boy shot back.

'Listen, son, my name's Prophet. I'm not one for ceremony – but you call me Mr Prophet. Understand?' He stared hard at the boy's face for a moment, then said, 'One more thing. You gang up on the Eddys – I'll be all over you like a bad rash.'

Hector started to say something, then thought better of it and started back through the hedge.

Prophet swung Zacharias up on to his back. He could feel him trembling. Samuel was nervously watching the hedge.

'What happened?'

'Nothing,' Samuel said. He turned and headed for the garden gate.

'Looks like something.'

Samuel whirled and faced him. 'We don't need thy help. What thou did is just going to cause more trouble.' He started back toward the house. 'Thou don't belong here.'

Prophet set Zacharias on the ground.

'I want thee to stay,' the boy said.

'Thanks. Tell Josh and Luke I want to see them.'

*

'Keep it up – up, up!' Prophet said. 'Keep poking it out. Keep it in his face. Jab and jab and jab.'

He was behind Josh, holding the boy's arms up in a boxer's stance, then shoving his left forward hard and sharp. Luke and Zacharias were watching and practicing their own jabs, while Samuel was sitting on Jack's corral watching.

The twins had been through the mill. Both had black eyes, and Josh's lower lip was split.

'That ain't going to stop anyone,' Josh said, carefully moving his swollen lips. 'Just sticking my arm out like that – it ain't going to stop anyone at all.'

'No. But it'll drive them to distraction.' Prophet straightened up and let go of Josh's arms, wiping sweat from his head with a rag.

They were behind the barn, the three boys stripped to the waist, their skin white like toad bellies. Their mother kept a tight rein on them, he figured. It was a shame. They weren't sissies, they were just made to look that way.

'I don't see what distraction is going to do,' Josh protested. 'Just get them madder.'

'It's like a fly keeps bothering you when you're eating,' Prophet said, moving his left hand around and over, behind and under Josh's face, the boy's eyes following it.

'That fly gets you distracted,' he continued, bringing a slow, soft left toward Josh's chin. The boy moved to block it. 'And you forget certain other things,' Prophet said.

'Like?'

'Like,' he said, bringing his huge fist over Josh's dropped guard to the boy's exposed chin, tapping it gently, 'where that fly's right is.'

The boy grinned.

They went back to practicing their lefts. None of them, except Sam, had noticed Mr Kishimoto. He was standing behind Prophet holding his shiny stick, watching intently. Strangest of all, Samuel thought, the old man seemed genuinely interested in the boxing lesson. Every once in a while he would raise one of his legs in a high step, then put it back down, as if he were limbering up.

Then Prophet stepped backwards and said, 'OK – let's try–' He hadn't finished the sentence when Kishimoto took a couple of quick hopping steps and let him have it with the stick across the back of his shoulders.

The sheer force of the blow knocked Prophet forward and he bellowed and rolled in a somersault across the ground. Then he was up and facing Kishimoto – ready to fight. The boys scattered.

The old man was taking his giant, high steps, moving back and forth, positioning himself against Prophet, looking for an opening, his stick held menacingly in his hands.

'You old bastard,' Prophet hollered. 'You're loony – but I'm going to give it to you anyway!'

Prophet began to circle the little man, forcing him to turn, feinting rushes and then continuing to circle. They were like two oddly matched gladiators, carefully taking the other's measure. The yard was quiet. Hercules stood at the corner of the barn watching, as if he might try and catch the Negro off guard himself.

Prophet was just about to lunge when he heard, 'Mr Prophet! What is going on?'

'Ask him!'

Pearl Eddy was tapping her cane fast and looking as upset as Prophet had ever seen her. He figured the old man saw this as well since he wasn't pursuing his attack any longer.

Pearl was moving her hands quickly over the boys' faces and bare upper bodies. Her fingertips carefully noted swollen eyes and puffed lips.

'When did this happen?'

'After school,' Josh said.

She paused. 'Thou were attacked?'

'Yes,' the three of them said in rough unison.

'And thou fought back?'

The boys looked sick. 'Yes. Josh and I did,' Luke said.

Prophet waited for her to console them. She didn't.

'Get thy clothes on. And since thou have such abundant energy, thou can clean the chicken shed before dinner.' She paused. 'And after dinner, I will have other more constructive things for thee to use thy energy on.'

The boys trudged off around the corner of the barn. Samuel hopped down from the fence and started after them. His mother heard him.

'Samuel.'

'I wasn't involved,' he offered quickly, raising his hands as if in surrender.

'Thou allowed whatever was going on here to happen. And thou are the oldest.'

Samuel stopped and looked at her, his face turning red. 'And Mr Prophet is thy guest. I figured thou would let him do whatever he wished.'

Pearl stood still, her face dead white in the evening light. The boy scuffed at the dirt with the toe of his shoe.

'I want to talk with thee in the house,' she said quietly.

The boy looked sick.

She turned back to face Prophet, but in her anger she had forgotten where he was standing and stood talking to the open prairie.

He couldn't help but laugh. It was only a small laugh – but she heard it.

'What is funny?'

'Nothing.'

'Yes. Obviously something is funny.'

'Just that you were talking to thin air.'

She began to tap her foot. 'I often suspect I'm doing that even when I'm talking directly to thee.'

'Nice,' he said.

She ignored him. 'What were thou doing with my children?'

'Talking about boxing.'

'Talk is not what I heard.'

He shifted uncomfortably. 'You mean when you walked around the barn?'

'Yes.'

He fidgeted.

'Mr Prophet.'

'The old man jumped me with his stick.'

Pearl stood contemplating what he'd just said. Then she straightened up some. 'Thou would have me believe that Mr Kishimoto attacked thee?'

'Yes.' Prophet looked for him but the little man was gone. Smart little bastard.

'Why would he do that?'

'I don't know why – just that he's crazy.'

She stood thinking. 'That's what thou said about Hercules – that thou didn't know why he attacked thee and that he was crazy. Is that not right?'

'They're both crazy.'

Pearl crossed her arms and shook her head slowly as if he were a hopeless soul. Prophet didn't care for her look of weary authority.

'It's the truth,' he offered, to shore up his arguments about the old man's and the bird's mental instabilities.

'And thou were teaching the boys to fight?'

'To defend themselves,' he said, thinking that sounded better.

Pearl put her fingers over her mouth as if she were trying to contain something she was about to say. Then she took a deep breath. 'To harm others.'

'That's one way to put it.'

'Is there another, Mr Prophet?'

'To defend themselves,' he repeated.

'It is the same. And I will not have it.'

He shrugged. 'Suit yourself.'

When she next spoke, her voice was quiet but there was no

mistaking her resolve. 'Thou will not teach my children violence, Mr Prophet. Is that clear?'

'They're taught it every day. What do you think happens to them out there?'

'Nothing that justifies violence.'

'You felt their faces – they've got black eyes, scrapes and busted lips.'

'I know the problems they face.'

'Baloney.'

'I know what it means to be different.'

'This isn't about being different. This is about being beaten up.'

'Do we understand each other, Mr Prophet?'

He watched her for a moment, letting his anger cool. 'They're your boys. It's just a shame.'

'Thank thee for thy concern, but it is what we believe.' She paused. 'I have spoken to their teacher many times. But it has done no good. I will try again.'

'That'll just make it worse.'

'I'm sorry, Mr Prophet, but it is what we believe.'

'What you believe, you mean, Mrs Eddy.'

'I am the children's mother, sir.'

The argument had taken more out of her than Prophet had figured and she turned now, completely disoriented, and started to walk into the side of the barn. He grabbed her arm and guided her around the corner.

'You OK?' he asked, releasing her elbow, but ready to grab her again.

She moved out into the evening sunshine without answering, her face empty of emotion, but deep in thought. Probably trying to figure some way to make certain her boys wouldn't try and protect themselves. He started to say 'handcuffs' but something in her unsteady stride kept him from it.

Pearl's thoughts were on Matthew. Then her boys. She knew the Negro was right. The belief was her own. Was it right for her to force her will on the children? To allow them to be harmed because she believed as she did? She climbed the steps of the back porch slowly, her thoughts on this troubling matter. Then she stopped.

It was not just her belief. Not just her will. It was the will and the word of God. She was simply a tool. She could not turn her back on that. Matthew hadn't. And she wouldn't. Even though the pain inflicted on her boys tore at her heart.

Prophet kicked at a stone, then began walking toward the garden, his thoughts on the one thing he hadn't said to the woman. It was true that the Eddy boys not fighting back caused them to be picked on by almost every boy in town. But there was more to it than just that. They were being bullied hard, he knew, because of the Chinamen and him. He'd made them targets. He shouldn't have come back. Samuel was right about that. He should have lost the money in the card game, tossed the picture off the back of the train, and kept going. But he hadn't. He'd come back. Still, it wasn't his affair.

He was just getting around to deciding he'd stay a couple more days when he caught a blurring motion out of the side of his eye. He grabbed instinctively at the movement, catching the old man's staff in the middle. He yanked. Then yanked again, surprised by the force it took to wrench it from the little man.

Stripped of his weapon, the old man went into a strange fighting crouch, his hands open and stiff like little meat cleavers. Prophet glared into his wrinkly face. If the tiny man had been surprised the night before when he missed hitting him, he was stunned now that Prophet had disarmed him, his beady eyes focusing with a slightly confused expression.

'I warned you,' Prophet bellowed.

Mr Kishimoto seemed beyond speech.

'Didn't I warn you?'

The old man was moving his hands and arms in a strange flowing motion that looked graceful and yet funny, like he was play-acting.

'Knock it off or I'll break your damn stick,' Prophet yelled.

Still the old man continued his strange pantomime of movements.

'OK. You asked for it!' Prophet brought his knee up and the stick down with a powerful jerk, then tossed the broken pieces at the man's feet.

'There! Now don't ever hit me with a stick again – don't even look at me – or next time I'll break it over your skull. Understand?'

Mr Kishimoto's eyes were glued on Prophet, his hands and arms moving in their strange gyrations. Then suddenly he yelled, 'Ei!' and flew forward with a kick of his sandaled feet that just missed Prophet's chin.

'You crazy old bastard!' Prophet yelped, surprised by the accuracy and height of the kick.

Kishimoto was back in his silly crouch again, then suddenly, in a surprise move that Prophet hadn't even remotely anticipated, this tiny warrior sprang through the air, feet first, with another savage thrust at his bald head.

Though caught off guard, Prophet was still on the defense and managed to catch him mid-air, feeling at once that he was all bone, tendon and hard muscle, and realizing that he had the quick reflexes of a youth.

At least forty years his junior and a good seventy pounds heavier, Prophet was still struggling to subdue him, the man squirming wildly out of one hold after another. Each time he freed an arm or a leg, Kishimoto thumped him a blow to the neck or the head, the last one a blast that caused Prophet to see sparks and the sky to go suddenly dark.

The Negro shook it off, shocked the old man had the power to stun him, then he put a headlock on the wild little Japanese, dragging him to a nearby water trough and tripping him so that he fell inside. He disappeared under the water. But in a flash, he was up and sputtering; then he gave Prophet a hard smash to the nose with the palm of his hand that started blood flowing.

Until now, Prophet had been trying not to hurt him. But he was hurriedly rethinking his options.

'That's enough, gawddamnit!' he bellowed, diving in on top of the little warrior, who at the moment looked like a half-drowned rodent. The weight of Prophet's body carried both of them under the water.

Ten minutes later, it was over. Prophet almost had to drown the old Japanese into submission. Even then, Kishimoto hadn't surrendered. He'd just flopped to the side of the water trough, vomited and then tried to get into his fighting stance and slipped on the algae, falling back under the water.

Afraid he might really drown – and that Pearl Eddy would blame him – Prophet yanked the old man up and tossed him out on to the dirt, then crawled out himself and limped off, gasping for breath and amazed at what it had taken to subdue this tiny man. He was crazy. But he was also a fighter. But what was he fighting for? Prophet had no answers. All he knew was that at an earlier time, he must have been a holy terror.

As he rounded the corner of the barn, Prophet heard squishing behind him and he whirled back, fists clenched, ready for round three. But there wasn't to be a third round.

When he saw Prophet, the old man stopped trotting and looked at him with his fierce countenance, then bowed. It was a deep bow that carried respect and obedience. Prophet didn't know what to do, wondering if it was a trick. He didn't trust anything about this man.

'Leave me alone,' he said, speaking slowly so the man would understand. Kishimoto bowed again 'Good,' Prophet said. 'Just leave me alone.'

CHAPTER TEN

It was dark in the room when Alfred Snipes rolled over and opened his eyes, the fire having died in the corner stove, the air cold. He could tell from the heavy silence that it wasn't more than two or three in the morning, and he wondered what had awakened him.

He could hear the deep purring of his cat on the pillow next to him, the sound at once comforting and sedating. He yawned and rolled on to his side, draping a thin forearm across the large cat, then dozed.

His sleep was disrupted by dreams. Beautiful dreams of water and wood nymphs who simply couldn't get enough of Alfred Snipes, bachelor, and small-town banker, who had never actually been with a woman. His inexperience didn't seem to faze these lovely maidens of myth. Beth and Joanne danced erotically before him until shoved away by Roxanne. Then Maryanne. Then Susan. Interestingly, on this night, these alluring phantoms had one similarity: they each possessed Pearl Eddy's classically handsome face. He smiled and moaned.

Alfred Snipes sat bolt upright in bed, his eyes probing the darkness surrounding him. He could see nothing but blocks of shadow. But he heard breathing and for a second, still groggy from sleep, he thought that he was continuing to dream. Then a chair scraped the floor and he knew he wasn't. Nor was he alone. He began to shake. His first thought was that someone had come to rob the bank. To murder him for his keys to the cash boxes.

'Who is it?' His voice broke from the fear.

Silence.

'What do you want?'

Still no response.

Snipes shoved his bare legs out of the covers and sat up on the edge of the bed. 'I'll scream,' he threatened.

'If you want your throat cut.'

Snipes froze then fumbled with a match, the flare briefly illuminating three shadowy shapes before his trembling fingers dropped the burning match and darkness flooded back into the room.

'Don't. Not stupid things.'

'What do you want?'

'Did you heard me?'

Snipes didn't say anything.

'If you scream, we'll take you somewhere and kill you slowly. I promise. And if you light another match, I'll put a cigar out in your eyes.' The man waited a few moments, listening to the frightened breathing of Snipes, then asked again, 'Do you understand?'

'Don't hurt me. I'll give you the keys to the safe. Just don't hurt me.'

'We aren't interested.'

'What then?'

'The woman who came into the bank this morning.'

'What woman?'

'The Quaker.'

'Yes.'

'We understand she came for a loan.'

'Yes.'

'She won't get one.'

'Fine.'

'And we want you to foreclose her property.'

Snipes wisely didn't say anything for a moment, just sat trembling and thinking. Finally, he said, 'But if she pays off her equipment loans – what am I supposed to do?'

He could hear the men moving out the door into the darkened hallway of the little house. 'I don't know, but now that you don't have to worry about your cat, you'll have more time to work on it.'

Snipes didn't move until he heard the downstairs door open and shut. Then he whirled toward the bed. 'Queenie, Queenie – where are you?' Snipes pleaded, his hands shaking harder as he hurriedly lit his bedside lantern. Then he let his breath out in a sigh of relief – Queenie was on the pillow with her legs tucked under her. Snipes wanted to cry with joy. Then he noticed the odd angle of her head.

The old man was getting on Prophet's nerves, following him everywhere. Even to the outhouse. He shuffled along in his baggy robes and sandals like he was on some important mission – like he and Prophet were a team.

Nothing Prophet did seemed to discourage him. He had fashioned a new stick out of white ash and Prophet kept his eye on him when he was close, just in case the truce was only temporary.

At the moment, he was sitting on the ground as Prophet dug the earth that the woman, Eiko, had told him to dig. The day was warm and Prophet was sweating. The old man was dozing in the sunlight, work obviously beneath his dignity.

Eiko hurried down the garden path carrying a wooden bucket of 'manure tea' that he had made under her careful instruction. She knew things about gardening. And inside this garden world she was boss: a little barefoot despot ordering him, Fumiko, the girls and the Eddy boys back and forth as she organized the work. The only one she left alone was her father-in-law. But even with him, she was more brazen in the garden.

Prophet didn't mind work, he had done it all his life. And he was learning some new things, like how to make liquid fertilizer by filling burlap bags with one part chicken manure, one part horse manure, one part rotting compost, and, finally, some ground-up dried fish that the woman carried in a bag. They soaked the mixture in a large trough of water overnight, and in the morning there was a nice yellow fertilizer for the young plants.

He'd also learned to build slug traps by cutting openings in old coffee cans whose bottoms had been filled with a solution of jelly and water. Once they were ready, they sank the cans up to the opening in the ground. The next morning they'd found dozens of dead slugs inside each can. She knew some things. He liked that. He liked to learn. Especially practical things.

Eiko was hurrying by him again. He had stopped digging and stood leaning against his shovel, catching his breath.

'Not difficult. Not difficult,' she said.

That was her answer to everything. But this was his fourth bed of mounded earth and he was beginning to tire, so he ignored her. He watched the girl, Fumiko, trotting by with two buckets suspended from the ends of a pole she carried over her shoulder. She'd been moving back and forth like this for a couple of hours. Like her mother, she was a workhorse, though an unhappy one. Even the little girls had been assigned jobs pulling weeds or straightening the rocks that bordered the pathways.

He was still leaning against his shovel as Eiko moved by him again.

'You not lazy – earth not lazy,' she said in a bright voice.

'Thanks,' he said. 'But I'm tired of digging.'

'Want happy garden.'

'Sure. Sure.'

'Earth hard. Water stand, drown rootos. Need home where rootos grow deep and plants be healthy. So you work.'

She grinned at him. 'Sky, earth and people – everyone hataraku. Work.' She held her hand palm up; he saw that it was filled with dark round seeds. 'You understand plants? Maybe little?'

He ignored the question, putting his foot on the blade of the shovel and pushing it deep into the soil. 'Why does the old man follow me around like a dog?'

She just giggled.

'Great,' Prophet said. 'Tell him to leave me alone.'

'You tell him. He no listen to me.'

'I tried.'

She shrugged as if she had lost interest in this brief conversation about her father-in-law, and pointed at the mound of freshly turned earth. 'Not difficult. Not difficult.'

Eiko had big ideas for the vegetables. And something told him she could pull most of them off – especially if he and the older girl didn't die of exhaustion first.

He went back to digging. They had been working steadily since sun-up. Pearl had brought them cool drinks and a big noon meal. She was still acting coldly reserved around him. He guessed it was over the money and the photograph and the boxing lessons.

While he might agree that she had a point over the first two, he surely didn't agree with her about the boxing – but he wasn't going to get anywhere arguing with her. She was as flexible as an anvil. Still, it seemed a heavy burden on these boys. Proof of just how heavy came an hour later, when the four of them trudged into the yard after school.

Josh had a cut cheek and Luke had a large mouse puffing under an eye. Zacharias was limping. And this time Samuel was sporting a bruised lip. They had taken a beating. Prophet felt bad, but there was nothing he could do.

They were standing near their father's grave, glancing from it to the vegetable garden. There was something lost-looking about them as they stood, bruised and battered, in the tangle of weeds and flowering plants.

'Going to work the flowers for a while,' he called to the woman.

'Not difficult. Not difficult,' she said. 'Strong man. When done – you come back. Isogu. Hurry.'

He looked at the enormous mass of tangled brush and plants, then looked back at her and shook his head. He started down the path, the old man hopping up and trotting after him like an obedient terrier. Prophet paid him no mind, hoping that he'd soon get tired of this silliness.

'Rough day?'

The three younger boys nodded.

'What do you say we clean this place up?'

Samuel turned and walked away.

'Sam?' Prophet called.

The boy didn't answer.

Zacharias came over and Prophet picked him up in his arms. 'Sam's got to take ma on her rounds,' he explained. 'That's how we make our living.'

'I see.'

'But even so,' Zacharias confided, 'I don't think we can fix the garden. Sam says it's too late.'

Prophet eyed him for a moment, then said, 'Nothing is ever too late.' He ruffled the boy's curly hair. 'What happened to your leg?'

The boy looked away from him. 'Nothing.'

'Maybe that's what you tell your mother – but not me.'

He looked back into Prophet's face. 'Harry Adams kicked me.'

'Why?'

The boy looked past him to Mr Kishimoto. The old man was standing with his little legs spread and his hands on his hips, looking like some sort of toy soldier on guard duty. Zacharias leaned close to Prophet's ear and whispered, 'What's he doing?'

'I don't know. I'm not even certain he knows.'

Zacharias thought that was funny and he grinned.

'Why did Harry kick you?'

'He called thee a bad name and I called him the same.'

Prophet pulled him close until their foreheads were touching. 'You listening?'

The boy nodded.

'Never. Never defend me,' he said, turning the boy upside down and holding him by his ankles. Zacharias was screaming with peals of laughter. 'Understand?'

'No,' Zacharias yelled, giggling.

Prophet pretended to drop him and the boy squealed again.

'Understand?'

'Mr Prophet. What are thou doing?' Pearl Eddy was tapping her way over the yard toward them.

'Just playing,' he said, smiling and setting Zacharias down on the ground.

Pearl was not smiling. 'Zacharias, thou have chores.'

'Yes, mother,' he said, turning and winking at Prophet, then trotting off toward the hen house.

Pearl let him get out of earshot. He could tell she was fighting her anger.

'We spoke about thy influence on Zacharias.'

'Yes. I can see it would be bad if he laughed a bit, Mrs Eddy.'

She started walking back toward the house. 'We have no time for idleness, Mr Prophet.'

'For fun, you mean.'

'As thou once said, sir, we see things differently.'

'That we do, Mrs Eddy.'

Samuel pulled steadily on the reins, backing Jack out of the Carlsons' darkened yard. This was the last customer on their delivery list for the day. He glanced at his mother. She was sitting in the shadows on the seat beside him looking small and clutching a new dress in her lap, and he could tell she was thinking hard about something.

She appeared lost again, the way she had the night the Negro stole the photograph. And while Samuel didn't exactly know what had happened on the Carlson's front porch, he knew she'd returned to the buggy looking dazed and carrying the new dress she had made for the Carlson's oldest girl, Ellen.

'Was it the wrong material?' he asked. That's what she'd been told when a blouse she had delivered to Mrs Jennings had been rejected. He was stunned. This had never happened in the four years that he'd been driving her.

He turned on to the road. 'Mother?'

She turned toward him as if just realizing he was there.

'I'm sorry, Samuel.'

'Was it the wrong material?' he repeated.

Pearl waited a moment longer, then said, 'No.' Her voice sounded distant. 'Mrs Carlson said she hadn't ordered any dress.'

'That's a lie,' Samuel said.

'Samuel.'

'I was there when thou talked about the color with Ellen,' he continued, a worried sound in his voice. 'She wanted red – just like thou made.'

Pearl turned back in her seat, clutching the new dress as though it were a dead child. Quickly she went over what had happened this evening, stunned by the enormity of the events.

None of the five women she'd spoken to about work for Eiko and Fumiko had been interested. It was a repeat of the night before. Each had a story about orientals who had worked for a relative or friend and who'd done something awful. Again and again Pearl had tried to talk their concerns away. It hadn't worked. She shifted uncomfortably on the buggy seat, running the tips of her fingers over the soft material of the new dress.

While those turn-downs had hurt, she'd been prepared for them. Over the past few days she'd come to the realization people weren't having the Kishimoto women in their houses, around their food, their valuables, their children.

What she hadn't been prepared for was the fact that in one evening's time, four of her seamstressing customers had not only refused to accept their orders, they had told her they didn't need anything new. She gripped the dress in her lap. She had lost four customers.

She trembled, recalling Rose Sherman's warning, 'You'll account for what you've done!' She bit at her lip. She desperately needed the money for these clothes.

She had accepted the food Prophet had brought in exchange for his room. But she knew with the work he was putting into the place he was being short-changed. She squirmed. Even so, the food he'd brought wouldn't last much longer. There were twelve people. Twelve people. The thought numbed her. She had been struggling just to keep her boys going, and that was when she had all her customers. Panic rose in her throat.

The food wouldn't last and she had no idea where she would get more. The eggs and the garden helped – but they needed to sell what they produced to pay bills. Thankfully, her garden business was flourishing. And Eiko had ideas for getting more production from the plants. But how much more? And how quickly? Her seamstressing had always been the real money-maker. Now that would have to change.

Pearl had not touched the $250. She couldn't. She was due to deliver it to Mr Snipes. That was part of what they had discussed in his office. She would deliver her $250 and take a loan against her farm for $600. The loan would be used to pay the remaining $250. The remaining $350 would pay off her other bills and provide her with living money until the gardens and her hens came into full production, and until she could rebuild her steam-stressing business. She shuddered. She had one dollar and fifty cents in her purse. All the other money she possessed in this world. And she owed almost every merchant in town. The thought of her rising debts, the loss of the house and Lillian's threat descended on her again. Yes. She had to borrow from the bank. It was the only solution.

Samuel stirred beside her. 'It's because of them.'

The words clamped on to the back of her neck like a cold hand. She hesitated a moment, then said, 'Yes.' She wouldn't lie to him. She waited for him to continue. When he didn't, she asked, 'Would thou have me turn them out?'

'Why are they our problem?'

'Because God gave them to us.'

'I don't believe that.' He slapped the reins on Jack's rump and the horse began to trot.

'Samuel.'

He reined the horse in. 'The Negro could survive,' he snapped. 'He's done it before – he's nothing but a fast talker and a thief. Thou knows he stole father's picture.' He paused. 'I don't know why he brought it back. But he's looking out for nobody but himself.'

'And who are thou looking out for, Samuel?'

The boy didn't answer.

Pearl folded the red dress neatly in her lap. Then she said, in a quiet voice, 'Please take me to the Phillipses.'

The Phillips family was one of the poorest in town. Old Rake Phillips was a giant of a man. The boys at school said he had the body of a Greek statue and the mind of one too. He cleaned out the slaughterhouse waste at night and mucked the town liveries during the day and, as a consequence, had a constant bad smell about him. His wife had been dead for a long time and he lived in a rundown house with his seventeen-year-old daughter, Sarah. Samuel glanced at the red dress and knew why they were headed to the Phillipses.

While Sarah wasn't actually ugly, Samuel thought of her as homely. And she and the red dress didn't go together somehow. She was always dressed in outfits he figured she sewed herself from cheap materials.

He let his thoughts drift, to Ellen Carlson and Fumiko. While Ellen was a beauty, Fumiko was somehow prettier, he thought. He wasn't certain what made her so. Again, he told himself it was simply because she was a foreigner. He wished she was friendlier. She was sour from the moment she got up until she disappeared at night behind the blankets his mother had draped in the barn for her. Still, she was pretty. He wished he was brave enough to say something to her directly, though he wasn't certain what he'd say.

He wiggled uncomfortably on the seat, not liking the fact that he wasn't brave enough to talk to a girl. He watched a possum scurrying along a nearby fence. But it was true – and further proof of what he was. He wondered who else knew about him.

Probably the Negro; he'd seen the man studying him in peculiar ways. And probably his mother – but she wouldn't mind. She'd just tell him wrath was one of the deadly sins. He clenched harder at the reins as they pulled up in front of the Phillipses' house.

'I couldn't, Mrs Eddy.'

'Thou certainly can, Sarah.'

'I haven't money – and I've got no use for it.'

Samuel sat in the buggy listening to them talking on the front porch of the old house. The night was cold and still and their words drifted clearly to him across the poorly kept yard. The possum was climbing the trunk of an old apple tree. At least Sarah had some common sense, he thought. She and the dress didn't go together. It would just hang in a closet. Either that or she'd look silly wearing it to school. She had no boyfriend and never went to socials, as far as he knew. She was right, the dress wasn't practical for her.

'Sarah, thou will graduate in two months,' Pearl continued. 'I have heard that thou are good with numbers. Like thy mother was.'

He had forgotten that Mrs Phillips had been a bookkeeper in town. He shook his head. His mother kept facts about folks cataloged in her mind. Not bad facts or mean ones – just facts that often came in handy.

He glanced at Sarah's tall, awkward frame as she stood bending to talk with his mother. Those must have been better years for her, he thought: having a mother at home and probably some money flowing in. Her father wasn't a bad man, he was just slow and worked so hard that Samuel thought he looked more like a beast of burden – filthy and wheelbarrowing loads of offal around town – than he did a man. He wondered what it smelled like in their little house. Pretty bad, he guessed. The boys in town called him 'the shit man'. Samuel always felt bad about that.

'I'm fair with numbers.' Sarah's voice had dropped some. Samuel knew she was shy.

Pearl paused. 'Stand up and let me see how this fits.'

Sarah straightened up awkwardly while Pearl held the dress against her. Even at a distance, Sam could tell it wasn't a bad fit.

'It's nice,' Pearl said. 'I want to take it in slightly at the waist and let down the hem some. And I think you could use a little more shoulder.'

'I can't afford it,' Sarah said, sounding like she wanted to flee back inside the little house.

'Thou doesn't have to afford it – it is thy graduation present. I want thee to wear it to graduation.' She paused. 'Then I want thee to wear it on thy job interviews.'

'Job interviews?' Sarah sounded as if she'd been slapped.

'Yes. This town has not had a bookkeeper since thy mother died.'

'My father is going to get me a job.'

'Where, child?'

'I don't know.'

Samuel could tell she was dodging. And he knew that wouldn't do with his mother. Pearl stood a good two heads shorter than the girl and Samuel watched now as she raised her arms and felt the girl's face and hair that hung down in shapeless strands. He squirmed as he always did when she touched people. It seemed so intimate and yet he knew it was the only way she could tell what they looked like. Still, it bothered him. It never bothered her.

'When thou go for thy interviews, wear thy hair up in a bun. Thou has a strong handsome face. Do not hide it.'

Samuel laughed to himself. She wasn't letting go of the job interview idea. He could have guessed his mother wouldn't let the girl go to work in the slaughterhouse without a fight.

'I don't know how,' Sarah said shyly.

'I will put it up for thee,' she continued. 'I will have the dress back in a few days. In the meantime, thou will go to the library and get a volume on bookkeeping. Promise?'

'Father has already gotten me a job.'

'I'll talk to thy father,' Pearl said firmly. 'I will also talk to Mr

Snipes at the bank and other business people in town. I am certain that with some work thou can build a nice business.' She paused. 'Sarah,' Pearl said, her voice more determined, 'thou must do this. For thyself.'

The girl looked uncomfortable again. But she didn't respond.

'Good,' Pearl said, as if Sarah, through her silence, had agreed with her.

It was Saturday and crowded on Main Street. Prophet trailed behind the three younger Eddy boys, as they headed for the general store, the old Japanese trotting behind him. The man still hadn't gotten it through his head that Prophet wanted nothing to do with him.

Prophet sneaked a glance at him out from the corner of his eye, thinking he looked damn silly in a crazy yellow outfit with long sleeves and tied like a woman's skirt around the waist. His legs were bare, making the whole thing more ridiculous. He carried his new stick tied across his back. But worst of all, he bowed like a cowed dog whenever Prophet happened to look his way. So Prophet had taken to avoiding looking directly at him.

The old man had attracted a crowd of gawkers and these were trailing along with them, making silly comments about how pretty his legs looked and whistling at him. Prophet tried to act like he wasn't with the old man – while Mr Kishimoto simply ignored them in his haughty way.

The Eddy boys had disappeared inside the general store, Prophet following. The old Japanese stopped on the sidewalk, taking up his wide-legged stance, a fierce scowl on his face – looking as if he was guarding the door to a king's palace.

'Get that Chinaman out of there!' the man behind the counter yelled to no one in particular, then he went back to a pile of paperwork.

'He's not a Chinaman, Mr Curtis. He's a Japanese,' Zacharias said proudly.

'I don't care if he's an Israelite, get him out of my doorway.'

Prophet walked out and motioned the old man over to one side. 'Stay here,' he said gruffly, as if addressing a dog. The on-lookers were watching closely, a few of them pointing openly at his face. Prophet paid no attention.

The old man bowed.

'And knock that off,' he hissed.

Mr Kishimoto bowed again.

'Hey look, Othello's got himself a nigger. And she's wearing a skirt,' somebody yelled from the back of the crowd. The whole lot of them roared.

Prophet ignored them, reminding himself that he'd only come to town to make certain the boys bought the thread their mother needed and made it home without being thrashed. It wasn't the time or place to start a riot over name-calling. He went back inside, pulling the last of his money out.

'Like to see what you have in shoes,' Prophet said.

The man behind the counter looked up from his paperwork and visibly drew in his breath. Prophet was used to the reaction.

The man squinted at him a moment, then asked, 'What size you wear?'

'For the boys.'

An hour later, he had the three little Eddys situated at a table near the front window of a dingy place called the Lantern House. They were wearing new straw hats and shoes, and Prophet was feeling good about things. He watched the woman bringing them their lunch and he could tell from their excitement that they weren't used to buying meals out. It made him feel extra good.

He leaned back against the bar and took a long drink of beer, letting his eyes drift over the men playing poker at a rear table, then out the front window at the gawkers eyeing the old Jap. As usual, the tiny man had stationed himself close to the door and was acting out his annoying palace guard routine, eyeing every-one as if they were assassins.

Prophet didn't see Pearl Eddy making her way through the crowd, but the boys did, and they darted out of the saloon like frightened cats. Zacharias left so quickly he forgot his new hat on the chair. Prophet shook his head and turned back to the bar, taking a long pull on his beer.

She was good at spoiling fun. Prophet ran his hands admiringly over his new suit. He'd ordered it from Kansas City and had just picked it up, discarding his old clothes in a trash bin behind the dry goods store. He stretched his sore muscles, realizing how hard he'd been working for the little oriental woman, and determined to have his beer and to enjoy himself in the sanctuary of the saloon. Then he heard Pearl Eddy's voice.

'Where is Mr Prophet?'

She didn't sound happy.

'In there,' Josh said meekly.

'Mr Prophet.'

He was facing the bar, determined to ignore her.

'Mr Prophet – I know thou are in there.'

'Another beer,' he said, smiling at the bartender.

The man tipped his head in the direction of the door. 'Mrs Eddy wants you.'

'She can wait.'

The man shrugged and started to pull the beer.

'Mr Prophet.'

'I'm busy,' he called over his shoulder.

The bartender was knocking the head off the second beer when the saloon's doors screeched and the tapping of Pearl Eddy's cane started across the floor. Prophet turned, unable to believe what he saw. She was standing inside the saloon and looking very angry. Angry or not, no self-respecting woman entered this kind of establishment.

'Mr Prophet,' she repeated, turning her head to try to locate the sound of him, her lips pressed hard together.

'Damn,' he said, slamming some coins down on the counter and grabbing a paper bag off the floor. He took her by the elbow and hurried her out on to the sidewalk. The crowd backed away.

'You can't go in a place like that,' he hissed.

'And why not?' she snapped. 'Thou took my boys in there!'

'That's different.'

'It certainly is not. That is a house for gambling and liquor.' She paused. 'And other things, I presume.' She stammered for a moment, her hands on her youngest's shoulders. 'How could thou do such a thing?'

He watched her for a few moments, the crowd pressing in around them. Then he said, 'Zach, here's your hat.' He held it out to the boy but Pearl reached and took it, feeling the new straw material. He could see her stiffen.

'What else did thou buy?'

'Shoes.' He paused. 'They needed them.'

'Mr Prophet, I told thee that I would not accept thy charity.'

'They need shoes,' he said stiffly.

'These don't hurt my feet,' Zacharias said.

This seemed to stop her and she waited a moment, then continued. 'We will discuss it later.'

Prophet started toward the buggy.

'Mr Prophet, I asked thee a question.'

'About?'

'Why thou would take my boys into a saloon.'

He shifted awkwardly, the crowd pressing in around him. 'It's the only place in town where a Negro can order a meal – and I wanted to treat the boys,' he said in a quiet voice.

Pearl looked stunned by some unseen blow, her face turning red. She held her cane in both hands and looked like she didn't know what to say, as if she might stand on this sidewalk in the middle of the gaggle of onlookers for the rest of her life. Then she said, 'I see. I'm certain the food is good.'

'It's decent,' he said.

'Yes. I'm certain it is,' she said quickly. 'Let's go home.'

As they started down the steps, old man Kishimoto darted ahead of them, his stick held diagonally across his body like a soldier clearing a path for officers. The crowd backed away from his menacing glower.

'Knock that off,' Prophet snapped.

The old man stopped and bowed, then fell in behind them. They were nearing the buggy now and a small collection of men who were hooting and whistling.

'What are they whistling at?' Pearl asked.

'My new clothes,' he said.

Before Prophet knew what she was doing, Pearl had stopped and with professional curiosity was running her hands over his new suit – over his chest, down the sleeves, feeling the material and the exaggerated cut of the lapels and shoulders.

'Get your hands off me,' he hissed. The laughter of the crowd had stopped as if someone had pointed a loaded cannon at them. The silence: sudden and unnerving.

'What's the matter?'

'People are watching,' he whispered.

Prophet tossed the paper bag in the back and hurried Pearl and the boys into the buggy, trying to act like a hired hand. But it was too late. Pearl Eddy had made a mistake – the kind of mistake that changes life.

The church bell tolled eleven o'clock, the sound drifting across the prairie stillness like something lost. Everyone but Prophet was asleep or headed there. He stood and picked up the paper bag and climbed the steps to where the boys had lined their new shoes against the wall.

Samuel's old ones were in their accustomed place at the head of the line. Prophet opened the bag and pulled out a new black pair. Unlike his old high-tops, these were for a man, plain-toed, low-cut and laced. He set them down and went back to his seat on the steps.

He was cold now and told himself so, but he didn't move. He had been sitting on the back steps of the house for the past hour, wondering where everything was headed. No place good, he figured. He tipped his head back and watched an almost full moon riding high over the darkened prairie landscape, seemingly escorted by bright white clouds. The dark flickering shapes of bats stitched through the air above.

The surrounding yard was still in a curious way, the silence broken only by the soft snoring of the old Japanese sitting in the dirt a few feet away. Perhaps it was this sound that tugged him from his thoughts, focusing his mind on a new and distant sound, slight but urgent. He stood slowly, but it was gone. He took a step down, then waited.

He was starting to turn back to the house – tired and ready for sleep – convinced that he'd been mistaken, when the tiny noise came to him once more. It was sharper and more desperate-sounding this time, coming from the direction of the barn and sheds.

Prophet grabbed the hammer he'd been working with earlier and jumped down off the steps, breaking into a run, followed just as quickly by Mr Kishimoto brandishing his stick.

Prophet was out of breath and dragging his foot badly when he reached the corner of the barn, kicking himself for not keeping his roadwork up. He stopped, peering at the surrounding shadows and standing absolutely still, ears straining to hear. Nothing. One of the little girls coughed inside the barn, the sound at once peaceful and disarming. He relaxed some, wondering if he'd simply heard some creature taken by an owl. He didn't think so, but wasn't certain why he felt this way.

He moved his gaze over the shadowy shapes of the sheds, peering carefully into the darker openings of the doorways. Nothing seemed out of place. He was moving slowly along the side of the barn – the old man following annoyingly close behind – when he heard it again: a shrill cry that raised goosebumps on the back of his neck. It had come from one of the sheds behind the barn. Somebody or something was hurt. The old man mumbled a few words in the darkness.

'Hush,' Prophet said, canting his head to catch any new sounds that would explain what was happening. But the cry was gone, as if snatched from the night sky by some invisible hand. Then he thought he heard a stirring in the smallest of the three sheds and faced toward it, taking a better grip on the hammer. The old Japanese said something else.

Prophet turned to reprimand him, and saw him pointing at the largest of the three sheds. Prophet shook his head and pointed his own finger at the smallest. The old man shook his head vigorously. Prophet was just starting to tell him he was wrong as hell when something banged hard against the wall of the bigger building. Kishimoto bowed.

'OK – OK,' Prophet said, irritated that the old man had been right. 'Just keep your mouth shut.'

He moved forward carefully, stopping outside the door and waiting. It sounded quiet enough inside – maybe too quiet – maybe quiet like a trap. He took a couple of deep breaths and saw the little man doing the same. The old Jap was a fighter, pure and simple, Prophet would give him that. Work might be beneath him, but a brawl in a dark shed was right up his alley.

He gave Kishimoto the professional courtesy of nodding when he was ready to move, the old Japanese nodding back. As annoying as he was, the tiny man knew about fighting. Prophet drew another breath, then put his hand on the door and shoved it open and went in fast. He swept the black air in front of him with a hard swing of the hammer, then backed quickly against the closest wall, ready for anything that might come at him.

The old Jap had followed fast behind him, he was sure of that, but he couldn't locate him anywhere in the dark air surrounding him. The tiny man was waiting silently in the same way he was. He just hoped he wouldn't make a mistake and clobber him with his damn stick. Something told him he wouldn't.

He held his breath, probing the darkness for sound. Nothing. He could sense something in the room besides the old Jap and himself but there was still no noise or movement. A few seconds later, Prophet heard Kishimoto yell 'Ei!' and the swishing of his stick, these sounds followed by a loud snapping noise and a pained yelp. Then it was silent again.

Prophet pulled a match from his pocket and struck it. They were standing in the chicken shed surrounded by piles of dead and injured hens, feathers floating everywhere. Kishimoto was off to his right, crouched and looking ready to take on the Mexican Army if need be – something lying motionless at his feet. The match burned his finger and he blew it out.

He struck another. In its light he saw that the old man had killed a dog coyote with a blow from his stick. How, Prophet wondered, had he done that in the pitch-black interior of the shed? Luck, he guessed.

Before the third match had expired, Prophet had counted thirty-two dead or injured hens, and that was just the beginning. The coyote had gone on a killing frenzy. The old man was dispatching the worst of the injured birds with his hands. Then Prophet saw the rooster, Hercules, wedged defiantly in the corner and the old Jap grabbing at him. The third match went out.

'No!' Prophet yelled, hurrying to strike another. 'Don't!' In the light of the next match, Prophet saw the little man looking at him with a puzzled expression, his small hand grasping the bloody neck of Hercules. Prophet held up his hand. 'Don't,' he said again. He lit the lantern that was hanging near the shed door.

The old rooster was in bad shape. The coyote had taken a bite out of his side and one wing was hanging broken and useless. Prophet took him from Kishimoto and examined him closely in the lantern's blaze. Nothing else seemed broken and the bleeding had fortunately stopped. Still, he looked half-dead. He didn't relish telling Zacharias.

While he was running his hands over the bird, the rooster raised his head and took an exhausted peck at his hand.

'I should have let him finish you – you ungrateful bastard.'

The old bird's hackles rose defiantly.

'Don't start with me!' Prophet snapped. 'You're in no condition to start anything.'

*

The James home was not what a person expected after meeting the Jameses. Expensive English and American furniture was grouped comfortably around a fireplace, and there were other soft touches of refinement – light lace on a pillow in a wing chair, wintry needlepoint designs, pink ruffles. These were faint remembrances of Simon James's wife. He had changed nothing after she left.

The men trooped quietly in through the foyer. They regularly held the Royal Order of the Redmen meetings here in the musty-smelling parlor, perfecting their plans to build a lodge bigger than the new Masonic Temple, discussing political candidates and government issues, planning events and fund-raisers. And when necessary, they also determined the Order's disciplines and punishments for certain people in the town. These were secretly carried out by the War Clan of the Redmen under Simon's direction. If severe enough, Simon usually led it himself. Patriots, the Redmen were dedicated to shared ideals of democracy and religion – each man sworn to take care of the others in time of need, to protect their town and institutions.

The men were watching Simon as he sat on the sofa, gently stroking the hair of his sleeping daughter. Then Cleopatra, Chrissy's big yellow cat, dropped off the top of the sofa, curling up on the girl's chest. Chrissy's breath stirred the yellow fur. Simon ran his hand over the cat's back. None of the men in the room moved to seat themselves – the secret oaths and fellowship signs had been exchanged and a deep quiet fell over the parlor.

Simon studied the faces of the men in the soft yellow lamplight like a general inspecting his troops before battle, his thoughts drifting back to the killing of the orientals' little pig. He had led that effort because he was the Supreme Chief of the Redmen. It had been his place – and he disliked Chinese. But this was different. This bore the seeds of a real threat.

The woman had turned her home into a sty for aliens – and immigration was an institution opposed by the Redmen. Worse, she had become intimate with the Negro, no better than the curs she succored.

They had taken up a collection and bought her $50 worth of trouble the other night. Unfortunately, the men they'd hired had been tramps, and they had been bested by the Negro. The thought of this – the Negro thwarting the Redmen a second time – caused his stomach to churn and gas to put pressure on his lungs. Forcing himself to calm down, he pulled a comforter over his daughter – Cleopatra snuggling closer into the sleeping girl's face. Simon cleared his throat and said, 'Thank you, brothers, for coming.'

He walked to the window and looked out at the clear night sky for a few minutes, studying the moon through the trees. Then he turned back and faced them. 'Some of you saw what happened on the street today.'

No one had yet noticed Chrissy.

The night was still with cold; enough so that the clothes on the line were stiff and Pearl had decided not to collect them. She stood motionless in the darkness, listening toward the hen house. Nothing. Mr Prophet and Mr Kishimoto had finished killing the last of the injured hens. She shivered; numb with loss.

Samuel was standing next to her, his hands gripping a large clothes basket. He set it down and shoved his hands into his pants pockets to keep them warm, then tipped his head back so he could stare at the black canopy of sky. He wondered what was up there. Wondered if any of what his mother said about it was true. Around them the tall grasses were swaying as if acknowledging the seriousness of what had happened here this night.

While his mother had never shared her worries with him, he'd known for a long time that things were bad. And he knew they'd been aggravated by the burden of the Kishimotos and the Negro. Now he was sensing the situation had perhaps been made precarious by the slaughter of the hens.

'What will we do?' he asked quietly.

Pearl turned to him as if she'd been distracted from some deep thought.

'What will we do?' he repeated.

'Wait upon the Lord for guidance.'

'Fine. But what else?'

'That will be enough.'

Samuel was starting to object when they heard the sound of a buggy charging wildly down the dark prairie road toward the farm. Someone was screaming: 'Mrs Eddy! Mrs Eddy! She's dying!'

Hector's cry had not been an exaggeration. Chrissy was almost gone by the time Pearl was brought into the Jameses' dining room. Simon was sitting in a chair beside her, holding his head between his hands and crying, while Mike and Dr Trotter tried desperately to give Chrissy a mixture of whiskey and tea.

Pearl sensed impending death in the room and battled her emotions trying to hear the girl. Nothing. She was barely struggling for air. Choking slowly. She put her fingers to the girl's carotid artery. The pulse was weak and fading. Eiko had come with her and she moved alongside the girl now.

'Doctor?'

'It's no use, Pearl,' Trotter sighed, turning his head from the table where Chrissy lay gurgling her last. 'They tried to handle it themselves.'

Pearl could smell the mullein smoke and the sharper odor of eucalyptus oil in the hot, humid air of the room.

'Ohhh, Chrissy,' Pearl moaned. She stood holding the girl's hand in her own. 'Peace to thee, child. God loves thee.'

'Shut up!' Simon screamed. 'She's not dead.' Then he saw Eiko. The woman was bent over and searching through her bag. 'What is that Chinese whore doing in my house? Get her out!'

Trotter whirled around and faced the man. 'Simon, at least have the decency to let your daughter pass in peace.'

'She's not dying!'

Eiko had found what she was looking for, standing up with a long bamboo box and leaning over the girl. She took the child's hand away from Pearl and straightened her limp body out flat on the table. Then she hurried to stand at the top of the girl's head and checked her alignment, squinting and shoving on one of her shoulders until the body was where she thought it should be. Then suddenly Simon lunged and grabbed her by the arm.

'I'll kill you if you touch her again – you damn yellow bitch!'

Eiko wrestled free of Simon's grasp. 'Leave me alone, man. She not dead yet. Leave me alone.'

Hector, Mike and Dr Trotter succeeded in pulling the enraged man back across the room, forcing him into a chair. Then they heard Penny James.

'You heard my father – get away from Chrissy.' He was pointing a heavy revolver at Eiko and speaking quietly, something deadly in his tone.

Pearl turned and stepped between Eiko and the man.

Eiko was ignoring the whole thing, concentrating hard on Chrissy's prostrate form, as if visualizing something that none of the rest of them could see. Then she removed a small three-inch-long needle from the bamboo box and bent over the girl.

'I'll kill you before I'll let you work your damn voodoo on her.' Simon's voice was cold and distilled-sounding, as if he had been saving up the drippings of his hatred over many years and was concentrating it now in his words.

'You kill – go ahead, man. You kill,' Eiko challenged, leaning in closer over the girl and rechecking the body's alignment. Chrissy's face was bluing now. Eiko took a deep breath and inserted the needle in her neck. Then she moved down to the girl's waist, pulled out another needle and stuck it into her hand. Everyone was watching, not certain what the woman was doing.

'Eiko?' Pearl asked.

'I working. No bother now.' Eiko was busy sticking pins in various locations around the girl's torso.

The noise of the pistol's hammer locking in the stillness of the room made everyone jump – everyone but Eiko. The woman continued to stick needles into the girl as if she were oblivious to everything else around her.

'Don't do it, Pen–'

Dr Trotter's voice was cut off by another sound: a piercing 'Eiii!' And suddenly Penny James was crumbling unconscious to the floor, the pistol sliding harmlessly over the carpet.

Then Mr Kishimoto was standing in his funny squat-legged stance brandishing his shiny staff in a menacing way at the rest of the Jameses. He had been followed into the room by Prophet who stooped now and picked up the weapon.

'You boys just sit tight,' Prophet said. 'Or Mighty Mite here will split your skulls.'

'Mr Prophet!' Pearl snapped. 'What are thou doing?'

'Wasn't me,' he said quickly. 'It was the old man.'

'Must thou always try and shift the blame to others?'

'Fine, Mrs Eddy,' he mumbled as if it wasn't worth arguing with her about. 'I just came to see if you needed any help and the old man followed along.'

'We do not.'

'I can see that,' Prophet said, shaking his head and looking around the room at the sweating fat man being restrained by his sons, then at the unconscious form of Penny James and the heavy pistol he'd been threatening to use. He shook his head. 'Yep. I can see you've got everything under control.'

'Nor do we need thy sarcasm, Mr Prophet. This child is fighting for her life.'

'Yes, ma'am.'

'My God,' Trotter gasped.

Prophet turned to see the James girl struggling to sit up and gasping for breath. She looked awful, needles sticking out of her in a dozen places.

Eiko clapped her hands together like a mechanical monkey. 'Good girl. Good girl. Big breathe. Big breathe.'

Simon and his two younger boys were bawling like babies. When he figured Pearl was preoccupied, Prophet bent over and pulled Penny James up bodily by his coat front and threw him hard into a large chair causing it to slide backwards over the floor. Mr Kishimoto was after him in a flash, standing at the ready in front of the man.

Trotter couldn't take his eyes off of the needles. He looked dazed, as if he'd just witnessed the raising of Lazarus.

'What are those things?'

'Those hari,' Eiko grinned. 'Needles.'

'But what did you do?'

'I poke yin-yang line. Arm sunlight yang. So girl breathe. Make good sense to you?' Eiko was nodding up and down vigorously as if consulting with a fellow physician. 'Make good sense, no?'

Trotter could not stop shaking his head. Pearl soon joined the Jameses in crying over Chrissy. Eiko continued to babble on about yin and yang. Old man Kishimoto just stood waiting for Penny James to make a wrong move. And Prophet scratched his head.

CHAPTER ELEVEN

Pearl had counted on the sale of the eggs for months, until it had become a mental insurance policy, one she'd dreamed would ultimately save her and the boys. But now with half the flock gone, that dream evaporated like mist in summer sunlight. There was no question left, she would have to borrow from the bank to keep going. To keep Lillian at bay. She shivered at the thought, wondering why Snipes had not sent word that he was coming to inspect the farm.

Pearl slowly lowered the bucket into the well, letting her thoughts drift. Though there had been problems, the two weeks since the slaughter of the hens had brought good things as well. Hercules had survived. The old bird hobbled around now with a permanently crippled wing that dragged pathetically along the ground, but his fierce pride remained unbroken. And in the garden there was a flamboyant explosion of new growth, spurred by warming weather and Mrs Kishimoto's care, growth so luxuriant that it promised to replace the revenues of the dead hens.

But it couldn't compensate for her lost seamstressing clients. She had only three steady customers left. The thought made her tremble. But again, there had been offsetting gifts of dispensation.

At the urging of Eiko, she had sold the silver frame and had purchased twenty-five young shoats to be fattened on the surrounding prairies, until the corn that Prophet had planted under Eiko's watchful eye could be harvested. Eiko claimed she was good with pigs – and Pearl believed her.

As she cranked a bucket of water out of the well, she reminded herself that things weren't half bad. God had seen fit to take, but He had also given, in all His glorious abundance. Pearl figured that Prophet and the Kishimotos were part of His gift . . . even if Samuel and the town didn't agree.

'Get lost – both of you!' Pearl heard Prophet order.

She smiled and picked up the bucket and started back toward the house.

'I'm warning you both – I'm sick of this,' Prophet continued. 'If I'd wanted kids – I'd have had kids.'

Again Pearl's face broke into a smile. The man was magical in his way, she thought. Zacharias and the other younger children followed him, Mr Kishimoto followed him, and now, after his recovery, so did Hercules. She didn't understand it. The man certainly didn't encourage it. He threatened and complained but it didn't seem to matter.

'Why don't you follow each other, you enjoy it so,' he grumbled, stepping over the rooster and heading for the barn. Undaunted, the bird and the little man trailed faithfully along.

Prophet squatted and began to rifle through a box of tools, pulling things out and setting them aside, until he found what he was looking for. He started to shut the lid on the box but Hercules had stuck his head inside and was carefully examining its contents.

'Do you mind?'

The old bird pulled his head out, standing with his legs spread and his head tipped, eyeing the man. His broken wing was hanging limply on the ground and Prophet noticed that all the dragging had rubbed the edge raw. He was going to ignore it, but couldn't. He stooped and before the bird knew what had happened Prophet had grabbed him up, holding him tight against his chest as the bird struggled.

'Knock it off,' Prophet warned, disappearing into the tackroom next to the barn. Mr Kishimoto took up guard duty at the door.

*

Daylight was fading when Prophet finally came out of the shed, still holding the squawking rooster tight in his arms. He squatted. Mr Kishimoto squatted.

'Behave yourself,' Prophet warned.

He held the rooster out at arm's length like he was a lit stick of dynamite, then let him go. While Hercules hadn't attacked him since he'd saved him, Prophet didn't trust him. The old bird didn't move for a moment. Then he tried to flap his wings. Only one came up – the other was held neatly against his body by a new leather harness that Prophet had fashioned for him.

'How's that?' he asked.

The bird turned his head and pecked at the leather a couple of times, then began to stride around with some of his old arrogance.

'Good,' Prophet said, heading back toward the barn. 'I did you a favor – now do me one. Get lost.'

Old Mr Kishimoto trotted behind him in his odd quick-step, followed by Hercules. Prophet shook his head. Short of murder, there didn't seem any way to get rid of them.

'That's silly, Lillian.' Pearl was dumbfounded.

'It's what I've heard.' The woman, Lillian Parker, paused. 'You have them tending your vegetables.'

'Mrs Kishimoto is a wonder in the garden,' she said hopefully.

'I don't doubt it.'

Something in the woman's tone snagged at Pearl. 'Lillian?'

'I wouldn't say anything excepting I'm worried for you and your boys.'

Pearl held her breath and waited.

'You know why those vegetables grow so fast, don't you, Pearl?'

She shook her head 'no', sensing from Lillian's tone that she didn't want to hear what was about to be said.

'They fertilize them,' the woman whispered, as if she'd just let Pearl in on some black secret of the universe.

'We all do.'

'Not their way.'

'Lillian?'

'With human droppings.'

'Lillian!'

'So help me God.' She flashed Pearl an all-knowing look. 'My husband says whenever they need to go – so to speak – they squat right in the field or in a bucket and save it to put on the plants later. I wouldn't dare feed that to my family.'

Pearl was no longer listening to her. She was having a hard time getting her breath.

The sun was dipping toward the wide horizon as Prophet and Zacharias stood in the field beyond the garden looking at the strange plants that the shoats were rooting out of the mulch. Mr Kishimoto was squatting nonchalantly a few yards behind, picking his yellowed teeth with a small stick, while Hercules scratched busily in the dirt nearby. Prophet knelt and took a closer look at them, Zacharias standing by his shoulder.

'What are they?'

'I don't know – I just know my pa ordered them from somewhere far away, and when they arrived we planted them. Took us almost a month there were so many. That was a couple of years ago.'

'Need to work – need to work,' Mrs Kishimoto called impatiently to him from the vegetable garden. When Prophet didn't acknowledge her, she trotted over as if to roust him out of his lethargy, then spied the little withered plants and squatted beside him. She was squinting her eyes. A moment later, she looked up and her face broke into a smile.

'What?'

'Hayberries.'

'Huh?'

'Right – that's what pa said,' Zacharias smiled. 'Strawberries and good to eat.' Then the boy frowned. 'But we never got but a few scrawny ones. They didn't come to nothing.'

Prophet ran his fingers over one of the desiccated-looking

tendrils. The little plants were putting out runners in all directions and small buds were forming on the stems. He ran his eyes over the field: row after row of them.

Eiko was sucking her teeth as if she'd just had a sumptuous meal, a habit he'd come to learn meant she was thinking about something. Prophet turned his attention to the woman. She looked excited.

'If they weren't half-dead, would they be any good?'

Eiko sucked her teeth again and said something in Japanese. The old man answered her as if he couldn't care less. She began pulling the straw off one plant, then the next. 'Oishii berry. Good berry.'

'These?' His voice was sceptical.

'Waking up,' she said, as if talking to herself. 'Need water and seed of cotton,' she mumbled, continuing to uncover the rows. 'Get!' she hollered at a shoat digging his nose among the little plants. She darted after him, giving him a hard kick on the rump and driving the lot of them squealing from the field. She trotted back and hunched down again.

Prophet made some quick calculations. There was some four acres of them, and from the spacing between them he guessed 5,000 plants. Five thousand plants!

'Valuable?'

'Plenty.' She held up her thumb and said, 'Grow two times bigger.' She smacked her lips, then asked the little man something.

'Cashee,' he muttered, as if the effort was too much for him.

She nodded vigorously. 'Hai – cashee crop.'

'That's what pa said, too, that they'd bring us cash. But they never did much.'

Eiko ignored the comment, clucking to herself in a satisfied way like a hen with a new brood of chicks.

'They don't look so hot to me,' Prophet said.

'Just leave winter.' She sucked her teeth some more. 'Good plants.' Then she was scurrying along the rows and pulling the rotting mulch off plant after plant. He had been right – there were thousands of them.

Prophet was helping now, his enthusiasm waxing. 'How much do these produce?'

'Much.' She knelt and stuck a finger into the dirt near one of the plants, frowning when she pulled it out. 'Need water.'

They watered until Prophet was about to drop and it was too dark to see and they were in danger of trampling the plants' weedlike creepers. Then and only then, Eiko called a halt to the work. Prophet hung back, waiting until she and the children had left. Then he stood in the darkness staring at the field of strawberries and thinking. There was a chance. Not much, but perhaps.

The old Japanese squatted patiently behind him, as if he had nothing in the world he'd rather be doing.

'Contaminated? With what?'

Prophet was helping Pearl and Samuel unload the last baskets of unsold vegetables from the buggy. The boy crawled up on to the seat and clucked to the horse, heading slowly through the darkness toward the barn. Prophet had seen him angry before but never like this: he looked physically stunned. The boy blamed him for what was happening to them. And Prophet figured he was partly right.

Pearl bent and picked up a heavy basket of young zucchini. Prophet took it from her. She looked weak and disoriented, as if she didn't know what to do next.

'Contaminated with what?'

'Waste,' she said, in a hollow-sounding way.

'What kind of nonsense is that?' He was angry. 'What waste?'

'Urine and feces.'

Prophet was taken back. Polite and proper about everything – angry if somebody swore a little word like damn – here she was boldly using words like urine and feces. He couldn't figure her – but that didn't keep the blood from rising to his face and he looked away, embarrassed.

Pearl hadn't moved, she was staring into the shadows in her sightless way. Prophet struggled to regain his composure and cleared his throat. 'Why would they think that?'

'Lillian Parker says people have seen the Kishimotos in our garden defecating on the plants to fertilize them.'

There she was again – bold as Jupiter. But the problem was far worse than her language. Nothing seemed to go right for this woman. Nothing at all. And he was a big part of the reason.

'That's crazy,' he mumbled finally.

'No one will buy now,' she said softly. She looked exhausted and as close to defeat as he'd ever seen her. This latter thing bothered him greatly. He wanted to say something to cheer her but couldn't figure what it might be.

She had lost her husband. She had lost her eyes. He'd watched her take one tumble after another trying to help people – himself and the Chinamen, the man who'd attacked her. And all she'd gotten in return was her nose bloodied. Even so, she had always bounced back up. But looking at her now, he doubted she would again. She was too far gone. There were some things even a fighter with heart couldn't do. She'd had her run. It was too bad.

Then she turned and looked in his direction and smiled and he knew he'd underestimated her again. 'What's funny?' he asked.

'Just how things work out.'

'Don't see that they have.'

'In some ways.'

'How so?'

'I had been wondering how we were going to sell more vegetables and still feed the family and others who need help.' She smiled again. 'Now we don't have to worry.'

He looked at her to see if she was making a joke, then realized she was not. He shook his head. 'Yeah, what a lucky break losing your vegetable business like that. It happened just in the nick of time.'

She started for the porch. 'Please don't be cynical, Mr Prophet.'

'I wasn't, I was being practical.'

'It sounded like the same thing,' she said, locating the stairs with the tip of her cane and starting up.

Prophet watched her as she stood at the top of the steps thinking about her problems. He was thinking, too. About her lack of common sense. He could feel trouble itching his skin like a wool blanket and he didn't like the sensation.

After he'd placed the last basket up on the porch, he turned and faced her. She seemed to be taking in the night air. 'What are you going to do?'

'Make dinner.'

He frowned. 'That's not what I meant.'

She held out her hands and he handed her a basket filled with lettuce, examining her face in the lamplight that spilled on to the porch from the kitchen. She was pretty but not smart.

'Things will work out,' she said.

'How?'

She walked slowly toward the back door. 'I'm not certain – but they will.' She paused. 'They do in right causes.'

'Keeping me and a bunch of Chinamen isn't some right cause – it's just plain rashness. And I'll be going. They ought to as well.'

Pearl turned fast and he could see that her temper had flared again. It made him feel better.

'Mr Prophet: the Kishimotos are Japanese, not a bunch of Chinamen. And while thou can leave if thou wish, they do not have thy abundant choices.'

'They've got enough.' He stopped talking and listened to the tapping of her small foot. 'If I was you I'd watch attaching a moral to everything. It isn't healthy.'

'Thou are not me, sir. And, as a minister, I am surprised at what thou preaches.'

'This isn't about me,' he said quickly. 'This is about you and foolishness. You've got no call doing these things.'

'Thou are wrong.'

'About?'

'My having no call, as thee put it.'

'Meaning?'

'We are called.' She emphasized the word 'we'. 'Each one of us – to establish God's kingdom,' she said with an edge to her voice. Then she turned, the basket on her hip, and tapped her way into the kitchen.

'Like I said, you got to stop with the morals,' he called after her. She didn't respond.

He stood watching her through the open door a moment then spun around and ran into Mr Kishimoto. 'I thought we had an understanding! You were going to keep out of my way – wasn't that our deal?'

'Hai!' the old man said, bowing hard.

'Then do it! Just do it,' he ordered, stomping off toward the strawberry field.

The old man shuffled along behind him, trying to maintain a three-pace distance as they headed for the strawberry field. Prophet ignored him.

From Pearl's back porch Judge Wilkins and Edward Johnson could see the lanterns moving in the distant darkness and they watched the shadows cast by the Negro and the oriental woman as they worked building a fence. From their expressions, the men might have been staring at lepers. Pearl was standing on the porch next to them. The Eddy boys were out back feeding and watering Jack and the pigs. A gust of night wind rose and whipped Pearl's long gray dress around her legs, the air cool and smelling of the verdant growth of the prairie. Spring had arrived.

She sensed something wrong in the men's silence, something more than their belief that she was stubborn to have done what she'd done. Steamy smells of cooking wafted out on to the porch.

'Gentlemen, I have fresh vegetable soup.'

Neither man answered.

'Judge?'

Edward and the judge had been friends of her husband. Together they'd organized Liberty's first chess club and spent many a night playing and arguing in her parlor.

'No, thank you, Pearl,' the judge said, taking a long draw on the cigarette he held in his bony hand.

Pearl didn't care for the tone of his voice.

'Edward?'

The attorney looked away from the moving lights and studied her features for a moment. 'Pearl, you've got the problem the judge was talking about the other evening on the road.'

'What problem?'

'There's talk your place has been turned into –' He stopped and looked at the old man, as if hoping he'd pick up the conversation for him. Judge Wilkins let out the smoke he was holding in a long breath, watching the wind moving through the trees at the far end of the garden. He made no move to assist the younger man.

'Into what, Edward?'

'An opium parlor. That the Asian women are for –' He stopped again.

'Yes?' Her tone shifted.

'Sale.' He shuffled his feet uncomfortably, then rushed ahead. 'That you've taken up with a black man, intimate with him in public. That you're unfit as a mother.'

'None of those things are true,' she said.

'No. But still it's a problem.'

'For others perhaps,' she said stiffly.

'No,' Judge Wilkins said quickly. 'For you and your boys.' He tossed his cigarette out on to the dirt behind the porch and turned toward her, pulling his large coat tightly around him. 'It's essential that you get rid of these people, Pearl Eddy. And quickly.' He had a gruff way about him normally, but now his tone was almost commanding.

Having known Pearl for more than a decade, the men were not

surprised when they heard the small, steady sound of her foot tapping against the boards of the porch.

'Being stubborn won't work this time, Pearl,' the judge continued. 'It's essential.'

She was silent for a moment. 'Judge, there are only two things essential in this world: God and the human heart.'

'Don't start your religious palaver, young woman. You're just being stubborn, and you must not be.' He stopped and struck a match to a second cigarette, hacking as he drew the smoke into his lungs. 'People are at risk – because of what you're doing.'

Pearl didn't respond, just continued tapping her foot.

'Don't ignore me, Pearl Eddy. You've put people at risk. Your boys, these people, Edward.'

'Edward?'

The attorney looked uncomfortable to be included.

'He stands for re-election in less than one hundred days. What do you think his chances will be if he's suspected of supporting this kind of riff-raff?' he said, pointing off toward the field. 'The sheriff, all the town council, Doc Trotter is running for county coroner. All these people are afraid to get mixed up with silliness and riff-raff like that,' he said, nodding his thin head toward the moving lanterns and blowing smoke out his nose.

A muscle had begun to twitch under Pearl's eye and she reached up a hand and touched it. It wouldn't stop. 'Judge Wilkins,' she said slowly, her voice lowered. 'Thou and I are friends, therefore, I excuse thy choice of words.'

'Of course, Pearl. I apologize. What we're talking about isn't riff-raff,' he hesitated, then quickly said, 'it's outrageous behavior, young woman. If you were my granddaughter I wouldn't tolerate . . .'

'Judge,' Edward intervened. 'Pearl, all we're trying to say is that this problem isn't going away on its own.'

Pearl was still tapping her foot. 'Edward, let me repeat: I don't have a problem. The problem is elsewhere.'

'Nevertheless, it's a problem.'

'For others, perhaps.'

'No, for you and your boys,' Edward emphasized.

'That's crazy reasoning,' the judge snapped. 'It's absolutely essential you get rid of these people, Pearl Eddy,' his tone more frustrated than before. He pursed his thin lips and looked her up and down for a few moments, his small gray eyes squinting to slits in exasperation. Then he seemed to seize upon an idea that would surely convince her. He hacked a cigarette cough, clearing his throat. 'Pearl, listen. A murderer comes into your house and threatens to kill you. Understand?'

She nodded, still tapping her foot.

'It's a problem, correct? A problem whether you invited him in or he broke in. Correct? It's a problem whether you admit it or not. Correct? No matter what you do or think – it's still a problem. So you deal with it. You escape. You shoot him. You knock him over the head. It doesn't matter. The point is: you deal with the problem.'

'No,' was all she said.

'Yes! Yes! Yes! It's a problem.'

'Only if I accept it as a problem. And even if I did – which I'm not – I would not shoot or strike him.'

The judge stared at her pretty face in the weak light of the moon, squinting harder and looking like he was going to burst. 'I'm going to use those words, silliness and riff-raff, again, Pearl, so I best be going. Edward.'

The men stopped at the bottom of the stairs. 'The town is against this, Pearl,' the judge said, looking up at her. 'Maybe a few agree with you – but I suspect those brave souls haven't beaten a path to your house to help out. And I promise you they won't.' He paused. 'You're standing alone.' The gruffness was gone from his voice, replaced by a tone of concern. 'You think about what we've said. Edward and I came as old friends. But you've got to save yourself. We can't do it for you.' He paused and looked around at the house and barn like he was looking at the inside of

Satan's living room. 'Edward is taking a chance coming out here to warn you. He's got kids of his own.'

The judge started for the buggy, then he turned back. He looked hot again. 'When they come for you, lassie, I won't stand up for you. No one else will either. And, Pearl, they'll come for you. Make no mistake.'

He turned back to the buggy. Edward waited until he was gone, looking up at Pearl who stared off into the night like she had no idea anyone was within one hundred miles.

'Pearl. Snipes came to me today and tried to get a foreclosure order on your farm. He says there's some interest for the land from some party in Rhode Island.' He paused. 'I told him that the judge and I wouldn't go along, that you would pay half the loan money and would raise the rest within six months.'

Pearl looked stunned. The 'interested party', she knew, was Lillian. She collected her thoughts, then said, 'Mr Snipes and I had discussed a loan.'

Edward shook his head. 'It isn't going to happen.'

'Why?'

'He says this place isn't worth $600.' Edward waited a few moments, then said, 'I don't believe that. It's just what we've been saying. Snipes doesn't want trouble.'

Pearl listened as the buggy pulled out of the yard, then she sat down on the top step and rested her head on her hands, the judge's and Edward's words playing over and over again in her troubled thoughts: 'People are at risk – because of what you're doing. Foreclosure, no loan. Some party in Rhode Island.' She was having a hard time breathing. Then she tensed and slowly sat up straighter, sensing someone had joined her on the steps. She could hear their breathing. Were the men back?

'Mrs Kishimoto?'

'It's me,' Prophet said.

They sat for a while without saying anything. He watched the moon rising over the trees beyond the garden and thought about ways out of the trouble she was in; while her thoughts stayed focused on the men's warning. Even as she had tried to keep people from being hurt – people were being hurt because of her. She shuddered, rubbing her face in her hands.

'They're right,' he said.

'No,' she snapped.

'Yes.'

They didn't talk for a time after that. Prophet finally sat up straight on the step and rubbed the back of his neck in his hand, then turned his head up toward her. Sitting in the shadows with her arms wrapped tightly around her knees, she looked small and lost.

'What are you going to do?' Prophet asked.

'I'm not sure.'

'You need money to take care of your boys and to hold on to this place – but you can't earn it because of me and those China-men.' He saw her tense and corrected himself, 'Japanese. And now the bank isn't going to give you a loan.' He waited a moment, then continued. 'There's no future in what you're doing. None.'

Pearl thought about this for a while, then folded her hands in her lap and asked, 'Why have thou stayed, Mr Prophet? Under thy logic, there's no future for thee either.'

He surely didn't want to tell her he'd originally stayed so he could rob her. Then he'd begun feeling sorry for the whole lot of them. Beyond that he wasn't sure himself. He cleared his throat. 'I don't know.'

'I don't believe that.'

He shrugged.

'Thou are a man who knows why he does things.'

He ignored her, tipping his head back and examining the wide spray of stars sparkling overhead in the black sky.

She didn't say anything and he thought she'd dropped it, but then she asked, 'So why have thou stayed?' She persisted.

He rolled his eyes but kept his mouth shut. She sat for a time in the shadows and he wondered what was going through her head.

Probably trying to figure out which poor misfit she could drag home by the scruff of his dirty neck so she could take care of him, whether he wanted her to or not.

Prophet cleared his throat. 'Your problem is that you believe in people too much. It's going to get you hurt.'

Pearl stood quickly as if the words had shoved her upright and went through the motions of straightening the pleats of her long dress.

'I mean it. You believe in people too much.'

She looked in his direction. 'There's nothing better in this world to believe in, Mr Prophet.'

'They'll break your heart.'

She smiled, looking as though she'd nearly recovered from her talk with Edward Johnson and Judge Wilkins. 'Thou are wrong, sir. They'll renew my soul.'

He shook his head: there was no reasoning with her so he changed direction. 'After I'm gone and the Japanese are gone, you could start over in another town.'

'Are thou saying goodbye, Mr Prophet?'

He ignored the question. 'You could make a fresh start.'

She shook her head 'no'.

'Why not?'

'Running is not right. Thou knows that now.'

'Don't go roping me into your foolishness. I told you, I'm off to Minnesota. I still got things left in me to do.' He stopped talking and looked into her face for a time, as if he was memorizing it, wanted to remember what she looked like when he was no longer here. 'Anyway,' he said, looking quickly to where Mr Kishimoto sat sleeping on the ground, 'there's no hope for it here.'

'There's always hope.'

'Well, if there is, it's gotten pretty slim around here.' He started up the stairs, moving stiffly. 'I'm going to catch some sleep. That old woman works me hard.'

'Mr Prophet?'

'Yes?'

She reached her hands out toward him. He felt the blood rushing to his face and wanted to turn and flee, but couldn't. He knew things like this were a big deal to her, so he filled his lungs full of air, shut his eyes and stepped forward.

Pearl Eddy's hands moved slowly over his face as if she, too, were memorizing him for when he was gone. He stood bent over slightly at the waist so she could reach him, his arms dangling limply at his sides. He felt foolish – but in a way he also felt something akin to family in the way this woman cared about him. He'd never felt that before in his life.

Finally she let go of him and when he opened his eyes he thought he could see hers watering. He turned away and tipped his head back and looked up at the night sky and blinked a couple of times.

'Mr Prophet, I thank thee.'

He swallowed and then cleared his throat. 'For killing your hen?' he tried to joke.

'For all thou hast done.' She turned toward the kitchen, stopping only to say, 'But thou must control thy violence,' then hurried into the house.

There she was again – just when he was feeling good about things – lecturing him like somebody had given her the tablets and Moses was a waiter somewhere.

He stood watching the back door for a long time. Samuel's new shoes were still sitting there. Mr Kishimoto had taken up his guard position at the bottom of the porch. The first summer crickets were beginning to chirp in the night.

Neither Pearl nor her boys heard Prophet climb the cellar steps that same night, letting himself out the kitchen. He stopped for a moment, swinging the door open and shut to test it, pleased with his repairs. Then he hoisted his pack on to his back and tiptoed away from the house, careful not to wake Mr Kishimoto who sat rigidly upright, but asleep, at the bottom of the steps.

When Prophet reached the little rise of ground and the trail

that led through tallgrass prairie to the railroad track, he stopped
and looked back: the outline of the house was visible in the moonlight, dun-colored, its clapboard covered with ivy and wisteria.
Something about it – the way it sat like some forlorn creature
adrift in an endless void of black – bothered him and for a
moment he had the desire to retrace his steps. But he heard the
faint train whistle and started away at a limping trot. He didn't
look back again.

CHAPTER TWELVE

'Of course I'll buy the asparagus, Mrs Eddy,' the barber, William Smith, said. He sounded slightly uncomfortable. 'Deal is a deal,' he continued. He was standing on the sidewalk outside his barber shop under a large yellow canvas banner that read: RE-ELECT GEORGE HAINES COUNTY SHERIFF. Smith's partner, Hank Fegan, and two other men stood watching them through the window.

Pearl looked relieved. She continued to sit on the buggy seat while Samuel handed her Jack's reins and started to get out. But before the boy could reach the ground, Eiko had hopped down and was carrying the basket of asparagus to the old man.

Mr Smith took a step backwards as the woman approached, as if he didn't want her to get too close. 'Put it down right there,' the barber said, curtly. He was counting out money in his wallet, and watching the oriental woman as if she might try and snatch it.

'Mr Smith, I'd like to introduce Mrs Eiko Kishimoto,' Pearl said brightly.

'Sure,' the old man grumbled.

'Mrs Kishimoto and her family are staying with us,' she continued.

'I've heard, Mrs Eddy,' he said, handing Pearl the money they had agreed upon.

'Thank thee. I'll deliver again next Monday.'

Smith got a funny look on his old face. 'Mrs Eddy, may I speak with you a moment?'

The old man took Pearl by the elbow, guiding her down the sidewalk in a gentlemanly way, out of earshot of the barber shop and the buggy. He looked uncomfortable, staring at a small cloud of dust floating over the dirt street, as though he didn't want to look directly at Pearl.

'We've been friends for a time.'

'Yes.'

'What I've got to say now has nothing to do with that.'

Pearl just listened.

'The way folks are feeling, Mrs Eddy, it would be a good thing if that woman didn't come to the shop.' He paused. 'And when you visit we ought to talk outside. Until this matter blows over.'

Pearl didn't say anything for a while. She wasn't angry or hurt, she was just shocked. She and William Smith and Hank Fegan had been friends for twelve years. Finally she drew a breath and said, 'Mr Smith. Whatever thou wish.'

'Just until this blows over.'

'Yes.' Pearl cleared her throat. 'And next week's delivery?'

He hesitated for a moment, then said, 'Let us see how we like this one and then we'll decide.'

Pearl felt dizzy and was having trouble staying on her feet. 'I understand.' She started tapping her way back toward the buggy, the barber hurrying alongside her.

'Mrs Eddy, we're just trying to stay in business.'

Pearl stopped and turned in his direction. 'Mr Smith,' she said quietly. 'Thou and Mr Fegan and I have been friends for many years. I have always cherished our friendship.' She paused. 'I see no reason not to continue to cherish it now. My best to Mr Fegan.'

William Smith swallowed hard as he watched the small buggy moving slowly away toward Main Street. Then he turned and picked up the basket of asparagus and started for the front door, the men inside still watching him. Smith stopped and stared at them, then he looked down at the asparagus. He turned and stomped off around the side of the barber shop.

*

Prophet was straddling the man, dripping blood from his nose down on to the prostrate fighter's chest. The man was out cold. Prophet had been hit hard on the side of his head by the fallen fighter's partner and his legs had actually buckled, but he had exaggerated the resulting swoon for effect. The crowd in the barn loved it, screaming and throwing coins on to the canvas. Most of the objects were aimed at Prophet. He didn't care as long as nobody threw anything big. The room was sweltering and smelled of stale sweat. Wooden bleachers surrounded the small ring and these were filled to capacity with drunken men and a few women.

Prophet took a tentative step forward as if he might finally tumble. The crowd screamed again, but Prophet wasn't paying them any mind. He was pretending to be hurt so that the remaining fighter would finally be suckered into committing himself, and hopefully into making a mistake. Prophet sensed the man moving behind him, and figured he would rush to one side or the other and try to land a cheap haymaker on him. The fight's purse was two hundred dollars, so Prophet wasn't going to let him succeed.

There were just three rules in two-on-one bareknuckle fights. One, you couldn't kick a man when he went down, nor anytime in his privates. Two, you couldn't hold a man while your partner hit him. And three, you had to be on the side or in front of your opponent before you could land a punch. A sudden searing pain in Prophet's lower back told him that the man had just broken rule number three, giving Prophet a thundering shot to his kidneys that drove him to his knees. The crowd roared its approval.

Then the man was coming at him from the right, his arm cocked to deliver. Prophet held his vulnerable position for three counts, waiting until the man had fully committed himself, then he whirled and drove his fist hard and deep into the man's middle. The fighter was big and tough, but Prophet had been watching him take long guzzles of water between rounds and figured his middle was a better target than his jaw. And it would certainly be easier on Prophet's knuckles.

He had calculated everything about right, except he hadn't expected the man to spit up on him. But he did. Prophet rarely fought mad, but he was now. The man was still bent over when Prophet stepped forward, grabbed his head, and drove a hard knee into it. The man collapsed, out before he bounced twice on the wooden floor of the ring.

Prophet stumbled to the corner, his mouth clamped tight against the slime that covered him, and poured a bucket of water over his head. Then he toweled off and collected his money. He was standing in a bright beam of sunlight that shone down from a broken spot in the roof. The crowd was reviewing his fight in graphic terms and tossing more coins, this time for him rather than at him. He had always been a crowd pleaser.

Prophet finished picking up the coins in the ring, and was standing and catching his breath when he saw her. He blinked, then ran his eyes back over the faces in the crowd, but couldn't spot her again. Still, he thought he had seen the old black woman, and she didn't look happy.

Prophet bent and stepped through the ropes and out of the ring. Then he stopped and searched for her one more time. She wasn't there, nor had she ever been there, he told himself. He had just been hit in the head again, causing him to imagine things that weren't right or real. That was it, pure and simple. The old black woman hadn't been in the stands, hadn't been on the dirt road near the Eddy place, nor been there any of the other times. She never had been, never would be. But maybe she'd been right anyhow. Maybe he was just muddleheaded. He took one last look over his shoulder, then began to move through the crowd.

From her seat among the vegetable baskets, Eiko watched the figure of the little barber, William Smith, receding behind the buggy and asked, 'What was wrong with him?'

'Nothing,' Pearl said.

'You lose another customer?'

'Mr Smith just wants to try this asparagus before ordering more. That is certainly fair.'

Samuel shook his head. William Smith and Hank Fegan had been two of their most dependable customers.

'Because of us,' Eiko said firmly. 'Warui. Bad.'

Samuel glanced at the oriental woman from the side of his eyes. She had more horse sense than he had thought possible in an Asian. She smiled too much but she had a good fix on things. He would allow her that.

'We cannot stay,' Eiko continued.

Edward Johnson and Judge Wilkins had been right, Samuel thought. Eventually Mrs Kishimoto would figure out this wasn't going to work and decide to leave. Only his mother was too naive to see it for herself.

'Thou can stay. The people in Liberty are just not used to orientals.'

'We cannot,' the woman repeated.

Samuel didn't hear her. His thoughts were on Fumiko.

It was warm in the sunlight and cool in the shade, the way early spring was in these parts. The sun, halfway to noon, burned out of a thin blue sky and hit Samuel in the eyes, partially blinding him. He was squinting hard and focused so intently on his disappointment over Fumiko that when they turned on to Main Street, he almost drove Jack into the middle of the accident. It was a bad one, and it had happened only moments before. Bystanders seemed frozen in different positions, staring at the tangled wreckage of the two drays that had collided, one tipped on its side and pinning the arm of a young man of around eighteen underneath. No one moved or said anything.

Samuel reined Jack in hard, causing his mother to tip forward on the seat.

'Samuel?'

Samuel was trying to find the words to answer her, when the

234

young man writhing in the street let out a scream and sat up, his sleeve empty. Still, nobody moved as the boy staggered to his feet, his sleeve seemingly exploding with a spray of blood. There was a frightened gasp from the crowd.

'Samuel?'

'It's Ernie Sherman,' Samuel said, as if the name was an explanation.

Suddenly the injured boy was staggering toward the crowd of people on the sidewalk, holding his one hand out. They backed away as if he were threatening them with a weapon.

'What's happened?' Pearl asked.

'He's lost an arm.' He sounded stunned.

His mother's sudden rush to get out of the buggy freed Samuel from his paralysis. He jumped from the buggy to help her. Ernie Sherman was still screaming and staggering after the crowd of people who backed away in shock, as if he carried some deadly disease. Blood was spraying like oil out of a broken pipe.

'Take me to him,' Pearl said. 'Hurry!'

Samuel grabbed his mother's elbow, then looked up just as Eiko grabbed the Sherman boy from behind, pulling him to the sidewalk. By the time Samuel had gotten his mother there, the oriental woman had a thong of cloth wrapped around what was left of Ernie Sherman's arm. Blood was still spewing. Eiko looked a fright, drenched in blood and straddling the boy's chest. Ernie was opening and shutting his mouth as if he were trying to say something. Eiko reached and snatched a paint brush from a man standing nearby and stuck it into the thong, and began to twist it. But the blood was still flowing and the boy was making a rattling sound in his chest. 'Sam-boy! My fukuro! My fukuro!'

'What?'

'Bag. Bag!'

Samuel rushed her old green bag to her and she pulled something out he couldn't see and began to work over the injured boy. Yelling loudly in Japanese at him – Samuel figured to keep him from dying.

235

Slowly, the flow of blood stopped.

Pearl was on her knees beside Eiko and the injured boy, checking the bloody stump with her hands to see that the flow had stopped.

'Quit?' Eiko asked, straining hard to hold the knot tight.

'Yes. We need blankets!' Pearl called. The boy was unconscious and looked ghostly pale. 'Blankets, please!'

One of the men rushed across the street to Collier's store, hollering for blankets. They were rolling Ernie over, Pearl cradling the young man's head and Eiko holding tight to the paint brush and the twisted knot, when the boy's grandmother, Rose Sherman, arrived. Seeing the blood-spattered oriental woman bending over her injured grandson, she began to strike at Eiko with her purse.

'Get her off! Get her off him!' she screamed.

'Rose! Stop it!' Pearl yelled.

But Rose didn't stop. She continued to strike at Eiko's back with her purse. Then a couple of men stepped forward and grabbed Eiko's shoulders, pulling her back. She fought them, struggling to hold the brush in the knot.

'Get away – leave her alone, you damn fools!' Dr Smith Trotter said. 'She lets that brush go and this boy is dead. Now get away!'

Night had fallen hard over Main Street when Dr Trotter and Rose Sherman walked out of his office. Ernie was inside with his parents and two nurses. Rose looked exhausted. The doctor untied her matched bays from the hitching post and then helped the heavy woman into her carriage. Rose had been crying hard, creating streaks that looked like streambeds in the thick powder on her cheeks.

'Rose,' Dr Trotter said, patting her thick hand, 'Ernie lost an arm but he'll live. We all need to go to church and thank God for that.' He stopped and looked into the old woman's face. 'He should have died.'

'Smith,' she said, shocked.

236

'He should have, Rose. That injury was massive.' He stopped talking and seemed to be thinking about something. 'Massive,' he muttered again.

'Yes,' she said, dabbing at her eyes with a handkerchief. 'I can't thank you enough.'

Dr Trotter put his hands in his pockets. 'Don't thank me.'

'You're too modest, Smith Trotter.'

'No. I didn't save Ernie's life. That oriental woman saved him, Rose.' He paused. 'I just don't know how she did it. That's the second time.'

'That's not funny, Smith.'

'Wasn't meant to be. Ernie should have bled to death in minutes, Rose. That woman saved him. She has a gift of some sort. She does something magical.'

'Anyone could have done it,' Rose countered.

'That woman and Pearl Eddy, Rose. They saved young Ernie.'

Rose looked upset. 'I think you grossly exaggerate the role those women played, doctor. You are a humble man. Thank you and good night.'

Dr Trotter stood in the street watching the woman's carriage pulling away. He shook his head.

Rose Sherman was sitting with her Ladies Conversation Club in the parlor of her large Victorian home, not conversing much, but rather resting on the sofa and being attended to by the other women of the club who fanned or mopped her feverish brow.

'Poor Ernie,' she sighed.

The women clustered around her nodded in sympathetic agreement.

'Thank goodness that Dr Trotter happened along when he did,' a tall, thin woman said.

Rose fanned herself. 'Oh, Ruth, I'm so glad that you said that. Dr Trotter, the blessed man, was so shaken he gave credit for saving Ernie to that horrible Chinese woman. Isn't that the silliest thing you've ever heard?'

The gathering of friends groaned in protest. 'That's absurd,' Grace Parker said.

'Of course it is,' Rose replied. 'The good doctor was just trying to be kind. And I'll tell you ladies a secret,' Rose said, lowering her voice. The women leaned forward toward her.

'What I saw,' she gasped, appearing for a moment as if she might faint, fluttering her fan faster.

'What, Rose?' Martha Forester asked.

'What I saw when I pulled that awful creature off of Ernie —' She stopped as if she couldn't continue. The silence of the room was broken only by the anxious breathing of the women.

'Rose?' Martha encouraged.

'I saw that Chinese woman sticking needles into Ernie's flesh. Like some ghoul.'

There was a collective gasp from the women.

'I swear it,' Rose affirmed. 'She was trying to put a spell on poor Ernie for certain. Doc Trotter claimed she worked magic of some sort on Ernie. She and Pearl Eddy are in league with the devil. Now Pearl pretends to be heavenly-minded but there's a certain unholiness to her — if you've noticed,' Rose said examining the faces around her. A couple of women nodded. 'A certain profaneness.'

Pearl stood in the barn listening to the sounds of packing. The little girls, Tamoko and Isi, were sitting on a bale of hay watching their mother and sister loading the family's belongings on to the rickety cart, and looking like they were about to cry. The younger Eddy boys were behind their mother, seemingly just as sad.

Samuel was in the deeper shadows of the barn, watching Fumiko, and feeling a vague sense that he was slipping over the edge of some dark abyss he didn't even know existed. He shook hard, trying to dispel this painful dreamlike feeling. For the first time, he admitted to himself that he had feelings for her.

But now she was leaving, going away just when he'd begun to understand things. Still, he didn't have the courage to talk to her.

A cold wind was blowing in through the barn door striking him full in the back, and heightening his sense of discomfort and loss.

The old man was a bundle of nervous energy, sitting in his accustomed corner, his eyes darting anxiously from the barn door to the windows. Every few minutes he would trot outside to search once more in vain for the Negro. From the strained look on his worn face it was apparent he was deeply depressed. He had let the man get away without him, and Muneo Kishimoto would have followed Jerome Prophet anywhere.

Pearl missed the Negro as well. When she thought about it, she realized that he had formally said his goodbye. She was just surprised that after all the times that he had threatened to leave, he'd actually gone. It left a hollow feeling inside her. Still, she was glad. He was searching, she felt, for something of himself that seemed to be lost. She hoped he would find it. Regardless, it was best for Zacharias. The boy was getting too attached to the man. And the man had problems with violence. Yes. It was best he was gone. Pearl heard the woman and the girl moving nearby.

'Eiko. There's no good reason for thee to go.'

'You lose everything.' She paused. 'Anyhow. We go claim rikuchi. Our land.'

'It isn't thine any longer.'

'It abandoned. We claim,' she said in her matter-of-fact way.

Pearl waited a moment, then said, 'Thou can't. There is a law in this country. Thou must be a citizen.' She waited, seemingly trying to catch her breath. Then she lowered her voice. 'And thou cannot be oriental and own land. I'm sorry.'

Eiko thought about this for a moment but seemed undaunted. 'We go. You no make money. Lose everything,' she said flatly. Eiko heaved a large canvas bundle up on the cart. 'No make money. Lose everything,' she repeated.

Samuel thought this little oriental woman's stubborn streak was a pretty good match for his mother's own. Then suddenly, Mr Kishimoto hopped up from his mat and bowed like the great

Buddha himself had entered the barn. Samuel turned toward the door and felt the familiar surge of anger pulsing through him.

Prophet was wearing a black fedora pulled at a sharp angle over his forehead. The hat almost covered the Negro's badly swollen eye, but did nothing to hide his battered lips. As far as Samuel was concerned, Prophet looked one hundred per cent like the fool he was.

'Nobody is losing anything,' he said.

'Mr Prophet?' Pearl spoke calmly, but Prophet thought he could hear the surprise in her voice. 'Thou have returned.'

Prophet bent and caught a shrieking Zacharias in mid-air, and said, 'Mrs Eddy, you've got the money you need.'

The old man scurried around behind him and took up his accustomed rear-guard position. Prophet started to say something to him, then he shrugged as if he knew the effort would be futile.

Before Pearl could ask the source of these miraculous funds, Zacharias asked, 'What happened to thy face?'

Prophet raised a finger quickly to his puffy lips. Too late.

'Mr Prophet, have thou been fighting again?' Pearl questioned, folding her arms across her breast.

'Some.'

'Thou promised to refrain.' Her concern for Zacharias came flooding back.

'Yes, Mrs Eddy.'

'Thou also forgot that I do not accept charity. And certainly not charity earned from the pain of another human.'

'I'd never forget that,' he said, with considerable dignity.

'Then where did these funds come from?' she asked with scepticism.

Prophet removed a piece of paper from an envelope and held it out toward Samuel. The boy hung back in the shadows for a moment, then took it, noticing that the Negro's large hands were badly swollen and cut.

Samuel was shocked by the name at the top of the document: 'Matthew Eddy Enterprises.' It made him feel warm on the back of his neck, then he shook it off, figuring the Negro had just done it to curry favor. He studied the paper.

'Read it to your mother.'

'Thou read it,' Samuel said.

Prophet shifted uncomfortably on his feet. 'I can't.'

Samuel looked embarrassed and glanced quickly down at the paper again. 'It's a contract of some sort,' Samuel said, squinting his eyes in the dim light.

'I went to see a man I worked for once in Kansas City,' Prophet said, 'produce wholesaler. It's a contract for your strawberries. All you can deliver. They're hard to come by in these parts.' Prophet looked at Zacharias' beaming face. 'Your father was a smart man.'

'Four hundred dollars for each crop, two yields. Eight hundred total.'

Eiko had walked over and was staring at him, listening and nodding her head.

'There are two yields, aren't there?' he asked her.

Eiko nodded vigorously. 'Cashee crop. Grow futatsu. Twice berries.'

'Good, because that's what I said we'd deliver.'

While she didn't say anything, Prophet could tell Pearl Eddy was thinking. It made him feel good.

Eiko turned and walked back toward the cart and her oldest girl. 'We go.'

Prophet looked stunned. 'You can't do that. You're part of the deal.'

Eiko heaved another canvas bag up on to the cart, and shook her head. 'We go.'

'You can't go.'

'We go to our land,' she said stubbornly.

'None of us know anything about growing these damn plants!'

'Mr Prophet, thy language.'

'I'll watch my language – but you tell them running isn't allowed,' he said. 'Tell them, Mrs Eddy. Running isn't allowed.' He walked over to the cart and returned the bag to the ground. The old man trotted along behind. 'Don't you know about running?' he asked Eiko, sounding tutorial.

The little oriental woman squinted at him for a moment as if he were daft, then snatched the canvas bag off the ground and stuck it back on the cart. 'We go,' she barked.

Prophet whirled toward Pearl. 'Tell her about running.'

'Mrs Kishimoto has her family to think about.'

Prophet looked like he'd been shot. 'Let me get this straight. You preach to me that running is never right. But that's just because I'm alone. If you've got a family it's OK to hightail it anytime you see fit.'

'It is not the same,' Pearl said quietly. 'Mrs Kishimoto is not running away.'

'Running is running,' he snapped.

Then Samuel did something that he even had a hard time understanding. As much as he wanted Fumiko to stay, he hated having the Negro back. The man was nothing more than a self-centered opportunist. Samuel glanced at Fumiko, then cleared his throat and said, 'We would still have to make it another two months before harvest. We don't have money for fertilizer. We don't have money to pay freight. None for food and other things.'

No one spoke or moved for a moment. Then Prophet reached into his pocket, pulling out a hundred-dollar bill.

'One hundred dollars. A fifty-dollar advance on each of the two crops,' he lied. The money was the last of his winnings from the fight in the barn. 'Shipping costs are paid by the purchaser.' This was true. 'All we have to do is ice them down and deliver them to the station.'

His eyes darted from Pearl to the oriental woman. 'But it isn't going to happen unless she stays,' he continued, staring hard into Eiko's face. The woman betrayed no emotion.

'Mr Prophet. That isn't fair.'

Mrs Kishimoto studied Pearl for a moment, then looked back at Prophet and began to suck her teeth. 'Contractee real?'

'Rock solid.'

'We make okane? Money?'

'Yep.'

She sucked harder on her teeth and thought about things for a moment longer, then raised her arms in her familiar strongman pose and said, 'You strong man. Unload cart.' And to Pearl, 'You no lose everything. I stay. Fixee everything. You no lose.'

Samuel continued to stare at the Negro; he was utterly convinced that nothing tied to this man would turn out right. The man was out only for himself. And that made him dangerous.

There was great progress made in the gardens during the next two weeks. The fence to keep the pigs out was finished, the thousands of plants were carefully cleared of weeds and the soil cultivated, then every plant fertilized with ground-up cotton seed. When they had completed these projects, Prophet dug irrigation ditches down each of the long rows. Everything was done under the watchful eye of Mrs Kishimoto. And as the spring air warmed, the berries came fully to life and began to grow and flower in earnest.

In addition to this work, Prophet spent his nights constructing a watering sluice from old rain gutters he found behind the barn. He sloped the trough down a wooden trellis that he built of two-by-fours, the device serpentining from the well to the edge of the field. The contraption saved hours of backbreaking labor, and Mrs Kishimoto and Mrs Eddy behaved as if Prophet were some kind of engineering genius. They embarrassed him with their praise, but it also made him feel good.

'Brilliant,' Mrs Eddy would say whenever she heard water coursing down the sluice. And if Mrs Kishimoto heard her, she would say 'Hai! Saino ni michita!' Which he figured meant something similar in Japanese.

In addition to all their hard work on the strawberries, they also maintained the vegetable garden and even found time enough to put most of the flower beds right. This latter effort was led by Prophet. All the boys but Samuel helped.

In the strawberry field everyone helped, including Pearl who quickly learned to differentiate the feel of the valuable vines from weeds. Samuel was seemingly content as long as Fumiko was nearby. Prophet knew the boy had thoughts about her, he just wasn't certain about Fumiko's feelings. She was tough to get a bead on, keeping things to herself. She never spoke and didn't smile unless it was during play with the little children.

The afternoon sun was burning down hard on Prophet's back as he bent over the plants, carefully spreading the heavy roll of netting that they had ordered from a company in Minneapolis. It had just arrived that morning at the train station. While the plants were showing only flowers, and therefore were of no interest yet to the wild birds, Prophet was taking no chance that there might be a flock of crazed flower-eaters out there somewhere.

He stood and stretched and looked at Samuel. The boy was standing a few feet away clearing piles of dead weeds from between the rows. He could work hard and he wasn't mean-spirited. Prophet just knew the boy didn't like nor trust him. And most likely, he never would.

'How's it going, Sam?' Prophet said, trying to make polite conversation.

'Fine,' the boy said in his curt way.

'You've done a good job clearing the rows.'

The boy didn't answer him and Prophet knew that would be the extent of their conversation and he bent down over his work, pulling back a thick matting of strawberry vine and finding himself staring straight into the blunt head of a coiled massasauga rattlesnake. Thick as Prophet's wrist, the heavy-bodied reptile was no more than a foot from his face. He froze. Smaller than the diamondback, the massasauga was more aggressive, and just as deadly. The fields around the farm crawled with these fierce gray rattlers. He had killed a five-footer earlier this week in the rhubarb patch, and he'd seen the young pigs eating another out behind the barn. They were easy enough to kill if you saw them first, but now the tables were turned in a deadly fashion.

Prophet was off balance and the snake had obviously heard him coming and coiled and was poised to explode. Anything might trigger the strike. Prophet fought the trembling in his body. He hated snakes of all kinds, but this was the worst kind and it was right in his face, its forked tongue flitting at the air.

'Samuel,' he hissed.

The reptile's tail buzzed louder at the sound of his voice. Prophet glanced from the side of his eyes at Samuel. The boy had seen the snake but Prophet could sense the fear and knew that Samuel had frozen up. Prophet had survived all his life by making quick decisions and he immediately dismissed the boy as a possible solution to the terrible situation he found himself in.

Samuel gripped the rake hard, his eyes locked on the snake. It had whirled into a stiff ropelike coil a few inches away from the Negro's downturned face. Its savage head was angled away from him, and Samuel figured he could strike it with the rake, but he couldn't move. Not a muscle. He wanted to – but couldn't. Fear surged through his limbs making them heavy and weak. He shuddered and stared hopelessly at the scene in front of him.

Prophet was no longer thinking about Samuel. His thoughts were on the tiny man. Kishimoto was fast enough and skilled enough to save him. For the first time since they'd met Prophet needed the old Jap, but he was sitting in his stiff-backed way, asleep, yards down the garden path. Damn lazy Chinaman! Prophet tried holding one arm behind him and snapping his finger quietly to awaken the old man. But the little Japanese didn't move. A nerve kept firing in Prophet's head, telling him time was running out, dangerously fast.

He tried pulling slowly away, even though he knew that once alarmed a rattlesnake visually locked on its victim, freezing the picture in its mind. He also knew that if anything in that picture moved, even slightly, blammm! But it was still his best chance. His only chance.

The agitated buzzing of the reptile's tail rose to a frightening shrill, warning Prophet that the rattler's picture was dangerously close to changing. He froze. Sweat began to drip from the tip of his nose. Then he heard Zacharias calling his name from somewhere behind him. He tried frantically to wave the boy back with his hand, but it didn't work. Zacharias would be there any moment, certain to startle the snake into striking. The boy would also be in danger. Prophet determined that his and Zach's only chance was to make a desperate lunge, a lunge that he knew in his heart was hopeless.

Trying to outjump this snake would be like trying to outjump a bullet fired into his face. Nevertheless, it was his last and only chance. Zacharias was running fast down the row toward him now. Prophet determined to move on the count of three. 'One,' he counted in his mind. 'Two –'

Just as he was about to lunge, he saw a blurring movement from the edge of his eye and the snake disappeared in an explosion of red. Prophet was numb for a second, then he hopped frantically backwards. Mr Kishimoto tripped the running boy with his foot.

Hercules had his one good wing out and his neck stretched forward, his hackles flared, defiantly facing off the coiled reptile. 'No!' Prophet said, but it was too late. The old bird wasn't one to just face an enemy – even a rattlesnake – and he took a lunging leap at the reptile in the same instant that the snake spread its jaws wide and punched its massive head forward.

Then Prophet yanked Samuel's rake away and it was over, the snake writhing headless on the ground. Hercules was standing and watching the creature coiling and twisting in death, ruffling his feathers as if to say 'That wasn't so tough.' The old man was holding Zacharias back. Prophet knelt down in front of the bird and it raised its hackles menacingly, then it took a faltering step and fell. The massasuaga had not missed. Zacharias was screaming and kicking at Mr Kishimoto to get free.

Prophet sat down hard and gathered the bird into his lap. It was shaking in rigid tremors. Prophet rested its head in the palm of his hand. The dark eyes were glazing fast. He wondered whether the old bird had come to his rescue or just couldn't pass up a good fight. Maybe it was a bit of both. The bird flared its hackles at him. Then it went limp.

Zacharias took Hercules from him, clutching it hard and sobbing. The tiny man was talking to the boy in Japanese, the words soothing and comforting, conveying a sympathy that transcended understanding and surprised Prophet.

Samuel wanted to hide. He dropped the rake the Negro had handed back to him and hurried from the garden. He was shaking, fighting back tears, conscious of the man's eyes on him as he stumbled down the rows. Once outside, the nausea overcame him and he vomited.

'Sam,' Prophet said as he approached the boy.

He didn't answer.

'It happens to all of us at times. I froze as well. It doesn't mean anything.'

Samuel started running for the house.

They dug Hercules' grave in a corner of the tiny enclosure where Matthew Eddy was buried. It was Zacharias' idea, but Pearl and the other boys agreed. Prophet spent the afternoon carving the words Zacharias wanted in a big wooden plank. He was faster at it this time.

HERCULES WAS MY FRIEND
Zacharias Eddy

It was just before sundown when the afternoon breezes stopped and the birds in the tallgrass ceased their noisy chatter, creating a calm and peace right for a funeral. The sun was low in the western sky and spraying golden rays horizontally over the flower garden. They'd all come. Prophet figured Mrs Eddy had ordered Samuel to be there. The boy avoided Prophet's glance and the

Negro did his best to try and act as if the boy wasn't there. He felt sorry for him.

Mrs Kishimoto and her three girls sprinkled pink and white flower blossoms over the small grave, and then each tied a little piece of white paper, that Eiko said were prayers, in the branches of the dying lilac. The baby was asleep on Eiko's back. Pearl Eddy and her boys just stood and watched, not saying or doing anything. Prophet guessed it was their way, but he didn't care much for it. It was too quiet for his blood.

He waited a moment, bucking up his courage, then said, 'Bless this bird. I did not like him. But he had heart.'

No one moved or said anything after that, until Pearl broke the silence. The sun was dropping behind the top of the barn. 'Samuel and Fumiko, thou need to bring the pigs in.'

Zacharias sat down next to the grave and put his hand on the freshly turned earth. Prophet squatted behind him, and the old man behind him. They didn't talk for a while. The garden was quiet in the thin shadows of late afternoon. The boy had quit crying but every once in a while Prophet saw him draw a breath and shudder hard. 'Thank thee for saying something about Hercules.'

Prophet nodded.

'Where do chickens go when they die?'

Prophet scratched behind an ear. 'Same place we do,' he speculated.

Zacharias shook his head in a forlorn way. 'Ma doesn't think so. She says that's just a people place.'

Prophet rocked back on his heels and thought for a moment. 'Your mother sometimes just talks like a mother.'

'What's that mean?'

'Mothers want their boys to be logical-minded.' He rubbed his chin. 'So I think they tell them things like that, rather than tell them what's in their hearts.'

'So thou think chickens go to heaven?'

'Makes sense.'

'Why?'

'I always heard heaven is just a better kind of earth . . . so things we love should be up there.'

Zacharias twisted his mouth and thought about this for a while. Then he wiped a tear from his cheek and nodded. 'Makes sense.'

Prophet nodded in response.

'Then Hercules is with my pa?'

'I'd say so.'

'Yes,' the little boy said in a voice that seemed to float over the still gardens, drifting out into the wide expanse of prairie . . . sounding if it might drift for a long time, a lifetime, if nothing stopped it.

The prairie was shading purple in the sunset by the time they found the pigs. The shoats had rooted their way down to the sandstone walls of the downstream gully, a good half mile from the barn. They were bunched now around a prairie crab apple, searching the grasses for remnants of last year's crop. Samuel had walked ahead of Fumiko for most of the way, carrying a stick in case they found any more rattlesnakes. The thought made him cringe. He doubted that he could use the stick now, anymore than he had that morning.

The memory was eating at him. Hercules was dead because of him. Gone because he was a coward. He shuddered hard. And wished he could say something to Fumiko about it, angry that they'd never spoken.

He had a feeling she might be mad at him for what he'd said the other night in the barn – about not having enough money. He wondered if that was it, or if she just didn't like him. Whichever it was, she wasn't much comfort to him. Still, he felt better with her around. Something stirred inside him as he glanced back at her striding along in her confident way toward the grunting hogs.

Samuel stopped unexpectedly to avoid the prickly branches of a coyote thistle and she accidentally bumped into him. She hopped quickly away and was off again. She hates me, he thought. She won't talk, can't stand me near her, and bristles when I accidentally touch her. He swallowed hard and started after the girl.

They were one pig short. Samuel had herded the animals into one of the blind turns of the gully and counted them twice, then he tried to convince Fumiko to stay while he hunted for the missing pig. She would have none of it, tossing her head and striding off down the crumbling walls of the gully to search. Samuel didn't like it but he stayed behind, knowing that if he let the shoats loose they would never round them up in the dark.

Samuel sat down in the sand and tried not to think about Hercules or what he had failed to do, watching instead a blue kingfisher darting after minnows over the shallow water of the stream, trying to guess where the pig had gone. They usually never wandered off alone. Fortunately, the animal was too big and tough for coyotes to bother and its arteries were encased in too much fat for rattlesnake venom to be a danger. He shook again at the thought of Hercules. The brave old rooster had faced death without hesitation. Samuel forced his thoughts away from the chicken. The only thing he could think was that the pig had fallen in a hole somewhere. There were a few dry wells around on abandoned homesteads.

Just before evening the deer flies got busy and they were pestering him now. He brushed them away with his hat and went back to watching the kingfisher again. Then he heard the shout. It could have been a hundred yards or a hundred miles away, it was hard to judge on the open plains. Still, any human sound out here in the lonely expanse of tallgrass caused a person to take notice. And he did so now, listening for a few more minutes, but hearing only the evening wind moving through the stiff pencil-like spikes of the blue vervain and leadplant lining the opposite ridge of the gully. But the voice had been real. He was certain of it. And it had come from the direction Fumiko had gone. Samuel stood and called her name. No answer. He weighed the problem of losing the pigs in the dark and his growing concern for the girl, and started trotting in the direction she'd gone.

They were holding her on the ground, hacking at her hair with sheep shears. Five boys struggled to keep her pinned, while a ring of men watched. Simon James' two older boys were among the watchers, standing off to one side as if to make certain that things were done correctly, while their brother, Hector, did the clipping.

The girl was thrashing wildly and it took them all to hold her down. Every once in a while she emitted a long scream, shrieking in pure anger as if letting out things that she had held deep inside her for a long time. The pig squealed seemingly in sympathy and began to run in panicked circles around the trunk of a cotton-wood where they'd tied it.

Samuel was certain they'd planned this thing. They must have watched the farm and knew that it was Fumiko's and his job to bring in the pigs at night. Samuel took a better grip on the stout stick he was holding and prepared to run down the hill from his hiding place among the grass. Then fear gripped him, and he froze, a nauseating wave of alarm splashed over him, there were too many of them. He couldn't hope to stop them. He needed help.

Samuel turned and started to run for the farm, his legs driving hard, groaning with the thought of leaving her. The thick grasses grabbed at his legs and arms as if trying to stop him. Then he quit running and turned around. He couldn't do it. He couldn't leave her. He couldn't run again. His stomach churned. It didn't matter that he wouldn't be able to stop them, didn't matter what they did to him. It only mattered that he reach Fumiko, and try. He started back.

Hector was still hacking at Fumiko's hair with the blades of the shears when Samuel burst through the ring of men. Most of the boys jumped away at the sound of him, and Samuel grabbed Hector by the shoulders and threw him off. Then he grabbed

251

Fumiko and shoved and pulled her toward a sandstone wall that stood a few yards away. Hector and the others watched them, following at a distance behind, the men urging them on.

'Stop!' Samuel yelled, pointing a trembling finger at Hector as if it possessed some magical power to impede. 'Thou hast done enough wrong.'

The men laughed, and Hector kept coming. He was in a crouch and cautiously eyeing the stick in Samuel's hand. Samuel pushed Fumiko behind him and took a step forward.

'I will not strike thee,' he said, dropping the stick. 'But I mean it, thou hast done enough.' His voice quivered.

Hector picked the stick up and flung it away, then he walked up close to Samuel. 'I'm not done shearing.' He brought a right hand hard into Samuel's face and the boy staggered but didn't go down. The men were yelling encouragement.

'Put your hands up,' Hector taunted. Samuel didn't move, just stood with his arms hanging at his sides. Hector hit him twice more before the boy sagged down on to his knees, blood spewing out his nose. Then Fumiko was clawing at Hector James, the boy pretending to be hurt and squealing in fake pain.

But it wasn't all pretend. Long red scratches showed on his bare arms and one side of his neck. After a rake of the nails against the side of his face, Hector took a hard swing and knocked Fumiko on to the seat of her pants. Then Samuel struggled back up on to his feet and pushed her behind him, the girl was gasping for the breath that had been knocked out of her.

'He's going to fight – hooolymaatheroffjesusss – the goddamn sissy is going to fight,' somebody teased. The men hooted.

But Samuel was not going to fight. Again, he stood in front of Hector, staring into the boy's eyes, with his arms down and taking blows to his face and chest until Fumiko couldn't stand it any more. She bent and picked up a handful of sand, tossing it into Hector's face, momentarily blinding him, then she jumped forward and brought her foot up hard between his legs. Hector went

252

down, clutching himself and gasping like he had been gutted with a knife. When he recovered, Fumiko was squatting and holding on to Samuel. Samuel was conscious but badly dazed. Still he struggled to control his body so that he could stand.

'Stay down! He kill you!' Fumiko screamed at him. Samuel stopped trying to rise and looked weakly into her face. She had finally spoken to him. He wasn't so groggy that he didn't know that, and hair or not, he thought she looked like an angel. Samuel tried to smile through the fog that clouded his brain and then shook her off, striving to stand once more, half-rising until his knees buckled and then sitting down hard as he lost control of his legs. The men laughed.

'Get up and fight,' Hector hollered.

'He doesn't fight because of his beliefs – but I don't believe in anything,' Prophet said.

He was striding down the incline, smiling and nodding at the men, as if approaching a group of friends. The little sap was artfully hidden in the palm of one hand. Mr Kishimoto trotted along behind, stick at the ready. It was the first time Prophet felt good about having the little Jap so close to him. The old man was chattering something that sounded like dried sticks being hit together. Prophet started to tell him to knock it off, that it was annoying, but he could see it was making the men nervous so he let the old man continue.

The men backed away as the Negro and the oriental moved through them, Prophet stooping casually to pick up Samuel's hat from the sand and then stopping in front of the boy and Fumiko. Kishimoto took up his wide stance facing the crowd while Prophet knelt and examined the boy and girl. Fumiko was shaking hard and holding Samuel's bleeding head, as if it might drop into the sand if she let go. She looked a fright, her hair hacked off unevenly, a few odd strands sticking out around her head, a large bruise swelling on her left cheek.

'That one hurt him,' she said, pointing at Hector.

Prophet recognized him as the ugly boy who'd chased the

253

Eddys home a few weeks back. 'I told you to leave them alone.'

Hector didn't respond, he just turned anxiously to his older brothers for support.

Fumiko's breath was coming in hard jerks and she was fighting back tears. The old man came over and studied her, feeling her cheek in a tender way that surprised Prophet. Satisfied she wasn't badly injured, the tiny warrior looked into her face and said something that sounded comforting. The girl nodded in response and forced a little smile. Mr Kishimoto bowed slightly to her, then turned back to the men.

Prophet propped Samuel against the sandstone wall. 'Can you hear me, son? I need you awake.'

The boy's eyes were rolling and showing too much white and Prophet sensed he was barely conscious. 'Never mind.'

Though Samuel was having a hard time focusing his mind, he knew it was the Negro. Then he wondered if he was dreaming, but the spurts of pain in his head told him it was no dream. The Negro's words were lost in the roar inside his skull. He shook his head to clear it, until the pain slapped back hard and he stopped. Difficult as it was to believe, Jerome Prophet had waded into this fight. Samuel couldn't figure why . . . there didn't seem to be anything in it for him. Nevertheless, he was here. Then Samuel felt himself drifting away again.

'Her,' was all he managed to mumble.

'You'll both be fine,' Prophet said, patting Samuel's hand. 'Just rest.' Prophet looked at Fumiko. 'Can you carry him?'

She nodded. He wondered.

He looked at her shoulders and arms, they were thin but wiry. Maybe she could. Then he looked into her eyes, and knew there was no doubt. 'Good. When the fighting starts, you get him out of here, back to the farm. Understand?'

She shook her head, no. 'I fight beside my grandfather,' she said resolutely.

The old man heard her and barked something over his

254

shoulder in Japanese. She dropped her eyes and nodded obediently.

'Good,' Prophet whispered. 'Wait for the fight to start, then get to the farm. Follow the stream. When you tire, hide in the tall-grass. But keep going.' He paused, looking at her eyes. She was staring at Samuel's face. 'Do you understand?'

'Yes.'

Prophet stood and faced the men. Mr Kishimoto had moved a few feet in front of him and was staring without visible emotion at an empty piece of air, somewhere midway to the men, his legs spread wide. The little warrior was chattering up a storm now and tapping his stick rapidly on the ground in a wide half-circle in front of them, as if inviting someone to try him. Prophet had the feeling that the tiny man had been in a fair number of these situations before and he didn't look the least bit troubled by the odds in this one. Prophet wished they were better . . . but he liked the fact that the old man didn't seem to really care.

'I don't know what you did, gentlemen,' Prophet said in an agitated voice, 'but you got old Kish pissed, and that's bad. Some of you may make it out of this gully but not many.' Prophet made a show of staring at the chattering old warrior, then shaking his head. The men were watching the tiny man as well. 'Seen him kill bullocks with that stick,' he lied. 'Not pretty. The way I figure it,' Prophet continued, 'you can back out now or take your chances with the little bastard. Your choice.'

Prophet was a pretty good talker and the men in the center of the line were actually looking at one another, uncertain what to do, then Simon's older boy, Penny, began moving in.

The men spread out, and it was tough to keep an eye on each of their positions. Suddenly one to Prophet's right made the mistake of trying a straight charge. He badly miscalculated Kishimoto's speed and range. The old man cut him down easily with a smashing side blow to his neck that stunned him badly. The old Jap was chattering now like a crazed monkey, high-stepping, slapping and twirling his stick like a baton tosser. The little bastard had style. Prophet had to admit that.

'Big mistake getting Moto fired up,' he yelled, trying to scare them into running one more time. It didn't work.

The men were on them in a rush. Prophet caught one of them with the sap alongside the skull and the man collapsed in the dirt. Then Prophet felt an arm around his neck, and he ducked his chin and saved his windpipe, just as somebody took a hard shot at his ribs. Another. He went down and the man holding his neck went down with him. Prophet was hurt but not badly. He moaned to let the pain out and then drove his elbow hard into the temple of the man who'd been choking him.

Prophet lunged back up, knowing that the last place he wanted to be was on the ground. He was trading punches with a couple of men when he saw it coming from the side of his eye and tried to dodge. He didn't make it. The board bounced off his skull and suddenly the sounds around him seemed to be moving away at an incredible speed, until he felt as though he were wrapped in silence deep under water.

He could feel his legs giving way. Before he collapsed he looked back to the place where he had left Fumiko and Samuel. They were gone. She was tough. Then he was falling and trying to hit somebody, but it was too late. He saw the old Jap go down swinging as well. Then things went dark for him and he was listening to the black woman saying, 'Life don't give nothing back when it turns on you.' It was the first time she'd ever spoken to him.

The men were cursing and kicking at him, and somebody spat in his face. Prophet felt his strength ebbing and knew it was over. He looked up and saw Penny James raising a heavy pipe to finish him. It was a killing blow, intended as such. Prophet tried to roll desperately away but couldn't. The world seemed to be floating by, and he was in the best seat watching himself about to get his brains splattered.

The familiar sound reached Prophet somewhere deep inside

some inner chamber of his mind, 'Eiii!' Then he saw the little Jap hop astride him, taking the downward blow of the pipe with his stick held high, but the pipe broke through and crashed into the old man. Then the world turned out its light.

CHAPTER THIRTEEN

Prophet woke with a hard start. He lay still and tried to figure out where he was and what had awakened him. Then he heard chattering in the darkness and struggled to move. Pain bit into him like the jaws of some feral beast and his eyes slammed shut with the hurting, and he fought a pounding feeling in his skull. He knew he was no longer lying in the dirt of the gully, but that didn't tell him where he was. Had they taken him to a barn or somewhere else to hang him? Was that the old man chattering? His mind raced. He thought he could hear the boy, Zacharias, calling his name.

The blackness surrounding him was silent now and he slipped back easily into his dreams, floating on a harsh bed of pain, in a vast world of nothingness, pain far worse than any he'd ever felt.

'Leave me alone,' he screamed, the words clawing out of his throat, but barely audible even in the silence, the movement of his jaws causing his head to throb again. Then the blackness began to slowly spin around him and he passed out once more, floating up above where he lay, floating into black space, flipping slowly head over heels, moving farther and farther away, searching in vain in this dark void for the old man. He could hear the old black woman's voice ringing in his ears but he couldn't make out the words. He heard other voices as well, Zacharias' a lot, and felt hands and ministering and knew that he had somehow survived. He just couldn't comprehend how.

Prophet no longer had any understanding of time, sensing only the cycles of light and dark in the room. He awakened slowly and stared at the ceiling. A lamp was burning low, the flame casting a dim light. He moved and felt the searing pain shoot through his body. The old Japanese was mumbling again.

'Cut the gibberish!' Prophet said. Exasperated, he forced himself on to an elbow and looked in the direction of the mutterings. His breath caught as his eyes moved slowly over the tiny form in the next bed. The voice told him it was the old man, but that was the only way he could tell. He couldn't see the little oriental through the bandages.

Prophet had once seen a photograph of an Egyptian mummy and it had looked like this. He suddenly knew how they had escaped. The men in the gully had left them for dead. The thought angered him, but he was in no shape to do anything about it. He let his eyes wander for a moment. They were in the Eddy home. Then the fatigue was on him again and he lay back and began to drift into oblivion once more.

Prophet didn't know how long he had remained unconscious before he heard the door to the room squeaking, but when he opened his eyes the lamp was out, the room in darkness again. Then he heard steps nearby and thought the black woman was finally coming for him. He always figured she'd come to collect him when he died. And he felt dead now.

Samuel Eddy leaned weakly against the wall for physical support. His eyes were badly swollen from the beating that Hector had given him and this forced him to squint at the black man lying in the bed. He could see Prophet's face clearly in a strip of moonlight that came in through the window and fell across the room, but it didn't look like the man's face. The swelling and cuts distorted his features until Samuel finally had to just tell himself that it was the Negro.

In the three days since the attack, the boy had regained much of his strength, though he occasionally felt faint. He cleared his throat and focused hard on the man. He didn't understand why he had risked himself. Why he had walked into a fight that he knew he was going to lose. And lose badly. Especially after he, Samuel, hadn't even tried to save him from the snake.

The old Japanese was just following the Negro – would have followed him anywhere. Plus the men were attacking his granddaughter. Therefore he had reasons for what he'd done. But the Negro had nothing. Nothing except things to lose. That fact confused Samuel's mind. But it didn't matter. He'd done it, whatever his reasons.

'Thank thee,' Samuel said to the still form. The Negro didn't move or respond in any way and for a moment Samuel thought he might be dead, but then he saw his shallow breathing.

'I misjudged thee –' He paused. 'I wanted thee to know that in case thou are going to die.'

The room's stillness was broken by a harsh sentence of Japanese uttered by the old man in his delirium. Samuel continued to study the broken black face. The boy drew in a long breath and held it. 'I was scared again,' he said.

Samuel jumped back. The man had motioned him with a slight crook of his finger. The boy watched him for a moment, then leaned forward. 'Yes?'

'Not going to –' Prophet mumbled, the words scratching out of his throat.

'What?'

'Die.'

Samuel nodded. 'That is good.'

Prophet moved his head slightly in agreement.

The boy leaned weakly against the wall and continued to watch him. Prophet was breathing hard as if the brief conversation had badly drained his energy, then he crooked his finger again. The boy leaned back over him.

'Me too.'

'Mr Prophet?'

'Afraid.'

Samuel looked like he wanted to run out of the room for a moment. Then he said, 'I do not believe thee.'

'Believe,' Prophet said, straining to get the word out.

'But still thou fought. And Mr Kishimoto fought.'

Prophet thought about this for a while. 'Practice. Old man and me –' He stopped talking and rested for a time, closing his eyes. When Samuel thought he had fainted, Prophet reopened his eyes and continued, 'Had lots of practice. Gets easier.' He laughed but the pained expression said it hurt too much and he quit.

Prophet didn't say anything for a long while. Samuel just continued watching him as if he didn't want to leave.

Finally, Prophet said, 'You aren't supposed –' He stopped and caught his breath. 'Your mother –'

Samuel nodded at the man, but in his heart he knew it was more than just not having practice or obeying his mother. He was a coward.

'Samuel?' Pearl's voice came out of the room's darkness. She sounded groggy. 'Is that thee?'

'Yes.'

Neither Samuel nor Prophet had noticed her asleep in the chair in the shadowy corner of the bedroom. She tapped her thin cane over the floorboards until she was next to the bed.

'I will tell thee when Mr Prophet awakens. Until then, thou needs thy own rest.'

'He's awake.'

Her surprise was evident as she bent over him. 'We've been worried about thee, Mr Prophet.' She looked tired and drawn, dark circles underlining her weary eyes.

'Tell the old man to knock off his jabbering,' Prophet said, straining to get the words out.

Pearl put a hand to his forehead to check for fever.

'Tell him,' he insisted.

'Mr Kishimoto wouldn't hear.'

'Why?'

'He is still unconscious.'

Something in the tone of her voice caught Prophet's attention and he asked, 'How bad?'

'I don't know.'

Prophet remembered the pipe, the blow intended for him, but taken by the little man. 'What's the doctor say?'

'He won't come.'

Prophet felt his head spinning and moved his body until the pain itself brought him back to full awareness. He repeated what she'd said in his head, 'He won't come.' Prophet knew what that meant. It was over. The judge and the attorney had been right. The so-called respectable citizens of Liberty were slowly – one by one – abandoning the Eddys to the town's rabble. He started to say so – then didn't. She had enough to worry about. He thought about the old Japanese again.

'He's just faking. He's lazy.'

'No.'

Pearl walked Samuel from the room. Prophet rolled over, ignoring the pain, and studied the bandaged head of the old man. Mr Kishimoto's lips were moving through a hole in the material that covered his face, but no sound was coming out. As he studied the little form in the shadows, Prophet wondered things about the old man that he had never given much thought to before.

When he finally stopped mulling over these, he realized that he knew almost nothing about him. Nothing about this man who'd saved his life. Something seemed to be pressing hard against his chest. He knew only that the little man was a fighter. Like him in some ways. Only better. He rolled slowly back down on to the bed, pain shooting through his ribs, and stared at the ceiling for a long time. When he finally spoke he had to clear his throat. 'Serves you right, old man. You've been asking for trouble since you got here.'

As if in response, Mr Kishimoto rattled off another heated sentence.

'Be quiet – you old fool.'

The little man suddenly stopped talking and Prophet listened hard for his breathing. When he couldn't hear it, he rolled over quickly, ignoring the pain, and watched the small shape until he was certain he was still alive. 'Damn fake,' he muttered, easing himself back down. 'You deserve what you got. Teach you to follow me everywhere like a damn dog.'

Prophet heard the muffled sound of Pearl's voice in the hallway. 'Zacharias. I'm not going to tell thee again. Thou must stop hanging around Mr Prophet's doorway.'

'He needs me,' the boy protested.

Prophet smiled.

'No. He needs his rest. And thou has other things thou are supposed to be doing. Now run along.'

Pearl entered quietly, tapped through the darkness of the bedroom to check Mr Kishimoto; Prophet lay watching her, listening to the sounds the old man made.

'How's he look?'

'The same.'

'He's faking.'

'No,' she said softly.

Prophet stared at her through the shadows. 'You don't know how bad he is,' he challenged.

'Only that he is in God's hands.'

'God doesn't take things into His hands,' Prophet snapped.

Pearl ignored him and straightened Mr Kishimoto's blankets.

A moment later, he said, 'You don't really believe that.'

'Mr Prophet?'

'That the old man is in God's hands.'

'We are all in God's hands.'

He shook his head. 'If that's true I've been dropped a lot by Him.'

'Do not make fun of God, Mr Prophet.'

He didn't respond.

'As a minister, I would have thought we shared similar beliefs.'

He looked uncomfortable and tried to change the subject. 'The old man will be OK. He's a fighter.'

'That is not a saving grace. It is, in fact, the problem.'

He had finally had enough. 'No,' he said sharply. 'We didn't start that fight.'

'Thou started that fight, Mr Prophet, when thou attacked Penny James in the street. Then again in his house.'

The wind had picked up and was banging a shutter against the side of the house. Prophet listened to this for a while, trying to cool off. Then he said, 'That's crazy. He attacked you in the street. And he was threatening to shoot the woman.' He paused and rested. 'And they were beating your boy.' He was angry and breathing hard against the pain rising in his body. 'Should we have let them, Mrs Eddy?'

'Rest,' she said.

'No. Should we?' he persisted.

'Thou must answer that for thyself.'

'I have. That old man,' he said, pointing at Mr Kishimoto, 'fought for the children. And was injured for the children. That's love, Mrs Eddy.'

'No, Mr Prophet. That's ignorance.'

He didn't say anything for a time, just lay looking up at her face, his frown intensifying. Finally, he said, 'You aren't the keeper of the holy book.'

'No. But I know that violence is wrong. That God would have saved the children.'

Prophet stared at her with a shocked look on his face. 'God would have saved them? Is that right?' he said, sharply.

'Yes.'

'When? Before or after your boy was beaten into snot?'

Pearl didn't say anything for a moment, then continued. 'Mr Prophet, thou wrongly confuse rescue with salvation. God would have saved the children in wondrous ways beyond mere physical deliverance from danger.'

'Your religion makes you loony,' Prophet mumbled slowly.

Then he drifted off again. In his delirium Pearl heard him ranting at some Negro woman. Telling her he had to get going to take his shot. Whatever that meant. She wondered who this woman was. Who this man was. Who he really was. She ran Zacharias away from the door again. The boy was becoming bothersome about seeing the Negro.

There were seven women sitting in her parlor. They'd come in two carriages and Pearl figured they were a delegation of sorts, Miss Belle Johnson and Mrs Isabel Tutt doing most of the group's talking. Pearl considered the two women friends. They'd worked long and hard on a number of causes over the years: raised money for Liberty's library and school book funds, led a failed crusade against intemperance. And Belle and Isabel had joined Pearl in collecting blankets and warm clothing for the Indian Reservation Relief Fund, when public anger had dried up desperately needed contributions after the Little Bighorn. They were good women. Good friends. She knew the others in the room as well, but was not as close to them as she was to Belle and Isabel.

Pearl leaned back into her chair and listened to their quiet breathing, the soft clinking of the cups and saucers, the fiddling of their parasols and knew they were uncomfortable.

'Pearl Eddy. How long have we known each other?' Belle asked.

'A long time, Belle,' Pearl said softly, waiting for the real questions.

'That's correct. For a long time.'

'We have, too,' Isabel interjected.

Pearl nodded and then folded her hands together in her lap.

'And, Pearl,' Belle continued. 'While we love Rose Sherman, we don't necessarily hold with the things that she says and does.' There was a murmur of agreement. 'I guess what I'm saying, Pearl, is that she doesn't run the women of Liberty. At least not the younger women.'

'I'm not certain I understand,' Pearl said.

Belle cleared her throat. 'Pearl. Rose is saying some hurtful things. That you're keeping time with the colored man. That the Asians are selling opium and other narcotics.'

'And thou?'

'That it's foolishness, Pearl,' Belle said without hesitation. 'We all know you. We're friends.'

Pearl didn't say anything, just sat thinking.

'Pearl,' Isabel said. 'We want you to come to your senses.'

'Meaning?' Pearl asked quietly.

'Talk in town is going against you, Pearl. People don't want these Chinese around. Philo Tucker at the hardware tells anyone who'll listen that they breed like rats. That today we've got six . . . and tomorrow we'll have sixty. And, Pearl, more and more people are listening.'

'They're Japanese.'

'Pardon?' Isabel said.

'The Kishimotos are Japanese – not Chinese.'

Belle Johnson pressed her lips together and shook her head. 'Pearl, whatever race they are doesn't matter. They just aren't right for this town. They aren't right for your family.' She paused. 'We understand there was trouble out here three days ago.'

'Some men attacked Samuel and a Japanese girl, and an old Japanese man, and the Negro,' Pearl said. 'The old man is hurt badly.'

'None of our husbands,' Isabel said hurriedly. 'But there are people willing to do almost anything to get rid of these people. And we're afraid for you.'

Neither Pearl nor the women said anything for a while. Then Belle broke the silence. 'You've been a good neighbor and friend, Pearl Eddy, no matter what Rose Sherman wants people to believe. We don't want you and your boys hurt. We'll handle Rose. We'll also see to it that you get your seamstressing business back. We've come today with orders for twelve new dresses and there will be more on a steady basis. Right, ladies?' There was a strong murmur of support.

Belle reached into her purse and pulled out an envelope. 'And, Pearl, we've taken up a collection in town.' She hesitated. 'There's money here to take these people to either coast by train. And more to help them get settled someplace.'

Pearl wasn't listening. She was thinking about Matthew and their Sunday dinners during the summer months. She'd loved those. The laughter and the fun. The boys running and playing afterwards in the yard while she and Matthew sat on the front porch and talked. That was all gone now. And Lillian and the bank were threatening to take what was left. Tears were rolling down her cheeks. The women watched and some of them began to cry as well.

Now her friends were offering her a way out. A way to save her boys and her home. Then her breath caught in her throat. Her mind seemed to drift. She tried to concentrate on Belle's words but couldn't. Couldn't stop this kaleidoscopic thing that was happening in her head.

She seemed to see them all – the Eddys, the Kishimotos and the Negro – sitting in a small boat in the middle of a dark ocean. Dying of thirst. The boat slowly sinking. Then suddenly her friends were there. Coming to rescue them. Smiling and bringing water. And she was crying and happy. But when she tried to give the water to the little girls, to the old man, to the Negro . . . nothing came out but dust. The only people whose thirst she could quench were herself and her boys. Nothing for the others. Not the little girls. Not the baby, Ituro. None of them. Then the little boat was beginning to swamp, and her friends were shouting at her to lighten the load by throwing the Kishimotos and the Negro into the dark waters. 'My God! Do it for your boys,' Belle Johnson was screaming.

Then the vision was gone and she could hear Isabel saying what a wonderful place Liberty was to raise children. She didn't disagree, but she couldn't think about that now. She could only think of the brutal choice they'd brought her: save thyself and thy boys. But no others. Cast them away. Cast them into darkness or hellfire or damnation – it didn't matter where. Just cast them away.

Pearl didn't move or speak for a long time. These women, her friends, wanted the foreigners and the Negro out every bit as badly as the mob in Main Street had. They just wanted it without unpleasantness. Pearl's stubbornness and wrath began to rise in her throat. A fly was buzzing in the room and she listened to the sound. Then she stood up.

'No,' she said flatly. 'Thank thee. But no.'

'Pearl, you are just being sill—' The word seemed to have been torn off at Belle Johnson's teeth. Then the room fell silent until Pearl heard Prophet behind her mumbling: 'You stay away from me, you old nigger woman!'

'He's just delirious,' she assured them.

But moments later, screams and pandemonium broke out and she could hear the women fleeing as if pursued by death itself. She couldn't figure it. Then she heard Eiko yelling in Japanese. Then English. Then back to Japanese.

'You go bed!' she hollered. 'Go bed now! Isogu! Isogu!'

'Eiko?'

'Mr Prophet. Oooooh,' she moaned. 'He break up party.'

'Yes. But why? These women have seen a Negro before.'

'Not like this one,' Eiko said. 'Go bed! Beddo! Beddo!'

'Eiko?'

'No clothes. Big naked!'

Pearl sat stunned and still for a minute, listening to Eiko chasing Prophet back to his bed. Then she began to laugh. The laughter exploded through the house, so loud that Eiko quit chasing Prophet long enough to peek at her, then shook her head and went rushing back.

'Beddo! Now! No dance! Beddo!'

Pearl was doubled up with the laughter. Then she heard Zacharias yelling, 'Thou just fought a big battle. Thou are a hero and thou needs thy rest.'

She stopped laughing and folded her hands together in her lap. Then, slowly, she began to squeeze them. Squeezed them until her knuckles were cream-white from the strain.

*

268

Inside the bedroom, in the soft warm air of an April night that drifted through the open windows, after Prophet had slept through another day, he shifted between the sheets of his bed and felt the pain dig at his soul again. He opened his eyes and knew immediately that he and the old Japanese were not alone.

He tensed, the contraction causing pain to spurt in a hundred places over his injured body. He fought it, and the feeling of faintness, rolling on to his shoulder toward the old man's bed.

Eiko was trying to give Mr Kishimoto water. Unconscious, the tiny man was nevertheless still cursing at her. Prophet watched them for a while then gruffly asked, 'How is the little faker?'

'He sick. Byoki no.' Then Eiko grinned at him. 'You big party-breaker.'

He didn't understand the last part of what she'd said. But then he often didn't understand her. He ignored it and focused on the old man. 'He'll be fine,' he said firmly. 'As long as he thinks he can pester me, he'll hang around.'

She didn't respond. When she was done with the old man, Eiko came over and looked down at Prophet's busted face and said, 'You not so strong. No tsuyoi.' She was smiling.

And he smiled back at her for the first time. 'Stronger than that old man.'

She looked suddenly serious. 'Now. Maybe yes. Once. Maybe no.'

They didn't speak for a while. Eiko had returned to the old man's bed and was sitting in a chair and watching his bandaged face, leaning toward him as if she wanted to tell him something.

'Who is he?'

'Muneo Kishimoto,' she said, as if the name would mean something grand to him.

'I know that. But why the stick? And why does he follow me like a dog?'

She stiffened. She was ready to defend the old man on this

269

quiet night. 'No dog. He follow like great warrior. Muneo Kishimoto. Great soldier.'

The old man was hard as scrap metal, but at something like four foot eight inches and maybe ninety-five pounds with his hair wet, Prophet had trouble swallowing that Kishimoto was some famous Nipponese gladiator. But he didn't feel like talking him down. Not now. Not while he was hurt and unconscious. And not after what he had done.

Eiko turned the kerosene lamp down until it cast only a dull smudge of yellow light over the bedroom. Prophet watched a mouse scurry across the wooden floor. They hadn't spoken for a few minutes, the stillness broken only by the old man's shallow breathing. Eiko returned to Mr Kishimoto. Prophet watched.

'He once chief retainer for second daimyo of Naga Prefecture,' she said with obvious pride in her voice. 'Okii samurai,' the words crisp-sounding as they came off her tongue. 'Big samurai.'

Prophet didn't know much about samurai. Only that they were mean. That certainly fit the old Jap.

'He's no longer whatever he used to be – so why's he always looking for trouble?'

She touched the old man's forehead through the bandages with the tips of her fingers in a reverent way. 'Itsumo. Always samurai.'

Eiko spent the next few minutes making up the old man's bed with him in it. Then she turned and looked at Prophet across the shadowy light of the room. 'He fight because samurai fight. Their way is shi. Death.'

'What the hell does that mean?'

'Samurai live like already dead. Iie osore. No fear. Only loyalty to master.'

Prophet shook his head. 'And he thinks I'm his master, right?'

Eiko ignored him. 'He try to commit junshi,' she said, drawing her fist hard across her stomach in a movement that needed no translation. 'To accompany master when he died.' She shrugged her shoulders. 'But junshi forbidden by shogunate.'

They didn't speak for a moment, Prophet studying the strange old man, Eiko whispering prayers in the small room. Prophet wondered about the little Jap and his willingness to conk out for other people. It was crazy. Prophet was almost a complete stranger. The only thing he'd ever done for the old man was beat the crap out of him and then yell at him every day. Things that hardly seemed worth dying for. Prophet promised himself he'd never die for anyone else. It was hard enough to do it for yourself.

Eiko stood and smiled down at Prophet. 'You new master. Shiawase na. Happy.'

'You tell him I'm not shiawase-whatever. I'm not his master. And I don't want him following me.'

'You tell him. He no listen to me.' She paused. 'Anyhow, he may die. Anyhow.'

'Don't sound too sad about it.'

She nodded vigorously and grinned. 'Not sad. He dead already. Anyhow, that what he like. Die for master. So why I be sad?'

'Very touching,' Prophet mumbled, feeling suddenly weak.

Pearl Eddy waited a while after she heard Eiko leave the sickroom before she tapped quietly inside. Zacharias was sitting by the door and she scolded him and sent him scurrying; his presence steeling her resolve that she was doing the right thing. She stopped next to Prophet's bedside. Neither of them spoke for a while. He could tell she had something on her mind and figured it was best to wait and let her roll it out.

Outside the bedroom window the hogs were fighting over the remains of a yellow gopher snake they'd killed behind the barn, squealing and snorting like it was a choice tidbit. With the curtains open, the room had pools of soft moonlight on the floor.

Pearl cleared her throat. 'How do thou feel, Mr Prophet?'

'Fine.'

'Good,' she said quietly. There was something in her tone that caused him to listen closely. She let the squealing of the hogs die down, then continued. 'Thou remembers what I said about Zacharias?'

'About?'

'How he looks up to thee.'

'Yes.'

Pearl had reached up and put a hand on the wall as if she needed support. It seemed an odd thing to him.

'Do thou also remember thy promise about violence?'

Prophet rolled his eyes, then said, 'I didn't start anything with Penny James, Mrs Eddy. He started it. Both times. And I sure didn't start things at the river.'

She looked suddenly exhausted. 'It doesn't matter, Mr Prophet,' she said quietly. 'I asked thee to control thy violence. To not expose my children to it. But thou have not.'

'Mrs Eddy. Only lesson I ever learned in this life was that weakness invites trouble.'

She seemed to tighten up with what he'd just said.

He pressed his advantage. 'You ought to think on that, ma'am.'

Pearl could hear him speaking but she was no longer listening to him, her mind flying back over the years to a painful memory: Matthew had once told her almost exactly the same thing. She shivered.

It happened in the first year of their marriage. Matthew was not yet living as a Quaker, had not begun his moral metamorphosis. She bit her lower lip hard, wishing now he had never tried, the thought tearing at her heart. They had been traveling west to Kansas when he'd gotten into a fight with a drunk in the dining car of the train, the man having made improper remarks about her. Matthew had a quick temper and hit the man hard enough to knock him unconscious. Pearl exhaled hard with the painful memory.

'You OK, ma'am?' Prophet asked, looking at her as if she might be sick.

'Yes.' She wrapped her arms around her waist, as if trying to hold herself, remembering that she had gotten angry and refused to talk the entire rest of the trip. For a thousand miles she had sat in silence. It was the first time Matthew had ever witnessed her stubbornness. She winced, as if struck. Her awful wrath.

After that episode Matthew had vowed to live as a Quaker,

adopting the clothing, the speech, the beliefs. Her breath snagged in her throat: the non-violence. He had sacrificed everything to believe like her. She knew now that he had done it because he had realized that they could never live together unless he did. She was fighting back tears now, turning and walking to the window so Prophet wouldn't see. And it had killed him. She had killed him.

Prophet watched her warily. He knew when she was in one of her moods she was tough to handle. A horned owl was sounding in the elm near the well, hunting mice along the barn wall, Prophet figured. He let his mind drift, wondering how they saw something that small in the dark. He knew they could spot a mouse in grass at a hundred yards.

Pearl leaned against the wall by the window, her thoughts still on Matthew. About a year after the train incident, on a lovely summer evening as they were sitting on the front porch watching the fireflies and listening to the sounds of their children playing hide-and-go-seek, he had turned to her and said: 'The passiveness, Pearl. It causes violence.' Pearl shuddered hard. Eighteen months ago, that truth had destroyed a large part of her life.

From the trial she knew that Matthew had been jumped by a group of men in front of the saloon. They claimed they had only been having fun with a Quaker, grabbing his hat, then his coat, and shoving him into a water trough, trying to get him to fight back. But he hadn't. She clamped her eyes closed tight as if to try and shut out the vision in her mind. He had lived up to his beliefs. No, she shook her head. She would not lie to herself. He had lived up to her beliefs. She was having a hard time breathing now.

The men had followed him to his horse, and when he started to mount, they had spooked the animal, his foot catching in the stirrup. Pearl was crying without sound now. The horse had galloped the three miles home. It had been winter and the roads frozen hard, and when Pearl freed the leg from the saddle and touched his face, she had not recognized him. Not recognized him until he had said her name. She was gasping for breath now.

273

'Mrs Eddy?'

It seemed unbearably hot in the bedroom and she wiped the back of her hand across her forehead. Yes. He had died because of her beliefs. Her stubbornness. Her wrath. She would have to live with this knowledge for the rest of her life. She'd never escape it. She set her jaw.

But Matthew had also died doing the will of God. She pulled herself up straighter and squared her small shoulders. And she would not – could not – allow his sacrifice to be cheapened by this man teaching his sons violence, leading them down the broad path to damnation. No. She could not allow it. It was no more complicated in her mind than that. She saw it very clearly.

'I didn't start that trouble, Mrs Eddy,' Prophet was saying.

'It doesn't matter.' She stood and listened to the wind and the owl for a while, then returned to the bedside and said, 'There is a saying in Proverbs, Mr Prophet. I'm certain thou are familiar with it: "A wrathful man stirreth up trouble."'

He didn't say anything more. Just looked at her face. He found it hard to believe. Or, maybe, he just didn't want to believe it.

'Thou must leave, Mr Prophet.'

After all the time he'd spent telling himself that he was wasting his time here, that he had to get on the road to Minnesota, he was surprised how the words made him feel. He watched her face for a long time and then said, 'I was going anyway. Soon as I can get around.'

She nodded but didn't say anything.

'I got things I've been putting off.'

She turned away slowly and left the room. Somewhere in the hallway he could hear her crying. He fought the tremors around his mouth. The old black woman was watching him from high in a dark corner of the room. Like she pitied him. He hated that.

It was early morning, just before the full light and before the birds cut loose with their endless singing for the day, the room cool and dimly lit, and Fumiko was standing and frowning at the rumpled mass of blankets that covered Samuel Eddy's bed. She had just entered the room, moments before, and stood staring down at him, Samuel too embarrassed to say anything. He studiously avoided her eyes, studying instead her closely clipped hair. His mother's work for certain. She'd turned Hector's ragged cuts into a smooth trim, shaped nicely to Fumiko's handsome head, a single lock of long hair draped stylishly down ponytail-fashion on one side, caught up in a pink silk ribbon.

Only his mother would have thought of this touch. Most everyone else would have just clipped off the piece, leaving the girl to look like a prisoner rather than a beautiful young woman with an exotic hair style. Even with the dark bruise on her cheek, she looked pretty. She moved closer. He pretended to sleep.

Then she was busily straightening his covers, and he was trying desperately to act natural. He cleared his throat. 'Thank thee.'

She stepped back, smiled and bowed slightly. The bow not cowed or obedient, just polite, as though simply acknowledging him. All traces of her former anger were gone. He raised his head off the pillow and bowed awkwardly back.

This seemed to embarrass her slightly and she began to move around the room, opening windows, adjusting curtains and, in general, making the place ready for the coming day. Done, she stopped and looked back at his bruised face, as if she didn't know what to do next. Then she bowed slightly once more, and said, 'Thank you.'

It was the second time that she had ever spoken to him. And it was wonderful.

'For?'

'Fusegu me,' she said in her strongly accented voice, pointing vigorously at herself as if he might not be able to understand her words. 'Protect me.'

He thought her voice the prettiest sound in the world, deep and full, like a cat's purring. Then the old feeling of shame returned. She didn't look like she was making fun of him. But he wasn't certain. She saw the darkness in his expression.

275

'I said wrong?'

'No.'

'What is the—' She struggled for the word. 'Matter?'

'Nothing.' He looked out of the window at the backyard. Jack was in his corral looking toward the house. Samuel continued staring at the horse.

'Something.'

He looked back and held his breath. 'You did the fighting,' he said finally. 'I just stood.'

She was nodding vigorously and he wondered if she understood what he was saying. 'You stand,' she said, continuing to nod, and holding her two hands in front of her, palms toward one another, like she might be measuring a very small fish, 'like this. Face – face.' Then she burst into a smile that he thought had the power to burn holes through things. 'For me. Fumiko.' She paused and the smile left her face. 'No one ever do that for me or my family. Never,' she said softly. 'Like we not really ningen. People.'

He watched her face for a moment feeling bad for her, knowing what it was like to be treated that way, and didn't want to hurt her more by letting her believe he'd done something he hadn't. He cleared his throat. 'I didn't fight.'

'You did this,' she said, putting her hands up again. She stared at him like he was a modern Lancelot. It made him squirm. She didn't understand. Still, it was wonderful.

'We've been here for almost two weeks,' Prophet complained. 'It isn't healthy. The old man needs sun. I need sun.' He was climbing out of bed, Pearl and Eiko were standing in the doorway. He looked shaky.

'Mr Prophet. If thou feel well enough, fine. But Mr Kishimoto is in no condition—'

'I've been watching him. He isn't going to get any better in here. Old man,' Prophet called toward the bed. 'Old man. We're going outside. You for it?'

Mr Kishimoto had been awake for the past week but he had not spoken. His words seemed to have stopped coming when he returned to consciousness. He moved his lips, but nothing came out. He was moving them now.

'He just said he's for it,' Prophet said, bending and picking the man up, surprised at how light he felt.

'Mr Prophet,' Pearl protested. 'Mr Kishimoto is not well.'

'You're a worrier, Mrs Eddy,' Prophet said as he moved through the house toward the back porch, Muneo Kishimoto in his arms. Prophet's legs were wobbling and there was a moment when he lost balance and almost fell, but he stabilized and continued forward, Pearl tapping along behind.

'For a little while only, Mr Prophet,' Pearl cautioned.

'Sure, Mrs Eddy.'

She listened to the Negro straining to bear the old man in his arms down the porch steps and then across the yard, talking steadily to Mr Kishimoto as he went, and got a funny feeling deep inside her that made her want to cry. She had been right. God saved in mysterious ways. Then she heard Zacharias running down the steps after him and knew that she had also been right about the man having to leave. To protect the boy. She was sorry. But that changed nothing.

The rays of mid-afternoon sunlight felt just as wonderful as Prophet had imagined they would; the day not hot, just flooded with brilliant light. He selected a place near the old stone well-house and Eiko and Pearl spread blankets on the ground for them.

Prophet leaned back against the cool, smooth stones soaking in the sunlight, while Mr Kishimoto sat in his familiar stiff-backed, cross-legged posture, still wrapped in his bandages and looking like the dearly departed at a picnic. As was normal, the old man did not speak. But he drooled, and Prophet kept drying his mouth with a rag, as if he were a large child.

'Moto,' he said, dabbing the side of the man's mouth one more time, 'you got to get a grip on yourself. You can't sit around,

277

spitting up like a baby.' He paused. 'They'll kick you out of the samurais.'

The old man seemed to stir slightly at the sound of the word.

Prophet turned his head slowly and took a close look around the farmyard, the gardens, the barn, the watering sluice. His eyes moved slowly over details that he had missed before. He wanted to remember this place. All of it. He might never see a place like this again.

He turned and looked at the house: gray and serious-looking as ever. Still, there was something about it he liked. That was funny. He couldn't remember ever liking a building before in his life. But he liked this one. He just didn't know why. It wasn't handsome or grand. It was just big and beat-up. But he liked it. He always would.

He felt like he'd lived here all his life. That was funny, too. Then his chest began to tighten and he shut his eyes and tipped his face up into the sunlight. 'Waste of time,' he muttered to himself. 'Get to Minnesota and get my shot.'

Zacharias was sitting cross-legged on the ground in front of them, his freckled face covered by the shade of his large hat.

'When thou are feeling better, we can go fishing.' Zacharias scratched his ankle. 'Thou ever been?'

Prophet's eyes were closed and he was leaning back on his arms, taking the sun and ignoring the boy.

'Thou ever been fishing?'

'Yes.'

'My pa used to take me. I'll show thee how to catch catfish. I'll bet thee doesn't know how. Would thou like that?'

Prophet squinted at the boy and then said, 'Sure. If we've got time.'

Zacharias grinned. 'We got nothing but time. It's summer.'

Prophet sat up, looking agitated. 'Don't talk like that,' he snapped. 'Time gets away from a person. Understand?'

Suddenly the muscles around his mouth had gone taut and he was turning away and putting his hand up to cover it and making

278

his pretend yawn. When he'd gained control of his face again, he said, 'You hear?'

Zacharias looked hurt. 'Yes, sir.'

'Good.'

'Zacharias,' Pearl called from the porch.

'We don't have to go fishing.'

'I want to go fishing. Now get before your mother comes storming down here after us both.'

'I don't want to now,' Zacharias said.

'Fine.'

Prophet turned and looked at Mr Kishimoto. 'You know I was right,' he said sheepishly. 'And you know time's running out for us, old man.' He stopped talking again, gathering his thoughts. 'We got to come to an understanding.'

The red shawl of the old Japanese had slipped to the ground and Prophet put it back over his shoulders. Then he looked through the holes in the bandages into his small eyes. They seemed to peer through him as if the little man were staring at a distant memory. Prophet sat back down and let him alone for a while. He figured the old man didn't have much time left for remembering.

Finally he said, 'You listen. I'm not your master. And you can't spend whatever little time you got following me. I got things to do. And you can't come.'

Prophet closed his eyes and thought that he had just day-dreamed for a short while about Minnesota, but when he awoke the sun was setting and night would soon be upon them. Someone had covered them with blankets. Pearl Eddy probably. The sound of children laughing drifted across the yard from the kitchen. He cleared his throat. 'You awake?'

The old man didn't move, but Prophet could see that he was breathing.

'Like I said. I got things to do and you can't come. I appreciate what you did. But you still can't come.' Prophet continued to sit and think, not certain what else to say to discourage him. 'You just can't come where I'm heading,' Prophet repeated. For some reason, it bothered him to say this. The man had saved him. But that didn't change anything. He couldn't have the old man trotting after him in his silly bathrobe all the way to Minnesota.

Prophet turned and studied the side of the bandaged face. He cleared his throat. 'You understand?' Prophet leaned over and dabbed at the side of his mouth again. 'Quit your damn slobbering.'

Then the old man's lips were moving and Prophet leaned closer. 'Master,' was all the old man said.

'No! You aren't some slave and I'm not some boss.' Prophet stared in frustration at the tiny man. 'If you got to call me something, call me friend.'

Prophet shut his eyes. When he opened them again, they were just standing there. Two of them. He could see three horses with their reins dropped near the barn. Two men and three horses. He wasn't great at arithmetic but he knew what it meant.

And they were big enough and rough enough looking that he also knew he couldn't resist them. If he'd been well, he could've handled them easily. But he wasn't. He leaned back weakly against the well and just stared up at them.

'Let's go.' The man who spoke had a bushy white beard like Santa Claus. But Prophet knew he wasn't. Prophet didn't move.

'Let's go, damn it. We don't like this any better than you do.' The man kicked a stone. 'But we been paid to do it.'

Prophet was struggling to get to his feet when he heard her.

'What do thou want with this man?'

His heart sank. He didn't want them involved in this mess.

'You just stay out of this, ma'am. Our business is with the colored. Not you. We got no interest in hurting you or your place.'

'Then leave,' Pearl said firmly.

'Leave!' Zacharias shouted.

'Zacharias, thou are to go to the house.' Her voice had an edge to it that neither Prophet nor the boy had ever heard before and

Zacharias turned and started off in the darkness. Then he stopped and looked back at the Negro.

'Mr Prophet.'

'Yes?'

'I want to go fishing with thee.'

'Me too.'

Zacharias broke at a run for the house. Prophet could hear him sobbing. Pearl had been sweeping the back porch and stood now clutching a broom in her hands. He could see her trembling in the darkening air of the evening.

'I asked thee a question. What do thou want with Mr Prophet?'

'We don't want anything, lady. We've just been paid to collect him and bring him in. If you've got any argument it's with those who paid us'

'Why do they want Mr Prophet?'

He could hear her voice changing.

'Lady. Don't ask questions. OK? Just get back into the house and let us get this done.'

'They're right. This isn't your business,' Prophet said. 'I don't need you nosing in everything I do.'

Pearl ignored him and squared her body to the place where she'd last heard the sound of the bearded man's voice. 'Thou are being used by Satan. Thou cannot participate in just part of this sin. Thou are involved in all of it.'

Prophet just shook his head. He didn't want to look at her. He just wanted her to turn and go back inside the kitchen, to make dinner, to sew, to have her boys read to her. Just to do the things she did. And to let these men get on with it. They were going to do it anyway. No matter what she said. This wasn't a time for her talk.

'Lady, get out of here,' the man warned.

'I will not.' She paused. 'I will be here while thee do this thing. Thou will not have the comfort of the night to hide thy acts.'

'I don't give a damn, lady. We're taking this nigger to the

people who paid us. What they do with him is their business. Not ours.'

Prophet was just starting to get to his feet, knowing they weren't leaving without him, and not wanting trouble for her or the others, when he saw her swing. He didn't believe it. But when he turned his head he saw the broom catch the man full in the face and pitch him backwards on to the seat of his pants. Then Pearl Eddy was standing over him and screaming and striking wildly with the broom like she was indeed fighting off Satan. Prophet couldn't move.

The second man was laughing hard and coming to the aid of his friend, his eyes focused hard on his fallen comrade so that he didn't see the shape moving in the shadows toward him. Didn't see Eiko swing. The iron skillet hit him on the side of the head and Prophet knew from the way he collapsed, he wasn't getting up for a while.

As quickly as she'd begun the attack, Pearl broke it off. But she was still screaming as if she'd witnessed something awful. The bearded man was bleeding from his nose and he scrambled to his feet and just stared at her, then he bent and picked up his friend and stumbled toward the horses.

'And no come back!' Eiko yelled.

Prophet couldn't take his eyes off Pearl Eddy. She just stood holding the broom in both her hands, shaking like she had malaria or something, or like she'd killed a man instead of just hit him with an old broom. Eiko stood quietly beside her, skillet in her hand, an arm around Pearl's waist, as if she were afraid the woman might fall down.

Then from behind them came another voice. 'Gosh!' Zacharias and his brothers stood staring at their mother as if she'd just done something amazing. Prophet wanted to laugh but knew he shouldn't.

Eiko was squinting hard at the boys now, then she pointed a finger at the house. The gesture needed no translation. They turned and started off, talking rapidly among themselves. 'Pow!

Whammm! Bammm!' Zacharias hollered from the safety of the porch, thoroughly impressed by his mother's performance.

Eiko said something to Pearl that Prophet couldn't hear. She shook her head. Then the little oriental woman reached out and put her hand on the broom and Pearl let go of it as if it were a viper. Then she started walking slowly toward the corral, looking like she was lost in a daze. Eiko started to follow, then stopped and returned to the house.

Prophet settled down slowly back on to the ground, watching the little woman through the gathering dusk, her smallness magnified by the huge barn. He would never have believed her capable of doing what she'd just done. And from the look of her, he guessed she'd never believed it either. He wanted to talk to her, to tell her things that he felt he should. But the time wasn't right. He stared off at the gardens for a while, thinking about catching the late train. He could just about make the tracks in time.

Prophet saw it when he turned and looked back toward the dark shape of the barn. At first he thought it was the last of the setting sun, a pink tinge of light running across the sky above the barn. Then, with a start, he realized that he was facing north, the western horizon to his left. Hurriedly, he stooped and picked up the small man and started at a run for the corral.

'Mrs Eddy,' he yelled.

She turned slowly.

'Mrs Eddy,' Prophet said, breathing hard. 'Get the old man inside.'

'What's wrong, Mr Prophet?'

'They're burning us out.'

It didn't take long for Prophet to realize that fires in tallgrass prairie don't burn, they rage, and by the time he made it around to the back of the barn, this one was storming in a blizzard of flame toward the farm. While he had no proof, he was certain it had been deliberately set. He figured when the two men returned to whoever had paid them to retrieve him, they'd decided to burn them out instead.

The flames were in the thickest grass, the wind blowing so that it would drive the fire over them; then once on the other side of the farm, it would burn out in the sandhills, sparing the town. Yes. It had been set. There was no doubt.

He studied the bright orange glow, choking in the smoky wind, watching in amazement as the flames exploded thirty and forty feet into the air. Fortunately the fire was a good two miles off. There was still time. He ran for the barn, forgetting the pain and soreness in his body. Samuel had gotten there ahead of him with the same idea and was hurriedly harnessing Jack.

'Where's the plow?' Prophet yelled.

'Under that tarp!' Samuel pointed to a darkened corner of the barn.

'This animal ever plowed before?' Prophet indicated the shivering horse.

'Just the gardens.'

Then the women and children were inside the barn, eyes tearing and coughing in the thickening smoke. Prophet glanced at Pearl. Whatever shock she'd felt after the broom attack was gone and she was moving and giving orders like her old self. She was a fighter.

'Get the chickens into the crates and up near the house,' she called over the building noise of the fire and the frightened animals and children. 'And, Eiko, let's pen the pigs up there as well.'

Then Prophet felt someone tugging on his leg and he looked down into the frightened face of Zacharias.

'I'm going with thee!' the boy yelled.

'No, you are not.' Prophet knelt and pulled the boy closer. 'You stick with your mother.' He lowered his voice as if confiding in the boy. 'She can't see and there's a danger she'll walk into the fire. So you stay with her. Hear?'

The boy nodded. Then he said, 'Mr Prophet. Thou will not die like my father, will thee?'

'No.'

When they drove Jack to the back side of the barn, Prophet stopped and stood staring, unable to speak.

'What's wrong?' Samuel yelled.

'Fast!'

'Horse can't outrun them.'

The flames had eaten up half a mile of grass in the time they'd been inside the barn, and he figured that, at best, there was no more than fifteen or twenty minutes before it was on them. It looked like the fury of hell.

'Damn!' he muttered, climbing the corral fence and tying a wet blanket around Jack's head. The old horse fought him until Samuel clamped his nostrils down hard with his fingers.

The man nodded at him.

The boy nodded back, keeping his hand on Jack's nose and watching the Negro's face. Prophet didn't like blindfolding the animal but it was the only way to make certain he wouldn't panic and bolt into the flames. The only problem was that if he went down, the horse was lost. But there was no other way.

'I'll plow,' Prophet said, grasping the handles and the reins. 'You get water up on the barn. Douse the roof. Then do the house. Stay with the house. I'll cover the barn.'

'I'll stay with you,' Samuel hollered.

'No. The house,' Prophet insisted. The barn, he knew, would take the brunt of the firestorm and Prophet didn't want the boy on it when the flames hit. But he didn't say this. 'The house. Your mother and the others will be in it. Make certain the door and windows are shut, that they have water inside, and wet blankets over every opening. Then get on top and beat out sparks. I'll join if I can.'

Samuel started to say something else to the man. But Prophet cut him off. 'Get going.'

Prophet turned and watched the flames roaring across the grass-land fanned by new wind, the air of the barnyard filling fast with drifting smoke, so thick that things were disappearing in it. Not much time. He yelled at Jack and headed toward the tall grasses, urging the nervous horse on with slaps from the reins. Then the wild animals came.

There seemed to be a living wall of them pouring through the grass, some on fire, all fleeing in mad desperation ahead of the burning. The coyotes and foxes were first, hunting along the front line of panic; then came deer, turkeys and prairie chickens. These were followed by the rodents and the reptiles. Even insects came, the night sky filling with lacewings, digger bees and midges; heavy-bodied grasshoppers zoomed low through the smoky air, crashing into the walls of the barn and house.

Soon the yard was crowded with thousands of creatures huddled in mixed groups, instinctively sensing that the clearing was their only chance to survive. Prophet and Jack were covered with frantically clinging robber flies, bees and butterflies, the horse twitching his skin and swishing his tail, but not dislodging the frightened insects.

But the worst, Prophet thought, were the birds. They came flying into the place in frantic waves, landing on the fences and the buildings until there was no more room, then covering the ground. They had been forced to abandon their young in the burning grasses and their shrill cries were rending the air and making it hard to hear. Prophet cupped his mouth and yelled at Jack, driving the horse into the towering brush toward the on-rushing flames.

He plowed fifteen furrows in front of the barn at one hundred yards out, then whipped Jack hard to the north end of the gardens and started to do the same in a desperate attempt to create a second firebreak. He had completed one two-hundred-yard run. Then he realized it was over. He stopped and turned and faced the oncoming holocaust of fire, stunned by the force of it.

Over a mile wide, the orange storm was still some five hundred yards from the barn, but when he faced toward it, he could feel the burning on his skin. He was having a hard time breathing in the smoke and heat, and he tied a handkerchief over his nose and mouth, then unhooked the plow and jumped up on Jack and kicked hard for the yard.

He checked the outer sheds to make certain all the animals had been turned loose, then he led the shying horse to the porch where the women and children had gathered in a frightened group to watch the final assault of fire. Samuel and Fumiko were on the roof, their faces covered with wet cloth, their clothes wisely soaked. Hot showers of ash and sparks were beginning to drift down, starting small fires in the short-stemmed red clover that covered the yard. Zacharias ran over and knelt and looked Prophet in the face.

'Are we going to burn up?'

'No,' Prophet said, with more confidence than he felt. He'd seen fires before, but never one like this, never one with this speed or intensity, a huge black cloud billowing out of the flames, drifting thickly across the land, obscuring the barn and other buildings in a dark and stinging fog.

'Can I help?' Zacharias asked.

The boy looked badly shaken.

'Yes. Get your mother and the others inside,' Prophet said, stamping out a fire in the shortgrass near the steps. The wild creatures moved slowly away from him as he walked amongst them, seemingly afraid of nothing but the roaring inferno.

'The children?' Pearl called.

'Take Jack and the twins in. I need Samuel and the girl on the house.'

Prophet pulled the harness and blanket off of Jack and pointed the horse toward the sandhills and slapped him hard on the rump, then he turned and started at a trot toward the gardens, the wild animals again parting slowly in front of him. He soon disappeared in the dark haze, unable to see more than fifteen feet in any direction. Zacharias tugged his mother toward the kitchen. 'Thou must go inside,' he ordered. Pearl nodded.

In the confusion and smoke-filled darkness, no one noticed Mr

Kishimoto sitting in the deep, smoky shadows of the porch. The old man's eyes were fixed on the Negro as he hurried toward the climbing roses, then Prophet disappeared in the drifting screen of smoke. The old man did not see him change direction and start for the barn.

Eiko caught Zacharias by the shoulder as he tried to slip back outside, then she shut the back door and nailed a wet blanket over the inside to stop the smoke.

'Let me go. I got to help Mr Prophet. He needs me.'

'You got to help no one,' the woman said. 'Go sit with other children.'

Something he couldn't taste, feel or hear told Prophet to stop. Whatever it was, it kept triggering a nerve somewhere deep inside his brain. While he didn't know the origin of the sensation, he knew it was real. And he knew he was in danger. Physical danger. He just didn't know why. Or what.

Prophet had turned and was starting back toward the house when he found out. The barn blew as surely as if it had been loaded with black powder and a match tossed into it, raining boards and farm implements over the yard, the roof sailing like some great ship of the night into the huge draft of the flames.

The concussion from the explosion hit hard like a board across his shoulders, knocking Prophet tumbling forward over the ground. He scrambled to safety behind the well, fighting hard against the sensation that he was passing out. He lay still for a time, his face pressed against the stones, trying to clear his head, the scorching flames searing the air around the edges of the well and illuminating the yard, house and gardens in a harsh, wavering light.

Then, for a fleeting moment, he thought he saw a shadowy shape trotting toward the gardens, then it disappeared in the smoke. But that was impossible. The heat was too great. And Samuel and Fumiko were up on the roof and had promised they wouldn't get down. Fortunately, they were far enough away that the firestorm of the barn hadn't reached them. Everyone else was inside the house. Prophet shrugged off the trotting figure as his imagination enhanced by pain. Either that or he'd seen Jack or a coyote panic and bolt into the flames. Animals would do that. Or maybe it was the old black woman. 'Good riddance,' he muttered. Five minutes later he tested the air above the well with his hand, then he began to pull back toward the house.

Prophet awoke on the floor of the kitchen, where Pearl and Eiko had carried him after he'd passed out. He studied the ceiling and smiled. The boy and girl had saved it, saved the old house. The room dark, Prophet thought it was still night, then he saw the crack of sunlight around the edge of the blanket. He was hurting badly. His face was burning and he raised a hand, gingerly feeling the blisters and the peeled skin. It hurt like hell. But he was alive. That was something.

Slowly, he pulled himself up, leaning back on his elbows, feeling dizzy and weak. Pearl was sitting at the kitchen table holding Zacharias in her lap. The boy was watching him closely, a worried look across his freckled face. Pearl was listening.

'Are thou OK, Mr Prophet?' Zacharias asked in a worried voice.

'Yes,' he said through the pain in his lungs. Zacharias grinned and made a growling sound, clawing the air with his small fingers.

'How do thou feel?' Pearl asked.

'Like a baked potato.'

'I put grease on thy face.'

'Thanks. Samuel and Fumiko?'

'In the parlor resting.'

He nodded, looking around the kitchen again. Then he smiled at her. 'They saved it.'

'Yes. I have thanked God,' she said as if to remind him of the watchful eye of providence.

They didn't say anything for a time, then Pearl spoke. 'Zacharias, go to thy bedroom with thy brothers. Thou has been up all night.'

Zacharias turned and looked at Prophet and growled, then clawed the air again. Prophet laughed at him.

She waited until the boy was gone, then said, 'Mr Prophet. I didn't want to ask Zacharias.'

'What's that, Mrs Eddy?'

'What it looks like – what survived.' She paused. 'Mrs Kishimoto could not tell last night in the smoke.'

Prophet struggled to his feet and pulled the blanket down off the window. It took him a while before he could say anything. And when he finally could, he didn't want to. He cleared his throat a couple of times.

'Mr Prophet?'

'Nothing.'

She stiffened with the word.

Maybe with another woman Prophet might have lied, softened the truth, but not with Pearl Eddy. 'Everything is gone. The barns and sheds. The fences. The wellhouse. The hens.' He stopped and studied the black desolation of the yard. 'The hogs panicked and stacked up on one another. They're gone.' He paused. 'Everything, Mrs Eddy.'

'The gardens?' She paused. 'The berries?'

He didn't speak for a few moments, he was staring at two thin lines of gray smoke rising like ropes into the still morning air from the charred remains of Matthew Eddy's cross and the sign. When he finally spoke, Prophet said, 'It's all gone.'

It didn't seem possible. Even the green plants were gone; the blaze so hot that it had melted the iron pump-handle near the well into a slumping mass of metal, and desiccated every living thing, sucking the moisture from each fiber, before consuming it in flames.

She stood and turned toward the sink. 'Coffee, Mr Prophet?'

'There's nothing outside,' he said quietly, not certain she understood the totality of the loss. 'Nothing – Mrs Eddy.'

'Yes.'

'No,' he said, speaking his words carefully in order to make certain she heard him and didn't smooth it over the way she did some things. 'Absolutely nothing.'

'I heard thee. We will just have to figure some way to do the things that need doing.'

'No,' he snapped, frustrated by her stubbornness. 'It's over.'

'Coffee, Mr Prophet?' she asked again.

He ignored her as well. 'You've got to leave. There's nothing here for you.'

She didn't say anything, but he sensed that leaving wasn't something she planned on doing. Prophet whirled toward her, ready to tell her again, and again, if necessary, then he stopped and just stood watching a shaft of April sunlight pouring through the window, staring at the floating dust motes that looked like galaxies in the light. He knew she wasn't going to listen.

Finally, he said, 'Where's the old man?'

She stopped moving and straightened up, holding the edge of the sink in a way he didn't like.

'Gone, Mr Prophet.'

The news hit like a punch in the gut.

'In his sleep?'

'Outside somehow.'

Prophet didn't move. It hadn't been his imagination. He'd seen the old man trotting for the gardens. He knew why. He just didn't want to tell himself. He stepped closer to the window and studied the devastation again. Searching for the old man's body.

'Perhaps he made it to the sandhills,' she said hopefully.

'No.'

'How can thou know?'

'Because he was an old fool,' he snapped.

'Not a fool.'

'He looked it to me.'

'He just believed in thee so much it made him look foolish.'

'Poppycock,' he said sharply. 'Don't rope me into your crazy ideas. He was a lunatic. That's all.'

Pearl didn't say anything more. Nor did Prophet.

He just sat and thought about the old man a while. In a funny way, he didn't feel like he was gone. He had shadowed him so much over the past weeks that Prophet felt like all he had to do was just throw open the back door and he'd see him sitting cross-legged and scowling at the bottom of the steps. But that was silly. He was gone.

A few minutes later, Prophet saw the horse walk by the window and then stop, looking at the rubble of the barn. The old animal had made it to the sandhills. He whinnied now for his breakfast.

Pearl turned toward the door and smiled. 'Jack survived.' Prophet sat down hard in a nearby chair, exhausted by the effort to stand, his thoughts on the little man. His eyes stared blankly at Pearl. He watched her taking the blanket down from the door, still not focused on what she was doing, but beginning to feel a nagging somewhere inside him that he didn't like. Something felt wrong. But it hadn't registered in his brain and he ignored it.

Slowly, churning deep in his gut, the nagging turned into a twinge, the urgency of it increasing now. Pearl had set the folded blanket aside, opened the door, and was stepping out on to the porch, when Prophet finally realized what was bothering him and yelled, 'No!'

It was too late. The massasaugas had been driven from their dens by the heat and had sought cover from the barren, smouldering earth and the sun in the shade of the back porch. There was a slithering mass of them, and Pearl was struck three or four times before Prophet yanked her back inside and slammed the door shut.

He stood holding her by her shoulders for a moment, not wanting to move or say anything. Holding her still as if he might be able to keep anything bad from happening if she didn't move or speak again. Then she stepped away and began walking toward the hallway that led to her bedroom.

'Please wake Mrs Kishimoto. I am going to need her assistance.' She said the words like she was about to clean rugs. Prophet watched her.

'Mr Prophet,' she said calmly.

He didn't move.

'Mr Prophet,' she said again.

'Yes.'

'It's best to attend to these matters quickly.'

'Yes.'

Something had snapped hard inside Prophet's head and over-powered his fear of snakes. He was standing on the back porch striking at the slithering mounds of rattlers with a garden hoe. Twenty minutes later, he had killed the last of them, without being bitten, but still he continued to strike out at the pile of writhing flesh, not in fear, simply to release an anger that threatened to explode inside him. Zacharias had come outside and was standing on a chair, crying.

'Is my mother going to die?' he sobbed.

'No. She's too tough.'

'My pa was tough.'

'Yes.'

'He died.'

Prophet didn't have a good answer for that. He bent and started to push the bloody mound off the side of the porch with the back of the hoe.

'My pa died,' Zacharias said again.

'Well, your mother isn't going to.'

'Promise?'

'Promise.'

Zacharias studied his face for a long time, then forced a sad smile through his tears. 'Thanks,' the boy said, as if convinced that Prophet had control over such things as life and death. Prophet nodded, squirming inside.

Samuel had been gone for a long time. Prophet had sent him to get the doctor, while he searched for Mr Kishimoto. He couldn't find the tiny man's body anywhere around the debris of the gardens or the sheds or far out on the burn itself, and he'd gone back to hunting snakes. Maybe she'd been right: maybe he'd wandered off into the sandhills or down the river and escaped the fire. He would look for him again when the boy got back.

He was poking with the rake handle under the back steps where he'd killed a good-sized snake a little while ago, wondering if the doctor would come to help Pearl, when he heard it. It was an odd sound, like the breaking of dried bread.

He stopped and listened.

Then he turned toward it, and couldn't move again for a while. It looked like the garden scarecrow had come alive and was walking slowly toward the house. He shut his eyes and just listened to the awful sound, hoping it would go away. When he opened them, Mr Kishimoto was sitting down hard on the blackened ground, and Prophet was running for him.

He'd been sitting in the sunlight holding the charred body of the old man in his arms for the past hour. Beneath the brittle flesh, he knew the little man was still alive, and wished he would just die. The lips moved in the horribly seared face, then an arm, and Prophet heard the dry bread breaking again, the charred skin around his elbow snapping open as he moved. But the old man would not stop struggling.

'Stay still,' Prophet said. 'You won.' He paused. 'Those men – they couldn't beat you. The fire couldn't. You won.' Prophet blinked his eyes a couple of time to clear them, then bit down on his tongue to keep from crying out. He couldn't take his eyes off the old man's face. 'When I said you couldn't come with me – that I had places to go where you couldn't—' He stopped and waited until he could go on. 'That was a joke. You can come. I'd like that. Anywhere I go.' He paused. 'You can teach me a few tricks. Maybe be my trainer. All you got to do is give me a little room when I walk. That's all.'

Eiko and the girl tried to take the old man from him, but Prophet shook his head hard and held him closer. He was dying because he had wanted to be with him and Prophet wasn't going to let him go now. Not before he was gone.

The women squatted in the dirt and mouthed prayers. Then Eiko stood and put her fingers over her mouth and stared at the old man for a long time. He could tell she wanted to say something. Farewell he guessed, but she didn't. She just looked at him. Then she said, 'It no matter. Remember?' She was crying softly. 'He samurai. He already dead.' She turned and trotted back to the house and Pearl.

'Why me?' Prophet moaned, whispering the word into the old man's ear. 'Why?' Then he saw the tiny lips moving again, struggling to say something. He leaned close.

'Tomodachi,' was all the little man said. 'Friend.'

They buried him that evening in the sand of the gully, in a place covered by calico aster and faced toward the river. Prophet figured he would have liked it: buried where he'd last fought.

Samuel and the girl offered to help dig the grave, but Prophet wouldn't let them. He waited until everyone had said goodbye to the old man, and gone back to the house, then he dug it. He shoveled it deep, talking quietly to the still form as he worked. Talking about things he'd never said to anyone else before in his life. The prairie night was chilly. Prophet shivered. The surrounding silence, the immense quiet of this grass world, bothered him for a moment. He wondered if he'd been right in choosing this lonely place to bury the old man. Then he realized that in the time he'd known him, the little Japanese hadn't spoken more than a dozen sentences to anyone. He listened to the soft sound of the night breeze moving across this empty land and smiled. It was the right place for Muneo Kishimoto.

He stayed at the grave until the moon was rising. Then he reached and put a hand on the mound of sand and said: 'Tomodachi.'

Prophet had talked to the boys for about an hour. They'd just sat in the living room and talked about their mother and what they wanted to do for her when she got better. Like him, none of them could believe that Pearl Eddy might actually die. They also talked about their father and Prophet promised to build a new cross and grave marker as soon as they got materials. He dodged Zacharias' questions about whether he was going to stay. Samuel seemed to have guessed but he didn't ask. And Prophet told them nothing. Nor had he told them what he expected was going to happen next.

He was standing in the corner in the weak shadows of Pearl's bedroom, thinking about all that had come to pass, while Eiko worked over her in the bed. Samuel and Fumiko were keeping the children occupied in the kitchen. He moved forward and glanced at her face on the pillow. She didn't look herself. He was used to seeing her with her purposeful gaze, thinking hard about something, lecturing or moving around like a steam piston. Just being still wasn't her. She was always doing. And it scared him to see her this way, looking like she was already dead. He returned to the corner so he couldn't look at her any more.

Things had turned out like he'd suspected: nothing good had come of any of it. Pearl Eddy had been wrong: right causes weren't any different than any other kind. The old man was dead. The farm gone. Her chances lost. And maybe her life. He sat down hard in a chair, then stood back up and paced the room. Eiko was talking quietly to Pearl as if she were awake.

He'd seen a fair amount of death – but he'd never been close to any of those people. So it hadn't mattered much. It did now. It had mattered with the old man. And it mattered with this woman. He let his eyes drift across the shadows to the bed, realizing that seeing this tiny woman near death was the hardest blow of his life. He'd been hit harder but none had ever hurt like this. He guessed it was because he'd begun to think of Pearl Eddy as if she were his mother. He knew that was crazy. She was white and close to his own age. But she'd done things for him. Things, he figured, only a mother would do for a son. Believed in him when nobody else did. Fought for him against bad odds. He smiled. Even made him behave. Prophet had never had any of that before in his life – before this woman – and it meant more to him than anything else in the world.

He took a deep breath and held it. If she died, the boys would be shipped off to places, and she'd be gone from the earth. He didn't mind her telling him to leave – he just didn't like the thought of her leaving. It felt like somebody had reached into his chest and grabbed his heart.

He watched Eiko mopping moisture from Pearl Eddy's face. Earlier Samuel had brought back snake-bite instructions from the doctor and also word that the man himself couldn't come. But he had given the boy two shotguns and shells and told Samuel to give them to him. Prophet knew what that meant. Nobody was going to help them.

He'd watched people on horseback and in buggies come out all day long to see the burn. They stopped on the road away from the house – like the place was quarantined – and looked. Just looked. None had come to offer help. He'd learned over the years not to expect much more out of people. But he knew Pearl Eddy deserved more.

They couldn't save her from the bites. But they could have asked to help. That would have been something. He shoved them out of his thoughts. They were what they were. Nothing would change them. That was the thing she didn't understand: humans. They couldn't be changed. They'd been that way since the world began.

He watched Eiko putting something on the bites. From what he knew, nothing much would alter the course of things. Whatever little there was to be done, the Japanese woman seemed convinced she knew. She'd read the doctor's instructions, sucking hard on her teeth, and then snorted and crumpled them up. Then she'd set about trying to save Pearl Eddy, looking like she was preparing the evening meal, mixing bowls of dried things she carried in her little bags. She also did a lot of ordering him around. She was like the Quaker woman in that respect. Prophet didn't mind. He wanted to be doing things.

Watching her working now he felt something he'd never believed possible: he was fond of her. He believed in her. He'd never had much truck for orientals. He did now. The old man and this tough little woman had changed all that. He watched her moving in her quick, no-nonsense way and felt better – remembering how he'd enjoyed her silly faces. Her corny jokes. Beneath all her teasing there was common sense and intelligence, and something of the same will that Mrs Eddy possessed.

She'd cut Xs over each of the bites on Pearl's lower legs and sucked on them for over an hour to get the poison out, finally sprinkling the wounds with powder from a small leather bag. After that, she'd had him split open three of the dead hogs to remove their livers, and these she pressed against the bites to draw more blood and poison. For the past couple of hours, she'd been carefully binding and unbinding the legs, then raising and lowering them to keep the blood circulating. She looked exhausted. But he knew she'd never quit. That was one thing he knew for certain.

The chills and sweats had hit first. Then came the dark, ugly puffing of her small legs as the poison began breaking down her blood system, swelling her legs so great that he thought her skin must burst from it. Pearl had remained conscious for a number of hours and she'd talked quietly to the children about things. About their schooling, about their father, about God and what they were were going to do to get the farm going again. Samuel had glanced at Prophet and he knew that the boy understood it was over here, that there was no future for the Eddys in Liberty. But he knew she'd never believe that. Would never believe that the people in the town could abandon her and her boys. It was her one great weakness.

She had talked to her boys through the pain like their tomorrows were going to be brighter than ever. After Eiko had ushered the children out, she'd lectured him about fighting and lying. He'd listened without objecting, just happy to be hearing her voice. An hour later, she had slipped into delirium.

He had asked Eiko if she thought she'd make it, but the little woman had dismissed the question. 'Hai! Not difficult. Not difficult.' But he knew that wasn't the truth. But he also knew that this oriental woman – her family rescued by this little Quaker – wasn't about to consider letting her die. As far as Eiko Kishimoto was concerned she was ready to do battle with any dark forces for this woman's soul. And she wasn't going to waste time talking about it.

He liked that about her. But it also scared him. As if death was in the room with them already and this woman was just whistling loud so she wouldn't be scared. He glanced back at Pearl's face. She was covered with beads of sweat. Yes, death was here somewhere. He could feel it.

Rarely did a rattlesnake bite kill a full-grown adult, but Pearl Eddy wasn't much bigger than a kid. And she'd been struck by three large snakes. He came close to muttering a prayer. He just didn't know what to say.

He stood and walked to the window and looked out at the night. The burned earth was as black as the vault of moonless sky above, making it impossible to tell where the earth stopped and the firmament began. Prophet shivered with the feeling that the old house was floating through empty darkness ... drifting somehow toward hell. Prophet swallowed hard against the feelings rising in his throat. Eiko had left the room and he sat down quietly in a chair next to the bed.

Pearl was soaked in sweat and breathing rapidly. He took a towel and wiped it gently over her face, studying the features. He'd never looked at her this carefully before. She was pretty enough to be an angel. Maybe in some ways she was. He knew she would scoff at that. Still, she possessed some magic things that angels have. Mostly, she could do good.

And until now, nothing had seemed able to stop her. Slow her but not stop her. Not the loss of her businesses, not blindness, not the town. It was strange, he thought, how she could do battle with the best of them ... and never raise a finger. He tipped forward, clasping the towel tight in his hands, his elbows on his knees, staring blindly at the floor between his shoes.

'Mrs Eddy—' he said, stopping to clear his throat and watching her still form from the side. 'There are some things I want to tell you.' He waited to see if she might respond. She didn't. 'I think you know some of it – but I've got to say it.' He waited a while, then said, 'I stole the money and the photograph.'

She didn't move.

'That's the way I been making my way since I haven't been able to fight much like I used to. I just steal whenever I can. That's how this whole thing got started. I tried to steal that man's wallet in the saloon.' He paused. 'We weren't arguing about church money like I told you.' He tipped his face up toward the ceiling for a while, then he looked back down at her. 'That was a lie,' he mumbled.

'I lie about a lot of things, Mrs Eddy. Like that French story and when I told you that I sewed robes for the choir and clothes for poor people.' He hesitated. 'Those were all just lies, too. I lie a lot. And I talk big, bragging about how I'm going to get my shot. I'm not, Mrs Eddy. I missed it. Whenever it was, I don't know. But I couldn't fight anybody good now. I just missed my time. So now I lie about that, too. Lie to myself. To you. To everybody.'

He waited a long time before he spoke again, clearing his throat hard so he could get it out. 'And that stuff about getting religion in jail and becoming a minister.' He stopped and looked off into the shadows as if he'd rather be saying anything but this. He knew what it meant to her. 'Those were lies too. I've got no religion. Never did.'

He jumped when she opened her eyes. Her stare was fixed and remote. 'You awake?'

She didn't answer but he could tell she was.

'You heard?'

'Thou lied,' she sighed against the pain.

He felt the blood rushing to his face, trying to remember the things he'd just said. 'About?'

300

'Minister,' she murmured.

He shook his head. 'No. That was the truth. I'm no minister.'

Pearl waited until she'd caught her breath and then whispered, 'Thou saved Zacharias and Mr Kishimoto.' Her face tightened with a new wave of hurting and she lay still, struggling against it for a moment. Then she slowly collected herself. 'Thou softened Samuel.' She stopped again and lay panting for breath, sweat pouring over her face.

There she was again. Believing grand things about him that weren't true. He squirmed. 'I'm no minister. I don't belong to any church.' He stopped and looked into her eyes. 'I've never even been inside one. I was never baptized.' He studied the boards between his feet again, ashamed about so much of his life.

She lay without moving or speaking for a long time, then she smiled weakly. 'Yes.'

She fainted.

'No,' he said quietly.

Prophet was sitting in a chair near the window watching them. The flames of the lamps looked like the lighted windows of a slow-moving night train coming down the darkened road. He'd been staring at the procession for a long time. Pearl was tossing restlessly in the bed behind him.

He walked over and stood looking down at her, not wanting to wake her, but knowing he had to. When his shadow fell across her face, she opened her eyes and stared up at him, and he could see her fighting the awful burning pain that was inching through her body, destroying the tissues of her legs.

'Mrs Eddy. They're coming again.'

She nodded as if she had expected it. That surprised him. But then a lot about her surprised him. He was holding the shotgun.

'They want me,' he said. 'But they want you gone too. If they're drunk, they may go for Samuel and the woman.' He paused. 'I can't let that happen.'

She stared in the direction of his face for a long time. He could

301

tell she was struggling to say something. He knelt down by the side of the bed and leaned close to her.

'Leave.'

He smiled at her. 'You mean run?'

'I mean leave. For me.' She winced at the pain. 'I've been wrong about a lot of things, Mr Prophet. About the children and my stubbornness.' She gasped for air. 'But I'm not wrong about violence.'

He gazed down into her eyes for a long time, as if trying to see things in them, then said, 'I'm sorry, Mrs Eddy. But you're wrong.'

They were wearing Indian outfits and sitting on their horses behind the house, their heads covered in canvas hoods beneath feathered headdresses. He guessed the hoods were to hide their identity. But it wasn't hard to make out Simon James sitting on a big yellow gelding, his daughter behind him. There were fifteen or twenty of them. Most carried lanterns, the light casting an ominous wavering glow over the house and porch.

Prophet was on the top step of the porch, breathing in the cool air and remembering things. Small things that didn't add up to much. Mostly, he wondered where it had all gone. Then his mouth began to twitch. He didn't try to hide it. He was done hiding things, pretending to be what he wasn't. He watched a nighthawk flit across the moon and wished for a moment he could fly.

When she came, the old black woman was floating in the night sky off to his right. He smiled at her. She frowned. He always knew she'd come to collect him on the day he died. She was too big a busybody to miss it. That thought made him feel better, but he shrugged it off. 'I'm not gone yet,' he mumbled under his breath.

Eiko was keeping the children shut in one room with Pearl, away from the windows, keeping them there no matter what. She'd promised him she'd do it. The only time she was to let them out was if they fired the house. After she'd agreed, the

302

woman had pantomimed like a strongman one last time. But neither of them had laughed.

He had shaken Samuel's hand. Whatever had been wrong between them seemed to be gone now. The boy had done a lot of growing. Prophet guessed he had as well. Samuel was wearing his new shoes and that made him feel good. Finally he'd held Zach until he had to go. He'd told him he was going to 'fit a tiger'. Told him that Hercules and his pa were together. The boy had just watched him. Watched him until he reached the back door, then he had said, 'Don't go, Mr Prophet.'

He could still hear the muffled sounds of his crying somewhere inside the house. He wished the woman would make him quit. It was harder when he couldn't concentrate.

He stood studying them and thinking about these things. About Mrs Eddy. Old man Kishimoto. About things he'd done. And things he hadn't. Zach and Samuel and the others. Minnesota. About the old black woman. Summer roads. But mostly about Mrs Eddy. He didn't want this thing to happen – but, somehow, she'd made it something valuable to him.

'You the Negro they call the Prophet?' Simon James said.

He took a step down the stairs.

'The one that steals?'

Prophet took another step. He'd been right: they were drunk, needing to be so they could do this.

'The one intimate with the white woman, Pearl Eddy?'

Prophet cocked the shotgun.

'Put it down,' Simon James said in a soft voice. His daughter was holding on to his middle with her thin arms, and peering around at him.

'You the Prophet?' he asked again.

'Just Prophet.'

'We've come to talk to you. No call for the gun.'

Prophet nodded. 'You dress up like Sitting Bull, just to come talk.'

Simon didn't say anything.

303

'The house,' Prophet said. 'It's filled with women and children. The old man is dead. Mrs Eddy and her boys are in there. You start it on fire or shoot into it. It's just murder.' Nobody moved or said anything.

'We don't want anybody in that house. Just want to talk to you.' He swung a heavy leg, crooking it around his saddlehorn, so that he looked almost friendly. 'Hell, I got twenty some men with guns. You gonna kill them?'

'No.'

'Good,' Simon smiled.

'Just you.'

The man was uncrooking his leg when Prophet heard the door open behind him and he glanced quickly over his shoulder at Samuel coming down the stairs carrying the second gun.

'What do you think you're doing?' Prophet hissed.

The boy didn't respond. Prophet studied the side of his face for a time. Samuel looked to be in shock as he stood beside him staring at the riders. Prophet shook his head. 'You know how to shoot that thing?'

He nodded.

'Then take the one to the right of the fat man,' Prophet said, raising his voice to make certain they heard. Penny didn't flinch. Having survived all his life by knowing who would and who wouldn't kill him, Prophet figured this man would.

He looked back at Simon. 'Where were we?'

'You aren't going to shoot.'

Samuel cocked the hammer on the old gun, the noise loud and convincing in the night air. Simon stopped talking.

'I'd get out of here,' Prophet said. 'Or I'd get that girl on another horse.'

'You aren't going to,' Simon said again.

Prophet figured things were a stalemate. Then suddenly Eiko and Fumiko came out of the house holding a sick-looking Pearl Eddy between them.

'I told you to stay inside!'

'She break my promise,' Eiko chattered. 'You know how she get.'

'Fine. So she broke your promise. Now get her back in there.'

But Pearl mumbled something and they half-carried her down the stairs. She looked like hell, her face ashen, her hair wet and matted, her eyes unfocused and dazed-looking.

'Samuel?' she called as if he might be a little boy and lost somewhere in the darkness.

He jumped like he'd just been struck by lightning.

'Mother?'

She didn't say anything more, just stood gasping hard for air.

Samuel shifted uncomfortably. 'Thou told me that I would have to decide those things that I believed as a man,' he said, not turning to look at her. 'And I've decided. They aren't going to burn us out. And they aren't going to take Mr Prophet.'

'Mrs Eddy,' Prophet said, 'you need to go back inside.'

She shook her head slowly and continued to stare in her fixed way. Eiko said something to Fumiko and the girl darted back into the house, returning with a chair for Pearl. Then Eiko was busy wrapping and unwrapping the bandages again. The stalemate was still holding but Simon and the others were beginning to grow restless.

'All we want is to talk, Prophet,' Simon tried again. 'There's no reason to involve women and children.'

Eiko rattled a sentence off in heated Japanese.

'Stay out of this, Chinawoman,' Simon warned. He looked back at Prophet. 'I'd have thought you'd have avoided that.'

Prophet knew this couldn't go on much longer. Some of these men were going to pull back into the shadows and drop him and the boy with rifles. They'd probably finish the woman as well. And maybe Mrs Eddy.

'I'll make you a deal,' he said. 'You leave these people alone and I'll go with you.'

Pearl said it first. 'No.'

Then Mrs Kishimoto and Samuel repeated it.

Prophet was just starting to respond when Pearl passed out, slumping in the seat and then sliding to the ground, looking to all the world like she was dead.

'Deal?' he hollered at Simon.

'Deal.'

'No,' Samuel repeated. 'I'm not putting this gun down.'

'Sam, I've never told you to do anything. I am now.' He paused. 'You take your mother and the women and get inside.'

'No.'

'Sam. They're going to put men with rifles out there in the dark. And they're going to kill me. You. Your mother. And the Kishimotos.' He paused. 'Is that what you want? Zach and Josh and Luke walking out and seeing that? They'll have nobody, Sam. You've got to go in. You've got to take your mother in. For her sake. For your brothers.'

'Very smart, Mr Prophet,' Simon said.

'Shut up!' Prophet yelled.

Samuel didn't move.

'Sam.'

The boy looked at the side of his face for a long time, then he bent and laid the gun down on the ground. He was crying but trying not to let Prophet see it.

'Mr Prophet,' Samuel said in a quiet voice.

'Yes?'

'I love thee.'

Prophet felt like he'd been kicked in the back by a horse, trying hard to get air but not getting any. He cleared his throat hard. 'Love you.' He realized that he'd never said that before to anyone. 'Your mother and brothers, too.' He hesitated. 'You tell them. Hear?'

'Yes.'

When Prophet fought his way out of his thoughts, Samuel, Fumiko and Pearl were gone. But Eiko was still there beside him. 'Get,' Prophet said to her.

She shook her head. 'They no scare me.'

Prophet glanced at the side of the little woman's determined face. He was certain they didn't. 'Just go inside.'

I stay. You strongman,' she said, making a small tight smile.

Then four of the men were around them, one giving Prophet a hard lick to the side of his head with a blackjack. He was badly dazed but he was used to being dazed and he stayed on his feet while they yanked the shotgun from him. Then Penny had a small gun pressed against his ribs. The other men grabbed hold of Eiko.

'Let her go!' Prophet hollered. 'We had a deal.'

'Not where she's concerned,' Simon snapped. 'She's a big part of the reason we paid this little visit.'

Prophet was calculating whether he could get a fist into Penny James and the pistol away from the man and stuffed into Simon James' face fast enough, when someone stepped out into the lantern light.

'Get the hell out of here before we take you too,' Simon barked. 'You had your chance.'

Prophet was as surprised as he'd been that night on the river when he watched Hank Meyers staring after the buggy in his shocked way. Then he'd figured the man's sudden conversion had simply been for convenience to save his hide. But that wasn't the case this night. Here he was unarmed and standing like a dumbstruck fool between Prophet and Eiko and a hanging.

'What the hell are you doing here?' Simon yelled.

The man didn't seem able to answer for a moment, as if he might be sleepwalking or something. Then he said, 'I'm a friend of Mrs Eddy.'

Simon didn't wait for any explanations. 'Then the sonofabitch can join these two!'

Prophet couldn't figure it. He just stared into Hank Meyers' eyes as a couple of men grabbed him and tied his hands behind him. He didn't resist. He just stared back at Prophet's face as if he was proud of something.

Then Prophet heard two new sounds. One he had half-expected. The other surprised him like nothing ever had in his life. The first was the sound of Pearl Eddy stumbling out of the kitchen and back down the stairs. Samuel grabbed Zacharias and pulled him back inside and shut the door.

'Dammit, go back!' he yelled, but she kept coming, hobbling off to the right, trying to orient herself to the sounds; then she sat down hard, falling back weakly.

Prophet was concentrating on the second sound now. At first he had thought it was another of Simon's riders, but then he saw the man dismount and start toward them through the shadows of the yard. He was tall and lean and dishevelled-looking.

Simon turned and looked at him, surprised as well.

'Evening, Mr Johnson,' Simon said. 'Come to join the Redmen?'

Johnson stooped and felt Pearl's pulse, then stood and looked at Prophet and the woman and the men holding them.

'What the hell are you doing?' he asked, directing the question at Simon.

'What you should have done, Mr County Attorney. Running these people out of town. That nigger robbed me and assaulted my boys. That woman is a whore and seller of opium. The other one is just a bum.'

Edward Johnson adjusted his glasses on his nose. 'No, you're not. You're not going to run these people out of town. You're going to take them somewhere and shoot them, then dump them in a well or someplace where nobody will find them.' The man was shaking with anger. 'Let's be honest. That's what you're going to do. And that's murder.'

Simon just sat on his horse smiling. Chrissy was making funny sounds and reaching a hand out toward Pearl's still form.

'Well, you're not going to!'

Prophet couldn't believe it. Never would believe it. Not if he lived to be a hundred. A white county attorney, up for election, facing off a crowd over a Negro and an oriental.

But it was over. The same man who had given Prophet the

whack gave Edward a shot just behind his ear, dropping him like a sack of oats. Whatever small glimmer of hope had been ignited inside Prophet went out with that blow, as Penny James and the others shoved them toward the horses.

Then out of the darkness, coming from the road, Prophet heard a team and a carriage, and a loud voice.

'Jessssussspriest, Rose! Can't you make these damn horses behave!'

And then, the haughty voice of the woman who'd tried to get him put in jail for stealing her pill box said, 'Judge Wilkins – if you don't care for the way I drive, you can just walk.'

'I'll consider it next time, Rose.'

Soon the old man was cursing at the horses and trudging across the yard in his raccoon coat, muttering and looking greatly agitated and ready to fight. He stopped and looked down at Edward Johnson, who had just managed to sit up and was trying to get his broken glasses back on his nose.

Slowly, the old man turned and looked at everyone. At the horsemen. At Prophet and the woman and the men holding them. At Pearl. Then back at Johnson, who sat trying to clear his head.

'Who hit Mr Johnson?' he barked in the stillness. 'Who was it?'

The men began to look uncomfortable.

'Get up, Edward. You look silly sitting down there. Try and remember that you are an officer of my court. Act like it.' Then he turned on the men again. 'Who hit Mr Johnson?'

Nobody answered.

Farther off near the road, clothed in the prairie darkness, a crowd was forming. Spectators, Prophet figured. Come to see a hanging. They were on horses, in buggies and on foot, standing silent as the breeze that was blowing in off the sandhills.

The judge had moved over and stood looking down at Pearl. He shook his head. She was awake and staring up at the old man.

'Lassie. You look a mess.'

She smiled weakly at him.

'Judge, you and Mr Johnson ought to take care of Mrs Eddy. She's been snake-bit, we hear.' Simon paused. 'We'll just take these folks and drop them off – outside the town limits.'

Prophet started to take a step backwards, figuring things had changed now, and he'd make a fight for it, when Penny jammed a pistol hard into his side. No chance.

'Penny James,' Rose called, waving her heavy hand in the air. 'You leave that man alone. He designs dresses for me and if you harm him in any way, I'll have you up on charges, young man.' Mother Rose was walking in her huffy way toward them, dressed in her evening finest, her grandson, Ernie, beside her. She stopped and looked down at Pearl, smiled, and said, 'I'll be back in a moment, dear,' then continued on.

Prophet's head was swimming. None of it made sense. None of it fit right. The crowd on the road was growing larger and it was beginning to look like a religious revival of sorts, people just drifting out of the darkness toward the house like they'd just been touched by the Lord. Maybe they had. He saw the two old barbers and a homely-looking girl in a red dress. Old men and women who looked too weak to do much resisting of anything. But they came anyhow. Prophet shook his head. He'd never have believed it.

'Let's go,' Penny hissed to him, cocking the pistol.

Then, from the line of horsemen, Prophet heard a shout: 'Gawddamnit – grab her!' He looked up to see Chrissy James scurrying across the ground toward Pearl, with Hector and Mike James in pursuit. They didn't reach her before she'd crawled on to Pearl, patting the woman's face and crying in a funny way.

'Bring her back here,' Simon shouted.

Hector turned and looked at his father. 'No, pa.'

Mike James stood by his little brother nodding in agreement.

'Get going or I'll shoot this bitch!' Penny hissed, putting the gun into Eiko's back.

'Let her go and I'll go.'

'No,' Eiko said, rattling off something in Japanese that needed no translation.

'Everything will be all right now,' Prophet said.

'No,' Eiko repeated.

Penny released her and was shoving Prophet forward when Rose Sherman suddenly appeared before them.

'Penny James. Did you hear me? This man works for me,' she said in her best high-pitched voice, as if even talking to Penny was something she found distasteful.

Prophet felt the man shifting nervously and waited for the blast. He figured Penny wanted him badly enough to do it.

'He works for me, too,' Judge Wilkins barked. He'd taken a place next to Rose, standing between Penny and Prophet and the horsemen. 'The woman,' he said, indicating Eiko, 'does as well.' The old man was squinting hard at Penny's face. 'Aren't you on parole in Mason County for assault, young man?'

Rose cleared her throat. 'Judge,' she interrupted, in her haughty way. 'The woman works for me on Mondays and Fridays. She can work for you any other day.'

'Fine, Rose. But that's hardly the point,' the old man said, continuing to stare at Penny James.

Slowly the man released his grip on Prophet and put the pistol away. The judge and Rose were squabbling again but Prophet wasn't hearing them any more. He just saw men turning their horses away and leaving Simon James sitting there alone. Rose was debating who got Eiko on the weekends now. And the tall attorney was standing and looking at his broken glasses, a dazed expression on his face. Alfred Snipes stepped up alongside him.

'Don't start talking foreclosure, Snipes,' Johnson warned, softly rubbing the side of his skull.

The little man grinned. 'No need. Woman's too lucky. Too lucky for words.'

Johnson looked at him and tried to focus his eyes. 'How?'

Snipes gazed around at the burned-out yard. 'This fire.'

'You got a strange idea of luck.'

'Nope. Not at all. Before I loaned her husband money for that equipment I made him take out a policy against fire.' Snipes puffed his chest out. 'So I wouldn't be stuck with a bunch of worthless land. Damn lucky I did. For me and her.' Snipes was beaming now.

Johnson shook his head to clear it. 'How much insurance?'

Snipes was scratching his cheek and staring around admiringly at the blackened farm, as if it was some masterpiece that he had somehow created.

'How much?' Johnson repeated. Louder this time.

The little man looked back at the attorney. 'Well, I guess since you're the Eddys' lawyer I can tell you. Twelve hundred dollars. Subtracting what she still owes on the equipment leaves $950. Tidy little sum.'

Eiko was standing next to the man listening wide-eyed as he calculated the money owed to Pearl Eddy. Suddenly, she grabbed him by his thin shoulders and planted an enormous kiss on his cheek. From the shocked look on his little rat like face, it could well have been his first.

'You very riko na man. Smart man. Smart man.' She squinted hard at Snipes' blushing face. 'I like that. Like smart man.'

Snipes pulled himself up a little straighter and said, 'I try and calculate risk. Keeps the bank out of trouble. That's my job—'

Eiko was listening attentively. 'Riko na man. Riko na.'

Snipes grabbed hold of the lapels of his jacket and looked suddenly very important. 'There was a time last year when a couple of speculators—' Eiko nodded enthusiastically and stepped closer to hear the man's story. Johnson turned and walked off to tell Pearl the good news.

William Smith and Hank Fegan, the old barbers, worked their way through the crowd until they were standing and looking down into Pearl's face. 'Mrs Eddy,' William said, studying her features.

'She ain't awake, Will,' Hank said.

'I'm awake.'

'We just wanted to say that fire don't kill asparagus. You'll have a new crop finer than ever. And Hank and me want to put our order in early. Deal?'

'Deal,' she said, smiling weakly.

Prophet stood off by himself trying to collect his thoughts. But couldn't. He just stood wondering how he could have lived so long and been so wrong about something like this. Something so important. It didn't matter. It had happened. He'd just been wrong. And he figured this was a good time for him to get going. Maybe not Minnesota. But somewhere. He saw Zacharias on Samuel's shoulders. They were both laughing. He'd leave them that way. It looked nice.

When he finally got his legs to move again, he made his way through the crowd and stood staring down at her. He wanted to say goodbye to her. She looked gone. Eiko was working on the bandages and some other women were covering her with a shawl. Then her eyes opened.

'You OK, ma'am?'

'Mr Prophet,' she murmured.

'I figured I'd be on my way.' He paused. 'Just wanted to say goodbye.'

'Mr Prophet,' she said quietly.

'Yes, ma'am.'

'I'm not pleased about those guns.'

'Yes, ma'am.'

She waited a moment, then said, 'If thou are staying, we will have to have a talk.'

The old black woman was floating above the garden, looking down at him. She smiled. The first time ever. He looked back down at the little woman.

'Yes, Mrs Eddy.'